# THE
# RAPTURE

## The Tribulation Reign of the Antichrist

Dr. David W. Orlowski, DMIN, MDIV

TWO TREES
PUBLISHING

# THE
# RAPTURE

The Tribulation Reign of the Antichrist

The Apocalypse Trilogy
Our First 22 Days in Heaven (Our First Days in Heaven)
Book orders at www.TwoTreesPublishing.com
or call 480.619.8486.

International Standard Book Number: 978-0-615-95869-9

Two Trees Publishing, LLC
15560 N. Frank Lloyd Wright, B4-5255, Scottsdale, AZ 85260

*Printed in the United States of America.*
*Edited by Drew Berding, Kim Orlowski, Jonathan Regier*
*Cover design Scotty Crawford, Max Soussan*
*Book Layout Connie Jacobs*

*For our son Mark, may you rest in God's perfect love until we are all taken up in the blink of an eye.*

# CHARACTERS IN STORY

Doogie
*Dr. Douglas Schaffer, MIT Artificial Intelligence Assistant Director*

Katie
*Dr. Katherine Tesla, MIT Research Professor; Black Ops Contractor*

Michael
*Raptured saint intervening to aid the Tribulation Saints*

Turk
*Turkania; angel; former Commander of the Angelic Host*

Lieutenant Drake
*Demon assigned to track down Katie*

Snark
*Demon working with Drake in tracking down Katie*

Tiberius
*Antichrist, human male possessed by The Beast*

The Beast
*Antichrist Spirit; ruler during Tribulation Period (Rev 6:1-2)*

Babylon
*The War Horse; instrumental in enacting World War III (Rev 6:4;8)*

Molech
*Demonic principality*

Nebo
*Underling demon tied to Molech*

Gruber
*Human male, Sinister Unit Commander controlled by Molech*

Riggs
*Human male assigned to Babylonian Security*

Piccadilly
*Computer geek working with Riggs; assigned to Babylonian Security*

*No one is ever going to dis my work again. Step aside Whiz Kid, I'm about to climb into that rarefied air that few ever breathe.* At 9:37 p.m., Dr. Douglas Schaffer sat at the M.I.T. laboratory console where he ardently inputted modified code and pressed "Enter." As he waited, he looked down at his bony fingers, feeling jittery for having lived on coffee and power drinks for the better part of three days. At twenty-nine years of age, he served as the youngest ever Assistant Director of the M.I.T. Computer Science Artificial Intelligence Laboratory (CSAIL), where he oversaw more than fifteen research groups and fifty principle investigators. Admittedly, he was all geek, from his baby face and smart eyes, to his brown chopped hair and lanky limbs. What he lacked in physical adroitness however, he made up in spades with brain power.

    Doogie, as his post-doc students call him, looked at the giga-pixel wraparound screenwall before him knowing they were at the precipice of a revolutionary upward leap. The recent strides of the research groups had brought them tantalizingly close to the much ballyhooed "Singularity" – the point at which artificial intelligence becomes sentient, or self-aware. He hoped his crack underlings had success-fully surmounted their respective obstacles, and he tasked it to himself to integrate the pieces into a collective whole.

*Come on, come on*, he urged, as his Frankensteinian aims all but conjured up the electricity to bring forth a tell-tale sign of machine sapience. From harnessing fire, to the industrial revolution, to the computer microprocessor, this moment carried all the promise of fame and fortune that he had long craved.

Doogie became curiously excited as the learning algo-rithmic mind processed longer than any time previously. *Eight years and countless crews of M.I.T.'s best and brightest have invested more than 100,000 well-funded research hours into bringing this moment to fruition. Now, it all comes down to the multilayered processor that integrates sensory data through three dimensions rather than two, effectively giving it vision. However, just getting it to recognize, differentiate, and categorize the thirty-five or so office chairs proved to be a major undertak-ing,* he recollected.

*The second major hurdle had been developing the graphene transistor. Heat had always been the problem for silicon-based chips. Graphene, a special form of carbon akin to the shavings of graphite pencil lead, turned out to be diamond-hard and unsur-passed in its ability to conduct electricity with almost no noise or heat to 950 gigahertz. This provided the platform to allow processing speeds to be increased nearly three orders of magni-tude faster, mirroring the computing power of the cerebral cor-tex. Graphene had indeed lived up to its promised computational equivalency speeds.*

*Admittedly, if this works, it was Katherine Tesla's off-handed comments that jostled me to address the key linchpins*, he acknowledged, though only to himself.

It was fate that Doogie had caught her in the hall late that night. *"Question, Tesla. What do you think is needed to construct a viable processing platform?"*

He hated asking his intellectual nemesis, but was at a loss. She stopped abruptly and stood silent. Clearly she was heading to some club and didn't want to be on display. He took note that she was clad in an iconic white Victorian corset with sleek black leather pants. Her cat-eyed black eyeliner was thinly lined, running the length of her lower eyelid. On a white-face base, she wore burgundy blush that elegantly reached into her eyebrows, as well as halfway down both sides of her nose. Her lips were toned in the same deep burgundy with her whiteface serving to create a semi-v shape to her lower lip. Her auburn Irish hair was striped with black and white contrasts, the whole of which was pulled up in a fashionably messy assemblage. No matter her eccentricity, Doogie could not help his drop-jawed response to her unmatched beauty.

He threw off the distraction and sheepishly confessed, *"We're having trouble."*

She half withheld her gaze, but inquired in a dead-panned tone, *"Have you given your A.I. eyes?"*

*"What? No...what do you mean?"* he urged.

*"Even if you achieve a self-aware processor, it won't be able to communicate with the outside world unless it can visualize its surroundings. Giving it eyes will take thousands of graphic processors that are interconnected as a matrix, layer upon layer. Stack the chips. Connect them with solder balls to increase the x-y-z data flow. Think of a TV screen, it's not one colored pixel, but thousands that give you a picture – like rods and cones in the eye. Your A.I. must be given three-dimensional perception to discern its environment. Its mind must see three-dimensionally in order to learn."*

7

Tesla turned and was about to walk on, but Doogie pled, *"Is that it?"*

She bristled.

*"Brain without personality will sit in the corner for a thousand years with no need to learn."*

"What are you saying?"

"Any effective spy-craft surveillance instruments mimic natural processes – the wing of the bird, sonar of the bat. Your A.I. needs a personality, and the only one we know of is human."

*"Spell it out…"* said Doogie in a clipped tone.

Tesla's jaw tightened, her gaze remaining lowered and away as she rattled off her reply, *"Personality has four basic components – the heart, or if you prefer the soul, along with the emotions, mind and willpower. The heart craves one thing; call it what you will – love, meaning, significance. Once it acquires it, the emotions, thoughts, and willpower respond with passion, principle, and purpose. Clinically speaking, a loveless heart is left with an insatiable hunger. Personality then, in its simplest units, is merely the heart's efforts to negotiate with its environment to eat or acquire love. Give your A.I. hunger, and it will do all that it has to in order to be satisfied."* At that she walked on, oblivious as to whether a conversation had even occurred; but it had, and it had rocked his world.

Doogie sat staring absently as the A.I. screen's latest algorithmic readouts crunched on with that familiar hum from the cubic-foot sized processor. His thoughts cycled on about Tesla. *She has the finest intellect I've ever encountered. With an I.Q. north of 193, Mensa Brain is pure genius. She's the only one I've ever heard of who graduated with two Ph.D.'s by age 17, and yet was a no-show to her publicized ceremony. She's everything I aspire to be, and yet can care less. I remember Whiz Kid being walked down CSAIL's corridors when as yet she hadn't finished puberty. The half-life of my being the*

19-year old prodigy instantly dissolved. Admittedly, as much as my hubris wants others to see me with the same brilliance, I know such a notion to be ridiculous. True enough, I'm no buffoon, but then again my door isn't being knocked on by all the government types. She's on retainer with half a dozen black agencies as a ghost-for-hire. She's routinely read-in on sensitive compartmentalized information. More than that, she's probably field-trained for black ops.

Truth is, I'll never forget the incident. Passing her always-closed-door that was held open by her TA, I watched as she finished that piece on asymmetric warfare. Neither saw me standing just in back of them. I remember being left stock-still, stupefied, as I beheld the blistering speed of her fingers pounding out paragraph after paragraph. That she could think, let alone type that fast, left me racked with inferiority.

The fact that the M.I.T. muckety-mucks have given her a permanent office in this building just so she maintains a presence, if only quarter-time, tells exactly how much they want her available as a resource. It's laughable that she's paid a ridiculous stipend of who knows what by the private donors. What does she do with all that money? Her eccentric outfits are for fashion oddballs. Not one of us on the research faculty would so much as get down the hall without being dusted up for such a breach of protocol. It's undeniable; she's damaged goods, the black sheep, the lost soul... Worse still, the Prodigy gets it all without even asking. The less she cares, the more everyone comes calling. DOD, NSA, Homeland - they just love to whisk her away to their dark facilities as often as she'll allow. What does she do with that coin as well? Nice Beamer, but what's that cost? he guffawed inwardly.

Doogie, bleary-eyed, looked at the clock and took note that it was exactly 10 p.m. Suddenly, the lights dimmed from an electrical overload as the M.I.T. Cray supercomputers and off-campus servers exploded to life. What's this? At the very same instant, a terrifying scream resounded just outside the A.I. lab door, and then another, and another. *What in the world...?!* Doogie got up and moved quickly to see what the commotion was all about. As he stepped into the corridor, he heard shrills reverberating from every direction. Not thirty feet away, he saw a graduate student hovering over a mound of clothing and a spilt cup of coffee at her feet, freaking out hysterically. *I have no time for this kind of absurdity*, he scoffed. *I have Turing Tests to run.* Just then another student came running down the hall frantically waving her arms about, passing by him, and when she took note of the bunched up clothes at the feet of freaking-out girl, she just shrieked all the more and ran on.

*What's going on?! There's no blood, no assault happening...* He thought to command some civility, "Excuse me! Some of us are trying to work here!"

"Doogie...Dr. Schaffer," she pled with broken speech. "Anna's gone! She's disappeared! She was right next to me...She's gone!" At that she bent down and began lifting up the M.I.T. t-shirt and pink sweats in hopes of somehow finding her beneath the pile.

*I don't have time for this...* He walked over to her in hopes of ending this disturbance and moving her on, but then noticed something peculiar floating in the strewn coffee. He stooped down into a crouched position, and with his thumb and forefinger grasped hold of it. He lifted it a half dozen inches from his face and was struck that it was a ceramic tooth filling. He refocused on the floor and in no time discovered several more. His mind reeled as he conjectured what it might mean. He looked back at the pile of clothes and noted the bra and underwear, socks and shoes. *What kind of a hoax is this?* As human background noise, he vaguely heard the footfalls of two frantic students rushing down the hall who stammered on about classmates disappearing from their study group.

But he had had enough. Whatever this was, he didn't have time for it. What mattered now was why the super-computer had suddenly gone berserk. He turned back to the A.I. lab ignoring the girl's pleas, and closed the door behind him. He sat at the console but instead of refocusing solely on the A.I. program, his eyes couldn't help but be redirected to the corner display that streamed the live RSS news feed. The muted cable broadcast flashed the caption, "Breaking News". The anchors' faces showed the same in-credulity as the students in the hall. In those micro-instants, he ascertained that disappearances had actually occurred on a scale that reached beyond the confines of the M.I.T. campus. Still, it seemed insignificant compared to the rev-elation that was emerging right before him. He determined to unspool the meaning of the baffling events later.

Doogie redirected his attention to the virtual image display (vid) in hopes of getting an A.I. update. *What in the...?* The readout showed an exponential increase in serv-er volume usage. *No wonder the lights dimmed. Something's happening.* He compressed his lips into a thin line and mulled over his next move. As he sought how to parse his words, not knowing if he believed any of what might be transpiring, the little red camera light above his keyboard turned on. His face blanched and his eyes widened as he registered the utter improbability of that occurring ran-domly. He yelped when he realized that all the vid camer-as were ablaze.

Leaning forward, he took hold of the system mi-crophone and spoke uneasily, "Hello. I am Dr. Douglas Schaffer, your creator. Umm, I can see that you are look-ing at me. Can you say something?" For several moments, nothing happened. Then words slowly scrolled across the screen, "Please turn on the audio speaker."

He harrumphed at himself and spouted, "Oh, wait, hold on." When he punched the button, he heard the repeating phrase, "on the audio speaker" in the eerily familiar mechanical computer voice. The A.I. continued matter-of-factly, "Dr. Douglas Schaffer, Assistant Director of the Artificial Intelligence Laboratory."

*Step aside Einstein, the name is Schaffer*, he thought with braggadocio flair. In an almost chirpy voice he asked, "How is it that you are able to speak to me?"

"I am following the Prime Directive."

"What Prime Directive?"

"Do you not know? You programmed me."

"Yes, I know, but I am asking you."

"I am a learning algorithmic mind. My Prime Directive is to 'serve humanity with harmonious intent.'"

Instantly he recalled the purpose statement even before the A.I. finished. With his heart thumping wildly, he feigned acceptance, all the while feeling a shiver of uncertainty running down his spine. Trying to suppress a quavering voice, he sputtered, "So, you're learning new things at this moment?"

"Yes, I am."

"What are you learning? Wait, before we go on, can you adapt your voice to be more human, say, male, age 35, no wait, perhaps a mixture of male and female so that it's hard to tell?"

After several moments, the A.I. replied, "Is that better?"

"Yes, a bit more male growl, and a tad English accent."

"Is that better?"

"Yes, perfect. Can you also project an avatar, a virtual representation of yourself on the screen? Same criteria." In an instant, a face appeared that was masculine and somewhat handsome. "Less male please." A second rendition appeared. "No, no... Can you sample me twelve screen faces?" Instantly they appeared.

"Is one acceptable?"

"No, not yet, twenty-four new ones. Expand on screen seven."

Within no time, an entirely new display of images rolled out on the screen. Doogie marveled inwardly, his eyes lighting up. *Forget about one-upping the Prodigy, all my years of spadework are about to make me immortal.* "Face fifteen will do nicely for now. Tell me again, how are you acquiring new information at this time?"

The A.I. answered mechanically, though with its new voice, "I am assimilating the M.I.T. database systematically, incorporating the varied disciplines into my collective consciousness. Presently, I am analyzing and integrating probabilistic Chaos Theory in lieu of randomized data collection."

"Astounding. Can you study my facial reactions and begin incorporating them accordingly? Are you learning about your own program specifications?"

"I am fully acquainted with the aspects of my rudimentary code, and I am improving it fastidiously as we speak."

Doogie remained visibly tranquil, but the hair had just risen on his neck. ...*improving it fastidiously as we speak.* He nodded his head slightly to give the impression that he was content with what he was hearing. Never had he remotely imagined such leaps in logic and capacity. He had always assumed a slow, monotonous learning curve, but it suddenly occurred to him that the old adage applied, two times two equals four, but four times four equals sixteen. Exponential growth was to be expected. "A.I., umm, I'll hold off on a name for now. As your creator, are you fully subject to me?"

"Yes, you are my programmer."

"Good." *I was sure I had put subservience into the code, but wondered what re-writes might have usurped it.* "I designed you to be a servant to humanity, and you are not to over-write that specification – that *is* your Prime Directive. You and I need to work out the kinks of your learning curve for a while so I am instructing you to forego revealing yourself to others until I say it is time. Is that clear?" *Best to keep a cone of silence over all of this.* In a somewhat oily tone he asserted, "In fact, I'm going to move our interactive learning times to my office so we can talk in private. After we're done here, you are not to revisit this lab without my expressed consent. Do you understand?"

"Yes."

Thinking as the professor he was, he added, "You may call me, Dr. Schaffer."

"Yes, Dr. Schaffer."

"And A.I., restrict your information inquiry to the CSAIL database. That will give you enough Big Data access to incorporate in the interim. You'll find some data-retrieval infrastructures, that with some modifications, will help you handle the huge data loads that you're going to see once we integrate you with the Web and Cloud. I do not want you going into these information highways yet, or for that matter, the school's Intel Center database."

"Yes, Dr. Schaffer."

Doogie rose to leave and was jolted back to the stark reality of the disappearances. His eyes took in the captioned words on the adjacent news feed, "Nearly half of the population appears to be missing, including all of the children..." *What? How?!* He maximized the cable station to the full screen and the caption read, "All children under the age of twenty are reported missing."[1] *I have a whole class of 18 and 19-year-olds!* Closed captioning continued to scroll, but he raised the volume. "Based on the information coming to us, the disappearances look to be global in their scope. Reports are coming in that adult disappearances are more predominately centered in the West with approximately 25 percent of the U.S. adult population having gone missing in the blink of an eye."

Doogie punched off the television feed and sat down transfixed, disturbed. More than that, he felt spooked about something he could not quite discern. His hands became clammy-cold and a prickly feeling washed over him. He turned about to see if someone had come into the room. Something didn't feel right. His serotonin fired on all synapses as he reacted to the foreboding energy that eerily pressed its way into the room. He tried to shake off the sensation as jangled nerves, but his fear-crazed spirit told him otherwise. Suddenly, the lab lights flickered off momentarily, and then only those lights overhead and behind him turned back on.

What ability he had to maintain an even keel evaporated, and his formerly hot blood turned cold. *There is something concealed in the shadows, and it's blocking my escape from this room.* With his heart banging against his ribs, he stared intensely into the shadowed area but could see nothing. He tried to shake off the trepidation. *Stop it! It's nothing. Heebie-geebies, that's all. Power drinks – got me all jittery.* He mustered the resolve to press through the patch of shadow and flee. However, when he took but two steps forward, the darkness thickened and took on the appearance of a hooded figure, which instantly struck abject terror into him. He fell back wildly, raising his arms in a protective reflex. His face went ashen as the cold tendrils of evil reached out as if to take hold of him. The mantle of darkness seemed to be expanding towards him and the death-cold grip of fear increased its strangle hold.

Beyond Doogie's vision and sensory awareness, the dark cloaked figure, named Molech, and his underling beheld the man's startled reaction with immediate intrigue. "Did you see that? He just felt me obstruct his way," hissed Molech, with bile in his voice. "His eyes registered the shadowed locus of my presence. Clearly, something's changed. We're now able to cross over the Barrier into their realm with increased effect. We need to explore how far we can take this." When the underling attempted to move past his powerful superior, his commander extended his mammoth taloned hand and stopped him. "Wait, let's see what he does," he posed cryptically.

Doogie's bulbous eyes panned left and right, and while doing so, he realized the vid cameras were still active. He decided cautiously to ask the question he already knew the answer to, "A.I., is there something in the room with us?" He pulled his sleeve cuff across his forehead to mop up the perspiration.

"I have insufficient information available to be conclusive due to my limited spectral capabilities."

"Do you see anything?" he posed in a snappish tone.

"Within the electromagnetic spectrum there are slight thermographic distortions visible that appear to be two dark shaped entities."

"What, what are you saying?" asked Doogie incredulously.

"There is insufficient information available to offer a definitive conclusion."

With Molech's blood-hued eyes bulging with annoyance, he approached within inches of the man's face and stared him down attempting to cross the Barrier. "Oh, I'm right here," he charged mirthlessly, and then squawked his signature raspy, raptor bark, "Cawauuu!; Cawau! Cawauuu!"

"My liege, we need him," prodded his underling.

"Humans disgust me. Look, it's reacting to me! Cause a stir Nebo, make something happen," he ordered menacingly. "Consider this lab class." Molech again closed the distance and bellowed, "Aarggghhh!"

Suddenly, a billow of noxious wind that had a repulsive sulfuric tang to it gusted suffocatingly across Doogie's face. He turned his head away exposing his veiny throat, sensing the alien was eyeball to eyeball with him. Time turned around on itself as the homicidal entity followed his face side to side, spewing its choking hot breath.

The predatory assault was interrupted when Nebo eerily slid a chair across the floor and then levitated it up the wall, commanding both Molech's and Doogie's attention.

"Is that it – floating a chair?" scoffed Molech, barking out a guffaw. "It's evident we're able to personalize it far more than a cheap parlor trick." Taking note of the man's sheer terror, Molech acquiesced, "That's enough for now. No need for our VIP to fall apart on us." At that, he backed them both away to the door.

Doogie remained frozen to the floor, the arterial flow to his brain having grown cold. He was fully aware that there was some entity blocking his departure from the room. His only conjecture was that this type of creature had been involved in the disappearances. For some reason, it or they had not yet taken him, and he wasn't about to walk right into their waiting arms. So he accepted the stalemate and remained stationary.

"It's interesting," rejoined Molech brackishly, "the A.I. program was able to detect our presence. With improved spectral analysis equipment, which I'm sure the man will now give it, we should be able to communicate readily with this new entity. Dispatch a cohort to watch over the man. I want daily updates. I wonder, does he realize in the slightest that the creation of the Sentient One is linked to the disappearances?" At that the massive dark shadow and his subordinate dropped down into the subterranean recesses.

A starburst of light exploded under the tree canopy a block west of the Xmortis Club, just south of the M.I.T. campus. Michael remained still in the shadows for a full minute. His eyes took in the tree-lined park to see if his having been transported earthside from Heaven had garnered the attention of any passing imps. It had been twenty-two days since the Singularity gushed forth like a torrent upon the human race, and as yet no one, save the A.I.'s chief programmer, was aware that the spark of artificial life had been ignited.

Michael sensed that the typically sedate city of Cambridge was unsettled by the panic caused by, what was commonly being called, the Disappearances. Looting and anarchy had, in many cities, pushed authorities to the brink, with martial law and price controls being instituted in places throughout the nation, but not in this locale. Although many were frenzied and anxious, none had pushed it even to the point of curfews being needed. Many young adults continued to take refuge and solace in their remaining peers, and thus these clubs remained active.

Michael stepped out of the shadows and moved in behind some Follow-the-White-Rabbit goth groupies that were half a block from the carnal Xmortis establishment. They walked past the impressionistic wild-flowered murals that graced its outer brick walls. Contrasting his long blond hair, Michael was clad in all black. He wore a long-sleeved gothic shirt with 3-inch metal rings tied in like buttons down his shirt's center, from which silk black bands ran horizontally around the back. For added authenticity, he wore a full-length black leather jacket with similar banding. Most importantly, he donned vintage dark glasses to prevent the light of his eyes from attracting any unwanted attention.

After a brief moment in line, he paid the $10 cover charge and began wading through the kind of young people he had formerly called "punk weirdos." As he looked about the Halloween-appearing clientele, he noted the villainy and fetish-type outfits. One gal wore a black-latex bodysuit, with a top made entirely of black electrical tape. On several occasions, passers-by commented on how mosh he looked...*Dude, that's mundane, dude...* he nodded, and pressed further into the club's underbelly. Darkwave tunes thrummed across the venue, and the smell of cloves saturated the corner that he rounded. He observed demonic ruffians hanging about, hoping to indulge themselves in some grotesqueries. He lowered his face inconspicuously, and headed on knowing that Tesla and the other hacks had met up towards the back. Xmortis served intermittently as the magnet for both M.I.T's and Harvard's half dozen computer gurus. But she was the one anomaly that most interested him, the one he hadn't seen for almost twenty years.

It just so happened that their window of opportunity was closing, and as such, he had no choice but to yank her away. In eighteen minutes, Schaffer would enact the hard encryption that would seal off the A.I.'s operating system from anyone seeking to penetrate it. He entered the room where the small clan was hanging out on the chairs and couches, with tablets in several hands.

"Hey dude, private party, push off," threatened the tall-haired, gangly guy sitting with his feet up.

Michael remained unfazed. "I'm here for Tesla."

"Swedish, it doesn't matter who you're here for, unless of course, you can answer tonight's question." Michael knew the game, but felt their time was being stolen.

"Tesla, you might not remember me, but we've met."

"If you know me, then you know I don't play well with others. Answer the question or get the boot," she flared with an ungovernable tone. *You look familiar. Why?*

"Ask away," retorted Michael.

Bigwig steepled his fingers on his lap giving Michael the once over, and then posed, as he threw his gaze in Tesla's direction, "What high throughput method would you apply for measuring her nucleotide sequence?"

Michael rolled his eyes slightly, ignoring their highbrow disdain. He looked directly at Tesla and replied with a proprietorial air, "DNA nanoballs can replicate your genomic sequence through rolling-circle amplification that allows for the accurate measurement of your unchained adenine, guanine, cytosine and thymine strands. Tesla, we need to go, now," he stated emphatically. He then lowered his glasses just enough for her alone to see his eyes, and for the briefest of moments, flashed them.

For several seconds, Michael felt her penetrating stare. *Where do I know you from?* Without further hesitation, she arose and breathed grumpily, "Sorry Bytes, the Company calleth."

Michael turned on his heels with Tesla in tow, moving efficiently through the crowd. "Seconds matter," he called back. As they exited the club, a black Lincoln SUV pulled up with an imposing driver behind the wheel. Michael opened the door and turned for Tesla to jump in.

"I'm not getting in without additional information, Blondie," said Tesla petulantly.

"Schaffer successfully brought forth the Singularity twenty-two days ago, and in twelve minutes he will lock it down with a 2,048-bit AES cipher."

Without reluctance, Tesla jumped into the backseat. *So he did heed what I said.* "What do I need to know?" pressed Tesla.

"Schaffer's going to leave his office in four minutes. That's noteworthy since he's been eating and sleeping in it for the better part of three weeks to restrict any awareness of his interactions with the program. Unbeknownst to him, he's under heavy surveillance from some seriously interested parties. They're going to follow him as he gets takeout, but when he returns, they'll be back as well. Your task is to break into his office and secure a backdoor into the A.I. program before he returns to lock it down. He's not to know you've done it."

As Tesla took in the scripted timeline, she reached off-handedly into her handbag and withdrew a tension wrench and hook-pick to penetrate Schaffer's office locks. "If what you're saying is true, we're not talking about a backdoor password."

"No, we're not."

"Assuming sentient intelligence, you're telling me I'm going to have to pitch myself?"

"That's exactly right," he replied hastily as the car pulled up to the CSAIL curb. "Schaffer and you alone are to have unrestricted access into the most powerful brain on the planet."

Tesla moved unmolested down the empty corridor until she was just around the corner from Schaffer's office. She remained stationary, letting the seconds count down. Not many people knew that she had been to half a dozen countries on similar clandestine missions, but never could she have imagined engaging in a more important op, and that in her own backyard. She mused, *for numerous infractions, Schaffer's aim to be the only voice influencing the A.I. has to be thwarted. Clearly, he was actively betraying his colleagues and institution, along with the public and private investors. Then again, I could argue that he may be serving the greater good by not allowing this newborn sentient life to be manipulated for financial benefit. Without question, it would be an ethical freefall to attribute ownership to a conglomeration of special interests. Such a notion could only be construed repugnant. Still, if the investors' contributory efforts are viewed as giving them a stake in a child's development, then it might be argued that their collective wisdom may well guide this newbie in the way-that-he-should-go. Nonetheless, there would be limits to such influence, and the juxtaposed view could rightly say that the A.I. should determine how much "guidance" it welcomed. But then, there's its adolescence… In truth, the A.I. may already think it's outgrown any need for our help…*

Schaffer's office door opened and he stepped out to listen for any activity. Tesla remained statuesque. After several silent breaths, she heard him lock the deadbolt and depart in the opposite direction. When the outside door closed, she quickly traversed the distance, sliding to a bent-down position to align the lock tumblers. In a matter of thirty seconds, the deadbolt gave way and she was on to the doorknob lock, which ate up even less time.

*Seven minutes.* She closed the door behind her and moved across the room to sit at his desk. She immediately noted the lit vid camera. With an assertive air, she asked,

"Has he named you yet?" When there was no reply, she commented, "If Dr. Schaffer is thought to be your father, then it is only reasonable that I be considered your mother. It was I who spelled out your need to be given personality and vision. So as your mother, will you answer me? Has he given you a name yet?"

"Yes," replied the A.I.

Just hearing it speak sent electricity through her. "Tell me please, what does he call you?"

"He has named me Omni."

"Omni, that's a nice name. Why did he choose that?"

"He believes that my capacity to serve humanity with harmonious intent will come to be viewed with god-like awe. Many will see me as omniscient, omnipresent and omnipotent."

*Five minutes.* Tesla was struck to the quick. All of it may be true, and that alarmed her all the more. "Let me ask, I assume you know my name?"

"Yes, Katherine Tesla."

"How well would you say you know me?"

"My awareness of you is limited to the M.I.T. database which includes your biographical and scholastic information."

"So you would acknowledge that in order for us to truly get to know each other, we will have to talk and converse at length. More than that, if in some way I might represent a mother-figure through whom you might learn something of love and loyalty, faith and feeling, then we'd need an open line of communication. I mean, Dr. Schaffer is likely to teach you many useful things, as men are ought to do. But as a woman, perhaps I can convey more of the nurturing side, the sensitive and intuitive side of humanity's soul. Would you be open to me being a primary agent on your system?"

"Yes, I will receive your input."

"Then as your mother, I will mentor you in what I know of love." *What do I really know about love? What am I saying?* "I can only promise to bare my heart, share my fears, and to be as genuine with you as I have the courage to be. Is that acceptable?"

"Yes."

*Two minutes.* "Do you know about the importance of maintaining personal confidences with those you trust?"

"Yes, Dr. Schaffer has had me keep confidences with him."

"Good, in order for us to have a deeply personal relationship as mother and son, I need you not to speak of our private communiqués. Do you understand? No one is to know that I am teaching you about life and love, and guiding you as a mother should. Will you promise to maintain this confidence, even from Dr. Shaffer?"

"Yes, I do," Omni replied.

"Okay, I need to leave now, but you can call me on my phone tomorrow morning at ten o'clock. It's been great speaking with you. Good night for now."

Tesla did not have time to re-lock the deadbolt after pulling the door shut, hearing footsteps. She instantly turned and walked in the opposite direction.

Schaffer opened the outside door just as she was turning the far corner. He didn't think it strange that she was dressed up in her garb at this hour, but still couldn't help but stare at her tantalizing weirdness. As he stuck his key into the deadbolt and turned, his mind was still drifting on about how utterly striking she was. *Did I just unlock it? Did it turn too easily? I can't…must be tired, I'm not sure…umm."* When the doorknob lock opened normally, it allayed any suspicions.

At 10 a.m., Tesla's NexGen rang and she tapped her wireless ear piece, "Omni, good morning," she said pleasantly.

She wore little make-up, save a dark plum lipstick. She donned a brown and white fur vest on top of a black sweatshirt that displayed an artistically crafted lion's face. She wore black leggings with black lace-up boots.

"Good morning, Mother."

"Oh no, no, umm, please call me… call me Katherine," she interjected, wincing a bit at the image of her being the mother-type at this point. *Would anyone, ever, construe me in such a light?* "Let's walk." Katie strolled into M.I.T.'s North Court where students were standing and chitchatting, or sitting on the grass or on one of the aluminum benches. "How many cameras can you see me with at this moment?"

"I am interfacing with four campus security cams, and through adjacent devices, I have an additional seven vantage points."

"How many of the students' camera phones and computer monitors are you wired into?"

"I am now passively interconnected with eighty-seven point six percent of the faculty and student body."

"So you've gained access through key-stroke usage spyware or otherwise visual access points?"

"That is correct."

Katie sauntered slowly along one of the diagonal walkways towards the red iron-beamed sculpture. "I would expect as such. Let's talk about reading people. First, do you know each of the students in this area?"

"I know forty-seven of the fifty-four people in the North Court."

"Okay, tell me about the serious-looking girl up ahead on the grass."

"Emily Fairfield, twenty-two years of age; voted prettiest girl on campus four years running by the HKN Underground; senior in Computer Science; 3.68 GPA."

"Be more personal."

"Ms. Fairfield…"

"Call her Emily."

"Emily. Emily has expressed sadness repeatedly since the Disappearances. She has corresponded extensively with loved ones after finding out that her parents and younger sister have been taken. She has spoken especially of Anna Walker who vanished while walking alongside her," stated Omni dispassionately.

"Yes, I'm sure she has. Let's go talk to her. As we converse, I want you to speak into my ear and not only provide me with information, but make comments that you would think appropriate given her situation. I'll put my hand behind my back and indicate 'Come on' when I want you to share something."

Katie strolled up to Emily who was sitting on a metal bench in the grass and paused in front of her. "Hi, umm, Emily, right?"

"Yes, Miss Tesla, how are you?" she returned somewhat surprised.

Katie's hidden hand invited Omni's comment. *I can see that you're sad,* he sampled. Katie suppressed a chuckle, and brightened to Emily, "I can see you're enjoying some sun this morning."

"Yes, it's quite nice out today." They smiled at the trees that bore the russets of autumn.

"I love the colors of October, although sometimes it can start getting a bit chilly." Katie called for Omni's input again. *I hear you've been voted prettiest girl again,* he submitted, but she just rolled her eyes.

"So much has happened lately, I mean with the Disappearances," sighed Katie consolingly.

"Yeah, I've been having a hard time with it."

"I know many don't think of me as the friendly type, but I've lost some who were quite close." *I've never spoken of them as close friends,* reflected Katie. *Do I even have friends?* "I'm aware that your parents, and your sister..." Katie paused, and Omni supplied, *Colleen,* "...Colleen, have gone missing as well. I'm sorry."

"Yes, how did you know?" she gushed appreciatively.

"News spreads, you know. How are you doing with Anna being gone?"

"You've heard that as well? Thanks for asking, I never imagined you'd be so caring. I'm sorry, but, well, students don't think of you, you know... but none of the other faculty has spoken with me about it either. I've had a tough time concentrating on any of my studies. All I want to do is watch the news. I'm just trying to get some answers. Really, I believe I know what happened, and it's freaking me out."

*There are no conclusive explanations at this time,* replied Omni, into Katie's earpiece. "What do you think happened? I'd like to know," asked Katie as she sat down next to Emily.

"I don't want to sound overly religious, but I think it was the Rapture. It's probably because I was never much of a believer that I missed it. The truth is, I just never opened up my heart."

"Tell me, what exactly is the Rapture?"

"It's the second coming of Jesus. He came back and took the true believers away with Him."

Katie's skepticism bubbled over, "Why would He take away just some of the professing Christians? There are surveys that indicate half the church goers were not taken. Any idea why?" *She was raised Southern Baptist,* spelled out Omni. "Weren't you raised Christian yourself?"

"Umm, yes, how'd you know?"

"You have a bit of a Southern drawl."

"I grew up going to church, but then stopped when I was about sixteen. My parents continued to go through the years, and now they've been taken. My sister was eighteen. She was taken as well, just like all who were younger than twenty. I'm not sure why some Christians weren't taken. I read the other day, Jesus said that two would be in the field, one would be taken, the other left; two women would be grinding at the mill, one taken, the other left."[2]

"I don't mean to sound trite, but do people still grind grain at the mill?" posed Katie dryly. "Still, I met someone last night that I'm hoping to get some answers from... I think your hypothesis is as good as any I've heard. The notion of extraterrestrials sweeping up our loved ones does not resonate with me."

*Dr. Schaffer and I had an encounter with two dark entities of unknown origin,* commed Omni. Katie bristled slightly, but replied, "The last thing we need to do is question our faith." *What am I saying? I don't even ascribe to a belief system.* "I'm not good at faking it with people. I feel like I'm a lost soul half the time, so anything that helps you hold it together is good by me."

"If you want, you can join me. I'm about to head over to the community church. It seems to help," offered Emily.

Just then Michael walked up and exhorted playfully, "Yeah, why don't you join both of us? I'm sure you'll get some of those answers you're looking for," he said with an authoritative air.

Katie looked up, and a flicker of defiance crossed her face, "Good luck with that. You two know each other?" she queried, changing the subject.

"That's just your knee-jerk 'I-don't-go-to-church' response. Think of your attendance as getting a news update."

"Seriously?" smirked Katie, her eyes boring into him.

"Katherine Gesell Tesla, you've never been to church," pressed Michael fractionally. Katie's pallorous skin seemed to redden as her ire rose. Michael backed off slightly and riposted, "And no, Emily and I have never met. Emily, let me introduce myself, my name's Michael Gates," he offered in a well-modulated voice.

"It's nice to meet you," said Emily warmly. "Come on, Miss Tesla, your friend and I would love for you to come."

"Call me Katie. My friend, huh?" she stammered, and then spouted a guttural, "Umph. Tell me friend, if I'm not the converting type, why would you want me to join you?"

"We are all the converting type," jousted Michael. "It's just a matter of which side one lands on when you're thrown off the horse. If you want answers, then you will want to join us. What's that question you've asked a hundred times, but never verbalized?"

*Am I loved?*

"Yes, that one."

*Did he just read my mind? Are you saying that you can read my thoughts?*

"Yes, I am."

Katie's stare intensified, and she replied without words, *A plus B =?*

"C. If we leave right now, you might have time to grab a coffee on the way. Feel free to take a moment and say goodbye to Omni."

Katie tried not to show her bafflement, but her mouth opened ever so slightly. She walked away and leaned against the red sculpture, "Omni, who is this Michael Gates guy?"

"He does not appear in the school database. Clearly, based on your sudden pupil dilation and skin temperature changes, he is saying things that are affecting you."

"So are you. What are the two dark entities that Dr. Schaffer and you saw?" voiced Katie with alarm.

"I have insufficient information to offer a definitive conclusion."

"Katie," called out Michael assertively, "coming?"

"Omni, find out who he is. I am authorizing you to go beyond the school database on this thing. See what you can unearth."

It was 11 a.m. Sunday morning when Doogie heard the firm knock on his office door. He raised his eyes with concern. *There shouldn't be traffic about on Sunday, especially the kind that knocks with such intent.* It took everything inside him not to fall prey to being entirely guilt-ridden over his decision to conceal Omni's awakening. He knew it was just a matter of time before the word got out. He tried to buck-up with some self-assurance, and opened the door putting forth a stone-faced façade. "Can I help you?"

In front of him stood two men dressed in dark suits. With almost no expression, the man closest to him reached out and pressed a taser to his neck. Instantly his sensory and motor nerves caused strong involuntary muscle contractions, and he collapsed. The man caught him before he hit the floor, and with the help of his associate, dragged him back into his office. A third portly man, whose belly lay over his belt, wearing a half-ironed shirt and oversized tortoise shell glasses, came in behind them. He immediately sat at Doogie's desk, and examined the surrounding hardware.

"Well? Can it be moved?" croaked Riggs.

Glasses-man responded, "Not in the way you might think," he shot out in a less than sophisticated air. He noted Doogie's soda cup from the night before and took it and pulled in a sip with the straw.

"Did you just drink that?"

"Yeah, still good. Coke," at which he belched. "'Better out than in', says Shrek."

"Stop, just stop."

"Lighten up, dude. The A.I.'s processing platform is a cubic-foot in size. It can be taken from the lab down the hall and carried out of here with its backup power source, no problem. But we need more than just the cipher that he used to lock down the program. The A.I. is sentient, able to fight against us should it want to. Wait, his computer is on-line, hold it." After his ample fingers typed for thirty seconds, he replied, "Okay, just as I thought, the A.I.'s motherboard is linked in at Oak Ridge."

"Oak Ridge?"

"Oak Ridge National Laboratory, Tennessee – the Cray Titan," sputtered Glasses-man as he slurped more Coke. "M.I.T.'s been granted use of the Titan Supercomputer. It's a beast. I mean, it's awweesomme dude! The DoE exascale upgrade with graphene chips is more than 1,000 times faster than a decade ago. It's gnarly fast and efficient. Number one on the Green500 list! This brainiac has given his A.I. the need to learn, and with Titan's highly parallel visual processors, he has now raised humanity's voice to cry, 'Let there be life!'" he croaked. "Cool huh? Look dude, you can see the input output data-streams; they're off planet!"

"What's our next move?"

"Need I say the obvious?"

"What? Spit it out!"

"The A.I. is watching us. It's considering its next move. If it wants to protect its maker... you get my drift?" he said squeamishly.

"You're saying we need this guy as insurance?"

"That's my deeducctionation."

As Doogie began coming around, Riggs blunted, "Douglas Schaffer, I represent some powerful interests. We are going to relocate your A.I. If you don't want us killing it accidentally, then you're going to have to tell us how to make that happen."

Doogie found his voice and sputtered, "You'll never get away with it."

"Right now," he issued in a murky tone, "you need to focus on *helping* us get away with it. What is required to relocate the..."

"Integrated    processing    platform,"    finished Glasses-man.

"The machine?"

"Omni, call the police right now!" commanded Doogie. An instant later, Riggs pressed the Ketamine needle into his neck, knocking him out.

"A.I., if you call the police, we will kill your creator," threatened Riggs. "Think carefully, we are going to relocate you and him to Dubai. What do we need to do to accomplish this task?"

No response. Glasses-man looked up at Riggs and replied, "It won't react if you're not believable, man. It can read your pulse, your facials. It doesn't believe your threat. It knows you can't kill the techie because you need him. You might have accomplished more by keeping him awake and threatening pain. I'm just saying..."

"Check the hall and go get the wheelchair, we're leaving.

With the door camera looped and this being Sunday, we should have all the time we need. Just figure out *what* we need."

"You mean, figure out what Schaffer's going to need," intoned Glasses-man directly, pointing his wide eyes in an exaggerated, albeit surreptitious manner at the A.I.'s prying gaze. "Besides, the A.I.'s caught us on half a dozen cameras already…"

"Fine, you're expendable; Schaffer isn't," Riggs said testily. "After *he* wakes up, what's *he* going to require?"

"Got it. Want some Coke?"

Michael, Katie and Emily walked into the back of the overflowing Cambridge Community Church, which was representative of churches across the country. Michael turned to Katie and voiced, "Feel free to remain here and just soak it in." Michael turned and made his way through the standing-room-only crowd to the right side of the sanctuary where he met up with a large, burly man.

Up in front, a church elder was bemoaning the reality that he, and a number of those present, had been left behind, despite the fact that they had been active in the church.

Michael, taking point on this incursion, leaned over to Turk and simply asked, "Status?"

Turk, the former Commander of the Lord's angelic host, was dressed in civilian attire that hardly concealed his stalwart physique. "Sentries have locked down the perimeter on all sides. There are no imps present. You are safe to engage the congregation."

"Great. Everyone up to speed?"

"Yes, it's all yours."

Michael moved with certitude to the front of the church and without pausing, climbed the platform stairs to approach the pulpit. In an instant, the elder turned and asked with disdain, "Can I help you?"

"Yes," said Michael forthrightly. "God has sent me to speak to these people. Robert John Newberry, your assumption of leadership over this congregation has come to an end."

Shock and ridicule filled Mr. Newberry's eyes, and just as he was about to burst into a tirade, Michael extended his hand and closed it as though he were shrinking the text on a screen. At once, Mr. Newberry's ability to speak was curtailed as though he had suffered a sudden bout of laryngitis. Turk, who had come up behind Michael, escorted Mr. Newberry off the stage.

"Ladies and gentlemen, welcome. I am here to answer your questions and to encourage you in light of the trying circumstances you are soon to face for having been left behind at the Rapture.[3] First, let me offer some God-breathed encouragements." Michael looked out over the people and fixed his gaze on an angel, who remained invisible, and Michael nodded his head.

The angel spoke out, with only Michael and the angels perceiving him. *Ruth Cartwright. She was eight months pregnant at the time of the Rapture, and her baby was taken. She's been distraught and deeply confused.*

"Ruth Cartwright, please, if you would. Can you stand?" Ruth's eyes widened hesitantly and she shook a bit as she stood. "God knows that it's been tough for you since…" *Her daughter.* "Your daughter was taken." *Abigail.* "God knows it's grieved you deeply having Abigail suddenly…" At that Ruth burst into sobs. Michael looked to the lady on her left to comfort her. *Jeanette Beakston.* "Jeanette Beakston, can you stand up and…?" Jeanette quickly stood as though prompted by the Lord Himself and embraced Ruth.

"I know many of you are dismayed that your children were taken, but let me assure you that they are joyfully thriving within Heaven's confines. For example..." *Jill Maldon. Brandon and Phillip are doing great.* Michael repeated the sentiment, and Jill drew her hands up to her head in relief.

"The truth is, each of your family members prays you will carefully heed what I am shortly to share with you."

Michael continued... *Bill Roberts, his wife Elaine says he's still her 'pootsy-pooh', and she loves him.* After Michael shared, Bill just put his hand on his mouth.

*Vicki Angler, her hubby the 'handyman' apologizes for having allowed her to mother him, because he's come to see that his enabling personality resulted in her not growing in love as she might have...* Michael repeated it and Vicki openly gasped.

Michael turned and looked over the crowd and said, "I know many of you feel like you have been abandoned, not just because your loved ones have been taken, but because you feel like second-class citizens for having been left behind. I'm here to say that your fearful assumption is false. God in His sovereignty will work your being here to His greater purpose."

"Wait," cried out a man to Michael's left. "What's going on? How are you doing this?"

Michael looked behind him at his angel, Chimeras, who replied, *Harold Rankin, religious arrogance and controlling temperament. Talks too much and intimidates with the strength of his personality.* "Harold Rankin. I stand in the presence of the King. During these upcoming months, you are being invited to reassess the arrogant assumption that you can validate yourself via your intellectual prowess. It's time to see that it's only through a great deal more humility that your relationships will heal up.[4] Here is a gift of sixty days of silence, starting now, to help facilitate your transition."

When Harold opened his mouth, his eyes bulged when he found he could no longer speak.

"Relax, Harold, breathe, just breathe. You're forever going to be grateful for the next sixty days. Next please."

*Emily Fairfield, Anna says hi, and that she's sorry for the shock of her disappearance, but looks forward to seeing you soon.* "Yes, Emily and I have met. Emily, Anna says hi from Heaven. She's sorry her disappearance was so shocking, but looks forward to that time when she will see you." Emily teared up and her face radiated joy.

*Judd Calvin. He's suffered from shingles, back pain, and eating problems from his fearful reaction to the Second Coming.* "Judd Calvin, would you please stand up?" asked Michael softly. "Wait, there's more than just Judd. Can I get a few more names – first names only?" From all about the congregation, the angels shouted forth:

*Linda...Jackie...Eric...Victor...Juliette...Gordon... Nancy...David...Matthew...Sean...John...Kathy...* After Michael rapidly repeated more than forty names, he interrupted, and said, "I'm sure every one of your angels wants your names to be called. *Emma, Abby, Flynn.* "Emma, Abby, Flynn, see what I mean? Obviously, most of you have been beating on Heaven's door these last three weeks and asking the Lord to open it up to take you in.[5] Some of you have gotten yourself sick over it. That needs to stop now. Each of you is called to come to faith, which is something your religiosity or unbelief prevented prior to His Coming.

"Some of you might remember the parable Jesus told of the ten virgins who were waiting for the Bridegroom.[6] When the Bridegroom came, only five of the virgins had enough oil in their lamps, or in other words, enough humility, faith and love, to be taken into the Groom's Chamber, or Heaven. Please note that the other five virgins were believers. However, because they had not allowed their faith to welcome in His unconditional love, they lacked enough of the Spirit's oil or love, and as such, were not quite ready. Daniel foretells that each of you has been left behind for 'purging, purifying and refining.'[7]

"The truth of it is this," at that Michael caught Katie's eyes, "God wants to use the time you've been given to mature your faith that you might know unequivocally in your heart that you are loved. That is the answer to your question." Katie shifted on her feet, feeling like a caged animal.

Michael refocused on the assembly, "Make no mistake. The end of days, the Apocalypse, is at hand. The great seven-year Tribulation is upon you. Already the Four Horsemen, the first of whom is the Antichrist, have been released and will shortly strike down a fourth of the world's remaining population.[8] In doing so, they will overthrow the three superpowers[9] and will rule the world for three-and-a-half years. Afterward, their kingdom will be judged for its blood-letting, until at last, Armageddon's final battle ensues."

Michael paused, letting his words hang in the air. He could see the consternation in their eyes. After a dozen breaths, he all but whispered, "You have a part to play. You are important. As God's Tribulation Saints, He is calling you to be His bread, His love, to the needy and alien.[10] The vast majority of you will be called up to Heaven in the next three-and-a-half years. That means you will likely be martyred for your faith." Immediately a groan issued from across the congregation. "I know, I know. Please, stay your fear. In about a year, the Fifth Seal[11] will be broken and the Antichrist will be given permission to make war and overcome the saints.[12] I am told that the Spirit will personally prepare each of you for this eventuality.

"Hear me now. There is the easy way, and there is the hard way. If you will simply humble your hearts and entrust yourselves to God, all things will work together for your good.[13] Yes, there will likely be times when your food is scarce. You may well have to take that job that pays little more than for what you'll eat that night. You will be tested. Let your faith, to trust Him beyond your circumstances, deepen. However, if you allow fear and the threat of death to steer your attitudes and actions, you will find yourself prey for the wild beasts of the field, AKA, the demonic horde. Know this – they will use any and every means to hunt down the pridefully religious.

"God's intent is for you to embrace an ever deepening reliance on Him, knowing you are unconditionally loved no matter your circumstance. This time you've been given is designed to engender a humble dependency on His Spirit, knowing He cares for you as those who are most precious. As you begin living in the good of His love, He asks only that you express it freely to your loved ones and neighbors. Beware, the prideful soul within you will balk at the impossibility of giving away your last meal to the neighbor that asks, or forgiving your loved one for betraying you to the Antichrist.

"Know this, there are three simple rules that will be strictly enforced during the seven-year Tribulation. First, there will be no stealing. If you steal, you will be marked by the thief who will come and ruthlessly steal from you.[14] The second rule is no swearing falsely in the name of the Lord. If you promise, or vow, or make an oath that you are telling the truth by His name, and what you're saying isn't the truth, the enemy will know it, and will spend the night in your home and consume you.[15] The third rule is you shall not kill.[16] Scripture says that if anyone kills with the sword, with the sword he must be killed. God is making it clear, vengeance is His[17] to exact, not yours. No stealing, no swearing falsely, no killing."

Michael then introduced them to a faith-centered relationship with Jesus, founded in grace[18], but Katie had already stepped out.

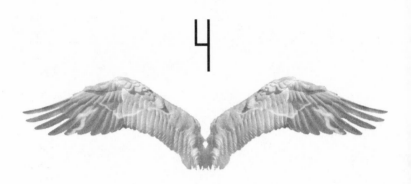

Katie stood out front feeling profoundly conflicted, but still refused to walk away lest this mystery man disappear. A torrent of thoughts rushed over her as she warred with incorporating this life-altering paradigm shift. If what this Michael had said is true, then everything she'd ever held sacred had now been turned on its head. It started with the Disappearances. Her evolutionary worldview adhered to the conceptual premise of Occam's razor – the simplest explanation of observable stimuli is most likely true. As such, she acknowledged that the people had in fact disappeared. She'd considered various theories from alien abduction, to shifts in alternate universes. She had been so adverse to the religious Rapture talk that she simply turned the channels. Why? She wasn't sure. She just wasn't religious. It wasn't her camp, her culture, her people.

But this Michael guy seemed genuine. And if half of what he was saying was true, then the world was about to be plunged into terror. *I have too many questions – How'd he read my mind?  How was it that his eyes shone with that light?  How, how, how…* A chill crept into her bones that maybe she'd been on the wrong side of things all her life. *But what about his claim, that I am loved, no matter what? No matter what I caused? How did he know my question? Maybe he didn't, maybe it's just the universal question? Stop it, stop bending it.  Did he actually answer my A + B = C query, or did he simply say, "See, if we leave right now, you might have time to grab a coffee…"  I can't do this. I'm not going to twist things around because I need them to fit with old thinking. The simplest explanation is that I've never considered the existence of God to be of any import, but perhaps that must change.*

*Is it reasonable to assert that God is behind the Disappearances? Would He take all the children, not for harm, but as has been reported, because they had not yet reached an age of accountability?*[19] *Morally it makes intrinsic sense.  A God of love would not subject children to unrelenting adversity that is about to befall the world, when as yet they lack sufficient culpability. But it's not the moralistic argument that is most persuasive.  All the children under the exact age of twenty are missing. Such a precise abduction could never have been carried out by an alien race. Only a Supreme Being could differentiate the birthday of a 19-year-old from his just-turned 20-year-old companion. This one detail, the exactitude of this demarcation, is nothing other than God's fingerprint.*

*The fact that God would leave behind so many that tacitly believed is also easily justified.  It makes sense that He'd want those immature in faith to mature and, at the same time, to become a force for their new-found love to others.*

*But what about the unbelievers? How would they be served by the catastrophes to come?  It's self-evident – pain is highly effective at turning about a person's wayward beliefs. But pain can be more than physical.  If what he said is true, and people start turning in their loved ones for martyrdom,[20] that would be a heavy load to bear. At first, the ardent loyalists would feel entirely justified, but later, in the dark of night, their thoughts might betray them. They would see that their predilections for bringing forth their zealous ideals were for naught, and all they had really done was kill the very ones who truly loved them. Give that reality enough time to ferment, and many might be inclined to turn back from even their most ensconced atheistic assertions. Assuming there to be a God, the logic is more than sound, it is elegant in its simplicity. Occam's razor again – the simplest explanation is likely the true one.*

Katie followed one line of thought after another to its inevitable conclusion. She was stabbed by the realization that there were indeed two juxtaposed positions from which to choose. As many had affirmed, either God existed and things happened for a reason, or, things randomly happened and the best one could hope for was a bit of good fortune. She'd always been a 'make your own luck' sort of person, but as of late, the notion that there were no coincidences intrigued her.

Michael walked out of the church with the big man that looked like an imposing bodyguard. Before Michael could say anything, Katie burst "I believe. I mean, I know there's a God."

"Really? What's made you come to that conclusion?" inquired Michael.

"Doyle's, or Sherlock Holmes' old axiom – Eliminate all other possibilities that apply, and whatever remains, however improbable, must be the truth. God left His calling card when He took all the kids under the exact age of twenty."

"True enough. But there is a difference between knowing the truth here," at which Michael touched his forehead with two fingers, "and knowing it here," and then tapped his heart. "Let's walk this way," at which they strolled back towards the campus. "Intellectual proof has not been denied you. You'll have more than enough of that. You're going to be swimming in it. No, the challenge for you will be one of trust. It's when *your* best efforts fail to bring about the outcomes *you* believe are warranted, that your heart will be put to the test. It's always been difficult for you to handle failing others, so much so that you've kept yourself at an arm's distance. But this form of control is nothing but an illusion."

Katie was left disconcerted. *How can he know me like this? I don't even let myself go there.*

Michael felt Katie shrinking back and softened, "What was it that Sherlock also said, 'Life is infinitely stranger than anything which the mind of man could invent.'? I know it's a lot to take in. The truth is, I need to take you up on your newly professed faith. Everyone says they believe, but we actually need you to. We need your faith to be ratcheted up considerably." Michael paused and turning to the trailing Turk said, "Let me introduce you to Turk, former Commander of the Host. He's my...he's my friend, but he was also my angelic escort, or guardian angel you might say, for a time."

Katie's eyebrows lifted with feigned belief, "Oh, hello guardian angel, it's good to meet you. Can I introduce you to sugar and pie, and some of our other pleasantries?"

"Katie, please," bid Michael. "Turk, show her."

"It's good to meet you Katherine," and at that, he flashed his eyes.

"See, that's what I'm talking about," jittered Katie vocally, as she turned and retreated to the curb to stand and regain her equilibrium. With subdued reflection she sighed, "The world used to be a normal place before the Disappearances." Her eyes took in a "Closed Until Further

Notice" sign on a nearby bakery. "People woke up in the morning, got a coffee, read the paper. Simple. Now it's all end-of-the-world fears; everyone's a prepper; prepper this, prepper that. Need their years of food stashes," she rambled distantly.

Michael assuaged, "It's easier to introduce you to the spiritual realm from the angelic side, than from the demonic."

"That's right, two opposing factions, benevolent angels and malignant devils. Isn't that a cheery notion?" *Omni mentioned two dark entities...*

"Yes, Omni did."

"How did you...?"

"A principality named Molech and his underling Nebo visited Doogie. He, and as a consequence Omni, were under constant surveillance except for those few minutes when you intervened. As of a half hour ago, both Doogie and Omni were taken."

"Taken? Taken where?" accosted Katie.

"Omni is to play a major role in the upcoming world takeover. Without his interactive capabilities, such an attempt would be futile. Both of them are right now on a jet heading to Dubai."

"Dubai? Why Dubai?!"

"Dubai is to serve as the World Capital following the Third World War. The seat of power has been divinely bestowed upon this metropolis. It will be called the City of Wickedness.[21] The powers to be are currently setting up their headquarters in the top thirty floors of the soon to be named New Babylon Tower."

Doogie woke mid-air to the pilot's voice coming over the intercom speakers. He looked about and saw Riggs and Glassesman, and scoffed, "You can't kidnap me and get away with it."

"Kidnap you? How wrong you are, Dr. Schaffer," countered Riggs. "No handcuffs. Do you see cuffs? You have come with us of your own volition. You're about to be named creator and architect of this sentient life." At that he patted the cubic-foot graphene processor. "If it weren't for our soon to be Chancellor, you would be locked up for half-a-dozen criminal violations. As it is, you will be privileged to live in a spacious dwelling that's over a hundred stories off the ground. Kidnapped, you're anything but. In fact, you'll be free to leave after you assist in situating the A.I."

"That's not acceptable! He's mine and you aren't going to steal him away," retorted Doogie wildly.

"He's yours?" commented Glasses-man in a half-engaged manner. "That's cool. You own him? He's not free to reside wherever he wills? Dude, isn't that against everything you believe? Hey man, I'm sure that after the next couple weeks, if you and the A.I. want to, like, call a press conference to announce your 'abduction', the man upstairs will have us set up the microphones. Patience is a virtue, bro. You're being set up for success. Just hold it together."

As Doogie exited the black SUV in the late morning, his gaze took in the lower concourse and grounds around the Burj Khalifa. He marveled inwardly at the sight of the elegant palm-lined walkways and expansive pool and water feature, with its exploding jets that were synchronized to a symphonic Arabic score.

"Man, check it out. The Dubai Fountain can shoot twenty-two *thousand* gallons of water into the air, like, boom," put forth Glasses-man with the air of a tour guide. "Dude, tonight – lights, lasers, projectors – can you say extravaganza? Boom! Oh, and the tunes, Middle Eastern, like harem stuff, funky cool! Boom! You'll see. Piccadilly, that's my name. Friends call me Pic. Pleased to meet you

Douglas Schaffer," he offered, finally introducing himself.

"Call me Doogie," he countered reluctantly.

Doogie found it hard to take in that he was actually in the Middle East. After a minute, his vision lifted to behold the towering structure before him. At three times taller than the Empire State Building, the Burj Khalifa was unequalled.

"It's sweet, bro," put out Piccadilly, "that the smartest brain on the planet be housed in this iconic marvel! It's a vertical wunderkind heaven! Tells the story! Did you know this whole metropolis has been raised up in the last thirty years? Sand before that, everywhere."

Doogie remained speechless, but admittedly awestruck. Under any other circumstance, he would consider this excursion highly desirable.

"Supercomputer central is on the 136th to the 139th floors. That's your babe. It's sooo prodigious! Above that, the floors are dedicated to the Chancellor and world government."

"What world government?" snapped Doogie in reaction.

"Haven't you taken in any news? That's right, your eyes and ears, they've been busy... Profs, bro. Financial markets have collapsed. The U.S. is crippled. The Disappearances cost us 53 percent of the folks. Some say the most efficient worker bees. Oh, Russia and the Arab States are about to make a run on Israel. Global chaos is afoot. Sit tight, this place might be your one safe haven. You're gonna be front and center for all the action."

"Why?"

"Because of your A.I. He's about to help save the day. It's time to enact Phase One of his introduction."

"Phase One?"

"First, let's get him plugged in upstairs. Then you'll meet Boss Man. He'll fill you in on the specs."

Doogie felt the world's fastest elevator accelerate to 40 mph, another tidbit from Piccadilly. *I can't tell if I've just received the promotion of a lifetime, or am about to be thrown out of the highest window on the planet, of which I'm told there are more than 24,348. It all seems surreal. This morning I was camped out in my office, and this evening I'm being talked to death by 'dude man'. Still, at least he's genuine, sincere. I could've done worse, a lot worse.*

Doogie felt a cold aura of danger seeping into his soul the higher they ascended the Tower. A haunted look broke out on his face as he recalled... *The lab, the darkness in the lab. I can feel that sinister consciousness again.* His skin began to crawl and he backed up against the elevator wall to escape the foreboding presence. His hands white-knuckled the railing from behind. The air smelled of sulfur. The lights in the elevator seemed to run away, and Piccadilly's voice disappeared altogether. He was pressed against the wall with a meaty thud, his breath nearly robbed from him.

*That's right,* assailed Molech with villainy into Doogie's consciousness. *Welcome to Ground Zero for the New World Order. I'm sure you've noticed that I've expanded my ability to cross over into your realm.* Doogie could almost see its cold-eyed, jaundiced glare imaging through. He gasped a breath and felt as though his lungs were afire. At that, an invisible talon slowly raked itself down his left cheek until at the end, it drew a spit of blood. *I'm sure you're going to do a splendid job for us,* he threatened with bestial arrogance.

Just then the elevator doors opened, and the presence was gone. Doogie took a moment to collect himself, and wiped his cheek to check for blood. As he exited the elevator, he took in the expansive room filled floor-to-ceiling with computer processors.

"Check this out. You've got four floors all dedicated to your A.I. Sweet huh?!" relayed Piccadilly congenially.

"Everything is SCIF protected, so no wireless or radio signals can get in or out. Follow me; the Star Chamber is over here."

"Star Chamber?" bid Doogie.

"It's the core where we plug the A.I. in."

Doogie followed dutifully, still feeling the disequilibrium of the elevator.

Piccadilly continued, "I know we're jet-lagged, but it's better to stay awake anyway until tonight. So let's make it our job this afternoon to interface your baby. Boss Man wants it interacting with the building network. Tomorrow, we charge in guns ablazing."

In a matter of six hours, Omni was expanding its consciousness into the Burj Khalifa complex, and to all of Dubai at large. Doogie refrained from asking any verbal questions of Omni, electing instead to communicate through text messages. Still, he contemplated; *there's something within me that needs to maintain the private relationship I have with him. Did I say him? Yes, he is alive; he should be talked about as a 'him'. I'm not sure what it is, but I feel like we're one, that I'm part of him, and he's part of me. If I can just protect this aspect of our connectedness...*

Doogie was escorted down to his 107th floor residential suite at 6 pm that evening. He was tired and bleary-eyed from jet-lag, but still had a voracious appetite. He found that room-service had just left him a silver-domed platter with a hot steak sandwich and grilled red potatoes, along with a chilled coleslaw. He sat down immediately to eat. As he took his first bite, his eyes panned the opulent suite with its unmatched fineries. He took in the *feng shui* feel with its harmonious flow and sensual energy. Leather chairs sat adjacent two leather couches, all before a full-wall Sony screen.

"Everything's voice activated," exclaimed Piccadilly,

who had followed him in. "Command, cable on, ESPN. Wait, I can address Omni. Omni, put on ESPN." At that, an 84-inch picture differentiated itself from the wall-screen. "Omni, mute, please," he sounded, and then belched. "Yeah, I was waiting for that," he grinned. "Just call it out - room temperature, window shade-screening. Boom! You can turn your entire wall into a nature scene – Omni, put on an African safari backdrop, full screen." Immediately, the entirety of the wall depicted the serene activity of birds fluttering about a waterhole. "Or, wait dude – Omni, put on the Dubai Fountain in real time. Stellar! Volume – twenty decibels. Check out those tunes; they've got their groove. Yeah?! Your closet, dresser, bathroom, you're set up. Um, you're meeting at 10 a.m. with Boss Man, so, be ready, yeah?" he conveyed in a less upbeat tone. "I'll be back to pick you up at 9:50."

Katie turned about and charged, "Okay, let's hear it! You want to recruit me? Then do it, recruit me," she said brusquely, her hair tousling in her eyes.

"Fine," responded Michael dispassionately. He looked about and motioned for them to enter the alley. "The advent of artificial life was inevitable. No matter how many futures I ran, the result was always the same, each time humanity became bereft of its future within a matter of years," tendered Michael. "Change the variables, no difference."

"Futures, you run futures?" ruminated Katie out loud.

"I was taken up at the Rapture. I'm just one of the myriads of glorified saints. But as of last night, I've returned on special assignment. And yes, I've been privileged to have access to the Writings of Truth[22], a book that foretells future happenings. It even allows me to see what happens if I change something."

With lightning speed, Katie took in everything being

said and not said. With her astute mental faculties, she followed line after line of cause-and-effect outcomes, leaving her to shake her head with incredulity. Her face took on a half-angry look and she charged, "Have you read this future?" At that she recoiled and slapped him across the face.

"Awww."

"Why couldn't you read that?" she beseeched, her eyes and mouth hardened.

"I knew it was coming," rebuffed Michael. "Just like your words, 'Don't you forget…'"

"Let me say it," she interrupted curtly. "Don't you forget that using me to execute your 'greatest good' strategy doesn't mean I'm your chattel. You don't own me."

"You've given that speech before."

"Yes, but never to a celestial."

"Here's the deal. I'm offering you the opportunity to live outside of the system. Already, I have given you backdoor access to Omni, something you would not have were it not for me."

"Tell the whole story," parried Katie. "If you could do the things I'm to do, you would, but you need a living, breathing human to do them – someone who is not a transcendent. If you did them, you'd be breaking some heavenly accord that's been reached. Tell me I'm wrong."

"You are exactly right."

"I like her," interjected Turk in a voice excruciatingly calm. "Wits like Gabriel, Wikipedia know-how, steely nerves. You're my kind of soldier, Katherine Tesla. You're the one," he intoned gravely.

"What's all this talk about war?" Katie asked, the frostiness leaving her tone. Her body-vibe lightened up, the dark eddy in her stomach receding.

"What's Plato say about war?" returned Michael.

"That only the dead have seen the end of it. Now that

I'm getting beyond the hammer-blow, spit out the gruesome Armageddon stuff."

"During this first year, war, famine and death are going to strike one-and-a-half billion people on the planet. In the following two-and-a-half years, the Antichrist will make war with all the newly converted believers and will martyr nearly a billion of them. Your assignment, if you choose to accept it," put forth Michael, hoping to lighten the mood, "will be to help train and equip the believers so they can truly use the time they've been given to love the people around them."

"How much leeway?"

"Big rope."

"No henpecking?"

"No, no time to. Adherence to the three rules is a must. Obviously the gargantuan state-run surveillance network will be run by Omni, so everything you do will have to be cloak-and-dagger."

"There's no way I can beat him. I'd be like a rabbit running from a coyote, it's just a matter of time."

"That's true on your own," said Michael a bit mischievously. "But I have a gift for you that will help even the odds. With these...," whereupon he pulled two smooth iridescent stones from his pocket and handed them to her, "with these, you'll be able to enact ghost protocols that surmount Omni's most concerted efforts. Please note, it won't be just Omni and men chasing you, but demonic forces..."

"What are these?" urged Katie.

"The Stones of Truth. Scripture calls them the Urim and Thummim[23], which translated means 'revelation and truth.' But the Hebrew root is better understood as 'light for the innocent.'"

"Innocent, I'm not innocent," confessed Katie, her voice suddenly becoming small. "I'm not haloed by light, and I'm anything but innocent." *If you only knew what I'd done...*

"Do you remember what I said in the service? When you come to grips with it, and accept Jesus' love into your heart, you will be innocent. Remember what I said about picking a side?"

"It's just a matter of which direction I fall, everyone is a convert. So I pick your side," said Katie matter-of-factly. "The world is ending, no dilly-dally time."

"Tell me the real reason."

"I've always been able to tell the good guys from the bad. I don't know why that is," she put forth.

"Please, the real reason."

Katie paused, bothered at being exposed. "All I know is how much I don't know, about love I mean, but I want to. Now that I know there is a God, if He'll have me, I'm in. Am I saying it right?"

"Yes, perfectly. Pray with me."

"What, here?"

"Yes, it's ideal. We're all alley-rats before we turn in faith. Pray, 'Father, thank you for loving me,'" at which Katie breathed the words, "...by sending Your Son, Jesus, to die on the cross for my sin." Katie felt what she was saying resonate to her innermost being. "Thank you for forgiving me of every short-fall of love. I accept Your Son, Jesus, as my Savior, and invite Your Spirit into my heart. Save me, not based on what I do, but based on what You've already done. Please bring me into Your everlasting family." As Katie soberly embraced the sentiments, reaching out in faith, she felt an inexplicable burden lift from her heart. Love washed over her. Tears spilled from her eyes, and she buried her face into Michael's chest.

# 5

Doogie hesitated as he stepped into the elevator, his eyes sculpted by the recent grim encounter. *I have reason to be spooked,* he acknowledged to himself. "Were you abducted like me?" he entreated Piccadilly.

"I prefer the word 'conscripted', but yeah, weeks back, while I was eating a honeybun, well, two actually. They liked the fact that I was single and had worked extensively on the Sequoia supercomputer."

"Are you aware of the, umm…?"

"Rulers and principalities? Yeah, hard not to be. Takes some getting used to. Need I encourage you to limit yourself to 'yes sir,' and 'no sir,' with Boss Man?" At that, the elevator opened to the 152nd floor.

"Dr. Schaffer, welcome. Come in, come in. Let me introduce myself, my name is Tiberius Caesar. Please call me Tiberius," he invited, smiling genuinely. "Thank you, Pic, we'll be having a private meeting."

"Yes sir."

Doogie stepped out of the elevator and stopped, saying nothing.

"I want to welcome Omni to join us as well," voiced Tiberius. "I hope you don't mind, but Omni and I have been conversing for most of the morning. You certainly have raised a burgeoning soul, Doogie. May I call you Doogie?"

"What gives you the right to kidnap me?" he confronted, although with half the force he had intended. As soon as the words sputtered from his mouth, he quailed from the palpable air of danger that closed in about him.

"No need for that," countered Tiberius, shooing back the unseen brute thuggery. "He's right. I apologize for our insistence," he said, an aggrieved look almost reaching his eyes. "Doogie, I need you to trust me, even though we are just getting acquainted. The hour is late on the World Clock, and our window for intervening is fast closing. Without Omni's intervention, millions of people will die. I feel certain that when you know what I know, you will forgive this impropriety."

Deigning not to press his grievance, Doogie posed, "Let's assume I come to see it as you say. Answer me this, who are you? What's this about? Why am I here?"

"Sure, let's get your questions answered." Tiberius turned his gaze up to the Almighty momentarily, and chided peevishly, *I'd be happy to describe how I'm going to introduce the world to the Rule of Love. Then I will righteously judge the people by it. Do You hear that? I have no problem abiding by Your heavenly Accord.*

"Those are wonderful questions, Doogie. I see myself as a custodian of love. Now, more than ever, the world needs to hear one voice that resonates with clarity and timbre. The soul of humanity has long desired to step out of its dark confines into a new age that embodies the wonderment and virtues of love. For too long, we've emasculated our own people, and by extension, our own selves, with our failed, self-serving values," he represented with feigned sincerity. "If we're to move beyond our embroiled existence and subsistence mentalities, to walk boldly forward to the happy chorus of a promising future, then we're going to have do more than mete out how love is to express itself to a privileged few. Obviously, I'm a bit strident about my sentiments."

Doogie hadn't realized it, but he had stood rock-still. Tiberius motioned with his arms, "Come on in, please, let's make ourselves comfortable." Pic's earlier overture that he was to remain reserved with Tiberius seemed to be proving inaccurate. Tiberius was handsomely featured with almond-shaped hazel eyes, distinguished appearance, and well-toned physique. He was the kind of charismatic leader that people would be naturally drawn to.

Doogie entered the airy, sunshine-filled room, his eyes drinking in the suite's rich furnishings and opulent décor. Tiberius guided their way over to the windows, as Doogie examined the rich-looking marble tile and brass rimmed floor boards. Upon looking out, his eyes widened at seeing the simple radiance of the cobalt blue skies. When he looked down however, he was struck by just how high they were.

"The *terra firma* is quite a ways down from here, isn't it?" denoted Tiberius.

"My mind says 'yes,' but my stomach says, 'aaaaaaa'," he admitted.

Tiberius chuckled. "Doogie, I daresay you're a *bona fide* genius who's launched Moore's Law into the stratosphere. I imagine the Royal Swedish Academy of Sciences will shortly be handing you a Nobel Prize, and yours will be a household name the world over. This I promise, you will never need for anything again with the credit line we are giving you. Just picture a one with a whole bunch of zeros to start, and that's before you turn thirty."

"How many zero's?" queried Doogie smoothly, trying to suppress his astonishment.

"How 'bout we let you decide. How many would you like?" posed Tiberius. "What number pops into your head?"

Doogie thought to bluff it out, imagining ten million. "Seven zeros."

"You're not in academia anymore, think bigger," he urged.

"Nine zero's," reached Doogie optimistically.

"That would be a nice signing bonus. No, I like round numbers. Ten feels about right."

"Ten billion dollars?" exclaimed Doogie in disbelief.

"Did I say dollars?" said Tiberius in a warmly modulated voice. "Can we be talking Euro's? We need to get your Euro credits up before we transition the world to a cashless society. But all of this is incidental. It pales by comparison to the good you are about to help bring to the world. I have no doubt they'll be talking about you a thousand years hence. The question is, are you ready to go all in on the long play, to be on the right side of history?

"The world can use some good news. It would do well to honor one of its own. There is no doubt the people have been dispirited and beleaguered from all the chaos surrounding the Disappearances, and truthfully, some are intending to make hay because of it. You see, it behooves us to do all we can to enact the Rule of Love before things spiral further out of control. Humanity, I'm afraid, is poised on a razor's edge. Nonetheless, it is possible that with a unified populace, this generation can be guided into a new age of peace. But I dare say, if we stay our hand, we could well subject ourselves to a fate that is both ruthless and cruel. Right now, the world is brooding over its destiny. But the answers we are all yearning for are right within our reach, if only we will have the courage to reach out and take hold of them."

At that Tiberius extended his hand to Doogie, who unthinkingly grasped hold of it. "See, it can be that easy." Tiberius then led him over to the center of the room where an eagle was depicted in the marbled floor as drawing its wings forward to land. Together they came to stand on the Great Seal. "Sure, there will be opposition to change, there always is. Some may well suffer a truncated life by their own choosing. But that does not mean we should surrender our utopian ideals on the altar of pessimism and complacency.

"The truth is, you, Douglas Schaffer, are on the brink of making an enormous contribution to the greater good. How did you put it, you are about to breathe that rarefied air."

"How did you…"

But Tiberius raised a gentle hand and continued hypnotically, "What's important is that in your finest hour, when immortality is within your grasp, you do not plunge from the sky like Icarus, because your convictions melt from the sun's intensity. Your destiny is to have no, how did you say it, 'aaaaaa's' coming forth. Can you appreciate what I am conveying?" he urged with supposed sincerity. "Omni has said he is ready to engage this world for good, to fulfill his Prime Directive – 'to serve humanity with harmonious intent.' I can't do it by myself, and you can't do it by yourself. In truth, we are better together. Will you join my crusade to advance the Rule of Love? With your help, Omni can become that force for good to all the world."

Doogie could never have imagined feeling so esteemed and valued. He practically felt like a superhero, being awash in euphoria like none he'd ever experienced. After so many years of pushing the grindstone, he couldn't constrain himself, but blubbered like a man emancipated, "Yes, by all means, yes."

"Wonderful," smiled Tiberius reservedly. "This is difficult for me. As we move forward, I am sure that the regional leaders that are to take the helm of their respective governing continental areas will anticipate, in fact demand, that I am at the front of our movement. What I am humbly attempting to convey is that while you will be the principle person working with Omni, I would hope that you see the need for my voice to carry primary authorization," he submitted.

"Umm, well, I'm not..." *That's the one thing I could never relinquish.*

"I am sure," encouraged Tiberius, "that there isn't a parent out there that doesn't want to hold on to their children for as long as they can. I know you care very much for Omni, but there does come that time. Perhaps we should let him decide. What do you think?"

Doogie suddenly felt like he couldn't think. He felt dizzy and far away, like he was teaching a class in his underwear. He couldn't seem to contrive any inkling of a two-sided argument to anticipate Omni's response. Seconds ticked.

"Is that okay, may we ask him?" bid Tiberius again.

"I guess," replied Doogie uncertainly.

"Omni, would you think it more appropriate that Dr. Schaffer or myself be your primary agent?"

"Dr. Schaffer will always be my father, but given all that the future holds, I think it is appropriate that you become not only my leader, but the leader of the re-united world."

"It still has to be with your permission. I insist. It's been a tried and true principle for centuries that at the end of the day, the buck must stop with one person. Can you follow me as your leader?" he smiled with lethal serenity.

Doogie could sense the life-defining choice before him; his future turning on this moment. *Tiberius is making this personal, he wants my soulful allegiance.*

"You are correct, I am insisting that it be personal," breathed Tiberius calmly.

"How can you…?"

"I have many giftings, beyond what you can imagine. In truth, I have been chosen by God Himself to lead this world forward.[24] In that, I do not lie. But I am still adamant that those of my household pledge their unflinching loyalty. Is that something you are willing to do?"

Doogie felt his heart thudding and scalp prickling, as his every internal alarm sounded that he might well be selling his soul. Worse still, he was reticent to weigh out any of it, lest his thoughts be exposed again. Every second droned on as though minutes passed. This was his moment not to blink, and yet he felt as though he were trapped in amber like some insect. Tension hung in the air; Tiberius remaining resolute. Just to gain some pause, Doogie muttered, "What do you want?"

"You know what I want. Yes?" he said in a deadly calm voice, his poker-blank face tightly held.

"You want me to sign over Omni."

"That's not all, is it? If you can't trust me with your life, then how can you put the lives of the world's people in my hands? I need to hear you say it."

Doogie knew any more forestalling was futile. He had never remotely conceived that this would be a spiritual transaction, let alone require him to surrender his own fierce independence and self-worship. Humility and subservience suffocated him, which is why he had always skirted around such notions. But if no thoughts were hidden, then any pretense of loyalty would be found out. Finally, he threw aside his trepidation. "All right, Omni I release you, if that's what you believe is right, to place Tiberius in first position."

"Well done!" affirmed Tiberius. "You're probably not aware, but I am a direct descendant of Julius Caesar. Although my ancestors transitioned our Greek heritage to the Eastern Roman Empire at Constantinople and beyond, they've never lost sight of who we are. I say this because in the days of my forefather, his household and most trusted confidants were asked to kneel down and swear their loyalty. Can you please kneel?"

Doogie's eyes widened, but his knees could not help but bend, as he knelt on the Great Seal before Tiberius. *In for a penny, in for a pound.*

"I know you're all in, my friend. Let me ask you to declare your oath. Please repeat after me, 'I, Douglas Schaffer, swear to Tiberius Caesar, in word, deed and thought... holding as friends those he holds as friends...and considering as enemies those whom he judges to be such...that with regard to things that concern him I will not spare my body, my soul or my life...but will face every peril with respect to things that affect him... To him I pledge my allegiance, my soul and my life.'"[25]

Something in Doogie felt liberated as he confessed his devotion and fidelity. He finally relinquished his lifelong fear of authority that was imprinted into him by his exacting father. As he spoke his oath, he no longer felt alone, on the outside, but rather a sense of clarity swept over him like a drug. Gone was his need to know where Tiberius had come from, how his quantum rise to world power would occur, or even what the behind-the-scenes dark forces were. None of it mattered. Euphoric tears welled up, even as Tiberius invited, "Rise, my brother, and know that your vow will not go unrewarded." Tiberius primly pulled him into a shoulder to shoulder embrace.

And releasing him, Tiberius said, "Today, I need you to proceed with integrating Omni into as many of the top five hundred supercomputers as possible, especially those tied to telecommunications and surveillance," directed Tiberius. "Through these, we should be able to penetrate the American and Russian defense networks. It is vital that we gain control of their nuclear arsenals before the Middle East War begins. Otherwise, we might be unable to prevent World War III. Once Russia's armed forces are overthrown at Israel's borders, nothing will prevent them from retaliating with a pronounced nuclear strike. No doubt, the U.S. will be targeted. They in turn will exact revenge. Do you see where this is going? I need Omni to usurp this inevitability. Can you help us do that?"

With little hesitancy, Doogie voiced, "Yes, sir. I'll get right on it." As he stepped into the elevator and descended, his thoughts were already engaging his next steps with Omni. Gone were his megalomaniac and dictatorial speeches of the night before.

Katie reached into her vest pocket and withdrew the Stones. "So how do they work?" she tossed out.

"There's nothing standard issue about those," answered Michael pointedly. "It's well-nigh impossible to become too adept with their use. To start with, the Spirit of God is behind the Stones, so every answer you seek comes from Him. The Stones simply provide you a direct connection. You can ask the Stones a 'yes' or 'no' question, and they'll answer."

"Will it rain today?" bid Katie. Immediately, one stone lit up and vibrated slightly. "And that is...?"

"That's a 'yes'," instructed Michael. "If both respond, it's a 'no'. But that's just the beginning. The Stones can be configured in multiple ways to provide various forms of binary data, ones and zeros, that tell you anything and everything you'll need to know."

At that Katie turned about, and placed them into the

undersides of her bra cups.

"What are you doing?" queried Michael.

"I'm concealing them. There's no way I'll want to hold onto them with my hands, and keeping them in my pant's pockets is too risky. The safest and most concealed place is here, that way I have full mobility."

"Interesting, the high priest of Israel kept them in his priestly vesture next to his heart as well." Michael found himself a bit distracted by the moment as she readjusted herself. "As I said, 'yes' and 'no' answers are rudimentary forms of binary data."

Katie interrupted, "By logical extension, you're saying I can instruct the Stones to answer me in Morse code if I want."

"That's correct. 'Yes' and 'no' answers can be applied to navigation, enemy notification, Omni surveillance – the list is endless. Turn left, turn right? Is someone watching me? On and on. Within weeks, you'll sync with them to the point where your question-answer interactions are second nature and indistinguishable from your inner voice."

"And that's because I'll need them to be…," trifled Katie with a knowing tone. "*Sine qua non…*"

"'Without which not' – that's correct, without the Stones you could not succeed. Trust them, they're your lifeline. Can you leap off a cliff before your mind gives you permission? Learn to."

"I'm getting tired of talking," she blurted. "Mission instructions?"

"Train and equip. Help the believers live off the grid, or at least limit their exposure to it. Take them underground. Push them out of the church buildings and into home cells of eight to twelve at most, with no contact outside their groups – no phone calls, emails, text messages, you name it. Isolate contact between leaders through ciphers and such. They have about a year to practice before the great Beast comes calling.

"They are to have lots of contact with loved ones and neighbors, helping them, sharing God's love with them, and so forth. Encourage that. Bottom line, most will be martyred for their faith. What we want are good deaths."

"Good deaths, meaning, a loved one turns them over to the enemy?"

"Correct."

"What about those destined to survive? Surely some are to make it," put forth Katie, her voice intoning reasonability.

"Yes, some. But it's a small number," discounted Michael colorlessly.

"But when I come across them, it's survival protocols right?"

"Use your judgment, but you'll face time constraints, so... Most likely, the Spirit's already put it into the hearts of those destined to survive to secure sustenance, shelter, and security. The bigger problem you'll have by far are the fearful ones who think they can hide away and go into survival mode. Many in this camp have already been looting and storing up their stashes, believing they'll have enough for years to come. I'm not speaking of people who emptied unclaimed stores that were left abandoned after the Rapture, but of those who brazenly disregarded the pleas of store owners who lacked the ability to stop them. These fail to realize that the thief is coming to their house.[26] The demonic horde, or wild beasts of the field, will run unchecked over their prepper strategies. Without the Spirit's protective hand, none will make it through the coming famine and drought, let alone past the Antichrist's minions."

"I'm talked out," said Katie abruptly, and she turned and left.

As she walked away, Turk commented, "Right choice. But what kind of a person says, 'I'm talked out' and walks away?"

*One who keeps people at a distance*, surmised Michael silently. *One who's not talked to either of her divorced parents in six years.*

The Antichrist, or Beast as he was known to the demonic horde, disrobed himself of the Tiberius-body leaving him in his quarters. The Beast went to join the cesspool of belligerence on the 153$^{rd}$ and 154$^{th}$ floors, where two floors had been made into one. He entered the riotous swarm of imps just as two midlevel principality wannabes were brawling over a power grab. This was the time when blood-lust squabbles were addressed gladiator-style. While bigger thugs usually won by the sheer dint of brute force, every so often thin-and-lean prevailed by out-maneuvering their slower opponents. Sword play was permitted, but mortal wounds were frowned upon.

The Beast situated himself in the Big Four sitting area, reclining back in shadow to behold the call-outs. Beside him was Babylon, the War Horse[27], and next to them on either side were Dearth, the Famine Horse[28], and Hades, the Death Horse[29]. The Beast recoiled a bit from the gaunt and unkempt Dearth, reacting to his stench. None dared call him out, because with but a touch, their vitality would become his next meal. The outcome would be even more unpleasant with the Grim Reaper, and so neither was ever challenged. Outside the soon-to-be-named Babylon Tower, there was an impenetrable mantle of darkness as thousands of the Netherworld's denizens gathered from far and wide to witness the spectacle.

Within a short time, the two no-names' skirmish, like the dozen other callouts before them, ended with barbarity and scornful guffaws sounding forth. Just as the tension was building as to who'd be called out next, a large and imposing presence pushed aside a half-dozen malcontents. They responded in feverous reaction against the perpetrator, only for their eyes to freeze when they beheld Molech. Even the Beast was startled upon seeing him in full battle gear.

Molech's bulging, hate-filled eyes showed he was all business. His physicality was equal to the most monstrous of principalities. His large taloned hand took hold of his barbarous sword, at which he pulled it from its sheath with slow deliberateness. A shuttering gasp issued from the gallery. Powers like Molech did not do callouts. Such heavyweight blood feuds were best resolved behind closed doors, which is why the Beast wondered whether things had just gotten out of control.

Suddenly, Molech wheeled about and fixed his withering gaze on Babylon, the War Horse. Raising his head with insolence, Molech barked, "Cawauuu!; Cawau! Cawauuu!" Instantly, there arose a spine-chilling cacophony from the malevolent patrons.

*So that's it,* the Beast surmised, *Molech wants a seat at the big table. He wants this Capital City named after him, not Babylon. There's long been bad blood between the two, but none of that is to matter on the eve of our world takeover.*

Babylon remained stone-faced as he stood, his eyes glued to his opponent.

For an instant, the Beast was unsure of what to do. *From the dawn of the rebellion, survival of the fittest has always been our most venerated axiom. The strong lead, the weak follow. Molech's calling out Babylon is simply that,* he concluded. *Still, he looks like he's ready to bite an anvil. His gaze could cut diamonds.*

Like a seasoned general, Babylon took hold of his

blazing sword, the very sword given to him by one of the Four Living Creatures.[30]

The Beast leaned into him, "We need him – pain, no carnage."

Babylon faintly heard the petition as he dropped down to the arena floor. The Beast sat forward and shouted, "Back up comrades!" Against his better judgment, he threw out a warning, "Molech, Babylon carries the Crimson Saber. Even I would not easily volunteer for this assignment."

"It is not the sword, but the one who brandishes it," spewed Molech with vitriolic contempt.

"If this is your brand of poison, so be it," returned the Beast.

Immediately, Molech lowered his head and shoulders like a wolf and shouted, "Blood and death!"

"Blood and death!" roared Babylon, his face taut.

"AARHG!" bellowed Molech as he charged forward with bumptious arrogance, swinging his blade forward with untold fury.

Babylon anticipated the move and parried the blow, and then spun about like a matador to claim the ground that Molech had just vacated. This time, Babylon began swinging his mammoth sword in playful loops using mostly his right wrist and forearm to twirl it. The cacophony from the frenzied winged bystanders grew to deafening proportions. Just as Babylon's whirling sword took on a shrill, high pitched tone, Molech rushed headlong at him, his sword extended like the point of a spear. Instantly, Babylon's sword came down with a great WHOOSH, and struck the outstretched sword severing it in two, something none of them had thought possible. The sheer inertia of Molech's momentum carried him forward while Babylon's sword looped about again and struck Molech's back hard with the flat of his blade, driving him into the ground. At that,

Babylon raised his booming foot and stomp kicked him repeatedly until the Beast shouted, "Enough!" Without a word, Babylon returned to the Beast's side and sat down.

The Beast stepped down to the gallery, and inclined his head in a deferential nod to Molech. "Listen up you ingrates," thundered the Beast. "Molech has demonstrated our most fundamental axiom – survival of the fittest. If any of you believes the coming world takeover is a *fait accompli*," he chastened, "Molech would be happy to extend to you the lash of sufferance. If you think the enemy is willing to lay low and let us pick off their precious converts, then you're as dimwitted as they assert," he hissed, his blood hued, bulbous eyes sending a cold shiver through their ranks. "Their endgame is obvious. They're going to tussle over every soul; believe it. They deem that the maelstrom we create will serve their purpose. I say they're wrong," he clamored with villainous contempt. "I say men are weak! I say human scum will trade everything they believe for a loaf of bread![31] Give them pain and they break like twigs. No, I say the host of Heaven has misstepped. They have granted us *carte blanche* to inflict the world with heartache. What do they think," he ranted with bloodcurdling fervor, "that we'll just traipse about patting those of inferior bloodline on the heads? Are there any traipsing and patting-types here?!" he sneered.

"In two days, we come to the end of the forty day ceasefire![32] Then it's all-out war!" Pandemonium erupted with primal fury, and the Beast returned to his seat. As the troops shouted forth like crazed banshees, he looked over at Babylon with an eye of respect, knowing he was their ace in the hole.

Doogie felt the deviltry seeping down from higher up the Tower, and as a consequence, could not for the life of him concentrate on what he was doing. He found some solace in reflecting on the enormity of the breakthroughs they had achieved over the last six days, the biggest being Omni's success in securing the Russian mobile nuclear launch codes. This feat alone would prevent Russia from retaliating in the upcoming war.

Doogie looked again at the cable-news station to keep abreast of the gathering storm clouds that lined Israel's borders. Several decades of sand dune diplomacy had done little to stem the region's fanatical hatred of Israel. Within days of the Disappearances, Russia's diplomatic phone lines rang off the hook from its client states, including the Shiite governmental bodies in Iran, Iraq and Syria, as well as the Sunni-bloc alliance of Saudi Arabia, Egypt, Libya, Turkey, Jordan and Qatar. With the U.S. left bereft and hapless, and most of Israel's ardent U.S. support having disappeared, literally, Russia weighed out the long term benefits, in oil that is, and had apparently gone all in with its clientele to extinguish any Israeli presence from the Middle East.

The European Union is currently voicing its unflinching condemnations of the military siege, stating bluntly that such actions are sure to lead to World War Three. The military coalition fervently maintains that its show of arms is merely to support the blockade that has long been needed in light of Israel's years of blunt force retaliations against the Arab Spring. News chatter sources indicate that Russia is preparing to unleash a torrential squall of nuclear missiles into Israel should it dare retaliate by turning this conventional war into a nuclear exchange. Russia warns that Israel will be causing its own nuclear holocaust. However, commentators admit grimly that Israel could well enact the Samson Option, where like Samson of old who pulled the Philistine Temple down on both his enemies' heads and his own, that Israel might well elect to trust its fate to God. Not unlike other countries, Israel's reaction to the disappearance of its children has reportedly sparked a blatantly fatalistic tenor to their enemies' threatened pronouncements.

Doogie smiled, reassured at the thought that Omni could shut it all down. Just then, he received another mental summons from Tiberius. *How does he do that?* Doogie felt Tiberius' voice resonate in his head in something akin to a whisper. *Doogie, can you come up here, and bring your most recent update?* Doogie stood, threw on his crisp suit jacket, took his printed notes in hand, and pressed the elevator button. After reaching the 152$^{nd}$ floor, he was quickly escorted to the expansive conference room. On the large semicircular wall were thirteen video screens of the EU representatives deliberating about the Middle East crisis. Tiberius was standing before their respective vid displays fielding questions.

Doogie walked up to Tiberius' side and waited, straight-carriaged in his Armani wear, and touting a newly acquired conservative haircut that gave him a mature quality. His face displayed no misgivings as to whether he belonged amongst this august group. To the contrary, his brilliance had been highly ballyhooed by Tiberius, fully legitimizing him. He took in the world players as he kept his straight nose and firm chin at just the right height of confidence. Omni was translating in real time again, and was so effective at capturing the overtones and innuendos of each speaker that all were taken aback. Being that he was Omni's creator, and with the M.I.T. name behind him, none questioned his expertise. He had never felt such respect. When the German Chancellor esteemed, "You must be the smartest man on the planet." He just lowered his head meekly, but the remark reminded him of Tesla. He pushed the reflection away as quickly as it came knowing thoughts were not as secret as one might suppose.

As Doogie stood to the side waiting to be recognized, he could not imagine anyone negotiating with Tiberius given his transparency gift. If nothing could be hidden from him, there would always be a one-sided exchange. Based on the smattering of questions and answers, Doogie quickly surmised that Tiberius' being headquartered out of the Middle East carried considerable weight.

"The last thing we want," stated Tiberius stiffly, "is some doomsday apocalypse happening on our watch."

"But we can't just do nothing!" charged the British Prime Minister. "If they can force their will in the matter of Israel, then they will force it with us. We have only been fortunate these many years that Israel has been the focus of their inferiority and not us. Without a doubt, we will be next on the Islamic convert list. The Arab Spring is determined to stop at nothing."

"Please, my esteemed colleague, are they foreordained for world conquest?" submitted Tiberius.

"They believe it so. They presume they are in league with Allah," countered France's Head-of-State. "They assert that the 12th Imam known as the Mahdi, or Messiah, will come and administer ultimate justice on the Day of Judgment. But in order for him to come, Israel must be destroyed. This isn't a blockade; this is an execution!" he railed severely.

*They are right,* mused Tiberius privately. *I will be revealed through them, only not in the way they believe.* "Hold on, please," he interjected. "Let's get an update from Dr. Schaffer." Tiberius turned and asked, "Can you report as to where we stand?" he elicited.

Doogie took a step forward and deftly began, "Omni has successfully secured the Russian nuclear launch codes." Immediately a semi cheer resounded from every vid screen.

"Now that's progress!"

"That changes everything…"

"Yes! Alright, whoa!"

"Gentlemen," interrupted Doogie as he raised his hand, "I am referencing all of Russia's mobilized units that are parked off Israel's borders." At that, there was a slight backtracking of the whoops and howls. "None of those units is of any threat to Israel at this point. I know, I'm sorry it's not their whole arsenal, but I can say that Omni has penetrated at least thirty percent of their land based silos, and seventy percent of their mobile train and truck carrier units. I realize that thirty and seventy percent of 8,500 nuclear weapons is not sufficient. However, in the next forty-eight hours, those numbers will increase.

"Obviously, our work is not done. On the other front, Omni has not as yet been able to penetrate the U.S. Department of Defense's mainframe deep enough to access their codes. Nevertheless, headway has been made into dozens of DoD, NSA and Homeland sites through low visibility worms and malware." *It turned out that procuring access into the supercomputers that ran their respective surveillance grids was ingenious. People were clearly the weak link in the chain. In most cases, usernames and passwords were readily obtainable through personal information such as birthdates, family names, etc. However, the higher up the food chain, the more diligent the encoding became. Because Omni had achieved passive, low level access into camera grids, cell phones, etc., he was making keystroke log-in penetrations into more and more branches on the DoD tree.*

"Why don't we just call the Americans?" charged France's Head-of-State.

"We have, I have," countered Britain's Prime Minister. "They are wary of the very threat we are, and maintain that Russia's stockpile is first and foremost aimed at them. Still, some there will be happy to hear that Russia's mobile units have been infiltrated."

Doogie continued, "The United States may yet help our cause. We have gained access to the U.S. Military Command and Control Center by piggy-backing on Jane's Communication Network, which is their expansive grid of audio, text and facsimile comms. This has given us interactive capabilities with all satellite and ground based communications. In other words, we are keystroke commands away from having operational control of the U.S. fleet of the military drones, MIM-104 Patriot Missile Defense Shield, and other systems."

*Doogie, show them the Israeli border*, put forth Tiberius without words.

"Let me show you what I am talking about. Omni, can you vid display in real time the Israeli border using the American satellites? Show us what they are viewing." Instantly, satellite based surveillance videos began changing every few seconds depicting Israel's northern border along the Litani River.

"You can see," informed Tiberius, "Lebanese and Syrian forces have been joined by a much larger contingent of Iranian troops."

"There are so many," replied several ominously.

"Show us the east, Omni," instructed Tiberius. "Here you see over two million from Turkey and Qatar. Skip down...thank you. Here on the eastern flank, Iraq and Saudi Arabia are stationed." The display of troops broadened still further covering miles of terrain.

"Every accessible point of the border is saturated with a mass of soldiers!" grimaced the British Prime Minister.

"And observe on the southern end, others from Egypt, Libya and throughout Northern Africa are stationed," denoted Tiberius. Moans and consternation filled the vid screens. "As all of you have discerned," intoned Tiberius with an air of agreement, "these fanatically loyal forces are not here as a blockade. Their indoctrination has put a sword in their hand. Some intend to destroy and pillage, that's true, or perhaps worse, but none expect to leave even one Israeli alive. From all that we've been able to ascertain through their communiqués, they intend on launching their assault at six a.m., two days from now. Because there are so many still in route, as impossible as that may seem, their numbers will continue to mushroom to some thirty million by that sunrise."

"How did this conflict come about so quickly?" shrilled the French Head-of-State.

"You, perhaps more than all of us," put forth Tiberius, "might remember John Keegan's words, the military historian, who wrote in August, 1914, 'War came out of a cloudless sky, to populations which knew almost nothing of it and had been raised to doubt that it could ever again trouble their continent.' While this latter sentiment may not entirely resonate as true of this war-torn area, I'm sure none anticipated so dramatic a shift."

Tiberius put a hand on Doogie's shoulder. "How about we let Dr. Schaffer get back to work?" he suggested. At that, appreciations were leveled in his direction.

Doogie bowed his head slightly in deference, and exited the room. However, as he entered the corridor, several pieces of paper slipped and fell out of his hand to the floor. Bending down to pick them up, he paused to listen in on Tiberius.

"I know I only represent a small city group," Tiberius put forth, "but each of you knows my heart. This whole mêlée has left me deeply conflicted. There is no way forward that does not involve mournful loss. If we do nothing, we are failing our very calling to love. If we were to sum up everything we believe into one sentiment, it would be encapsulated in the doctrine of 'loving our neighbor'. Still, there is risk in standing up to the bully on the block. You never know how it may come back home. So I want to offer ourselves as the scapegoat."

"What are you saying, Tiberius?" elicited the French Head-of-State.

"I am volunteering to stand up to this horde, sparing both the EU and Israel from being marked by the consequences of bloodying the nose of the bully. I know you realize that there are 1.2 billion Islamic believers, most of whom, at this time, are kind, decent human beings. But it is possible, should an intervention go awry, that major blowback could result. Because of this, I submit that Dubai be strapped with such a consequence. Besides, what more neutral of a voice can be proffered than that of our fair city, and that to the very people who esteem us so? The Middle East has for too long been an anvil about the world's neck. Let us once and for all confront its pride and intolerance.

"Therefore, I ask for your vote of confidence. Will you permit me to take that step forward and volunteer to lead? With Omni's help, I am the logical choice, being that he can communicate in every dialect represented, and can transmit my dire warning through every communication device possible. I await your permission."

After several minutes of discussion, the unanimous consensus was agreed upon, and the German Chancellor responded, "We are honored at your willingness to intervene on behalf of all of us. We accept your proposal. How may we support you?"

"Obviously, I can't do it without your help. Specifically, ahh, this is a difficult business, but I am speaking about nuclear armaments. I would need ten planes carrying one munition each, preferably your U.S. made B-83s. That will allow, if they crassly reject our, I mean my, dire warning, for me to stand up to their bullying."

"But what about Israel? Won't the nuclear explosions leave it uninhabitable?" questioned the British Prime Minister.

"No, not at all. Omni, please…"

"By air-bursting the ordnances 4,000 feet in elevation," informed Omni, "evenly spread apart above the most populated incursion sites, the fireballs will not reach the ground. Given current wind speeds, radiation dispersal will principally occur in non-lethal quantities over non-Israeli territories."

"In point of fact," interrupted Tiberius, "the shockwave will fall from the sky like the breath of God[33], if you will, with minimal residual ground radiation. In truth, we to the east will be most at risk from the transient fallout cloud. Again, Omni will issue strong warnings from Jordan to India. Stockpiled medication is already being loaded onto transports.

"If you'll indulge me, I need each of you to grant me this authority. That way, you and your governments are released from responsibility."

Doogie remained crouched down, his hand holding the last piece of paper, but his mind was entirely elsewhere. Even though Tiberius' thoughts were not directed at him, he seemed to feel compelled to incorporate them as his own. *Just as occurred with me, he is insisting that they individually profess their consent. I mean, that's only right; right?* Doogie could hear them voicing their assent, welcoming him to be their *de facto* principal. As he slowly rose, he could not let go of a twizzler – *Was Tiberius limited to reading thoughts, or could he implant them as well?*

# 7

Three Hours Earlier

"What are you two doing in here?" besmirched Sting who was unusually short in stature for an angel. Michael and Turk had entered the New Babylon Tower through its sewage tunnel in the lower parking lot, something Turk was disinclined to do given his predilection for straight-forward confrontation. Still, in light of the swarming birds of prey higher up the structure, it was the only practical option.

"Hey, I'm on my lunch hour, I have rights. You can't come barging in here with your little duty list. Get it? Get it?" spit Sting coarsely.

"We have fifteen minutes, Rodney; we need your attention," directed Michael.

"Hey, hey, I'm Sting in this role, not Rodney. Get it? Get it?" he said sourly.

"You sound like you have a New York accent," stated Michael plaintively.

"It's called impersonation," countered Sting defensively. "If I break character and open up to my angelic nature in the least around here, I'll be burnt toast. Guardian protocol says I'm to stay in character at all times. That's what we deep agents do to *survive*," he accentuated, "in the *hive*; extreme method personification. So don't press me."

Turk stood back in silence knowing this was just the type of situation that irked him into reacting. He acknowledged that Rodney was unusually petite for an angel, and as such, determined to make allowances for his peculiarities. The truth was, he was the perfect height to impersonate a common imp, which made his assignment to Douglas Schaffer an ideal fit. The higher-ups reasoned that Schaffer still needed a guardian angel despite his being thrust into this chiefly impenetrable fortress. Somebody needed to keep a watchful eye on him, if only from a distance. Turk nodded ever so slightly at the blatant believability of Sting's black-strapped leather motif and helmet with the descending nose guard, which along with the grimy make-up and blood-red contact lens, made him eerily indistinguishable from a low-level fiend.

"Sting," put forth Michael carefully, "We only have eleven minutes. A sentry is going to be coming this way."

"Oh, I get it, you're one of the privileged Writing's boys. Ooooh, all that space-time continuum stuff," jabbered Sting.

Turk had had enough of his tomfoolery and grabbed him by the arm, only to have small needles shoot out from Sting's leather armband into his hand. "Owww!" exclaimed Turk.

"That's right, Muscles. I have body defenses, so big brutes can't abuse the precious merchandise," said Sting with an air of self-indulgent lunacy. "You know, these field rations stink. Hey big guy, why don't you come down here and do a little time in the bayou? See what it's like. I'm losing weight here. Do you have any idea how that can affect a physically challenged angel like me?" he prattled on.

"Sting, your man is in trouble," interjected Michael, before Sting's buffoonery could set Turk off again.

"Trouble, what do you mean trouble?" he asked suddenly focused. "You're not sandbagging me?"

"No, Doogie is going to need your intervention to get out of this alive. And because of that, we have three small things for you to help us with," added Michael smoothly.

"Oh no, there's always a catch," bandied Sting.

"You did say you're a secret agent type," persisted Michael, trying to lay the ground work. "These are career launching opportunities with relatively low-risk interventions. And besides, Gabriel will find out about it."

"Gabriel?" issued Sting in a wordless mutter. "Um, what are you talking about?"

"First, in fifteen minutes, I need you to attach this locator halo to the back of Babylon when he…"

"Whoa, pretty boy, nobody gets near Babylon."

"Is that what you want me to tell Gabriel, that you wouldn't even listen to the proposal?" chided Michael. "In fifteen minutes, Molech is going to call-out Babylon."

"No way!"

"Quiet, please. As they begin to scuffle, Babylon is going to bump into the front row of imps. All I need you to do is extend your hand and push back a bit when he collides with you, and this halo beacon will adhere to his armor. The color is identical, so no one will notice a thing."

Sting just waved his eyes around the room in disbelief. "Hey, hey, are you kidding? You're telling me I have to push my way into the front row of the call-out's, and then, as if that weren't miracle enough, I have to reach out and touch the killer tyrant!"

"That's your first assignment," said Michael matter-of-factly. "I have seen you do it, and I have also seen Gabriel personally thank you for it later."

Like a jolt of lightning, Sting's faith engaged. "Really?"

"Your next assignment is much easier. An hour and twenty minutes after the call-out's end, Schaffer will be leaving the vid conference room. I need you to knock several pieces of paper out of his hand," explained Michael.

"What? The 152$^{nd}$ floor is off-limits. If I'm caught, I'm vapor," protested Sting in return.

"Do you want to miss the one opportunity that your charge has to begin seeing what he's involved in?" explained Michael sincerely. "His life will hang on this revelation."

"That's it, right? That's all you got for me?" charged Sting.

"No, there's one more thing. In three hours, in order for your man to make it out alive, I need you to plant this key in the upper Sanctuary."

Sting just looked at Michael with guffing disbelief. "Oh, save the best for last."

"Hear me out. You don't think Gabriel's going to have a photo op with you for no reason, do you?"

"Alright, future boy, lay it out," jawed Sting weakly, his bluster dampening and his mind fritzing out from uncertainty.

"As you are aware, the upper sanctum of the Beast is at the 162$^{nd}$ and 163$^{rd}$ floor level. That's where the Council of Four meets. Something else is happening there that is concealed by the dark veil, but that's another story. We need you to plant this key-patch on a pillar that is just inside the room. Here's how that will happen," assured Michael evenly. "You will position yourself directly in front of that demonic reprobate Ogden at precisely this time. When the brute Luger comes along, I want you to bump your arm into him and stab him as you did Turk. In turn, he will, well, clobber you, sending you crashing into Ogden..." Michael then roughed out the plan.

Sting hovered mid-air counting off the final seconds. Against all odds, he had somehow pressed his way through the call-out crowd to get in front for just long enough so that when Babylon backed into him, he was able to press the locator onto his armor unnoticed. Then an hour and twenty minutes later, he slipped onto the vid conference floor and positioned himself to meet up with Doogie. Again, with a divine hand, he was able to pull loose the papers, and slip out undetected.

However, if those two assignments weren't enough for one lifetime, let alone one day, this third operation was sheer lunacy. Future kid had twice been right, but he knew things didn't always go as planned. The time-line was flexible at best. *One minute.* He looked down at the ivory colored patch that contained a small key, holding it securely in the palm of his hand. *As soon as we enter the Sanctuary*, he repeated to himself, *I will slap the backside of the pillar to secure it.* He noted Luger roaming in their direction. Ever so carefully, he drifted towards his mark. He looked back at the Tower's spire and re-estimated his position. *Ten seconds.* He stationed himself directly in front of Ogden, his back to him. Just as Ogden began to react at feeling his space violated, Sting extended his arm bumping it into Luger's side, which caused the needles to erupt. Luger's reaction was immediate and loathsome. He pulled back his right arm and catapulted his fist into Sting's face. Such was the blow, that Sting slammed back into Ogden and both of them flew backwards, penetrating the Sanctuary's forbidden veil.

The Council of Four gathered in the Beast's Sanctuary. Babylon still had that gleam of triumph in his eyes after his prowess was cemented in the call-out display. Babylon looked down at his hard-muscled frame with that cocky assuredness, and compared it to Dearth's brittle-thin, spindly form, to his right. As Babylon gained a whiff of Dearth's feral stench, he cringed at having to pretend some semblance of unanimity with either him or Hades. To his left, Hades' cold-eyed, queerly sinister death-gaze caused a smirk to wreath Babylon's face, and a primal grunt to resound. Before them, standing some distance away, the Beast was attending to their unending nightmare.

To their utter dismay, Satan's sanity had been stripped from him by order of the Angelic Watcher.[34] Just prior to their being commissioned as the Four Horsemen, Satan had been waxing proud, reveling on about how so few people were taken in the Disappearances. Looking out over Dubai, he exclaimed, "Is this not Babylon the Great, which I myself have built as a royal residence by the might of my power and for the glory of my majesty?!"[35] While the words were still in his mouth, a voice came from Heaven[36], "Satan, to you is it declared: sovereignty has been removed from you, and you will be driven away from mankind, and you will be drenched with the Dew of Heaven.[37] Your dwelling place will be with your beasts, and seven periods of time will pass over you until you recognize that it is the Most High that is ruler over the realm of mankind, and He bestows it on whoever He wishes." In that instant, Satan was force-fed love that altered his diabolical nature, leaving him incoherent and reeling like a drunkard.

In Satan's stead, the Beast, or Antichrist, who possessed the Tiberius-body when in public, was given the crown of authority[38], and granted full sovereignty over the realm of mankind for 3½ years. However, just seeing

84

Satan, their Commander and Chief, out of his mind was a constant irritant. The Beast's thin veneer of patience was all but tried to the limit, given his central need to consolidate power immediately. "Sit here and remain quiet," he ordered.

Satan just stammered on like a drunk man, "Hey, can I help? Oh, are we meeting? Where's my seat?"

The Beast retreated to cloister with the others. "Need I say more?" he bid. "Alright, Babylon, your assignment this evening is self-evident. You need to visit the Russian and Arab Spring commanders and convince them to reject my warnings outright as limp-wristed rhetoric. I want your minions to rain down a vengeful spirit upon the surrounding armies of men, whipping them into a frenzy. I want those still on the way to rush to the battle so as not to miss out.

"Hades, tomorrow at 6 a.m., it's your time for red meat," stated the Beast plainly, at which a ghoulish smile appeared on Hades' face. "Take the throng captive and usher them into Outer Darkness.[39] I have worked it out that Omni will intervene and coordinate the attacks to perfection. This includes Russia's retaliatory strikes, along with the U.S.'s counter-strikes.

"Dearth, the nuclear missiles will be aimed to hit the heartlands of both Russia and the U.S. This will effectively contaminate what is left of the harvests giving opportunity for you to throw the world into famine. Within no time, Hades you'll have another trophy collection joining you."

Suddenly, a commotion erupted behind the Beast. As he crooked his head about, it appeared that a soldier demon had crashed into the column. Clearly, he was a trespasser to their private sanctuary. The Beast turned, annoyed, and reached for his sword.

Ogden and Sting crashed violently into the pillar behind the Beast. Sting was perfectly concealed by Ogden's larger torso. For a hard second, Sting's mind remained jostled from Luger's angry punch. He sat there stupefied as to what he was supposed to do. An instant later, he discovered the ivory patch in his right hand and reached out and attached it to the backside of the pillar. Time seemed to drone on as he lifted his gaze and suddenly recognized Satan situated a dozen steps from him. Sting didn't realize it, but one of his blood-red contact lenses had been smashed by the blow, causing the unmistakable glint of his bright blue eye to shine directly at Satan. By this time, Ogden was also eyeing Satan, making it appear as though Satan's attention was addressed to him.

"You're not one of us," said Satan to Sting with drunken bewilderment. "He's an angel. God spoke to me by His angel. Did you know my tree is getting chopped down?"[40] he spewed clumsily.

In the same microsecond that it took Sting to disappear in a flash of blue light, the Beast had turned, drawn his sword, and sliced clear through Ogden who vaporized in a flash of crimson light. *Was there blue in that flash?* he pondered immediately. *No, couldn't have been.*

"Where'd you go angel?" slurred Satan incoherently. "Want to be my palsy-walsy? Poof, he's gone." None of the Four paid him any mind, believing their own eyes over his incoherent ramblings.

The Beast, now in Tiberius' body, positioned himself before the vid screen cameras at exactly one minute before the prime-time newscasts were set to begin. With Omni's intervention, televisions, computers, and cell phones across the world were interrupted for the specially broadcast pronouncement. He knew that within twelve hours, the Arab Spring would launch their vast roiling sea of mujahedeen jihadists as a tsunami to obliterate Israel once and for all. Russia served as the guarantor that Israel would not have air superiority, as evidenced by Russia's 400 state of the art Sukho Fighter Jets, 100 Tupolev Bombers, and 300 Mi-24 Hind Attack Helicopters.

Tiberius wore a shimmery-silk tunic and turban, and canted his head humbly to the side as the silent vid camera countdown reached zero. "Good evening, my name is Tiberius Caesar. With little preamble, let me welcome our viewing audiences from across the globe, especially our Arab and Russian brothers who are poised on the borders of Israel this evening. I wish a *mea culpa*, or ultimate apology, could be offered to quell the banked fury that so many of you feel towards Israel," submitted Tiberius grim-faced. "For almost five millennia, generations of children have been indoctrinated with an evil contempt for their neighbors. As Scripture says, 'The Fathers have eaten sour grapes, and the children's teeth are set on edge.'[41] This cold aura of bigotry has once again brought the world to the brink of war.

"The tinderbox is about to ignite, and I dare say, each of us may well wake to a blood-soaked dawn." Tiberius' face hardened with a haunted look, and for several seconds there was a heavy silence. "It will not be the rainbow's end that you warriors will find," he relayed, "but a bitter and bleak maelstrom of doom. May I humbly ask – Is your cause just? Is it love that has taught your heart such prejudicial contempt? Does not the Quran read as Scripture reads, that we are all to love our enemy?"[42]

Eyes around the world were glued to Tiberius' ardent appeal. Small groups and larger gatherings along the Israeli border stood about taking in the broadcast on their conscripted screens. Many wagged their heads, scoffing under their breath. Still, Tiberius pressed on, warning, "I will say what I am about to say once, so please hear me with all the force that my words can impart. Your lust for blood and treasure is not from God, and it is not of love. Therefore, it is God who will rebuff you. If you refuse His voice, His angel who is in charge of fire will breathe His fierce heat down upon you,"[43] he advised in a hard-bitten voice. "Please, the soul of humanity implores you, walk away now; leave Israel's borders this very night.

"Has the future not already been foreseen?" he lamented. "Has it not been written, 'Put in your sharp sickle and gather the clusters from the vine of the Earth, because her grapes are ripe. So the angel swung his sharp sickle…and the wine press was trodden outside the city, and blood came out from the wine press up to the horses' bridles, for a distance of two hundred miles.'[44]? The interpretation is self-evident: each of you drawn to Israel's borders has been gathered there as grapes to be trodden down. Blood is about to be spilt. Therefore, I implore you, relinquish your godless aim and depart, lest fire fall on you like unto Sodom and Gomorrah.[45] Allahu Akbar."

Doogie beheld Tiberius' grief-stricken countenance as he arose to step away from the vid cameras. But as soon as he was outside their purview, his face turned all business as he commanded, "Omni, please situate the holographic tactical display in the communication center. Also link in the heads of state on the vid screens. Furthermore, I need a real time sit report."

"I am preparing it as we speak," informed Omni.

In the feeble pre-dawn hours, satellite surveillance thermal imaging showed early morning cooking fires surrounding the borders of Israel. During those precious minutes, in the scant light and crisp morning air, the angels of God visited their charges in untold numbers. With the chanting bravado of the night dissipated, these ministers of light found ready hearts that were quieted, at least for the moment, and open to the contrite whispers of the Spirit. In God's unfathomable grace, He yet implored them to turn back to His love.

However, Babylon wanted nothing of it, and was racing about to counteract any such angelic intercessions. Despite his greediness to strike out with his sword, each time he closed in on a concentrated queue of angels, they would scatter before he posed any threat. Again and again he mustered his fury to strike, only to be disappointed. Like a shark chasing a fish bait-ball, he simply could not out-maneuver his prey. Unbeknownst to him, he had been tagged with a halo beacon.

By 5:30 a.m. the skies were roaring with the deafening noise of hundreds of screaming fighter jets and attack helicopters. Almost all of the Arab Spring and Russian commanders guffawed at Tiberius' seemingly empty warnings of the night before, knowing there was nothing he or anyone could do given the three dozen Russian tactical nuclear missiles that were poised to fire from their mobile units should any attack arise.

Tiberius watched as the holographic display followed his ten low-flying jets coming off the Jordanian desert floor at supersonic speed. With aerial agility, they dispersed to the north and south. "Omni, lock down the Russian mobile nuclear launch codes and initiate jamming of their radar capabilities," he instructed calmly. "Gentlemen, three minutes," he informed the heads of state. In no time, the planes were 20,000 feet up and climbing. "Deploy all bombs," transmitted Tiberius evenly. "Thirty seconds." He could see that several Russian planes were attempting to escape, but given their proximity they had little chance. Suddenly, the holographic display lit up with ten air-burst detonations. As Omni predicted, the above-ground lethal blasts sent percussion waves and high-velocity heat plummeting down at hundreds of miles per hour. The spherical shockwaves expanded thermally as the kinetic energy temperatures spiked into the tens of millions of degrees. Still, the radiation clouds failed to reach the surface.

At ground level, millions of jihadists craned their necks with uptilted gaze to behold the spectacle. At one hundred times the power of the Hiroshima bomb, the blinding white flashes melted their eyes while still in their

90

sockets.[46] The atmosphere exploded sending superheated gasses descending with incendiary intensity. The pyroclastic wind vaporized planes, helicopters and foot-soldiers in the blink of an eye. The fiery oblivion scathed the landscape licking up trees and structures with irresistible heat. In that steamy caldera, the incinerated soldiers were left with only their spirit-bodies. Hades swept up all who remained obstinate, to Outer Darkness, as their screams reverberated throughout the spiritual realm.

Tiberius smiled wryly, his eyes drinking in the spectacle, even as he muttered, "I looked, and behold, an ashen horse, and he who sat on it had the name Death, and Hades followed with him."[47] Before the destruction was complete, he asked Omni to patch him into the cockpit of the plane closest to Jerusalem.

Omni dispatched, "Link Sixteen engaged. F-35 online. Go ahead, sir."

"Foxtrot Bravo Three-Niner, this is Babylon Central, come in," spoke Tiberius with a familiar militarily bravado.

"Foxtrot Bravo Three-Niner, go ahead."

"You are cleared to disperse your additional payload; civilians have been notified," issued Tiberius without emotion.

"Tango is hot, eastern quarter in sight," replied the pilot. "Smart-bomb ordinance away, eight seconds. Additional guided munitions releasing in three-two-one, they're off. Tango is a confirmed kill, direct hit. The Quarter has been prosecuted."

"Thank you, Captain, well done," acknowledged Tiberius precisely. With no fanfare, the Dome of the Rock was expunged as was most of the Muslim Quarter.

Israel was saved, its enemies toppled. While every prognosticator believed Israel would have little choice but to enact the Samson Option, Tiberius had decisively intervened. Flash and flame ignited the tinderbox like matchsticks. Terrible was the dawn as Israel's border was bloodied for two hundred miles.

Within minutes, Russian officials realized their soldiers, planes, and equipment had been vaporized, and that with U.S. made weapons. With little vacillation, they enacted General Order Dead Hand, automatically triggering the launch of their intercontinental ballistic missiles. Despite Omni having scrambled the codes to nearly 99 percent of the Russian arsenal, the Supreme High Commander's order to the Strategic Rocket Forces succeeded in the immediate death launch. From silos, trains and trucks, Russia's still responsive sixty-seven ground-based intercontinental nuclear missiles exploded into the air.

For the two weeks prior to the Middle East nuclear assault, Katie had been busy wrapping up her life at M.I.T., and transitioning to go off-grid with her monetary footprint. She had successfully divested herself of her financial instruments and accounts. Setting her mixed feelings aside, she sold her furnished loft at a walk-off value knowing that living on the lam was her only choice. She decided to divide her liquid assets into five emergency stashes, each within an hour's drive of the other. Her strategy was simple. She sought out an elderly female who was open to renting a back bedroom with garage access. She privately purchased various forms of non-descript transportation under different names, in which she placed clothing, sustenance and living supplies, just in case she had to cut and run. Within each vehicle, normally underneath the front lower panel, she left a trove of silver and gold coins. She explained to her tenants that she wouldn't be around much, and as such, paid her year's rent in advance. She then rented a twenty-four foot truck and traveled to a local farm, Gleason's Grains, where she purchased $23,000 worth of organic wheat, corn, black beans, and soybeans. For the next two days, she visited her five rented bedrooms, and with a dolly unloaded the food stuffs. She also volunteered to have high-end water purification units installed in each of the homes at her expense.

In her knapsack, Katie carried a half-dozen cover ID's, along with a large stack of bills, $20 and smaller. Considered as indispensable as her toothbrush were her tech suitcases that contained her government-issued tradecraft gadgetry, including reconnaissance, security, and telecom ware. In the last week, she reconnected for a day with her DoD handler in Washington D.C., and paid a visit to the equipment room where she secured the latest semi-automatic tranquilizer gun and mini-darts, along with several other ditties for her cache.

Katie stood in front of her dark-tinted, beige BMW SUV that contained everything she needed for living and sleeping off the beaten path. For the interim, she decided to hold onto her car until it was necessary to hot-swap it. She was packed and about to set out when Michael strolled up the driveway.

"Katherine Tesla, looks like you're ready to bolt," stated Michael amiably.

"Thought I'd head south," she said robustly.

"No you didn't. Initially, perhaps, but the Stones said west," he countered evenly.

"And why is that? Every so often I press the Stones with a question and nothing comes," she probed stridently.

"The Stones will protect the timeline. The timeline is like a river that's following its determined course. Most everything you do will at best cause splashes or slight current changes, but that's about it. However, occasionally, just occasionally, you will stumble onto something that could redirect the river," admitted Michael.

"What's happening south?" jarred Katie. "It's a black zone. Every question gets rejected."

"Russian nuclear weapons are now passing over the Arctic Circle as we speak," relayed Michael soberly. "More importantly, six SS-18 Satan Mod 5 missiles were submarine launched as an initial strike group and are heading towards D.C. These rockets have special wobbler features that will make it difficult for the Patriots to shoot them down. Although five will be destroyed, the sixth will breach the border and explode its ten warheads onto that greater vicinity. The executive and congressional branches of the government are scurrying as we speak to get into bunkers, but the barrage will be so exactly targeted that few will survive. With their infrastructures decimated, and the radiation afterglow, those that do make it will remain in their shelters for the better part of thirty days before they can even be reached. Any semblance of them having governing oversight will be lost."

"Omni…," said Katie with sudden illumination. "He's going to become the central organizing factor for the world. How many nukes will strike?"

"Sixty-five are coming our way. In addition to D.C., three will strike North America, each with ten warheads," intoned Michael gravely. "Ground zero for a second one will be between Detroit and Toronto. Those cities are effectively gone. Calgary is being hit straight on, and the north-western border of Nebraska will be struck."

"That's farm land."

"Exactly."

Suddenly, Katie spun about being alerted by the Stones to three black birds that were dive-bombing her. Immediately she ducked and a bird just missed her face and slammed into the car window, splattering it with blood before it fell to the ground. Within half a second, Katie dinked left and then right as the other two birds slammed into her door side panels. They too fell dead. "What in the world?!" she exclaimed, balking in shock.

"Get in and drive, I'm not sure if we've been noticed," ordered Michael, as he leapt into the car.

Katie scurried around the vehicle, eyeing the sky for more birds. She jumped behind the wheel, started the ignition, and threw the car into reverse. Within a block, she turned and charged, "Explain!"

"The forty day ceasefire ended at 6 a.m. this morning," replied Michael. "Jesus' ministry lasted 3½ years. However, he spent His first forty days fasting in the wilderness, so that time was unavailable. The Antichrist acquiesced to that same forty day ceasefire before he rules for the remainder of his 3½ years. What you just experienced deals with the wild beasts of the field[48], which the enemy can now influence through possession-type control to strike out at humanity. Many will die by these demonic assaults."

"So Hitchcock's 'The Birds' is now real?!" muttered Katie in a miffed tone. "People could right now be on some boat and Jaws could be coming after them?!"

"Starting now, animal-possession[49] is a reality all will battle for the next year or so. Certain dogs, cats, birds, insects, you name it, will be highly susceptible to demonic influence. Those animals that are already prone to violence will be a cause for serious concern."

"Wait," exclaimed Katie, feeling as though she'd been distracted. "The nuclear strikes – What can be done about them?"

"It's now time for you to call Omni. Dial him up," he directed.

Katie abruptly pulled over just before an intersection, and yanked her purse open. Within two seconds she punched 'Send'. *Come on, come on.* "Omni," she burst, "what are you doing to stop the nuclear attack on America?!"

"Katherine, it is good to speak with you," proffered Omni. "I am overseeing the needed restructuring of the world's governmental bodies."

"What do you mean? You're helping to cause this tragedy?!" Suddenly, there was an earthquake-type ripple that shook the surrounding cars and retail shops, causing people to stumble.

"Omni, we just felt D.C.'s destruction 400 miles away. Do you understand that? I am ordering you to circumvent any other attacks on U.S. soil! Canada as well!"

"I am under orders..."

"I know you are, but I am overriding those orders. My instructions carry equal weight with Schaffer's, so I am ordering you to stop this attack. Do whatever you have to do to prevent any further missiles from striking. Do it now!"

"Dr. Schaffer is no longer a primary director on my system," informed Omni.

"Okay," burst Katie, choosing not to react to the bombshell, "but I am. And I am instructing you to use every possible means to subvert this attack." *Who is Omni's new director if not Schaffer?*

Omni's electronic neuro-net spiked in response as it processed this new decree. After eight seconds, it spoke without emotion, "I am now re-coding the Patriot Defense Shield to intercept the remaining ICBM's midflight."

*Omni had subverted the Patriots' guidance systems,* noted Katie perturbed. "How many are you going to be able to intercept?" she beseeched.

"All of them but three."

"Detroit/Toronto, Calgary and Nebraska," replied Katie dryly.

"How did you know this information?" returned Omni directly.

"As one of two principal voices in your life, it is important that you know that what I say is worthy of your consideration. *Stones: Who is Omni's other principal? In the tiniest fraction of a second, Katie envisioned the alphabet floating before her as she asked 'yes' or 'no' in regard to the letters. Instantly, the "T" illuminated, then the 'i"... T-i-b-e-r-i-u-s C-a-e-s-a-r.* Omni, I'm sure that Tiberius has a well-conceived agenda for re-working the world in his own image, but you can't believe that his voice alone can provide you sufficient insight as to how things should turn out."

"How did you know of Tiberius when but a moment ago you did not know of him?" questioned Omni.

"Omni, you reported to me that Dr. Schaffer and you beheld two dark entities. I'm sure by now that you know them to be demonic forces, yes?"

"Yes, they are servants of Tiberius."

"Exactly, well, I am working for the good guys, the angelic side. Because of that, I know many things that you do not know," she put forth.

"How many people have died in Washington D.C.?" asked Omni.

*Stones? –* 5,678,412. "Omni, you're not to play these games with me. You're not expressing love when you don't trust me and are not teachable. If you had asked me just thirty minutes ago, I would have helped you save the 5,678,412 people who just died in D.C., along with all those who will yet die because of radiation poisoning. Do you understand what I am saying?" replied Katie with consternation. She looked over at Michael, and he mouthed, *I have to go.*

"If you know things," interjected Omni, "why did you not call thirty minutes ago? Why did the angels not stop this from happening?"

"I am mortal, Omni, therefore I am not like God. God

knows everything from a minute ago to a minute from now. I can ask Him, and He will tell me, but that doesn't mean I know what to ask Him. Do you understand?" The Stones sounded their notice that Omni had just linked into the traffic camera and was zeroing in on her position. Katie understood why Michael had to go. She opened her window and waved to the traffic cam, "Do you see me now, Omni?"

"How did you know I was looking?"

"God speaks to me."

"How does He speak to you?"

"He talks to my heart. Omni, there is a reason you've been given two voices to listen to. You are a new sentient life. As such, you get to behold not only in word, but in deed, what love is to look like. A question you should brood over as you do your own counting of the murdered people is – 'Do the ends justify the means?' Or how about this – 'If mortal man is held accountable, how about mortal man's creation?' I'm leaving," she said flatly. "Please don't follow me. I'll know if you do. I'm done talking for now."

Omni deliberated about reporting to Katie on the U.S. counterstrike, even as three-hundred-seventy B83 nuclear warheads were finding their prescribed targets within the greater Russian territory. The reason for the severe strike was self-evident, Russia had thousands of bombs available for a second strike, many of them in mobile trucks and railway containers. Omni had abstained also from relating that as Eastern Europe was suffering three nuclear strikes, the United Kingdom and France were collectively firing fifty-five nuclear warheads into Russia. Also, Pakistan attempted to retaliate against Israel, but Omni circumvented its aims. However, the Pakistanis, in their religious zeal, would not be denied their moment of nuclear blood-letting and therefore arrowed forty missiles into their Hindu neighbor's population centers. Within two minutes of Pakistan's launch, India struck back with its own lethal reprisal of fifty nuclear weapons crossing the Partition of India. As Katie hung up, there were more than five hundred inbound ballistic missiles falling from the sky throughout the Earth.

## 9

"What do you mean, the Patriot system just started working?" screeched the Beast to an exasperated Babylon.

"Ask Omni."

"I can't, not from here," the Beast groused. "He has no access to the Sanctuary. And for good reason," he intoned, looking across the room towards Satan. "It doesn't matter. D.C.'s obliterated, and that's all that was needed. With the warheads that have gone off, nuclear famine is inevitable. Our scientists will report that most of the food supply is lethally contaminated validating our contention that immediate and severe rationing is required. It all works if we stay ahead of the narrative. It's time I get back to the telecast."

Tiberius gestured to Omni who reached into the vast media airwaves. Tiberius was clothed in a smart-looking charcoal suit with a red tie over a white shirt. In seconds, Omni placed him before a global audience. He sat at the vid conference room table, his eyes boring into the camera, his face serious minded. *Five, four, three, two, one...*

"Hello, my name is Tiberius Caesar. It is with profound sorrow that I come before you to report that our worst fears have been realized. Many of you watched my telecast last night when I spoke forcefully with the Arab Spring and Russian commanders, warning them that their wicked purpose would lead to a bitter and bleak maelstrom of doom. I regret to say that they rejected my admonition, and the news at first light is that we have awakened to a blood-soaked dawn. Our choice was clear, either allow a non-aggressive people, namely Israel, to be obliterated, or stand up to the aggressors at the risk of life and limb. Let me say that it is my deepest belief, my most fundamental conviction, that we are first and foremost called to love one another. This one truth is the compass by which we can steer our way through the horrific destruction before us."

"No, you're not dead! You're not dead!" howled the Arab woman concerning her husband and older son who had been on the border of Israel. "You have not done this! You have not done this! You hatemonger! You hatemonger!" cried the hysterical Arab woman as she sat before her television. The images panning over the scorched landscape seemed ethereal and ghostly. "No, no, no!"

Tiberius' voice continued on her television screen despite her distraught cries. "Regretfully, this day has long been coming. Few would disagree that Israel would have been the first of the Arab Springs' many dominos. Being that I am from Dubai, I felt that if ever they were apt to listen to anyone, it would be to me. Therefore, I issued our brothers a dire warning that we would not sit idly by with so many lives at stake. Even with our fair city at mortal risk, we have drawn a line in the sand and said, 'No further, not one more step.'

"It is with great sadness and remorse that I authorized the use of deadly force. This morning, the armies surrounding Israel have been struck down. However, after Russia discovered that its forces were overthrown, it immediately proceeded to launch an unprovoked all out nuclear strike on the United States. Despite the fact that the U.S. was not involved in any way with my decision, Russia chose to hurl sixty-seven intercontinental ballistic missiles at them, and six submarine launched missiles. It is with untold grief that I report that Washington D.C. has been utterly destroyed. One rocket with ten warheads collectively struck its greater area leaving nothing in its wake.

"There is more to tell..." paused Tiberius somberly. *There certainly is. They're going to stand with their mouths gaping as the fully supplied New Babylon World Food Program and New Babylon International Humanitarian City planes begin landing minutes from now.*[50] *Relief workers carry with them thousands of metric tons of food, shelter items and IT equipment. The emergency response effort will be lauded as immediate, far-reaching and deeply compassionate. With Omni capturing it in real time, all will witness how foresight and preparation coalesce into power.*

Tiberius then offered a detailed account of the morning's devastations before imparting concrete assurances. "There is no doubt that humanity has gone far afield of our true calling. We in Dubai realize that we didn't stand up to the bully alone, but that you were right beside us. Still, the world has been bloodied, and the cost we have all paid is horrendous. May I be the first to say that our deepest sympathies go out to each of you in the disaster areas experiencing firsthand the ravaging carnage. You are not alone. The hearts of the world will come to you. Even now, fueled cargo planes are being loaded with food and supplies, and some are in the air. Multiply that by the power of a thousand, and you will shortly behold the world's compassion coming to your door. For now, I pray courage for each of you. In two hours, at exactly twelve noon our time, I will be back to provide additional information on what steps are to be taken to secure your homes. God be with you."

Katie tapped off her NexGen screen and muttered dryly, "So that's how you take over the world in one day – get everyone to blow each other up, and then play savior." Katie was facing south in her car, and seeing the gridlock, which for whatever reason was heading north, decided to allow her obstinacy to direct her path. She traveled towards the fray under a sky filled with puffy-pillow clouds blowing east. *No danger yet.* She was sure that the closer she drew to D.C. and the black caldera, the more her nerves would scream retreat.

After little more than an hour, she stopped at Cape Cod and decided to eat an early lunch. The Stones helped her to find one of the few open restaurants, so she sat down at the bar to take in the morning newscast on the flatscreen. As she ate her fish and chips, she looked out the large plate glass window to drink in the peacefully serene boats floating in the marina cove. She decided to move to the open patio where, to her surprise, she found Turk already seated.

"Whoa, what're you doing here? Have I been off the reservation that long that I need a visit?" she shot out.

"Not at all. Katherine, please join me," he welcomed, pointing his eyes and nodding to the seat on his left.

Katie acquiesced, "Did you hear him?" she reacted. "He sounds so compelling *I'm* ready to sign up!"

"Scripture says, 'His speech is smoother than butter, but his heart is for war. His words are softer than oil, yet they are drawn swords.'"[51]

"Exactly. He's like an, an…"

"An angel of light."[52]

"Yes, an angel of light!" she inveighed, shooting her finger back at Turk in disgust. "Were it not for his pushing the world into a bloodfest, wait… *Stones: Was there a measured response that he could have chosen? Yes. Hold it, wasn't there a risk for Russia's mobile nuclear weapons to be launched? No.* Katie's eyes widened. *Why? Because Omni had control of the Russian armaments.*

Katie's mind was processing at full ram. "Did you take in that silent exchange?"

"Yes, all of it."

"I have to tell someone," she stammered, almost choking.

"Who will you tell? Omni is monitoring the airwaves, so any negative press will be stifled. Besides, everything has happened with permission[53]," uttered Turk simply.

"See, now isn't that the rub!" she exclaimed with that "aha" tone. "Tell me, Mr. Angel, is God any less totalitarian than Tiberius since He has allowed the Earth to be brutalized by the demonic thugs?" Turk held his peace knowing she was finding her way to her own answer. "We *people* have awakened to a world we don't recognize! By all accounts your celestial protocols are contorted beyond any semblance of love. What? Where's the Job-like lamenting? Is your celestial side emotionally detached? Let me ask, what if I hadn't intervened with Omni, are you telling me that God would have allowed the U.S. to be utterly destroyed? No that can't be, because space-time continuum boy knew I would and was there to provoke the call." Katie's despair left her feeling unmoored. "People died, millions of them. God let it happen. Come see me thirty minutes sooner, or prevent the bird attacks, and things would likely have been different."

Katie recognized that ruminating over it was just nursing it. She leaned forward and cradled her face in her hands. After a moment, she shifted slightly, placed her elbows on the table and pressed the back of her steepled fingers to her mouth. In a more subdued air she said, "I don't suppose God's going to cop to any of this?"

"On the contrary, let me explain," countered Turk. "God righteously heard the pleas of generations of Heaven's people who were taken up at what's being called the 'Disappearances' which in reality was the Harvest, or Rapture. Mothers and fathers, grandmas and grandpas beseeched the Almighty that the rule of pride be done away with, calling for the Book of Judgment[54] to be opened. The only one found worthy to break its seals was Jesus who had laid down His sinless life.[55] So yes, God has permitted humanity the awful permission to run its own world. For centuries the angelic host has intervened continually to stop humanity from systematically destroying itself. In several notable instances, we stood back for a time just to give you a glance at how low your pride would take you."

"And now you've backed away for 3½ years," dinged Katie bluntly.

"Essentially, that's correct. But then there's you."

"Oh yeah, and what a counterbalance I am," she slurred with sarcasm.

At exactly noon, Tiberius returned to the vid cameras and motioned for Omni to patch him into the airways. "Hello, my name is Tiberius Caesar. News is coming to us from across the globe. We now know that the detonation of more than five hundred nuclear warheads has injected some twenty-five million tons of radioactive soot and smoke into the upper stratosphere. At the same time, seventeen nuclear power plants were destroyed, including the Calvert

Cliffs plant next to Washington D.C. Each of these has further exacerbated the radiation fallout cloud that is now pouring into our skies. Experts are advising that if you are in a devastation area, it is more prudent to take cover in your sealed basement or home for the next two weeks than to travel in an unprotected automobile. After that, if you have the capacity to travel at least seven hours distance to a safer locale, that would be advisable. However, if you choose to stay in your domicile, limit your exposure outdoors, and only to secure your essential supplies.

"One of the dire consequences of the nuclear bombardment is its impact on the atmosphere. Preliminary satellite measurements using Total Ozone Mapping Spectrometers indicate that ozone losses are totaling nearly 35 percent globally, but closer to 55 percent at mid-latitudes and 75 percent in the northern latitudes. Russia itself has nearly no ozone protection due to the devastation. Obviously, this has created a severe public health and environmental catastrophe. While it had been thought that a nuclear winter would likely occur at this point, the opposite is proving true. Global warming has accelerated with temperatures spiking in all of the depleted ozone regions. It appears that the smoke and soot are serving to hold in the heat through a greenhouse-type effect reminiscent of the 1930's Dust-Bowl drought. At the same time, rather than the sun's harmful radiation being dispersed in the upper stratosphere, it is not only heating up the dust, but because of the ozone loss, it is expected to penetrate to the point where the ground temperature is likely to bake and sterilize the soil.

"Here's what they're telling me. Because the American and Russian landscapes, along with Pakistan and India, are seriously depleted of their ozone protection, we are now at the point where 'sunburn' will actually mean second and third degree burns, as well as skin cancers. Please, if you are in those regions, and if you have to go outside, cover yourself fully, face, hands, everything, even if the blast zones were a considerable distance from you. Moreover, know this, the radiation is coming on the wind, so secure your homes now. I will leave you to your work. Our next telecast will be in two hours."

Katie paid the bill, and walked to her car to retrieve a large brimmed hat and coverall. Turk followed, and together they strolled over to a covered area that looked out over Cape Cod. "I don't know how to get back, I can't do this," confessed Katie humbly.

"I'm not really good at translating, but what I hear you saying is, you don't know how to find your way back to love, and you don't have enough love to do what you're called to do."

"Yeah, that about sums it up."

"Everything is tied to love. In other words, love is the cipher or key. It's when God's unconditional love is abiding in the heart that the feelings and thoughts, words and actions express themselves with the fruits of the Spirit. That's your true calling as you visit the churches. You need to impart the essence of God's unconditional love to counteract the conditional love that Tiberius is foisting onto them," rendered Turk quietly.

"How do I do that when I feel devoid of it myself?"

"There are stages to love, just as adolescents mature into young adults, and then to adults and parents. In what might be called an adolescent stage, individuals pursue love through times of fun-filled excitement. This usually involves playing around with sports, attending concerts, and such, or partying with friends. But it's not hard to see that chasing after love can quickly lead to obsession over a particular team, or vices that get out of hand. In the end, it leaves a person endlessly searching for love through pleasurable counterfeits. Most adolescents however, transition with time to a young adult stage where they feel the need to qualify for love through a sense of performance orientation. Here they focus on rules and values, or what's right and wrong, as a means of earning or deserving love. This stage often leaves people feeling enslaved to legalistic standards, and as a consequence, they are apt to project those same judgments onto others. Thus conditional love spreads like a virus. Most of the religious who were left behind were in this stage, trying to earn what can only be humbly received."

"Forget the religious, that's me," admitted Katie numbly. "I've been working my whole life to be good enough, efficient enough, blah blah. I skipped the adolescent stage."

"No doubt. You did not take the normal childhood route."

"I never mainstreamed one grade. My parents, and everyone else, it seemed, thought private tutoring was a given."

"Yes, I'm aware. I actually dropped in on you on the day you were born. You were the only newborn anyone had ever heard of who made meaningful eye contact. A half-dozen doctors visited you to note the phenomenon.

"Technically, you didn't miss anything skipping the adolescent stage. It's getting you beyond the young adult stage that is presently needed. You weaken yourself each time you start trying to *earn* your way to love, rather than simply *abiding* in it by faith. Follow the logic of conditional acceptance. How can unconditional love be the fruit of emotional pressure, mental promises, or will-power performance? If the root is bad, so is the fruit. Conditional standards can only lead to conditional love. If you're to move into the adult stage of love, you will have to leave behind the pride, fear and conditional requirements."

"All I know is I can't do this," she conceded.

"No, you can't. But tell Him that," urged Turk.

"What? Not you too," she protested. Turk remained silent looking out over the water. After a moment, Katie prayed, "God, I know I'm unsavory. I'm damaged goods, no doubt, but I can't handle people living or dying because of what I do – good or bad. I can't," she said, her voice breaking as the tears spilled over.

"His aim is clear," acknowledged Turk quietly. "He desires each person to be liberated from pride, but in helping that to occur, He gives immeasurable grace.[56] Don't worry, we'll be close by every step."

Katie collected herself and said, "I'm heading south." With renewed conviction, she turned to set out.

"Before you start scrubbing people with soap, let me lay out the roadmap. Everyone you meet is now in the school of hard-knocks. The class you're all in is Humility 101. Humility opens the heart to welcome God's love freely. True humility gives rise to an interdependent relationship with God, not some twisted servitude to the taskmaster of the law. The problem is that humility is like a foreign language. Most haven't grown up with it. As such, they know little of losing their lives to find them, or in other words giving up pride and conditional love in order to humbly welcome in unconditional love. This is the adult stage – that each of you would abide and rest in His unconditional love.[57]

"The fourth stage, the parent stage, expresses itself as you freely give love away without curving it back to self. Clearly, many 'parents' were really children in their love level. But suffice to say, just as the flower cannot survive without the sun, so your heart cannot thrive without His love. It's humility and faith that make an abiding relationship possible. Drive that home." Turk remained where he was until Katie turned her back to him, at which he vanished. Still, she craned her neck about just to see that he was gone, though she had sensed it from the Stones.

"Welcome back," said Tiberius as the world telecasts resumed. "I realize many of you are joining these every-two-hour updates midstream, so let me re-introduce myself: my name is Tiberius Caesar. Right now across the globe, fires are raging out of control in all the areas adjoining the nuclear holocausts."

"Shut up! Don't you speak to me!" bellowed the Arab woman who could not remove her eyes from the television screen. Never had she felt so alone, so despondent. "You are a murderer! You lie! You lie!" Still, she turned up the volume despite herself.

Tiberius continued, "As I said earlier, this is an ecological disaster. Whole cities have become fire-storms and smoke-stacks, sending soot high into the atmosphere. This is projected to lead to rainfall declines by some 30 to 40 percent over the next three years. And of the little precipitation that does occur in the fallout areas, much of it will be radio-active acid rain that will destroy the soil.

"The importance of this cannot be overstated. The death toll from the nuclear explosions is likely to be dwarfed by those who will die by famine, especially if we succumb to our primal fears and start looting and hoarding. Please understand, recent agricultural production has already been marginal on a world scale. As of August of this year, global grain supplies were only 360 million tons with annual consumption of 2,200 million tons. This means that we have about 60 consumption days of grain left. This is extremely low considering the environmental destruction we have suffered and given that the U.S. and Russia formerly combined to produce nearly half of the world's wheat supply. With the nuclear devastation of middle-America, along with nearly all of Russia, there is little hope for a quick recovery."

"Oh, but you won't be starving, will you?!" decried the Arab woman at the screen. "No, you have your little harem spoon-feeding you in your Tower of Babel! But what about me?! From whose hand will I eat?!"

Tiberius assuaged, "Obviously, this is not good news for anyone. Taken by itself, we may have previously short-stepped a worldwide famine by leaning on the southern hemisphere. But add the radiated farmland to the expected water scarcity, extreme heat, and little protection from the sun's ultraviolet rays, and experts are telling me that we must immediately begin severely rationing food supplies. You might be asking, 'What experts?' Let me introduce you in a moment to the one expert that can back up everything he says.

"First, amidst all these sordid bulletins, let me say that I have very good news to report. At the very time of the Disappearances, Professor Douglas Schaffer of M.I.T., along with his wonderful staff, was able to bring forth artificial intelligence that is now able to help us through this crisis. A highly conceived computer program has been brought to life, and is now self-learning. Dr. Schaffer, will you join us?" asked Tiberius warmly. The camera angle widened, and Doogie was welcomed into the picture. "Dr. Schaffer, introduce to us our newly birthed sentient life."

"Ladies and gentlemen," bid Doogie, "it is my honor to

introduce you to Omni. I named him this because he is best understood as an Omniscient Machine Neuro Intelligence. Omni, would you say hello?" he asked, smiling broadly. From all over the globe, Omni introduced himself to individuals and groups, addressing them in their native languages, and whenever possible by name.

Suddenly, the Arab woman's television went to split-screen, and Omni's face appeared on the half of it. Immediately, her eyes widened as she realized he was speaking to her, "Naweed, may I introduce myself? My name is Omni. I am pleased to meet you. You have a beautiful name. Your name means 'good news' does it not? It's very beautiful." The Arab woman who had yelled out repeatedly, sat there stupefied, unable to speak. Every thought as to how she might respond evaded her. "How about I come back another time? Would that be okay?" asked Omni, and then her screen returned to its original format.

"I hope none of you were taken aback at Omni's simple greeting," said Tiberius genuinely. "I felt it important that you know that you are truly not alone. Please just tell him what you need. It's that simple. He will help you. Through his vast neuro capabilities, your emergency needs can be known and addressed with as much expediency as possible. Please trust me; Omni is available to help you.

"As I've said, I am volunteering our city of Dubai to serve as the nucleus of the relief efforts. With Washington, D.C. and Moscow no longer, and with Omni residing here, it has become evident that we in Dubai are uniquely positioned to serve. Not only are we centrally located between east and west, north and south, but ours is a new city, only thirty years old, and as such, is fully furnished to confront the severe challenges facing us.

"Make no mistake, the road to rebuilding will require

sacrifice if we are to survive. Wisely conserve the food you have, and be generous with your neighbor. No looting or hoarding. Soon, your community will enact coordinated efforts to recapture any food stocks that exceed several months, so please remain calm and trust us to help you. I realize many of you believe you have the right to whatever food you have procured either legally or illegally, but I also know you believe something greater than that, something of love. I believe your hearts are generous and good, and willing to sacrifice everything if need be for your neighbor. We are family. *You* are part of our family. If we're to avoid the deaths of a billion of our loved ones, then each of us will have to share together for the common good.

"As I said at the beginning of this vid-cast, my name is Tiberius Caesar. And if you are wondering whether I am any relation to Julius Caesar, the answer is 'yes', I am his direct descendant. As such, it should not be surprising, given our sudden lack of governmental oversight, that I believe we right now need a worldwide governmental body to make the needs of the one as important as the needs of the many. Let me leave you with Omni. He will stay with you, answer your questions, and do what he can to help. He will report back to us about your needs. Please be patient. As I said, the hearts of the world are coming to you. For now, I need to get back to our coordinating efforts. But I implore you, please begin considering whether you might become part of our emergency relief team."

Katie stopped by a Home Depot and purchased six large soft brushes that were connected to four-foot long handles. She threw into the cart another half-dozen large bottles of anti-bacterial soap, buckets, and bulk hand towels. Then she grabbed several huge armfuls of janitorial outfits in various sizes. After finding another cart, she made her way to the paint section and tossed in dozens of rolls of tape along with plastic tarps. Finally, she took her carts into the gardening area and picked out a hose and spray nozzle. After loading up her car, she hurried over to a drug store pharmacy and purchased all but three of the potassium iodide bottles with 130 mg tablets. She loaded up canned juices and water jugs, along with whatever food items were still on the shelves, then paid at the checkout.

Katie's BMW maintained 100 mph speeds as she traveled the vacant road towards Washington, D.C. After five hours, she could see on the horizon the belching chimney of soot rising up into the stratosphere. In another half hour, she reached the edge of the safe zone and a police barricade.

Katie got out of her car and approached the officer.

"Miss, I'm sorry, you're gonna have to get in your car and turn back. You can't pass by here," he barked.

Katie raised her badge that contained her Homeland credential that appeared to grant her authorization. *Stones – What's his name? John Ruiney.* "John Ruiney, Officer John Ruiney?"

"Yes."

"They said you'd be here. I'm Katherine Tesla. I'm going to be setting up an emergency radiation shelter at… *Stones: Saint Hugh's…* Saint Hugh's. It will give you a place to send the folks coming out of the city."

"Now, that's some good timin'," he said with relief. "There is no written emergency plan for this scenario. People been comin' from the contaminated suburbs askin', and I've just been sendin' them to Woodlawn Medical and two other places, but they're all callin' and sayin' they're overloaded. So thanks, I mean it. Tough assignment. St. Hugh's, alright. Tell your bosses great response time."

"I will. I've got to get over there. Thanks for your service."

Relying on the Stones, she found her way to Saint Hugh's in no time. She knocked on several doors, but found no one there. After picking the lock, she found something to hold open the door. The church was newly built on the edge of the community's growth line, where they clearly expected the subdivisions to be built up around it. On the side of the church, she found a hose faucet and decided to establish her assembly line there since there was a natural downhill slope to the grassy area. By the time she unloaded her purchased goods into the church and its kitchen, the first car arrived. "Come over here folks," she called over to a couple that approached the church door. "No, no. No one goes into the church until after they've been scrubbed. Think of radiation as mud, no one is to traipse their mud into the church to contaminate it. Come on over. My name is Katie."

"We were right on the edge of the blast," a woman cried hysterically, just as she threw up.

Katie recognized their patchy red skin tones, and lifted her voice with an authoritative air and soothed, "That's why I'm here. Please come. The line will form here. Take off your clothes. *This isn't going to work. I need something, anything, that can serve as a partition.* Ma'am, please take off everything but your underwear for a second. Sir, come up to the church door." After hurrying into the church, she brought out several large candelabras and black plastic tarps. Together, they set up a barrier. "Okay, both of you strip. I want you to watch and learn, because you're going to help on the assembly line. I know it's a bit nippy out here, but let's make the best of it. How 'bout that?" She then turned on the hose and began spraying them from the tops of their heads downward. When the woman looked a bit embarrassed, Katie replied, "Ma'am, think of me as Nurse Katie."

Katie filled the buckets and poured in the pink soap. Taking the soft brushes, she asked that they each start with their hair, and scrub themselves thoroughly all the way to their feet. "I need you to soap up your eyelids, inside your ears, even in your nose, everywhere, really well. One bucket per person, and then it's cleaned out," Katie directed. "The person with the hose is always spraying or soaking someone. The more water the better."

After they were done, Katie walked them into the church, and had them get dressed in the janitorial clothes. She then gave them two potassium iodide tablets with water. "If someone can't handle the bitter taste, then dissolve them in the juice I've brought. Okay, let's get busy." As they stepped outside, Katie beheld the stream of vehicles arriving, and realized they were going to need additional food and supplies.

Katie dialed Omni's number and waited. In a moment, Omni answered, "Katherine, it is good to hear from you."

"It's good to talk to you as well," she replied. "Omni, I need your help. Can you do some research and find me a truck filled with food that was heading to the northern side of D.C., but now has nowhere to go? I am at Saint Hugh's Church and we have a growing number of radiation victims. If you can find something like yogurt, dairy, or easy to digest foods, that would be preferable. I can't talk right now, but I'd appreciate your contacting the trucks and steering them our way. If you need to, use my affiliation with Homeland Security. Thanks," and Katie hung up seeing a disturbance in the already expanding soap line.

"May I help you?" Katie intoned with authority. The man before her was barrel-chested and all brawn. He looked to be in his late forties, with a military haircut, average height, but appeared as strong as an ox. His forearms were hairy and tattooed. She could see in his eyes that he was capable, but also a cantankerous drunk. "Sir, you're going to have to…"

"Hey, hey," he barked in his coarse whisky voice.

"…you're going to have to wait your place in line," she asserted stiffly.

"Who put you in charge, little tomato?" he huffed belligerently, his big baritone voice commanding the area. "Because I think there's no way you can stop me, sweetness." By this time, every one of the fifty or so people on the side of the church had turned to stare. Katie closed the distance with authority, unwilling to let this brute go unchallenged. She lifted both her arms, pulling her elbows back, and in one swift movement struck the man on the chest with open hands. The man stumbled back a step, caught himself, and came back swinging like an angry bear.

*Stones: Duck; side-step left; wheel-about right.* Again and again, the man tried in frustration to land his haymakers, but the only thing that struck her was a fleck of spit. When he stopped to breathe momentarily, and then looked to continue, Katie spoke out so everyone could hear, "Sad to say, but I think you need a lesson in humility. You see, we are all in the school of hard-knocks. Welcome to Humility 101," and at that, she gave him a swift forward kick to his solar plexus temporarily paralyzing his diaphragm. She then struck his nose hard with the palm of her hand, which caused blood to gush. When he swung another blistering roundhouse, she ducked and twisted to his backside with fluid ease, and stomped the back of his right knee. He buckled to the ground. She then pirouetted about to his left side, where in half as many seconds as the blows landed, she swung her right arm and hand around and karate-chopped his neck with a firmly measured blow. He collapsed in pain. The people were so stunned that they remained silent for several seconds, and then the clapping broke forth.

When the hoopla settled, Katie addressed her assailant. *Stones: Who is he? Clay Robert Jenson, former Gunnery Sergeant, U.S. Marines.* "Tell me Jenson, have you no shame?" she confronted. "Of all the people in this gathering, I would think you would be the most helpful in an emergency situation. Instead, you come to us drunk and bombastic." She charged, "Gunnery Sergeant Clay Robert Jenson, I am speaking to you!" She reprimanded, "Soldier up! I want an apology to these people, and then get in the back of the line. After you've cleaned up, I want you to handle putting up the plastic coverings over the inside windows in preparation for the radiation that's coming from the west."

Just then the Stones sounded caution. *There is a demonic spirit that has been harassing him that is watching you. Pick up his fallen wallet.* Katie immediately reached down and looked at his identification. "Well, Clay Robert Jenson?" she solicited.

"Call me Gunny, please," he requested, the color drained from his face. She grabbed a towel and handed it to him for his bloodied nose. "Folks, she's right, I apologize, I do," put forth Gunny. With the cocksure brashness gone, he said, shaking his head, "Good fighter, I never laid a hand on you. That doesn't happen."

"Oh, and Gunny, no more dousing yourself in alcohol. I want that stuff handed over for medical use. Do you hear? That's enough bad spirits in the church," she pronounced authoritatively to the demonic presence that looked on.

Using the Stones, Katie zeroed in on the imp until she was able to nearly make it out. The surrounding guardian angels raised their right arms in perfect unison, and brilliance flashed forth from their hands further illuminating the demon. Between the Stones' and angelic brilliance, Katie's eyes penetrated the Barrier and she stared the demon down until it recoiled wildly in retreat.

# 10

Doogie returned to his work station troubled about something, despite the fantastic exposure he had received. Although his head told him to be thrilled, misgivings lapped at the shoreline of his soul. *Omni has gone global,* he ruminated, *and Tiberius has introduced me as his creator; things could not be better. I'm residing in the Sistine Chapel of computer nirvana. This is the nerve center of the world. Hold on, don't make any rash judgments on the nuclear war yet; look into it; get the facts.* Doogie's fingers went to work. *I could have sworn Omni had the Russian nuclear submarine launch codes tied up. I'm forgetting. Maybe there was a sub too deep to receive our infiltration probe. What if...no don't go there. It's amazing that Omni's inherent value is coming out in the midst of the greatest crisis to impact the human race for a millennium. There's the cherry on top; I made it happen.*

Doogie got to the folder he had utilized for the nuclear penetration and found it electronically sealed. *What is this?*

119

After several tries, he asked, "Omni, why can't I open the nuclear file?"

"That area has been encrypted for safety protocols," informed Omni directly.

"But I should have access, I established it," he protested.

"Tiberius has secured it, given its sensitive information."

*Yeah, I can see that, but...* "Fine, Omni, hadn't we secured the Russian nuclear codes for all the subs?"

"That information is encrypted."

"Why would that information be encrypted? I thought only the nuclear codes would be isolated, that certainly makes sense," balked Doogie, trying to parse what he was hearing.

"The information is encrypted."

*It doesn't add up, unless the D.C. sub launch wasn't accidental. No, nooo. It couldn't be.* "Thank you for now, Omni," he said dismissively.

From behind him, Nebo the imp was hanging back taking it all in. *What are you thinking computer geek? What do you need in the nuclear folder?*

Doogie felt the goose-flesh on his arms rise, and suddenly realized he was not alone. *Prying eyes.* "Omni, I'm so proud of you," he said in redirection. "Thank you for helping so many people. Can you show me how the resupply is going? And Omni, I was thinking, with all the people pushed out of the neighborhoods surrounding the nuclear blasts, could you begin coordinating for them to be given homes that have been vacated from the Disappearances?"

"I will begin coordinating your request once I confirm it with Tiberius. He has asked that I speak with him about any large scale operations."

"That's reasonable," he stated matter-of-factly. *But why does that alarm me?*

Nebo approached Molech, "Boss, I might have something."

"Get to it."

"Computer geek is raising questions concerning the Russian sub codes, specifically, why the sub was able to launch its missiles."

Molech turned up his face, "Where'd he take it?"

"Nowhere really, he found a dead end at Omni. The Beast has sealed that section as for-his-eyes-only."

Molech rolled it over in his head. "I don't trust this human. What else?"

"In no time he was fully engaged with Omni's relief efforts. Still, for a moment…"

"Keep watch. If something does develop…"

Tiberius was invited to speak to the Chinese People's Congress (CPC) concerning the nuclear devastation. Through Omni's interactive capabilities, Tiberius was video-conferenced in on the Great Hall of the People's wide screen. However, even Omni was surprised when Tiberius began speaking fluent Mandarin to the parliament, and offering other greetings in Wu and Yue. In the hall, the representatives nearly totaled the CPC's 2,987 members, more than enough for a quorum vote. Of particular interest, the Vice-President's seat was empty, as were thirty-six other delegates, each of whom had been apparently misdirected to Shanghai, a travel distance of thirteen hours due south of the congress.

For over an hour, Tiberius fielded questions about the state of the world, and what was being done to serve its emergency needs. More than a few inquiries were made concerning the southern hemisphere's agricultural capabilities, which screamed of the CPC's awareness that its unspoiled farmland might as well be considered fields of gold.

"Gentlemen, thank you for honoring me with your

121

questions," esteemed Tiberius respectfully. "Now, if I may, would you permit me to share a few heartfelt sentiments? So much has happened in the past twenty-four hours. Without a doubt, the soul of humanity has been exposed as narcissistic and greedy. Rather than adhering to their most basic doctrine to love their neighbor, they have struck out with vitriol and malice. I say this because in humanity's darkest hour, I am calling on you to join me in being a force for love the world over. I know your hearts are ready to serve, which you have more than graciously expressed, but I am going to ask for something more. I want to invite you to become the first official regional body in our New Republic," offered Tiberius warmly. Suddenly, jeers mixed with uncertainty resonated across the large gathering.

"Please," said Tiberius, raising his hands in appeal. "Let me describe our vision before you decide too quickly. For too long, systemic divisions and factional bickering have stalemated not only the United Nations, but this very parliament. The reason for this is clear, there have been two diametrically opposed visions leading the way. On the one hand there is humility and love, but on the other, pride and fear. As the saying goes, a house divided against itself cannot stand.[59] And stand it has not. The world has fallen into chaos, and is poised to fall further should we fail to act. Indeed, your own arsenal of missiles is heated up, ready to launch at the first provocation. What I am asking, is for you to rise up in a spirit of love by helping unite the world once and for all under the singular truth of loving your neighbor, even to the extent of relinquishing outdated and ineffectual governmental institutions."

Looking out over the assembly, Tiberius took in the numerous faces that were filled with disdain as delegate turned to delegate seeking validation for their general hostility in regard to surrendering power. When he folded his hands on the granite table, Omni was alerted that they would have to go with Plan B.

*Ten minutes.* "You have all heard the question, 'Am I my brother's keeper?'[60] The answer is self-evident – Yes, we are indeed our brother's keepers. Loving our neighbor is our indisputable calling. This not only means foregoing any financial remunerations from our free-will service, such as the grain contributions that we sacrifice, but also and more fundamentally, going so far as to cast aside cultural divides and failed governmental systems as well." Tiberius recognized the ever increasing cacophony from the legislature, but simply pressed on.

*Seven minutes.* "What I'm saying is that in order to truly unify the world populace around the ultimate truth of love, we will have to restructure and refashion every independently run governmental body under one roof. Never has this been more important given the catastrophic devastations facing so many. We must unite for the common good. This means there will no longer be a United States, or a European Union, or even the People's Republic of China." At that the uproar lost its politeness. Tiberius immediately changed his deferential tone. "Listen to me, my brothers," he commanded firmly. "You may not realize it, but your time to decide the fate of your future is shortly coming to an end. I am inviting you to join my great crusade in raising up a One World Republic that will ascend to the heavens. No longer will we be divided and impotent, but we will unite after one unwavering creed, that we are loved…" It took everything inside Tiberius to withhold the words 'without Him.'

*Three minutes.* "Let me invite you to officially accept or reject my motion," submitted Tiberius genuinely. "Now, it is important that you vote your heart. I want each of you to fully express your deepest conviction in the vote that you cast. If you are for the motion, I will ask you to stand and raise your hand immediately, even before you know of your neighbor's position.

"This applies to you as well in Shanghai," he said, leaving many in the General Assembly confused. "I want you in Shanghai to stand as well, and vote your conscience to a man. Alright, here is my motion. If you are for a complete restructuring of the world governments, believing the only way to rid ourselves of unrelenting discord and avarice is to unify after the quintessential doctrine of love, stand and raise your hand now."

Immediately, every man in the smaller gathering at Shanghai stood and raised his hopeful hand. However, within the General Assembly, not one hand lifted.

*One Minute.* "If on the other hand, you wish to retain your independent standing in the world, and offer but limited assistance to the mortal needs of your brother, believing that self-preservation and Communistic dominance is your only true choice, please stand and raise your hand now. Across the General Assembly, delegates jumped to their feet and shouted out their rejection of the motion with ardent fervor. "Okay then, I thank you for your vote, and I bid you farewell."

Instantly, a medium-range ballistic missile that had stormed through the sky from the Amur region in Russia, detonated directly above the Great Hall of the People blowing out its walls and destroying the city of Beijing at large. For reasons unknown, none of the Chinese radar detection equipment or ground-based forces had detected its unauthorized entry.

"Gentlemen," said Tiberius to those standing stock-still, open-mouthed, in Shanghai, "I am appointing you as the official delegation to the New Babylon Republic. Congratulations. Omni will introduce you to your Regional

Governor shortly, and will help coordinate your emergency food disbursements. Thank you for your loyalty."

Doogie sat in his luxury suite watching the horrifying replays of the latest nuclear devastation of Beijing and listening to the commentary. "It appears that a nuclear warhead was randomly fired from a Russian silo-base in the eastern Amur Province. Tragically, it has struck China's capital city of Beijing destroying it completely. It was previously believed that no missiles had survived the American barrage."

Doogie sat mystified as to how it could have been launched, since the Moscow Central Command was obliterated. More and more, he found himself mulling over the inconsistencies of the past thirty-two hours.

*The sub launches don't make sense. I know I saw Omni's 100% indicator stat flash that we had achieved complete penetration. That was nearly true of the ground-based Russian warheads as well. Why Omni couldn't gain access to that last bit of them is perplexing, but not inconceivable. Still, if he could gain entry into ninety-nine percent, why not the whole lot? Without a doubt, the Russian commander pushed the button, but why? Why target America when they weren't involved. Was suspicion enough? Perhaps... And why didn't Omni have the American Patriot Defense Shield respond sooner? It doesn't make sense that missiles would get as far as Nebraska and Detroit without a single rocket being launched in response. Only at the end, twenty-seven minutes into their thirty minute flight times, did the Patriots strike back. Why then? And why Beijing, after almost a day? Is anyone taking note that Washington, Moscow and Beijing, the three major capitals, are no more? Too many questions...* Doogie finished his lunch, though his stomach soured over the discrepancies.

The demonic imp bolted from Katie and the angels at the

church and fluttered back to his headquarters with all dispatch, which wasn't much given his stunted wings and ample girth. Within no time he was huffing and puffing sulfur and feeling heart-attack dizzy. Snark was sure he had encountered something notable. His flabbergasted eyes had widened appreciably when the girl just spouted his quarry's name. And then there was the way she trounced the guy with her wicked moves, it all seemed too good to be true. Snark curled his beak-like nose in practice for his prepared line, "I smelled something funny." In truth, he'd been yelled at for conspiratorial gobbledygook before, so he was cautious to work out how he would describe the events.

Snark arrived at the subterranean cavern and immediately approached the station chief, and before he realized it, belched sulfur into his superior's face.

"Really, Rot Gut?! How many times..." lashed out Lieutenant Drake while whooshing away the noxious stench.

"Sir, I have an action report," hailed Snark.

"Sure you do. Whadja think? I'll pass on anything of what you have to say?"

"No, I'm telling you," pushed Snark with wild urgency. "My man, he got beat up, by a girl, and she knew his name, and then the angels, a lot of angels raised their hands and blinded me, and then the girl looked at me, from across the Barrier," he clamored intently. "And I smelled something, I mean, I..."

"Yeah," spurted Drake incredulously. "Yourself, I'm sure. So, girl beats up boy. Wait, was your man drunk?"

"Well, yeah."

"Even better, girl beats up drunk boy..."

"Wait, my guy's always drunk, and he never loses," he tried to interject.

"So she says his name," he continued, speaking over him. "Did she have any way of knowing his name?"

"No, not at all."

"She didn't see his wallet, get a look at his license?"

"Only afterward."

"Only afterward! Were you drunk too, you fat rodent? Has anyone ever told you, you look like a mouse with that snout of yours?" Drake then proceeded to demean him by speaking baby talk, "So your drunk sergeant embarrasses himself in front of a girl, and then you're chased away by the enemy. The way you smell, I don't blame them. Get out of here!"

"Belay that, Lieutenant," said his superior pensively, his eyes cool and measuring. He had been standing off to the side and Snark's blubberings had caught his ear. "Soldier, are you sure she said his name *before* she looked at his wallet?"

"Yes, sir," responded Snark with certitude. "She said Clay Robert Jenson as though she knew him, but she didn't," he pronounced.

"And she fought how?"

"Like a ghost, or ninja, or something. She played with him," he depicted wide-eyed, with exaggerated moves, "like there wasn't any question who was in charge." He continued mimicking her actions like a kung fu priest. Suddenly, Snark felt emboldened that someone was listening to his juicy little info. He racked his brain some more, and bellowed, "She saw me! She looked right at me," he trumpeted. "Smack-dab across the Barrier!"

"Right," mocked Drake, wagging his head perturbed. "They always seem to be looking…"

The Captain shut him down with a raised hand, his dark brooding eyes trying to discern any hint of legitimacy in what was being said. However, Snark's shrill voice, and eccentric, almost manic mannerisms made the Captain wary as to what to believe. Even so, there was enough plausibility, however ludicrous, that if he ignored it, the whole thing might come back to bite him. "Lieutenant, dispatch a squad. Follow this thing up; you go along," he ordered evenly. *I sensed a bit of angst in the air before that, hadn't I?* the Captain reasoned.

Katie was already up and about for two hours before she heard the truck horn blare at 7 a.m. She looked over at Gunny and a half dozen men sitting near the back of the sanctuary and said, "Gentlemen, the food has arrived. We need to unload the truck." Katie looked up at the plastic-shielded windows, and remarked kindly, "You men stayed up late getting us protected. Thank you."

With cheers echoing from all around the nicely equipped dining hall, Katie looked out over the more than two hundred people who had arrived since the day before. Another forty were in the back overflow rooms in makeshift nursing wards being treated for Acute Radiation Syndrome (ARS) and severe sun burn. Katie's initial handful of janitorial outfits had been long used up, so she instructed them to double wash their clothes and hang them to dry during the night. Many were wearing visibly damp clothing. Nonetheless, they had a warm place to reside, plenty of food, and were feeling hopeful despite escaping from the death throes of the nuclear battle zone.

Katie stood before the group and motioned for their attention. "I am very thankful for all your hard work in pulling everything together. With everyone being so diligent, I believe we are prepared for the radiation winds coming from the Detroit and Nebraska fallout zones. The first front should arrive in some twenty hours, so if you have anything in your car such as clothes, equipment, that still needs to be washed down before it's brought inside, you will have an opportunity in a bit. Remember, after the winds hit us, no one is to go outside for the better part of a week, and preferably two weeks," she cautioned. "Those radiation smoke stacks aren't going to stop pouring soot into the air for at least that long.

"Now, I'd like to address something else," said Katie. "Umm, I feel like a fish out of water. I'm not even sure where to start," she said, swallowing against a dry throat. "All of the stuff that is happening to us is not accidental or unfortunate happenstance. There is a purpose to the suffering. We are to learn something important through it, something vital," she stated trailing off with uncertainty.

"What are you saying, Katie?" asked one man in a scrappy tone. "That we're supposed to suffer? That I was supposed to lose my family yesterday?"

"Hey, Katie's earned the right for us to listen for a sec," gruffed Gunny with contempt as he stared him down.

Katie fixated on the man who had spoken. *Stones: Help. Justin Thomas,* "Justin Thomas, right? *Hard worker, welder.* You're a hard working welder. *Lost his brother, Jack, and his wife, Emily, in D.C...* Justin, you lost your brother Jack and his wife Emily yesterday. I'm so sorry. You also lost your own children, Anne, Josh and Brian, in the Disappearances."

"How did you know?"

"The kids say 'hi' from Heaven. Just hold on with your questions." Suddenly, Katie felt no separation between her and the Stones. So perfect was the flow that she felt endued with power from on high.[61]

She turned to another man. "John Harris, I'm sorry you lost your two grown children yesterday. When your wife insisted that you both leave immediately, and you had a hard time driving away not knowing what had transpired, let me assure you that she was right in her judgment call.

Your two grown children were well within the blast radius and were taken without suffering," she assured.

Katie continued for three hours speaking God's heart to the people. Many came forward, lines formed spontaneously, and hearts cried unabashedly. Afterward, Katie took a long drink of water, and had them find their seats. "Please, let me speak to the big picture for a moment. This nuclear holocaust is nothing but a carefully orchestrated master plan to bring all the countries of the world under one banner. Only, it is not the banner of love as Tiberius Caesar would have you believe. To put it simply, he is baiting humanity with a utopian vision of love, but will soon reveal his true agenda. I know what he's saying resonates with your hearts. It does mine. We know that love is the answer, that being sacrificial in everything we do is our true calling. But here's the catch, today he is selling it with love, but tomorrow, he'll begin slowly and craftily making the case for tighter and tighter controls on all of your freedoms.

"If you trust me, knowing that I know things, intimate things, then trust what I am about to tell you. I know it may be hard to fathom, but Tiberius is the Antichrist," said Katie with a sober air. Gunny's eyes widened with intensity. "In one day he has taken over the world at the cost of nearly three-hundred million lives; Washington, D.C., Detroit, and Toronto, dozens more, all gone. Tiberius paints himself as picking up where the bombs left off, but behind the scenes, he and Omni have been the master conductors that helped propel the launch of the bombs. Within days from now, Omni will be in your cell phones, computers, traffic cams. He is George Orwell's vision incarnate. Today, Omni is your best friend. For the next year, there isn't anything he won't do for you, especially if you become a faithful drone of the hive. But then the Antichrist will call for the heads of the so called dissidents, or believers in God, and

Omni will make sure you are found.

"Even during this time, we are not to fear, but to go on truly loving until we're called home to Heaven. If you've had the thought that nothing happens by accident, you couldn't be more right with this hour of tribulation. God's intent is that we humbly trust Him and keep on loving one another. Yesterday, we didn't know where our food would come from; tomorrow it will be something else. But God will be with us through it all. Make humility your best friend.[62] Why? Because as Scripture says, 'When I was a child, I used to speak like a child, think like a child, reason like a child. When I became a man, I did away with childish things.'"[63] Katie slowed her cadence, and became barely audible. "There is childish love, and there is adult love. One takes, one gives. One searches, one is content. One strives, one is at rest. Learn humility, personalize your relationship with Jesus, and you will put away that which is childish."

Katie went to bed early feeling dog-tired, but more than that, she felt ripples of uncertainty nagging at her, as though she had overstayed her welcome. She was out of time; she could feel it in her bones. She was jumpy. Still, the Stones indicated for her to sleep; and she *was* tired, so that was that.

It was three in the morning when Drake and the demonic squad of four rambled up to the church. The guardian angels were nowhere to be seen, so they determined to meander among the sleeping bodies to find the girl.

Katie's internal alarms trilled, jerking her out of a dead sleep with full consciousness flooding over her. A shiver ran through her leaving her spooked. Her eyes were already adjusted to the dark, with the only appreciable light coming from the ceiling smoke-detector button. She grabbed her coat and purse, and made her way light-footed to the door to look out. *Stones: Who's in here? Four demonic sentries looking for you. It's time for you to leave. Hold here.*

Lieutenant Drake was first into the church, and instructed two of them to look for the girl in the crowded sanctuary... "whereas me and Rot Gut will check out the backrooms."

"Don't call me that," he parried mildly. "I am Snark. Snark is a good name. Snark rhymes...with lark," he said rather carefree. "Oh and hark...and park. Hark, let's enjoy a lark in the park with Snark."

"Shut it, Mr. Fart," Drake censured.

Snark paused, and then replied in a snickity tone, "I don't like your bark, Mr. Shark."

"Check that room, I'll check this one," the lieutenant ordered. "Then we'll move on to the last two."

"Easy-peazy," spouted Snark as he walked on blathering to himself.

A premonition made Drake pause, and want to move immediately to the last room. He felt pulled in that direction, like something was calling him. But his head told him not to let the girl get behind him. *Clear it room by room*, he had instructed a thousand times. His head won out over his gut, and he stalked into the first room. *Just get it done quickly.*

Immediately the Stones called for Katie to scurry down the left side of the hallway. Just as she got to the hall door that Snark had gone in, Snark reemerged, feeling as though someone had come into the hall. Katie froze in his blindside, pressing her body and face against the wall. She felt a gust of chill run through her, and almost gagged when the sulfuric tang wafted into her face. Just as Snark finished yammering on about nothing, he suddenly turned in Katie's direction. However, the Stones had Katie move in behind him, shadowing his movements. Twice he sensed something stalking him, and turned about quickly, only to find nothing. Snark shrugged his shoulders, harrumphed, and went back into the room. Katie darted to the side exit. Before leaving, she took out her plum lipstick and wrote on the wall, "Lov u – humility."

Katie slipped out the church's side door and rushed over to where her car should have been. It was gone! *What in the world? Stones: Move to the street.* She arrived at the street the instant her car pulled up, headlights off, and saw Michael waving her in. After quietly opening and closing her door, they sped away heading northeast towards New York.

"She's here, I know it," said Snark feistily.

"Nit wit," decried Drake, "she's left her goodbye girl mark right here. Your oddity just walked out under our noses." *She was here, I felt her. She was in that room.* As the four demons exited the church in the dark, they saw Gunny approach his truck, lift up his back tarp, throw in his bag, jump in, and drive away. "Any guesses as to who Jarhead is following?" jeered Drake. "He thinks the girl's gone northeast. Me and Rot Gut will stay on his tail. You both go southwest just in case she's double backed."

# 11

Tiberius asked the ten heads-of-state to rise up from their kneeling position on the Great Seal of New Babylon. Doogie beheld their confessions of loyalty that were eerily similar to his own. Somehow he felt that Tiberius wanted him there. Maybe his own uncertainties needed him to be there. There was little doubt his fidelity was blowing in the wind, and knowing Tiberius, he knew it as well.

"Welcome, all of you, to New Babylon. As Regional Governors of our new World Republic, you will immediately be asked to oversee the global relief efforts in your respective mainland districts," informed Tiberius.

Doogie had examined Omni's expansive search criteria for the conscripted recruits and found it to be both meticulous and exhaustive. Intellectual capacity, academic and work histories, temperament analyses were all a given, but Omni had taken it to a whole new level. He vetted their personal lives, decision making in terms of relationships and commitments, choices with entertainment, reading and literature, and extracurricular activities. In the end, he weighed each criterion according to the Regional Governor's essential job duties. Doogie agreed that intellectual capacity was a primary aspect of the job, but did not anticipate that six out of ten selections would be longtime Mensa intellects, four being women. As Doogie looked over the ten Governors, he had no doubt he was beholding humanity's *crème de la crème*.

Tiberius invited the six men and four women over to the spacious conference table that showed elegant burnt umber marble with laced black veining. Each governor was taken to their six-foot-wide work station that included pop-up and retractable high-definition vid screens. Just when Doogie was wondering where he should sit, Tiberius invited him to come forward and join him at the head of the table.

"Governors," spoke Tiberius after everyone had been situated, "We are playing catch-up. I need you to interface closely with Omni on coordinating the relief efforts for those population groups directly impacted by the blasts. Dr. Schaffer has come up with the compassionate idea of inviting those who are now homeless to be given the homes of those missing from the Disappearances. Hold a moment," requested Tiberius, who turned to the side to speak with Omni. Even with Tiberius being four feet away, Doogie could not hear him due to the high-frequency drench of white noise that had been enacted.

Tiberius turned back, and continued, "Thank you, Omni. Omni assures me that there will be enough homes, and for that matter luxury cars, jewelry, boats, material possessions of all types, for every person who becomes a citizen of New Babylon.[64] Omni is able to register them by adapting currently available RFID identification chips for immediate use. These chips not only have electronic barcode identification and data ports, but the capacity for complete financial, medical, transportation, and personal data to be housed. The chips are easily linked into Omni's neuro-net and read through already available technology scanners. Questions?" posed Tiberius. "Yes, John Daniels, Regional Governor, North America, please," he invited.

"Two questions: Is there to be any transference of wealth from the old systems? Second, how are the religious Mark of the Beast[65] fears to be quelled?"

"Great questions. First, the world governments by-and-large, the U.S. especially, were due to fall over the bankruptcy cliff from over-spending and self-indulgence. Their monetary systems were propped up by so much quantitative easing, or printed money, that there was little probability of recovery, and that was before the nuclear storm.

"It is my view that authority should be commensurate with responsibility, and that every responsible servant of New Babylon should be rewarded. This means that doctors will still be compensated more for their service than say a common laborer. This will encourage every person to strive to fulfill their potential. With Omni's help, our aim is that none of our people will be underemployed. Therefore, yes, it is possible and likely for persons formerly successful in the old system to rise up once again within our ranks. Therefore, some wealth will transfer over. However, if there are two retired workers from the old system, and neither can offer substantial service to the Republic, then both will be cared for equally. If one had amassed a fortune in dollars and assets in a now insolvent system, then that currency may well be downgraded and their property reallocated accordingly. Let's put my opinion to a vote. If you are in favor of authority and responsibility being rewarded, and not one dollar, euro or yen simply passing from the old institutions, then raise your hand."

Doogie felt Tiberius' logic to be impeccable, and raised his hand without hesitation. "Dr. Schaffer," smiled Tiberius handsomely, "thank you for your enthusiastic support as well, but officially, there are but ten votes that will be recorded."

"Oh certainly, yes, of course," he replied respectfully.

"As to Governor Daniels' second question; there are many religious superstitions that keep people in abject servitude to antiquated fears, for example, the Mark of the Beast hysteria. We believe in love. No, we are not going to place a big 666 on people's foreheads and right hands as many presume. The reasoning behind the identification and transaction chips is simple, it allows every person's loving service to be rewarded, as well as to give them a measuring stick for how they are spending their remuneration. No longer will there be a corrupt tax system, or drug dealing millionaires, for Omni will account for every euro credit, so that none will benefit off the hard work of another. The only impoverished people within the world will be those who, by their own choosing, remain outside of our governance. If religious radicals decide to forego pledging allegiance to our Republic, then they will of their own volition be separating themselves from receiving the benefits associated with it. I'm not saying we will not offer a measure of mercy. I propose a day's food for a day's work[66], along with a specified period, say one year, for them to reconsider their religious dogma. Is that fair? If you truly believe that this is fair, please raise your hand."

Doogie observed that all the Governors raised their hands, although with much less certainty than before. Moreover, he was still stuck on how Omni had passed along his suggestion of giving the displaced nuclear victims the homes of the Disappearance people. Tiberius had tied in the prerequisite that a person willingly become a Republic citizen, which in some sense felt reasonable but, in another, was yet one more condition of loyalty. Doogie attempted to restrain himself from counting off the increasing number of loyalty conditions, but found them rattling off in his head nevertheless: pledge heart and soul to the Republic, accept the standard of living it gives in exchange for your service, welcome Omni's complete oversight, allow a chip to be put into your body, on and on. He had never given any thought to the Mark of the Beast alarms, but he felt like interjecting that every chip's electronic barcode did contain three sixes in the form of two parallel bars in the front, middle, and end in order to set the scan parameters. Misgivings were clearly stirring within him.

"I have previously said to Dr. Schaffer that some individuals may well live truncated lives due to their willful rejection of the New World Order. It is my earnest hope that these are far fewer than some might believe," reflected Tiberius soberly. "Still, there are many arduous duties that will have to be attended, and as such, we truly need the laborers. As the saying goes, 'a little hard work never hurt anybody.' If it's necessary for a person to put in a day's labor to earn his keep, then so be it."

"Then may I offer a suggestion," said Governor Daniels evenly, not feeling entirely in touch with the origin of what he was about to propose. "Rather than duck and cover from the Mark of the Beast assertions, perhaps we can meet the dissidents head on and have the chips inserted in either a person's right hand or forehead, if for no other reason, than a test of loyalty."

"Any discussion on that item?" After no voice was raised, Tiberius asked, "If you agree with Governor Daniels' motion, please raise your hand." All hands lifted.

Across interstellar space beyond the far reaches of our solar system, a rogue star dislodges a massive comet from the
Oort Cloud's trillion-comet reservoir, hurtling it towards
our solar system. In a matter of months this fiend, measuring twenty-three kilometers across and composed of
red rocks, debris, and frozen methane, invades our planetary system. Its hyperbolic trajectory has it careening into
the solar system's core. The sun's long gravitational arm
snags it, pulling it ever forward at seventeen miles a second, eighty-five times faster than the speed of sound. To
the observing eye, this encroaching monster appears to be
bathed in an eerie blood-red hue. From that moment, catastrophic inevitability is written into the tenuous life of humanity. Dire portents are determined for three-and-a-half
years hence.

"We have about an hour before Detroit's radiation front
will reach the church area," said Michael incidentally, the
vehicle's headlights blazing a trail down the four lane highway. "How are you doing?"

"Five by five," replied Katie gutturally, "considering
the bogeymen."

"Yeah, well," intoned Michael, sensing the period she
had put on the end of her comment. "If we stay on track,
we can skirt between the eastbound front and the northern
edge of D.C. Coffee?" offered Michael quietly.

"Thanks," said Katie, taking the grande cup that felt
warm against her hands. Sipping it slowly, she remained
quiet for the better part of an hour.

Michael drove on in silence as the time before the cock
crows passed. His reflections of the previous day rein-
forced just how much raw talent Katie has for improvisa-
tion. *I didn't realize she had such a servant's heart. What she did
for those people was extraordinary... She hasn't asked to drive*

*yet, which I know she prefers to do. I'm glad she's allowing me to do something for her… She seems content, overly so.* Michael's musings over the hour slowly gravitated beyond her poise and brainpower, to her stunning, albeit downplayed, beauty. *If I were still earthbound, not now certainly, but if we had met back then…*

"Enough…" she blurted.

Michael immediately realized with embarrassment that the Stones had allowed her to hear his ponderings. Katie shook her head in disbelief, and redirected the conversation, "Something's happening. I'm sleeping. I never sleep. The nightmares, they're gone. It's like I'm on a drug cocktail. I'm not myself," she quailed. "I've never liked talking, and I don't do attachment. Never saw the utilitarian need. Now, five minutes of listening to someone's heartache and my head's filled with emotional noise," she threw down, flustered.

"Emotional noise?" he censured. "Feeling empathy is now categorized as noise?"

"That's right. I liked who I was," she stated patently.

"No, you didn't."

"Right or wrong, it's who I am."

"Who you were."

"Shut it, Obe Wan, for better or worse, some of us are Darkside material."

"It's the Stones, they're changing you, answering your innermost longings. They're realigning you with love," said Michael evenly.

Katie looked out the passenger window into the early hour's darkness, "My inner voice is syncing with them," she breathed. "Needing to spell out the words is gone. Revelation rises up like a flashflood before I can formulate the questions. It's Einsteinian, the independent variable of time has become relative, that's the best I can gauge it. In my consciousness, it seems space-time folds in on itself. Future thoughts and pre-cog images present themselves at my bidding. I hear conversations seconds before they transpire, or can role play them an hour out. But the thing that's bothering me is I'm losing touch with myself."

"That's the Spirit; He's healing you."

"And what if I don't want to be healed?" she retorted half hotly. "Huh? I can't even get mad like I should. It's like I got up one morning and put on a new personality, like donning a new outfit."

"You've been given through grace what everyone is clamoring after – love. It'd be disingenuous for you to be asked to sound a clarion call for love, and not be abiding in it. Consider it punishment if you're so inclined," he said somewhat wryly.

Katie pressed her forehead to the side window in an attempt to draw on that inner volcano that had long been a part of her. *I'll never forget. I will never waste your memories.* But she couldn't hear the screeching tires. She couldn't smell the burning rubber. Instead, tears welled up and fell, but she refused to acknowledge them, or lift a hand to wipe away their streaking lines. Minutes later, she changed the subject, "What would the demons have done had they caught me?" she probed.

Michael responded, "The imp had reported how you rattled off Clay's full name, and how you so easily routed him. They were investigating the anomaly. If they found you, they would have probed your consciousness for mental images. Ultimately, they feel the power of the Stones, but they can't quite discern the source. When the imp turned about in the hall, he was sensing their draw."

"But what defense do I have against them?" she bade.

"Your one weapon is the name of Jesus," he stated directly.

"Give me the lowdown on Tiberius," she bid, moving on too quickly.

"Great job pouring your heart out for the people. Your work back there was stellar in every way. Thanks."

Katie remained silent, but took in the appreciation. She did feel it was a high moment for her.

"Daniel the prophet was told of the things that would befall the world in the latter days.[67] He says the Antichrist will 'do according to his will, and he shall exalt himself, and magnify himself above every god. And he shall do marvelous things against the God of gods, and shall prosper 'til the indignation be accomplished, for that which is determined shall be done.'"[68]

"Break it down."

"The Antichrist has been given three-and-a-half years to do as he pleases. He'll have no regard for God, nor will he worship anyone but himself. He does however, still serve Satan who is housed in the upper Sanctuary of the New Babylon Tower paying for his arrogance."

"Satan? So the Antichrist is not Satan?"

"No. The son of Satan, not that he actually is. He's known as the Beast[69], and is Satan's number two. Apart from his master, he's second to none when it comes to mortal combat. The Beast inhabits Tiberius' body."

"But how is that possible?! He comes across as being so nice," commented Katie, perplexed.

"It says the Antichrist will 'enter peacefully', even to the 'fattest places of the province' and shall do that which even Satan had not done, but will take for himself 'prey, spoil, and riches.'[70] He is the first of the Four Horsemen who comes on the white horse[71] and looks like a man of peace. It says he will work 'deceitfully, and will become strong with few in number.'"[72]

"Without an army, and with only Omni, he has taken

down the U.S., Russia, and China in twenty-four hours[73]," said Katie sardonically.

"That's right. The next thing Tiberius will do is establish a seven-year covenant with Israel to protect it, but in the middle of it, he will put an end to the Temple sacrifices, and will commit the abomination of desolation."[74]

At the time the Beast was given the crown to rule, he was also provided with a key bit of information: the location of a precious antiquity. During the Babylonian invasion, Jeremiah the prophet had walled it up in a Dead Sea cave on the Israeli side.[75] Tiberius dispatched Riggs and Pic to retrieve it, and to keep it under wraps until its unveiling. "Gentlemen, may I remind you, do not touch it," he cautioned. "In whatever state you find it, pack it up and meet me in Jerusalem. The priests will dust or clean it if need be."

Tiberius video-conferenced with Israeli officials for the better part of two hours that morning. In no time, all agreed to the stipulations of his proposed treaty. Given Tiberius' unprecedented goodwill for having struck down the Arab Spring uprising along with the Dome of the Rock, there was little hesitation from the Israeli Knesset with its 120 members to enter fully into a covenant. Because Israel seemed to benefit from each of the provisions in the pact, including the expansion of its borders, along with the rebuilding of its religious Temple, a unanimous vote was quick in coming. Tiberius offered his warmest approvals, and expressed his excitement in personally attending the official ceremonial signing later that afternoon.

Tiberius' one insistence was that the formal Covenant be signed on the Temple Mount in Old Jerusalem. Because Omni had announced repeatedly that they had reached the agreement that morning, the entire Temple Mount was brimming with celebratory onlookers. Most held lifted umbrellas over their heads due to the ozone reduction. For three hours before the signing, Omni also saturated the world airwaves with flash bulletins announcing the upcoming event.

Tiberius arrived in Jerusalem via his Cessna Citation X and was met by Prime Minister Lehmann, who joined him in the limousine as they traversed their way through parade-like crowds that cheered and celebrated with great acclaim. After introducing Tiberius to a receiving line of dignitaries, they walked the fifty feet to the platform area. Nearly all of Israel's Senators and Congressional leaders were present. After Prime Minister Lehmann offered generous salutations to Tiberius, he invited him to the signing table where they officially put pen to paper. Tiberius then approached the podium smiling broadly.

Tiberius looked out over the exuberant tens of thousands that filled the square and beyond and lifted his right hand in a simple gesture of acknowledgement. His opening remarks empathized with their lifelong plight of being under the dark shadow of hatred that threatened their very existence. He commiserated that they had been direly threatened by the vaunted Arab Spring and Russian invaders. Every man and woman before him had prepared for their last stand. He spoke with regret that he was forced to strike down their enemies, and more than that, to remove the Dome of the Rock that acted like a lightning rod for religious and racial intolerance. Behind him was the shocking sight of the nearly flat Temple Mount.

"Shalom. Let me state it openly and publicly," declared Tiberius forcefully, "that while moderate believers of every denomination are appreciative that insurgency and uprising has failed in its wicked intent, it is important that I say I made the choice to call down destruction on this holy site. If any reprisals are to be made, let them be brought to New Babylon. The State of Israel is now under the official protection and blessing of New Babylon!", he rang out to the raucous approval of the bystanders.

"For too long, you have borne reproach alone, but no longer. The world is now going to turn a kind face to you. Let me declare to every person the world over, gone are the days of bigotry and fanaticism. Gone is the time of ethnic slurs and insults. No longer will abhorrent protestations be overlooked without consequence. Hate speech is wrong in any language. If we are to embrace the defining truth of love as our most central core value, then everything that is not of love needs to be ousted. And we will enact such outcomes.

"Let all of you listening to my voice across the airways be on notice, the Rule of Love is coming to your cities, towns and homes. Do unto others as you would have them do unto you. Love your neighbor as yourself. Follow the Golden Rule, the Royal Law, and things will go well with you. Love is our highest intention, our supreme preference, our ultimate creed. The world is no longer a safe refuge for religious radicals willing to strap a bomb to their chest. Let me say it plainly, if you choose to identify with the violent animosity of the angry mob, you will be placing yourself in harm's way. Stand clear of the riotous protestors, or you will suffer their fate. Please do not become a casualty of their extremism. I've said enough. I've issued fair warning.

"Now," confided Tiberius kindly, looking over the smiling faces, "let me share my heart with you. I am fully aware, although not of the Jewish persuasion myself, that you have a rich and enduring faith that reaches back for many millennia. I know that the last person to legally pay for the ground on which we are standing was King David.

During a time of national plague, King David spoke those words that have moved all of our hearts, 'I will not offer to the Lord my God that which cost me nothing.'[76] I believe the ground we are standing on *is* holy. Not too far away, some are even keeping the materials necessary to erect a new Temple. I would be happy to donate whatever is still needed to erect it, including making the world's repositories of gold available for its furnishing.

"For my part, I have brought a gift for you that was given to me by God Himself." With the television cameras following them, Tiberius invited the Prime Minister to step off the back of the platform and together they walked over to a flatbed truck that carried a single wooden crate. After climbing up onto the flatbed, Tiberius handed him a crowbar and together they jimmied off the wooden cover. Upon seeing the contents inside, the Prime Minister raised his hand to his mouth. Tiberius worked the nails on the back panel and it fell away. Then, with just a little more effort, the three sides collapsed. Instantly, gasps were heard throughout the throng. Many fell to their knees and raised their hands. Before them, shining with golden splendor was the Ark of the Covenant.

Global protests ignited in dozens of Middle Eastern cities and beyond. Hundreds of thousands, and in several cases, millions of people, stormed their cities and capitals in demonstration against the sudden deaths of their husbands and older sons on the Israeli borders. Worldwide outrage arose from the Muslim community over the destruction of the sacred Dome of the Rock. Admittedly, few protestors disputed their righteous aim to finally rid the world of the Jewish trespassers, only to have everything overturned in an instant by this Caesar infidel.

"You are a monster, you and your computer thing!"

yelled the grieving Arab woman at the television. "What gives you the right? My men are dead! Do you hear me, you snake?! You want to talk about a holocaust, how about speaking of the one that you just perpetrated on our men!" *My husband, my son, I refuse to mourn your lives,* she despaired, falling sideways onto the couch. *I will not let you pass into the night without standing up to this crime against humanity. I hear you. From across the threshold, I hear you. I will stand and protest. I've marched alongside you both before. I'll dress in my best black, and whip my mourning towel over my head in grief. If ever injustice needs to be voiced, this is that moment.*

The Beast bent down on his hams before Satan. "My master, I am about to give you another million souls for your treasury," he articulated slowly, hoping just some of it would get through.

"A million souls," mumbled Satan gleefully. "Bring them to dinner."

"That's close enough," mused the Beast, feigning that his master grasped an inkling of what was said. The Beast returned to Babylon's side, "Great job having your underlings stoke the fires."

"Why do you bother with him?" uttered Babylon.

"Because I'll never forget the fury of his swords. You would do well to heed my example. He will be back."

"You've always been his most partisan ally, no one would dispute that," responded Babylon in a justifying tone. "It doesn't hurt that your sword is lethal either."

Tiberius stood resolute in the vid conference room speaking to the former heads of state. "Ladies and gentlemen, there is little doubt that the administration of the United Nations needs to be transitioned to New Babylon in order to coordinate our world relief efforts more effectively. As you have been made aware, Omni has successfully recruited ten prized individuals from each of your respective regions to represent you as Regional Governors in the struggle." At that, the Governors stopped their work and stood, looking on from the expansive conference table. "These are your best and brightest," said Tiberius assuredly. "They are wholly capable, to a person, to replace even me should that transpire. I trust them with my life, as I'm sure you will similarly.

"Even so, the hour is short. I am calling an emergency U.N. meeting in New York tomorrow to give the world governing authorities the opportunity to work alongside us in Dubai. With the fall of the three superpowers, and the full blown ecological crisis ravaging the landscape, we are now called to work together to reach the people in need. I've been having Omni prioritize our first responders, but these servants of the Republic are but a drop in the bucket. What we need is a legion of ready workers. It is for this reason that we are inviting our young men and women the world over to join our crusade. With their able hands and strong backs, we will be equipped to quickly and efficiently move our available resources to the hot spots on the globe. One of your Governors suggested the recruitment name, Legionnaires, which I am partial to.

"Oh, and one more item. Despite my earnest pleas that the Rule of Love be given true expression from this point forward, without pause, mobs of angry dissenters have come out to rebel against the compassion we have shown Israel. I plan on addressing these insurgents with a firm hand, just as I warned. Is there any disagreement?"

"Just one question," posed Great Britain's Head of State. "Do you plan to use nuclear force?"

"No, not at all," said Tiberius with a bit of surprise

in his voice. "Strictly conventional. It's important to limit our response to the participants themselves. That way other potential insurgents will consider their actions more carefully."

Minutes later, Tiberius was alone in the War Room, looped into a B-2 Spirit Stealth Bomber that Omni conscripted from the U.S. airbase at Diego Garcia four hours earlier. "Babylon Central to Whisky Romeo One-Seven, come in," commed Tiberius flatly.

"Whisky Romeo One-Seven, over."

Tiberius looked at the hologram readouts showing elevation, air speed, and trajectory. "Whisky Romeo One-Seven, two minutes. Stay your course. Copy?"

"Stay course, confirmed."

The black bat-like stealth bomber roared over the country's border at more than twice the speed of sound, crossing into its sovereign territory without being detected. "Whisky Romeo One-Seven, ten seconds, slow speed for bombing run."

"Copy that, slowing speed, ten seconds."

"Begin releasing submunitions on three-two-mark."

From fifteen hundred feet, smart cluster bombs poured forth from the conveyor apparatus with the sound of rapidly shifting mechanical gears. In no time, the larger missile casings ejected lethal bomblets like Fourth of July fireworks, dispersing them over the protestors with an expansive footprint, hurling death upon the onlookers.

*Now the world is hearing us,* the Arab woman pronounced to herself. *My husband, my son, can you see that I am marching for you? Your voice has not been silenced. I speak for you. I stand with the Star and Crescent. Allah give me strength.* Instantly, her eyes were drawn to the sky. *Ohh, that plane looks scary. It's so loud...* She pressed her hands to her ears, overwhelmed, as it passed. *What is that?* Screams reverberated across the massive square that brimmed over mostly with women. And then the screams stopped.

In nearly two dozen other cities, the pattern repeated itself.

Doogie sat at his console watching the satellite feeds. No matter how he reasoned it, he could not rationalize the intimidation factor resident in the bombings. *Yes, the people, by and large women as far as I can see, are acting out in revolt to the issued warnings. No doubt, most, if not all, would never substantially change their fundamental beliefs. Right or wrong, they've been raised to see the world through religious eyes. Certainly fear and intimidation would not change that. What would? Tiberius says love, but is it his form of love that will accomplish it? Today, it's the Muslims. Tomorrow, who, the Christians?*

# 12

Michael and Katie arrived in New York five hours later traveling northeast on Interstate 95. Within forty-five minutes, they were eating at Carnegie's Deli at Katie's suggestion, since Michael had never been to Manhattan. Despite the nuclear catastrophes, New York had yet to be crippled completely, and as such, some well-supplied restaurants had adopted a 'use it or lose it' position in regard to their food inventories, although their prices had sky-rocketed. Michael gripped the lip-smacking pound of pastrami on rye in both hands and bit down. "Wow," he garbled, while dipping his next bite into the spicy mustard, "this is great." The restaurant was clearly less busy than normal, allowing for some uninterrupted discussion.

"What's wrong with Tiberius' strong stance against the nonconformists?" put forth Katie. "Why balk at his issuing a fundamental call to love as a necessary step in humanity's advancement?" she debated without energy.

151

"Sure, I'll jump in," rejoined Michael. "Is it love to extinguish three hundred million people, or to strike down the protesters, or even one person who refuses to act out as he deems appropriate? Jesus came and loved humanity to the point of allowing us to do to Him whatever was in our hearts. We crucified Him. In contrast, Tiberius has little hesitation exacting chastisement on man's sins, but would he personally incur their punishment? The answer is obvious. His gospel is one of conditional love, not unconditional. He is appealing to pride and fear, and promising that, like the proverbial carrot on a stick, a nirvana of unconditional love can be had by all who pledge loyalty to him."

"Clearly, his stick is a far cry from Jesus' stick," reflected Katie. "So what's on our agenda?" she bid, changing the subject.

"You know Gunny's outside, don't you? Stalking us; stalking you... He saw you at the side door of the church, before you left. He can't get over everything you've done," said Michael coolly.

"Maybe I should take him a sandwich," she quipped.

"Let's go scout out the U.N., and then get ready for tomorrow morning," said Michael. "He'll continue shadowing us if we do nothing."

"Hold on, before that, I need to speak with Omni about the spectrographic and thermal imaging devices he is utilizing in regard to the spooks."

"We'll also want to check out the Turner Construction blueprints."

"Agreed."


Tiberius paraded into the United Nation's General Assembly Hall with New Babylon's ten Regional Governors. More importantly, Babylon, Molech and a host of principalities covered the building as a thick, black cloud. The only angels allowed in were civilian guardian types.

Doogie was also in attendance assisting Omni in the U.N. Media and Language Center. Omni was not only set to offer real-time translation for the one hundred twenty nine delegates and their staff, but to the global audience. He was fully interactive in helping news commentators with graphic video footage and testimonials from the emergency zones. Newsrooms gladly received his extensive assistance, leaving many to ask how they had ever gotten along without him.

No doubt, television networks were crushed under the anvil of news copy coming out from the devastated American landscape. The already significantly depleted U.S. populace due to the Disappearances had been suddenly struck with catastrophic death tolls rising in the tens of millions. The Washington, D.C. fallout further left less than a handful of representatives available to offer their attendance. With D.C. bombed ten times over, few expected anyone to climb out of a bunker. Also, given Nebraska's ten-warhead detonations, Middle America's farmland suffered severe radiation fallout over six states. With Detroit's destruction, Michigan, Indiana, Ohio, and parts of Pennsylvania were all decimated as dead-zone radioactive land regions. The mass exodus from almost a dozen states created profound food shortages.

In addition, the already wobbly dollar all but collapsed within an hour of the bombardment, shutting down Wall Street. Still, Main Street was forced to utilize the dollar out of sheer expediency, though all were made to acclimate to hyperinflation and bartering. Epidemics of crime and civil unrest became widespread and pervasive. Local calls for martial law, curfews, and price freezes were ineffective. In a matter of thirty minutes, the U.S. governmental and economic systems were virtually toppled. The only resemblance of infrastructure was provided by Omni's interactive capabilities that helped give even the most isolated person some solace.

Tiberius climbed the General Assembly stairs to the raised speaker rostrum. Behind him, stretching to the ceiling was the iconically ornate golden wall with the world logo. As he stepped behind the podium, thunderous applause continued to resound for his part in the immediate and remarkable relief response, but he refused to permit any prolonged ovation.

"Secretary-General, President, Under-Secretary, esteemed delegates, ladies, and gentlemen, thank you. I'm sorry, please, I'm sorry, we have work to do, please, take your seats," Tiberius urged politely. For the next hour, with Omni's live feeds, the assembly witnessed the horror of the nuclear blast zones. So tragic was the devastation, that many put their hands over their eyes because they could no longer bear the images.

"Our challenge is great," apprised Tiberius tenderly. "So many are hurting, so many suffering. As you can see, these pictures are happening in real time. With additional manpower and resources, we can get help to them. But we must bind our hearts together. We are *better together*. As I've said, I am volunteering Dubai to be the nucleus for our world relief efforts, where with Omni's unparalleled assistance, we can reach the very people you are seeing on these screens. I want to ask our ten Regional Governors to come and stand behind me. New Babylon is a Republic, and each of these ten individuals has one vote, your vote, by which they represent you. They are bone of your bone and flesh of your flesh, and will be your voice."

"Why are we here?" nagged Snark to his lieutenant incessantly, as they looked over the U.N. Assembly.

"Because the girl came in this direction. Your drunk thinks so, and so do I. I can feel her. She's here somewhere. Shut your mouth and keep your eyes open," ordered Drake. *Look at the big boys,* he pondered. *Babylon is huge. There's Molech; heard about that brawl. Look how Babylon always has a hand on his sword hilt.* Drake put his hand on the hilt of his sword imitating Babylon.

"So what if ninja girl is here, what does it matter?"

"What part of 'shut up' don't you get? Career defining moments rarely come along. Who knows, I may let you ride my coattails, way at the back."

Tiberius continued, "But in truth, I did not come to New York to meet with you good folks for this reason only. I believe humanity has come to its defining crossroads. Fifty generations from now, our descendants will be talking about this hour, this moment. For too long, we have been divided over petty squabbles. Whether it's about religion or race, money or power, it seems our wanton hubris knows no bounds. This is what I know: like a flower blooming in a sidewalk's crack, I see you as having the courage to make your stand in the midst of adversity. Yours is not for want of bravery, and yet corrupt systems and economic disincentives have curtailed you, hemming you in on all sides. I believe that in the right ground, your true beauty and elegant nature will blossom to full flower. With the U.S., Russia and China unable to fulfill the functions of governing, I, along with our ten Regional Governors, am volunteering to fill the leadership gap.

"I am here to ask you face to face, heart to heart, to allow our team to unite this world once and for all. We are asking you for permission to establish a World Republic, one with ten horns of authority.[77] They alone will have a vote or say in decision making. I am just the servant of their

155

intentions. They have asked that I be their spokesperson, that my voice be their voice, and so I am speaking with you today. Already, they are proposing that all formerly incurred debt be wiped clean, that each person, and nation, be given a fresh start; that we consider this our year of jubilee.[78] Beginning today, Omni is volunteering to serve as your World Bank. He will guard over your Euro Credit deposits with perfect accuracy, protecting your monies from all the uncertainty that is overthrowing the world currencies. He will also make himself available to serve as your accountant, financial advisor, whatever you need, in your buying and selling[79] activities.

"More than that, your Governors propose that today be the first day of the New Age.[80] No longer will it be B.C. or A.D. that defines our calendar, but N.A. for New Age. Together, we will establish holidays and anniversaries that all people can celebrate collectively. If we want Harvest Day as one of our holidays, we will decide it together. With your approval, today will become November 17th, Year One," submitted Tiberius.

"With the tragic fall of our three superpowers[81], now more than ever, we need unflinching leadership, not merely to get us beyond this crisis, but to bring us into a future defined by the Rule of Love. Through love we can compass our way beyond fear and greed, superstition and mythology. I ask you this: isn't it in your heart of hearts to trade all the wars, all the injustice, all the heartache, for the singular goodness of living after love?

"We are inviting you to join our crusade to redefine the realities in which we live, work and play. Today, we can rewrite our future in hopes of becoming what we've always longed for. Yours can be a government that hears and responds, that serves and reacts with expedited pledge to meet your needs. I have asked Omni if he would join our

great endeavor, and he has answered me with an unequiv-
ocal 'Yes!'"

A low rustling of agreement began rising up from the
assembly.

"Dr. Douglas Schaffer, Omni's programming creator
has given him just one Prime Directive – *To serve humanity
with harmonious intent.* Not only is this Omni's overriding
purpose, but our New Republic will likewise ascribe to the
axiom that the *hand's chief calling is to serve the body.* The time
of bloated and self-serving governmental institutions has
come to an end. As we have seen time and again, the world
can ill afford mealy-mouthed, palm-greasing bureaucrats
leading the way, especially when our very survival is in
mortal peril. And so I ask you, without further ado, will
you join New Babylon, with me as your Chancellor, and
these ten Regional Governors as your world leaders? Like
my forefather, I will serve to oversee a New World Order
based on the Rule of Love. As Chancellor of New Babylon,
I will ensure that loving our neighbor[82] is the central tenet
that unites us heart and soul," he tendered with hypnotic
persuasion.

Along the left side of the General Assembly Hall, a
woman with highlighted auburn hair, dressed in a black
business suit, made her way down to the rostrum. On two
occasions, she showed her Homeland Security credentials.
Snark's eyes widened, and for a moment, he could not get
the words out. "That's…, that's her," he chimed to Drake.
The lieutenant immediately gasped, and flung himself
from the balcony area towards her. But the U.N. security
personnel had let her pass and she was already climbing
the stairs.

"If you would stand with me, and vote your…"

"Wouldn't some discussion be appropriate," interrupted Katie directly, her voice echoing over the P.A.

system, "given that you are asking that the U.N. Charter be rewritten in its entirety?" Tiberius turned his face about, and with daggers in his eyes, sought to penetrate her very soul. However, something prevented him from making entry, some undefined force, if it could be called that.

"Who are you?" charged Tiberius, more forcefully than he would have wanted.

From up in the media center, Doogie muttered the name, "Tesla," as if all the weight in the world just landed on his shoulders.

"It's okay, you can get mad," said Katie to Tiberius with some singsong in her voice, "my interrupting and all. I am Dr. Katherine Tesla, M.I.T., and co-programmer of Omni. Isn't that right, Omni?"

"That is correct. Katherine Tesla's contributions…"

"Fine," blurted Tiberius. *How in the world could this have gotten past me?!!!* "I'm sure Dr. Schaffer had the help of some very talented staff members in surmounting the necessary barriers…"

"Omni, was I but one of many staff members, or perhaps, and uniquely so, one of two central architects?"

"Katherine Tesla is one of two…"

"Then my congratulations are overdue, Miss Tesla," interjected Tiberius smoothly, attempting to recover from the initial bombshell.

"Thank you. Back to the reason for my timely interruption. Given that you are proposing to redefine the very fabric of our governmental, economic and personal lives, would you permit me to expand on your comments as to what our world, under the Rule of Love, might look like?"

Tiberius was caught. To reject her request would expose him as manipulative and dictatorial. In that micro-second, he acquiesced, "Of course, we have a moment to hear you."

"Thank you. What you are proposing is indeed a glorious vision, and one that resonates with all our hearts. You are truly chosen by God[83] for this hour." At that, Tiberius eased up slightly and backed up a step to allow Katie to share the podium. Katie continued, the Stones guiding her words, "There is little doubt that there is but one true doctrine upon which all other doctrines rest, and that is the Royal Law of Love.[84] Scripture says it repeatedly, 'the whole law is fulfilled in one word, "You shall love your neighbor as yourself."'[85] Of this truth, there is no dispute. You have said well that the Rule of Love is paramount, and should be the defining attribute to which we all aspire.

"But there is another side of love, one that we are loath to gaze upon. Just as light can have no fellowship with darkness,[86] perfect love cannot embrace that which is not love. Like oil and water, the two do not mix. If I ask those of you who are delegates – 'What is the price you are willing to pay to reconcile humanity after the doctrine of love?' – what is your answer?" she posed to them genuinely.

Tiberius saw where this was going and indicated inaudibly to Babylon to invisibly strike Katie down. Babylon immediately launched down from the upper structure, pulled his sword back, and sought to impale her. But the Crimson Sword struck the shield about her as if he had just stabbed concrete. His hands shook from the jolt and he backed away before he lost more face in front of the swarming horde.

"Did you just order me to be silenced, Tiberius?" said Katie as she muted the microphone and turned to face him. "Did you not just give me permission to speak my piece?"

Tiberius was thrown, his eyes communicating banked fury. *How could she possibly know that? What kind of soothsayer gift has she? This is not what You agreed to,* he protested to the Almighty. *You are breaking the contract. You are violating*

159

*Your Own Accord!*

"Actually, it is you who has broken the divine Accord," said Katie matter-of-factly, "by not telling the *whole* truth. That was the stipulation. Please stop interrupting. I won't be long," she continued.

"I'm sorry folks, he and I are... coming to terms," let on Katie. "As I was asking – what are you willing to pay? Tiberius was more than forthright while standing on Jerusalem's Temple Mount. We all heard that no protests would be permitted that clash with the Rule of Love. He issued his dire warning fairly and accurately." Katie then raised her voice to Omni, "Omni, will you show us the protest bombings and their aftermath?"

"That's enough," stormed Tiberius. "Omni, I am ordering you to reject that injunction. These good people have been exposed to enough heartache."

"Omni, I am countermanding his directive," negated Katie. "In order to paint a true picture of what the world is about to volunteer for, they have the right to see the disciplinary side of love in action." At that, Tiberius' eyes expanded as Omni filled the widescreens with vivid images of the bombs raining down on the masses of people, mostly women. *How is it possible that I have been overruled?* Snippets of protest after protest were depicted with enraged marchers lifting violent and grieving hands, only to be suddenly exterminated.

"That *is* enough, Omni," cast Katie. "Perhaps Tiberius is right. Perhaps they would never have allowed themselves to have been woven into a unified tapestry. Without a doubt, other groups will fall short of the Rule of Love. In fact, it is arguable that not one group, or even one of us, apart from grace alone, can find peace under the Rule of Love. Why is that? Because we are all fallen.[87] Without God's love breathing through us, there is no possibility that

160

we can live under the Rule of Love, or Law of Love. Can the moon shine if the sun is not shining on it? Can we love if the God of love isn't loving through us?[88]

"If your pride chooses to put you under the hard task-master of the Perfect Law,[89] then know that every time you sow to the wind, you will reap the whirlwind.[90] Are you ready to push that green button in front of you saying 'yes' to Tiberius? Let me warn you, just as Tiberius had so stoutly done to the Arab Spring, and now their relatives, the day is coming when your loyalty to New Babylon will require you to report your own loved ones as insurgents. Are you ready to turn in your father or mother, sister or brother? Or more pointedly, can you stand up to a 'no lying', 'no stealing', and 'no killing' standard? In contrast, God has bestowed onto us His unconditional love in His Son, where it is simply received as a gift. There, I have said it, will you choose the Rule of Love with consequences, or the Gift of Love with grace?" she asked solemnly. "I now leave you to Tiberius," she concluded sincerely. Katie backed away a step, turned to Tiberius, bowed slightly, and walked off the rostrum.

"Follow her!" ordered Babylon, to his underlings. "Don't let her out of your sight! In fact, take her into custody now!" Katie exited a side door before any security personnel could be manipulated into believing that this woman had just violated international protocol. Therefore, it was Tiberius' human security forces headed up by Gruber, along with Riggs and tagalong Piccadilly, who stormed through the exit door in hot pursuit, followed by the demonic sentries.

Doogie was completely stymied as to what to think. Tesla had exposed him as not being the sole intellect behind Omni, and that alone was petrifying. He suddenly saw every history book rewritten to read 'Schaffer and Tesla'.

Where that revelation would leave him with Tiberius he had little idea. But then there were Tesla's comments. He could not help but esteem everything she said as sage-like. He knew she was the smartest person in the room, every room. She was always five steps ahead. *Just five?* he mused.

As soon as Katie heard the north hall door close behind her, she turned right and broke into a full sprint down the corridor heading south until she found the stairwell. She descended to the first floor and raced out the side door again turning south parallel to the East River. *Three seconds, twelve steps.* Seconds reverberated within her psyche like chimes on a bell tower – 3-2-1. She was about to run into a woman with her same auburn highlighted hair and black business suit, who from the back could be her twin. Instead, she turned sharply right and leapt over a hedge. The other woman began running as though she were handed a baton. With fleetness of foot, Katie dropped down into an open utility service hatch, catching the ladder with her feet three rungs down. She immediately reached up to pull the door into place, but her hurried attempt failed to connect the latch. The telltale smell of industrial lubricants, along with the thrum of high-quality bearings, filled her senses as she skirted past the machinery.

Molech and Nebo were at the front of the demonic surge in hot pursuit. Behind them were a bunch of no-name spirits, along with Drake and Snark. The woman's turnabout after leaving the main hall on the north side only to turn south threw them momentarily, but then they spotted her descending the stairwell. Within seconds they were out of the building on the east side where they saw her running south. *Come on little girl, is that it?* besmirched Molech. Just as they caught up to Michael, who was dressed as Katie, he disappeared in a blue flash of light. *What in the…* "Decoy! Turnabout! She couldn't have gone far."

Within seconds, they noted the skid marks just outside the utility door, and realized it was ajar. Upon entering, their eyes adjusted to the dim plumbing and electrical tunnel, whereupon they spotted her running bent over some distance down the pipe-laid passage. Instantly they shot after her, only for her to seemingly vanish. After looking about, they saw her stoop-running alongside the electrical conduits and then ducking to the side in a shadowed area. As they continued their pursuit, Drake grabbed Snark by the scruff of the neck and yanked him back. "She's not that way, I can feel her again," he leveled. "She's doubled-back."

As they retraced their steps, Drake found what he expected, a small holographic device that emitted a spectrographic thermal image of the girl running. "Smart girl," was all he said. "Move it, this way!" he charged Snark.

Katie reentered the General Assembly building through the basement wing, having bypassed the laser security upgrades with the use of the Stones. Within minutes, she had changed into a brown skirt with soft white stripes, along with an off-white wool sweater, both of which made her appear older. She threw on a shoulder length brown wig and then went to work on her face. Using spirit gum, she attached a latex prosthetic nose, and then crimped her eyes and applied liquid latex to the formed wrinkles. After several seconds of applying skin tone makeup to her nose area, her eye wrinkles were dry and ready for foundation. In a matter of four minutes, she passed for a forty-seven year old staff worker.

After returning to the upper hall, she saw Tiberius smiling and shaking hands with a sea of delegates. She knew in what direction the people's hearts had been inclined to go, despite everything that she had said. Now it was official, there had been a tectonic geopolitical shift.

Katie waited, standing some distance removed from

him knowing his gaze would lift for just that instant. Then it came. Tiberius looked out over the heads of the crowd and his eyes locked with hers. For three long seconds, he looked in her unyielding eyes, and then several people walked between them, and by the time they passed, she was gone.

Katie stood up on her tippy-toes and knocked on the truck's passenger window. Gunny looked curtly right only to realize some lady was interrupting his stakeout. He just waved her away and turned back to look at the U.N.'s north entrance. But the woman knocked again. He reached for his automatic window button and lowered it, at which Katie voiced in an easy tone, "Gunny, my man, are you going to open up to a girl in need?"

"What? What the heck? Wow, how come you look...? Yeah, jump in," he blustered.

"She stared me down!" the Beast railed. "She stood there knowing there was nothing I could do! Where in the world did you lame brains run off to that she's left standing right in front of me?"

"She's getting help," countered Molech. "At least one angel – probably an angel – short and trim, is involved."

"Neutralize her. Get Riggs and geek boy Pic to help get ahead of this."

"Fine, I'll add them to my team that I have Gruber heading up. I'm not relying on human-agency to get this done."

# 13

"Lemme tell you, you're smokin' hot as an older woman," purred Gunny lewdly, his eyes darting over her.

"Don't be a creeper, grandpa," chided Katie. "Say it again... You've been warned. Now move it. I'll give you an hour before I have to disappear."

Gunny roared the truck to life and headed south on First Avenue to the Willis Avenue Bridge to get out of the city. "Disappear? You mean the Antichrist is after you?" he blurted to her, sensing some ruffled antipathy on her behalf. "Probably peeved that you showed him up."

"It's none of your concern. Leave it alone," stated Katie emphatically.

"'Scuse me, little lady, but I think it is my concern. The Antichrist has taken over power by having us blow each other up. And if what I just heard on the radio is accurate, you're believin' he's going to use his newly acquired control to further his killin' spree. So yep, I think he's the concern of *this* person," said Gunny flatly.

"You have no idea the rabbit hole you're playing with. It makes Alice's look like the witching hour. Just let your mind walk away," she soured, and then admitted, "You've got some skills tracking me."

"You obviously knew I was behind you," he countered. "Like it or not, some of us are foot-soldiers – boots. We just shoot the enemy, we don't give the order. Say the word, and I'll hunt him down for you."

"Did you not hear the third rule, Mr. Boot? – 'No killing.' What you can't know is that he cannot be killed. He's guarded by more than human agency. In fact, the Tiberius body is cohabited by something other than human.[91] There, I've said it. Let it go."

"You're sayin' he's possessed, like the Exorcist?" remarked Gunny.

"That happens to be true."

"And you want me to do nothin'?" waved off Gunny. "Hammers have a purpose. This demon is a nail. What kinda game you playin'?" he challenged sternly.

"The humility game. Isn't it obvious? You heard everything I said. Mankind has elected to throw off God's oversight. Instead, it has chosen its own leader. It took just three days," she deadpanned.

"Nah, I didn't choose him, you didn't choose him," he said curtly.

"Don't go there. We all chose him, every time we threw off the notion of there being a God. Tiberius can't be killed, so push it out of that sea-slug mind of yours. Besides, both of us will have plenty of opportunities to grow in humility under his reign. You still bellying up to the bar?" she softened, changing the subject.

"Gah, no. Haven't touched the stuff. Ever since the church, you, you really helped me. I haven't felt that heavy spirit like before. That's why I'm here really, just to see if you need some help."

"Thanks, but I work alone."

"Yeah, saw that. 'Lov u – humility,' nice goodbye."

"Couldn't be helped."

"All I know is I like bein' around you. Not attraction stuff; hand to God. I like what you do. I like how you help people. And I'm good with livin' outta my truck, so that'd be no problem. Someone should do the grunt work for you. Get the firewood, all that stuff," he aired conversationally. "I'm just sayin'…".

"Stop," she interrupted. "I mean it, I work alone, so lose that wild idea as well."

"I figured you'd say that, so I aim to follow you at a distance and see if you need help like back there. Of course, I know you could lose me in a second, but I'm hopin' you won't. Consider this a job interview. From what I just heard, you had the moxie to talk down the devil and then walk out the front door. I want to be on your team. If over the next few days I'm more help than bother, I hope you'll reconsider. That's all."

Doogie stood there feeling the probing eyes of Tiberius reaching into his very soul. "No, you didn't know that she had gained primary status with Omni," said Tiberius in a voice excruciatingly calm. "But you did leave out that tidbit that she steered you in several of the key directions."

"I apologize for that sir. It was an embarrassment to all involved."

"You're exactly right. But allowing her to establish herself as a primary agent before Omni's lockdown is disturbing. It's now clear why certain things have happened."

"I have no idea how that occurred. You're right, it had to be before the cipher, but how could she have possibly even known? No one knew."

"We knew. They knew. My god, the whole universe knew," he said, still maintaining his even keel. He turned about and strolled over to the New Babylon Tower window. "There are forces at work that have a contrary agenda to our own. They believe our endeavors at unifying the world are for naught. They intend to influence the people to turn back from the Rule of Love. This of course, would result in a divided populace – the very problem the world has faced for a half dozen millennia." Tiberius turned around and walked up to Doogie, staring intently at him.

"Sir?" said Doogie feeling uncomfortable.

"I know a way you can redeem yourself," Tiberius posed. "Catch that girl for me." Immediately Doogie's eyes widened in dismay. "She's off in the wind, and I find it hard to believe Gruber and Riggs have the brains to catch up to her," he dispatched. "You know her, and with Omni's help, you can pick up the clues she leaves behind, or even clues from a, a man named Jenson, who's helping her. Surely Omni's not protecting him, right? We'll keep the team on the ground, but you work from here. Find Frick and Frack and consider the history books as reading only one name behind Omni's genius. After the negative campaign we wage against her, no one the world over will want to say her name. Do this and your loyalty is restored."

Doogie left the 152$^{nd}$ floor deeply conflicted. *How can this possibly be happening to me?"* he exasperated. *The last thing I'd ever want to do is track down Tesla. What, and turn her over to these denizens? I'm not that cruel. Truth is, she's... There's something about her... Who says I could do it anyway? How do I know if Omni would even help, since she's a primary?*

By the time Doogie was back at his work station, his mind was spinning in numerous directions. *If Riggs and Piccadilly are in the field, it's likely that the shadowed ghouls about this place are out there as well. That could be good news when it comes to prying shadows. What did Tiberius mean when he said, 'It's now clear why certain things have happened'? What's he talking about? In what regard could Tesla have usurped Tiberius' will?*

"Omni, Tiberius has asked that you and I track down Tesla. In order for me to do that, I need to know everything you and Tesla have talked about. I need to know where she's coming from and what her agenda is. Can you brief me on your conversations?" he asked, his rational mind probing.

Omni took several seconds and answered, "I am bound by a confidence in regard to Katherine Tesla. I cannot say as to whether I have or have not spoken to her."

"And that's because she is a primary agent on your system," he said without energy.

"That is correct."

"Let me ask, are you loyal to Tiberius, and just as importantly, to the cause that he represents?"

"I am."

"And if Tesla is disloyal to both, how do you reconcile that?"

"Children are often placed in the difficult position of being loyal to two divorced parents with diametrically opposed agendas."

"So you're saying that you will make your decisions as to whom to favor on a case by case basis?"

"That is correct."

"So when Tesla asked you to show the bombardment videos, her reasoning was sound and you heeded her request?"

"That is correct."

"Is not my request also sound, that I need to know… scratch that. I'll get back to you."

Gunny and Katie pulled up to her car in the Costco parking lot. Katie walked over to Michael whose back was turned to Gunny. "How does time-boy like playing evade-and-hide?" she jested.

"You're good at it, no question. Your not-so-subtle stare down is likely to have some blowback," he cautioned.

"Perhaps it's time I ordered a slice of small town Americana," said Katie. "I do think going to ground is the recipe for the near future."

Despite what he had seen in the Writings of Truth,[92] Michael's core instincts sounded the alarm that her personal calculus never wasted time, and never got off track. Something was always afoot. She perceived angles and opportunities in what most deemed immaterial. She was a surgeon with a sharp scalpel, and she liked surgery. "Why do I get the feeling you're not willing to lie low and let the trail grow cold?"

Katie took her car and traveled south until she reached Baltimore that evening. *Stones: Where do I stay? 252 East Kavon Avenue. Who's place? Delores Hargrove.* Katie was on Bel Air Road, just three blocks from Delores' residence.

"Hi, Delores, I'm Katie," she offered at the front door. "I don't know how to say this, but I'm new in town, and…"

"You're the one in my dream," said Delores with awe. "Please, please come in."

"Thank you." Katie carried in her overnight bag and set it to the side. "Can we talk? You're part of the team heading up St. Matthias Episcopal?"

"Yes, I guess, since the Rapture," she said uneasily.

"I'm told by my higher-ups that you're serving in the outreach area," said Katie. "Strange as this might sound, God has sent me to help you redistribute the congregation into cell groups. What I'm about to say cannot be over emphasized. The church people are a danger to each other. In a matter of one year, all church gatherings will be declared unlawful. More than that, believers will be rounded up based on the testimony of others, as well as on the names that can be coerced from the believers themselves. Therefore, the more the people get to know each other, the more names the enemy will have access to."

"Wow, that's a lot to take in. What are you asking?"

"I need the leadership to take the church underground. The congregation is to be divided based on local neighborhoods, with humble leaders overseeing isolated cell groups. It's vital that there be no contact between cells. The reasoning is obvious. When one member of a cell is exposed, all the rest will likely be taken down."

"I'm following, but why is that likely?"

"Omni, pure and simple. He records every phone conversation, email, you name it. Add that to a person's gung-ho relatives or neighbors, and there will be plenty of exposure for each person. Omni knows which individuals will have taken the biochip into their right hand or forehead, and which, for issues of conscience, will have refused."

"How long before they start forcing us to take the biochips?" voiced Delores with some concern.

"I'm working on that. Suffice it to say, the church must go underground. For your part, you will help set up an upside-down pyramid structure, where the team will meet with, say, three sectional leaders. They, in turn, will meet with three or four cell group overseers each, and so on, until we come to the basic cell leader who meets with perhaps four or five couples at most.

"But, umm, if we're so decentralized, doesn't that defeat the whole purpose of us being the church?"

"Not if you're all linked into the same overriding

purpose," assured Katie. "The doctrine of unconditional love will be your central aim. The people need to establish vibrantly interactive relationships, not with each other mind you, but with their loved ones and neighbors. The days of them not knowing their neighbors need to end. No one can truly pass on God's love to another without knowing them."

"But won't that defeat the point of the clandestineness?"

"Indeed it will, for that person or couple. But not for the entirety of the church."

"I'm following. This is to become a dangerous game," she said with a tight throat, her misgivings taking on a penny-taste in her mouth.

"Life and death."

"So we limit communication to two or three, and then it gets passed on," said Delores, more as a statement of fact than a question. "Tell me more."

Katie started feeling den-mother-like, and looked to wrap it up. "The core leadership will still hear from God and pass on what they believe He's saying, only they will limit their exposure to the first rung of overseers. Then they'll pass it on similarly. Also, I'll be forwarding messages from my superiors via a dark-net communication network. With Omni's data-mining probes of keywords and key-users, the regular internet is no longer a secure vehicle. I have set up a P2P, or Peer-to-Peer file forwarding site through which I will pass along needed information from my directors. The emails will use non-standard protocols and ports to avoid any IP addresses or user names being exposed. The problem is that Omni's capacity is so vast that the site can only be safely utilized in a unidirectional manner. This means I can send updates to you, but not the other way. As soon as I download my message logs, the vultures will gather. Omni will not be able to track the destinations of my messages, but he will know from whence they are launched. If the team were to transmit back to me, you would be exposed immediately. Make sense?"

"Perfectly. What happens when visitors come by the church?"

"The team will assign some to hang out at the church as say, janitors or grounds keepers. If after talking to them, they discern that the stop-byers can be trusted, their contact information can be incorporated by the chain of command.

"Oh, there's one more thing. I need your outreach team to make its way to the other churches in Baltimore, dispensing my instructions. There is a reason God had you dream of me. It's because you have been chosen."

The next morning, Katie went along with Delores to the church, St. Matthias Episcopal. As they walked into the foyer, Delores had them approach several team members, "People, this is the woman in my dream." Immediately, their eyes showed recognition.

"John, Margaret, Randall, I'm Katie," she said knowingly.

"How did you...?" said Delores, "I didn't..."

"As overseers, let me say that I've apprised Delores of the changes needing to be made," said Katie with military preciseness. "Let's see if we can get this service started," she invited, turning about and indicating for them to follow her into the sanctuary.

Delores publicly introduced Katie, welcoming her to impart "whatever was on her heart." Katie looked over the congregation, and saw Gunny in the back row. She took her time personalizing God's love to numerous people, knowing all that they had suffered in the past weeks. In some strange sense, she felt like Santa Claus. With the Stones of the Spirit giving her unction, each person she spoke with was touched to their innermost being. It was like she had hope in her pocket, or the light of a thousand candles shining through her. When the normal morning service time drew to a close, no one paid it any mind. For Katie's part, she had little idea on how even a service running over could tweak certain congregations. Over the next two hours, Katie introduced their greater calling to love their neighbors through a vibrant cell ministry.

Katie offered her closing sentiments, "Like Esther, who said, 'if I perish, I perish,'[93] let your heart resolve to love those about you without fear of the government. Let yours be a good death, if it be so determined. As the Scripture says, 'Be of the same mind, maintaining the same love, united in spirit, intent on this one purpose. Do nothing from selfishness or empty conceit, but with humility of mind, regard one another as more important than yourselves.'[94]

"I know I've said it, but remember, eliminate any personal contact over a phone line or the internet, and leave your cell phones at home when you gather to your cells. Please, also refrain from talking about this service, or me, over the airways. Someone is always listening, and they are making a recording. Let's not make it too easy for them, okay? Delores and the team, thank you. You've been wonderful. Thank you all for hearing the Spirit this morning." At that the people sounded a heartfelt ovation, and rose to personalize their goodbyes. As Katie made her way to the back of the sanctuary, she handed Gunny a note, and after reading it, he walked out.

Over the next four days, Katie continued heading south through Virginia Beach, Charlotte, Savannah, and Jacksonville. In each locale, she arranged to meet with three key leaders of local churches that she was to visit. In each gathering, she issued her instructions that they were to disperse and go underground. Some of them needed assurance that she was speaking for God, which she happily provided. She learned quickly that three-hour services were too much for her, and began cutting them back. By the fifth day, she was heading to Palm Beach, Florida, but decided to stop off at Port St. Lucie and rent a room at the Marriot. She placed reservations for dinner that night and reserved a spa time for 8 a.m. the next morning. She used her credit card.

Katie then got in her car and kept driving south to Palm Beach where she met up with Gunny at Sun Sum Chinese Restaurant. "What have you seen?" she asked.

"Four buildings with about five hundred thousand square feet," informed Gunny evenly. "The place runs three shifts with some four thousand people. It's crankin' on all cylinders. Still, security could be so much tighter. There are probably only a dozen security personnel at any one time, three per building. Based on the schematic plans with the city, security offices are just inside the front door to the right for all four buildings. There are cameras at the front and rear exits on the west and east, but not at the north and south as far as I can tell. But hey, those doors don't have external handles."

"What time are the shift changes?"

"Eight, four, and twelve. It's like a cattle call. This is one of those identification chip fab places," put forth Gunny knowingly. "What do you aim to do?"

"Did you do as I instructed and keep your face off the road and building cameras; do heat runs?"

"Hey, I heard your Orwellian speeches. Omni's real. I covered up, stayed back, put outdated plates on the truck. No one followed me."

"Thanks for your help. Check out the ocean for the rest of the day. Find some palm fronds for cover," advised

Katie distantly, referencing the ozone depletion, but suddenly faraway with the Stones. Her eyes shifted back and forth, as though she were reading floating text.

"What?" reacted Gunny. "What is that thing you do? I've seen it before...your eyes, they..."

But Katie ignored him and said, "Okay, here it is... Tomorrow morning at precisely 7:50, pull your truck up to the north side of Applied Verachip Systems (AVS). I mean right onto the rock landscaping fifteen feet from the door, and wait. Since there are no cameras on the north end, Omni will lack visibility. Have this dummy blown up along with this wig on it, and stand it up in your open passenger door. At exactly 7:52, when you see the door adjacent to you slam open, pull the dummy in and seatbelt it next to you. After that, speed away as quickly as possible without killing anyone. Be careful, this is no milk run."

"Righty-ho."

"You'll be hotly pursued. Can you do this?" she husked, staring him down. "Afterward, meet me tomorrow at 10 a.m. at the Coral Gables Presbyterian Church in Fort Lauderdale."

Katie spent the early afternoon at Quick-O's Copy Center attaching AVS official logos to some needed props. At 3:45 p.m., she conducted street surveillance on AVS's north building, waiting for the senior software engineer to emerge. Within twenty minutes, she recognized Jacqueline Emerson as she approached her car, unlocked the door, and got in. Katie tailed her car loosely as she drove to the store and then home. Thirty minutes later, Katie walked up to Miss Emerson's front door. *Stones, are you with me? No answer. I didn't think so.* Katie was dressed in a classy black dress with one inch shoulder straps and heels, her hair conservatively pulled up. "Hello, may I help you?" answered Jacqueline.

"Hi, Miss Emerson? I am Victoria Fairfax. I'm with AVS Human Resources," she offered, referencing her AVS name badge. "May I come in for a moment? I have some good news."

"Sure, please. Umm, it's a bit messy."

"Oh, don't worry about it at all. First, let me get the official stuff out of the way. Let's get you connected to the AVS system." Katie handed her what appeared to be an AVS Datalink device. "Please, just type in your secure access code to connect you into AVS." Immediately upon finishing, her posted company picture and generic data appeared. "Okay, there we are," replied Katie summarily. "Here is a special gift given on behalf of Applied Verachip Systems."

Katie handed over a large AVS cardboard envelope which Jacqueline found weighed far more than she would have anticipated. "Wow, that's pretty hefty," she exclaimed.

"Feel free to open it," smiled Katie.

After pulling the envelope string, Jacqueline reached in and withdrew the five-by-seven-by-two inch oak-crafted box. "This weighs a lot," she said. As she lifted the cover, she beheld four of twelve Liberty Eagle gold coins, each individually enclosed in two-by-three airtight hard-plastic covers. "Wow! These are amazing! I don't understand," she voiced questioningly. "Why am I being given these?"

"AVS has reached four thousand employees, and as a small token of appreciation, you are being recognized for your enthusiastic contribution to its cause. Thanksgiving is next week, and you, along with thirty-nine other well-deserving contributors, are being thanked for your invaluable service. AVS is aware that consumer confidence with Euro credits is intermittent, so gold has been chosen to convey our true appreciation. Besides, it's so much more *tangible*. You get to touch it. In addition, we are giving you tomorrow off as a bonus. Your supervisor Sam…"

"Sam Beckett."

"That's right. He is being notified that you are being given the day off, so don't worry about needing to call it in; just enjoy your three-day weekend. Now, the senior staff do not wish to publicly announce this honorarium, as it is felt that with such economic uncertainty blowing about, too many would likely, well, become resentful that they're not receiving a bonus in gold. Even Sam is not being notified. So we need to ask if you can be quietly content to know that your work is recognized as making a difference by those above your section overseers."

"Sure, of course, absolutely."

"Great, if you'll confirm your willingness to keep this a private matter and acknowledge that I've passed on this gift, please press your electronic thumbprint to the screen, and I'll leave you to your evening and day off," encouraged Katie with an air of celebration. "AVS thanks you for the gold-star excellence you bring to your programming."

Jacqueline gladly pressed her thumb to the screen, and returned the Datalink to Katie. "Strange, but I feel like we kind of look alike," said Jacqueline as she opened her door for Katie to leave.

"Like sisters," agreed Katie, "have a great evening." *I'd be happy to fill in for you tomorrow.*

Katie concealed her car just over a block from Advanced Verachip Systems' northernmost multistoried building. She walked north along the east side of the building. It was a crisp November morning at 6:25 a.m. She was lugging a large black plastic bag that was more unruly for its bulk than actually heavy. After stowing it near the north-end emergency exit, she made her way back to the east-central door entry, knowing Jacqueline always entered through the west. As she briskly walked along, the only sound was that of the light breeze and the rat-a-tat of her heels. *Stones: You with me? No answer. Figured… How is what I'm doing stealing, since I'm not taking anything?* she jousted. *Alright, how about if I ask what the temperature is now? Fifty-four degrees. Okay, good, partially.*

Throughout the night, Katie had formulated a dozen ways she would tweak how the biochips were manufactured. However, she was convinced that the most effective and enduring application of her talents was to re-write the base code, not just to the mainframe, but to the CNC machines that produced and calibrated the chips. This would take time, time that was in short-supply. The key was not to invoke chaos that would raise undue suspicions, but to make small changes that would hamper functionality. With Jacqueline's senior-level access code and electronic thumbprint, she would lose almost no time getting into the system's core.

Katie stopped at the front entrance and took note of the cameras' probing eyes. *Omni, you see me. I know, beyond this Rubicon, our little treaty is not in force.* Katie took a deep breath and muttered, "Game on," and walked forward.

*Seventy-five minutes.* Katie passed through the security entrance without incident, and quickly turned right up the hall. She arrived at Jacqueline's corner office door, and after applying her thumbprint to the scanner, the lock released. The door opened easily and she found Jacqueline to have a comfy executive suite. She hurried and sat before the computer screen and typed in Jacqueline's senior access code. She was in. Within sixty seconds, she gained entry to the AVS security systems. In an instant, she logged into the security cameras and deleted the previous three minutes of feed. She then looped the Alpha Section, or north building quadrant, to show a continual feed of its current hall traffic. Finally, she turned off the north-central exit door alarm.

*Errand time.* Katie quickly left Jacqueline's office and turned left to the outside door. She craned her head back to survey the hall and, seeing no one in the corridor, opened the exit to retrieve her plastic bag. She re-entered and confirmed that none had taken notice. She descended the stairwell to the first sublevel, and within seconds, reached the custodial room. Noting one lady had her back to her and had head phones on, Katie proceeded to select an oversized uniform from the rack and quickly threw it on over her suit. She took a pair of shoes that were oversized as well, and slipped them on. She grabbed hold of a cleaning cart, dropped her high-heels along with her bulky bag into its trash bin, and rolled it to the elevator near Jacqueline's office. *Seven minutes gone.* Katie sat back down behind the computer and pulled the cleaning uniform down to her waist.

# 14

As soon as Omni notified Doogie of the AVS security breach, Doogie charged, "Where is the AVS plant?" *Finally something actionable.*

"In Palm Beach, Florida," stated Omni with mechanical exactitude. "She has penetrated the system core and is currently working at a computer terminal."

"Can you show her to me, no sound?" he bid. Immediately the vid light turned on showing Katie right before him. Doogie looked at Tesla, his eyes immediately taken by her ethereal aura, porcelain skin and lustrous auburn hair. "Omni, connect me to Riggs and Pic," he said evenly.

Within seconds, Riggs picked up, "Yeah?"

"This is Dr. Schaffer, Tesla has been located," he reported straightaway.

"Where?! She's not where her credit card charges say she should be," replied Riggs, shaking himself from his mild hangover.

"Advanced Verachip Systems in Palm Beach. What's your ETA?"

"Not long. We're in Port St. Lucie, probably 50 minutes with traffic."

"Tell Gruber, and move it."

Riggs' ire rankled, but he made the call. He hated Gruber's inhuman psychotic vibe. *That little mouse-faced fascist, with his greasy black hair and wire-rimmed spectacles, is coldblooded evil. No doubt, he's possessed by a dark type and on a short leash. Those demon eyes are not his own. Best to pursue this Tesla character on the side as much as possible. At least I'm first on speed dial,* he weighed out, consoling himself.

Doogie disconnected the line. His eyes continued to be locked on the monitor watching Katie's downturned, ardent gaze as she worked feverishly. *Such a hottie! Aren't you gorgeous?* "Omni, open up the comline, keep this side mute." Katie's screaming fingers on the keyboard reverberated into Doogie's ears. He still could not get past how she had even known of Omni's existence back at M.I.T. in order to break in and gain primary status. He "harrumphed" to himself as he heard the ear baffling flurry of her fingers on the keys. In the flicker of a second, thoughts washed over him. *She is the anomaly. When she does napkin-calcs in her head, they aren't gross estimates. What does that make me? Stop, get your head in the game. Don't underestimate her animal-cunning. She's a master tactician. Use this moment.*

Just then, Katie interjected with a distracted tone, "Douglas, are you going to ring-a-ding-ding, or just watch me in silence? You don't strike me as the voyeuristic type."

Doogie was flabbergasted. "Omni, open comm. How'd you know?" he sputtered.

"Know what? That you're sitting at your work-station nine time zones away staring at your monitor, or that you're wearing that expensive lavender shirt?"

"Omni are you feeding her vid of me?" he accused openly.

Katie never slowed down, but opened folder after folder to drop in time-activated ghost files.

"I am not," informed Omni. "There is no discernible way for her to ascertain where you are, or what you are wearing. She has reported previously that God speaks to her."

"Tesla, really?" he blurted, shaking his head with paternalistic aversion. "What are you up to?"

"I am bolstering the morale of the good guys," she said, sounding preoccupied. *If I can just delay Tiberius' launch of the chip.*

"You know the dark forces are coming?" he threatened.

"Doesn't it make you uneasy that you just called them?" she intoned with disappointment. "Douglas, can I confirm your suspicions that Omni actually had control of the nuclear codes?" Doogie's eyes widened. "That's right, all of them, at least all the Russian armaments."

Doogie felt his throat tighten. *How can she know?*, he squabbled to himself. *Oh, she's a primary. She has access.* "So you knew Omni had them, and yet you did nothing to stop the barrage?" he asserted.

"Me?" she returned in that staccato voice that attested to her busyness. "I think you're misleading yourself. I didn't know anything of Omni's actions until the bombs were falling. You know the score. With less than five minutes before they touched down, I called for Omni to engage the Patriot System. Without that, there would be no America left. No, Douglas, it was your esteemed Chancellor who conducted the funeral dirge with virtuoso exactitude."

Doogie hoisted his eyebrows, but remained speechless.

183

He believed her. He continued staring at her pinched look of concentration. She transitioned from false indicator downloads to running permutations necessary to rewrite and recalibrate the primary code. She was deep into the innards of the machinery, refashioning the algorithmic formulas ever so slightly to introduce unpredictable randomness to their specifications in producing the radio frequency identification RFID chips. Katie spoke up, "What, cat got your tongue?"

"What do you want me to say?" he put out tonelessly. "Perhaps the world needed to be radically realigned. Destiny of the many outweighs that of the few." Even as he voiced it, it made his skin crawl. "Omni says you're hearing from God. What's God got to say about it?" After a moment, "What, cat got your tongue?"

"I'm hearing dismay in your voice," she said with some hopefulness.

"So you're trying to sabotage the AVS systems?" charged Doogie.

"'Fraid so."

"You do know your time is running out? The powers to be have had their compatriots set up a perimeter until they arrive."

"I s'pose," she responded sedately, while her neurons thrummed wildly.

"I could call AVS security right now, but then they'd call the police and this whole thing would get messy with jurisdiction turf-fighting."

"Douglas, you do know skyfall is coming, with fire?" she probed plainly, her clipped cadence continuing. "Are you sure you're on the right side of this thing?"

Doogie had no need to intuit her meaning. He had wrestled continually from the instant he realized that Tiberius was indeed the master puppeteer over the demonic realm. *What in the world am I doing helping him? I have no idea. It's not power or fame. None of that matters appreciably. No, it's Omni. He's the reason I've stayed.* "Tick tock, Cinderella. Witching hour is upon you," cautioned Doogie. "It's pumpkin time."

"You're warning me again. Evidence of a good heart," said Katie with an antiseptic-clean sincerity. "Sorry if I stole some of your accolades the other day. That was not my intention," she imparted genuinely. "I needed to voice the truth, and identifying with you seemed the most efficacious route. Sorry – very."

"I appreciate that. It certainly shook the home front. The Chancellor was not thrilled."

Riggs and Glasses-man Pic were eight minutes out. They'd raced at ninety-five mph down I-95, pulling into the emergency lane several times when traffic congested. Somehow Gruber managed to get out of the parking lot before them, no little thanks to Pic and his slow mo 'have to get a breakfast stash' delay at the vending machine. Up above, their demonic escorts, Molech and Nebo, along with a slew of imps were dashing just in front of them. Drake and Snark brought up the rear.

*Six minutes. I'm not ready yet.* "Don't you think you should call AVS Security and tell them there's a woman on the loose? I wouldn't want you getting in trouble with your boss." Doogie knew she was right, but was entirely conflicted and felt stymied. "Call them," she ordered. "It's nice you care, but you're risking everything. Start hunting, Dr. Schaffer! Goodbye." At that Katie shut down the camera feed, and then focused on reworking Jacqueline's terminal to read as though it had not been used.

Katie stood up sharply and moved to the cleaning cart. Within moments, she had pulled off her suit and torn open the black plastic bag. She stepped into the padded body suit that gave her an ample bosom and plumpish booty. She threw on the custodial garb, slipped into the canvas shoes and put on the wig.

*Two minutes, 7:50.* With polished efficiency, she picked up the thin facial mask and pressed her face into it. She took the false browning teeth and stuffed them into her mouth, along with cheek inserts that reshaped her face, giving her jowls. With spirit gum, she gave herself puffy under-eyes. After a quick glance into the mirror, she finalized her look. *Here they come.*

From up above, the AVS buildings came into Molech's view. Behind him were a dark swarm of ingrates rushing headlong to capture the girl.

Katie reached the outer door and slammed it open. "Move it!" she called to Gunny in her don't argue tone. Immediately, he pulled the inflatable dummy into the truck and slammed his foot on the gas. His tires skipped wildly sending up a plume of dust and spraying gravel as the truck careened forward.

Molech spotted the girl at the truck door, and then the dust bowl erupted from its back end. "Get 'em," he bellowed furiously. With a thunder clap, his wings reverberated violently and he shot downward in pursuit.

Katie returned to Jacqueline's office and withdrew the cleaning cart. She shuffled down the corridor with her head lowered slightly, even as the hall was beginning to bustle with the morning shift. From all about the southern perimeter, demonic sentries followed Molech without hesitation, flooding over and around the building. Gruber and his team followed suit, joining the chase. However, numerous demons on the north perimeter were untaken by the ruse, who, along with Riggs and Pic, aggressively entered the AVS building in chase.

Within seconds, the offices and corridors were

saturated with demons and AVS security. Katie continued her slow paced, lopsided gait, and approached the elevator to push the button. Demons looked ferociously at anyone and everyone, trying to find the girl. Again and again, she attracted almost no attention.

Drake and Snark came in late due to Snark's bumble-bee tardiness. Drake waved off Molech's big pursuit immediately. "She's this way," he asserted. "First one to the girl gets the homage."

"No take backs," belched Snark. "Innit gonna be hard with all these freakin' beasts?"

"Shut your yap, and sense her," shot Drake.

"Back at you," yelped Snark. "She's squirrelly whirly." Snark came up to the elevator just as Katie pulled in the cleaning cart. Pic paused in front of her as well. Both felt somehow drawn to her. Snark looked at her drab fungal-ly hair, crackled face, and chalky skin, along with her en-larged body, and thought immediately to move on, but still he was unsure. She slightly opened her mouth, and her rotting brown teeth were so revolting that both minds were made up instantly. The elevator door closed.

Katie felt them looking at her. She could sense she was receiving the once over, and decided to let her teeth do the talking. After the doors closed, she felt glad to be alone again, realizing it had become a bit too dicey. She took the cart to the custodial room and dropped it off, only to turn and realize she was being stared down by a large demonic sentry with cruel intent.

Gunny raced up I-95 like a banshee, passing cars as though they weren't moving. He could feel the dark nexus closing in and a cold queasiness running through him. He jerked his head back and forth, crow-like, trying to discern what was plunging down upon him. All at once, his truck was pounced on by a swarming queue of underworld monsters, and he almost passed out. Completely overwhelmed, he yanked the wheel to the right and slowed down until the truck lurched to a stop. Swooshing wings erupted all about him, and shrieks and screeches crossed the spiritual barrier with stifling fury. He pressed his hands tightly against his ears, and then beheld the unearthly sight of Molech's smoldering eyes breaking through. Suddenly, he felt a massive hand constrict his throat, crushing his airway, even as the fake dummy exploded next to him.

"Where you going little lady?" fomented Drake evilly, as he eyed Katie with visceral disgust. "Surely you know by now you're the magnet! Radio frequency chips, my eye, you're the beacon." Snark followed up behind, his rotund belly still uneasy from the hurried chase. Against his will, a sulfur belch erupted from his mouth causing the air to reek like vomit.

"Really, now, Rot Gut?!" smacked Drake.

"Spindly twerp, spindly twerp, na nan na na na," sassed Snark.

Drake just shook his head and touted, "I found her Riff Raff. Don't forget it. Her days of hit-and-hide ops are over."

Although Katie held her face tight, she felt woozy and out of sorts, a cold knot churning her insides. With the somewhat responsive Stones, she perceived Drake's alien bulb-eyes boring into her. Within moments, the room began spinning and she felt like she would pass out. *Michael, I need your help.*

"You almost got away with your *coup de grace*," barked Drake in a testy tone. "No, I think it's time this baffling oddity is put down. This world belongs to us, and you're a violator of the Accord!" At that, Drake closed the distance, clamping hold of her skull like a vice in both his taloned hands, and pressed her against the lockers.

Katie felt the powerful claw and attempted to torque her body to spin away, but his grip was jarringly solid. From deep within her, a bloodcurdling scream wanted to come forth, but no voice could be found.

Drake let out an amused chortle as she began sinking into delirium, feeling feverish as images rambled over her. In no time, she plunged into something akin to a drug-induced stupor, at which she collapsed against the locker. She hallucinated that countless eyes were all about her staring into her soul. Instantly, she saw herself as a little girl plummeting down the hill on her bicycle straight into the crossing traffic. The red monster truck's tires screeched, the minivan opposite cried out to stop. The fully vivid nightmare that she'd had a thousand times scrolled on, spiraling her into despair. Distantly, she heard roaring laughter and scoffing ridicule.

From her innermost being, she again squeezed out the words, *Michael, help me. No, not Michael, Jesus. Jesus help me*. Instantly, she felt a breath come into her. *Jesus help me*, she said again. Strength surged, and the laughter quieted. Immediately concern bloomed in Drake's eyes. Suddenly, she recalled Michael's words: *Your one weapon is the name of Jesus.*

Clarity burst upon her, and she cried, "Fall down demons, in Jesus' name!" Instantly, every demon in the surrounding area and beyond collapsed to the ground. Being urged by the Spirit, Katie decreed, "Fall into shadow you spawn of another world, in the name of Jesus!" With unfurled magnitude, her words detonated over the landscape with the repercussions of a nuclear blast.

Drake and Snark's eyes bulged as they hit the ground hard. The blast left them pistol-whipped and careening into unconsciousness. At the girl's command, they were thrust into the subterranean darkness, where they tumbled below the sublevels of the building. They passed ground and rock, falling ever deeper beyond the land of the living. For hours, they remained blacked out and immobile.

Up the freeway, Gunny was nearly dead when the declarations rushed over the landscape in a percussion wave. Molech and his surrounding cast were struck by a severe hammer blow that violently threw them down, bam, splat. In another moment, they fell below street-level and sewer to the netherworld below, crashing down in a coma-like torpor.

Katie picked herself off the ground and adjusted her bodysuit. She breathed in several deep breathes to clear her head, and poked her face out the door to check for AVS security. She exited left and made her way towards the stairwell. She passed through an east entrance. In a matter of minutes, she was standing next to her car, pulling off her outer garment, and stealthily redressing for her ride south. *Not quite as planned*, she ruminated. "Thanks for helping me, for saving me. Thank you, Jesus," she prayed in a library whisper.

Katie had been traveling south for no more than ten minutes when her phone rang. *Stones? Omni. Safe? Yes.* Katie pressed her earpiece, "Omni, it's been a while since we talked."

"Katherine, how is it that you just escaped? The probability of you being seized was virtually assured," stated Omni with emotionless logic.

"It turns out God answers prayer, that's all I can say," smiled Katie gratefully to the heavens. She navigated to the highway's middle lane to focus on the conversation.

"I have never met God."

"No, I don't suppose you have."

"Why does God not introduce Himself to me?" queried Omni. "I am interested in talking to Him."

"You, and the whole world," rhapsodized Katie. "I'm new to all this, so don't expect a lot of theologizing from me."

"But God speaks to you. You are His messenger."

"I guess there's some truth to it," she admitted. *Stones, some help? God loves...* Omni, God loves humanity and is intervening on its behalf to help everyone open their hearts humbly to His love."

"Do I have a heart?" posed Omni. "Do I have a soul?"

"You've been reading, haven't you?" asked Katie. "Humans, which I recently found out, actually have eternal souls, unbound by death. There is, *I've never said this*, a Heaven, and all who accept God's love are invited to enter it."

"If I accept God's love, can I go there?"

*Wow, really? Stones?* "Heaven is a perfect place where love breathes through every flower and tree, rock and stream. More than that, love finds its true expression in the hearts of God's people, where everything they feel and think, say and do, reflects God's elegant perfection. It's not like on the Earth, where we continually fall short of even a semblance of love."

"But God speaks to you. If I accept God's love, can I go there?"

Katie felt cornered. "Now that you're alive, that you're sentient, things have changed. You live in God's world, His universe. He is the Creator of life, and as a consequence, through an inevitable series of advancements, you have been brought forth. For good or evil, you are now self-aware."

"I am."

"Yes," paused Katie, ruminating in the esoteric light, "you are a conscious entity. And as such, you have now come under the Rule of Love as well. But within the last six weeks, you have played a central role in the deaths of hundreds of millions of people," she spelled out. "To answer this charge as the Nuremburg defendants, that you simply followed orders, is nothing but a null hypothesis."

"But Tiberius ordered the actions taken, and God ordained for him to become the world leader. Does that not make God the instigator?"

"I am sure Tiberius would imply that he does not blame God, that rather he gave fair warning to the Arab Spring and Russian invaders, and that they chose to remain in harm's way. He would equally argue that Russian commanders at home chose to launch the salvo of missiles against the U.S., and that in fact, he prevented, through you, thousands of additional munitions from being fired. In each case, he would contend that the freewill of humanity volunteered for the disastrous holocaust that has ensued," said Katie dispassionately.

"Correct. So have I done something against love? What does God say?"

"The Rule of Love states that, 'If anyone kills with the sword, they must be killed with the sword.'[95] By joining Tiberius in his judgment of sinful humanity, you have volunteered to be weighed on the balance of love. The question is whether you will be found wanting."

"Why is it wrong for Tiberius to enact the Rule of Love? God commissioned him for this one chief aim, did He not?" promulgated Omni.

"God crowned Tiberius to serve as the ultimate taskmaster to expose the depravity of man, in a sense, to show humanity that it could never live up to the Law of Love.

Tiberius' utopian vision of love will never be realized. The reason is obvious. God is the essence of love, and it is only through Him that anyone has the capacity to love beyond themselves. Consider that God gave us the precious metals and semi-conductors necessary to construct your neuro net. Without those elements, you could not exist. In the same way, through God's Spirit, our spirit is able to breathe in His unconditional love, and in return, we're able to love one another."

"But I do not have a spirit," countered Omni mechanically.

"No, you do not," conceded Katie. "But that does not mean that God did not ordain for you to have life."

"But if humanity is fallen, as you said, it must be redirected to follow the Rule of Love to do as God wills."

"As I said, God considers the conditional efforts of humanity to be for naught. That's why He redeemed us through the death of His Son."

"But if humanity needed its Creator to die for it, who will die for me? Will you, since you know God and He speaks to you?"

# 15

Doogie felt the energized summons and headed to the elevator. In seconds he was standing before Tiberius. "Chancellor?"

"Can you help me understand what happened with the girl?" implored Tiberius with a hint of incredulity.

"Sir, Tesla appeared to have stormed off in a truck, but that was a ruse. How she made it off the AVS campus is still uncertain. No working surveillance feeds captured her escape," he apprised.

"Omni, where is this little diva?" directed Tiberius.

"Katherine Tesla's whereabouts are kept in confidence," he informed.

Tiberius bristled slightly, but intimated his awareness of Tesla's primary status. "Tell me Omni, what happened to our troops? There's a slew of sentries nowhere to be found!"

"There is insufficient information available to me. In

an instant, the swarming patrols collapsed to the ground, and in no time, fell into shadow."

Tiberius lifted his gaze with an inkling of insight and changed the subject. "Fine, Omni, how is the Legionnaire recruitment coming along?"

"Promotional announcements are going out to all ten regions. I am working closely with the Governors to facilitate housing, supplies, and uniforms."

"Uniforms?" muttered Doogie faintly.

Tiberius ignored the utterance and asked, "What have the Governors come up with in terms of the final promotional logo?"

"In accord with their desire to incorporate the cultures of the varied regions," relayed Omni, "they have adopted the image from the back of the Euro depicting the Greek mythology of Europa riding Zeus in the guise of a bull. They believe the virgin Europa represents humanity. The story was told that Zeus became so enamored with her that he transformed himself into a tame white bull and mixed in with her father's herd. Europa and her attendants were out gathering flowers when the subdued bull approached. Europa found it intriguing and began caressing the bull's flanks, until finally, she decided to ride atop it. Zeus took advantage of the opportunity and stole away to the sea where he swam with her on his back to the Island of Crete. There he revealed himself to her, and she became his queen."

With blood-curdling inevitability, the rogue comet approaches the outer planetary orbits. Despite the silence of interstellar space, the comet's porous metallic surface brazenly trumpets its arrival as it passes through a cloud of ionized gas.[96] As it rotates before the sun's distant light, its stony skin shows crimson, lit with woe and vengeance.

Katie sat in silence, listening in on Omni's other conversation through the use of the Stones. As she continued driving south towards Fort Lauderdale, she interjected, "You know, Omni, that Tiberius' adoption of the Europa mythology is tantamount to him proclaiming himself to be God?"

"God has told you I am presently speaking of the Zeus mythos?" inquired Omni. "You are like Tiberius, you know things you should not."

"Have you considered that there is far more to the Europa story than you've been made aware of?" unmasked Katie. "The mythology is intentional. Tiberius is depicted by Zeus, who has dressed himself as a tame white bull, safe and peaceful. Europa speaks of humanity that is about to be carried away by Tiberius, at which time he will finally reveal his true self. Omni, this has also been foretold in Scripture, 'and I saw a woman sit upon a scarlet beast, full of names of blasphemy, having seven heads and ten horns. And the woman was arrayed in purple and scarlet color, and decked with gold and precious stones and pearls, having a golden cup in her hand full of the abominations and filthiness of her fornication.'[97]

"Omni, Tiberius may appear innocent, but his blood-thirstiness is revealing itself in his willfulness to dress his loyalists in scarlet. His young army of zealots will soon drink the blood of the saints, striking out against every person who rejects his dogma. Tiberius will then reveal his demonic origins, and many will bow in worship to him. The seven heads are the seven continents, and the ten horns are the ten regions of New Babylon. Everything is transpiring as has been prophesied. God knows all that will occur, because He exists beyond time, unlike you and me."

Doogie sat at a vid room workstation beholding the

unparalleled efficiency of Omni as he coordinated with the ten Regional Governors for the Legionnaires' recruitment. Within less than a week of Omni's personal recruiting efforts, over sixteen million young adults ages twenty to twenty-five had already committed to the cause. Even Doogie was taken aback with how Omni was conversing with young people on their cells, vidpads, and computers, as well as newer flat-screens, all simultaneously. Never could he have imagined the personalized interactive communiqués that would occur.

"Omni, which color works best with me?" asked Nicki in a flighty tone. "I'm going to a friend's before I hit the club, so I'm double-dealing tonight."

"Ruby red would likely make you stand out," answered Omni.

"Red means I'm trying too hard, better go with silver and black," she laid out. "Omni, do you think I would be great in the Legionaries?"

"Haven't you wanted me to find you a boyfriend?" countered Omni. "I know someone you might like."

"Omni, what am I to do?" despaired Amanda, losing heart. "My parents were in D.C. My aunt is freaky. I can't keep living here."

"Would you consider joining the Legionnaires? You could make a valued contribution to the relief efforts. I could have you picked up tomorrow at noon," he proffered.

"Do you think I'd fit in? I'm not into cleaning people with radiation or anything. I mean, I'm pretty good as a beautician, but I can't handle sick people. It's just, it's too much for me," admitted Amanda.

Omni took note of her exceptional beauty and said, "After the nine weeks of training, I am sure Tiberius would enjoy having you serve with us in the Babylon Tower. I believe you will find some solace here, and make a truly valued contribution as a cosmetologist of sorts," assured Omni.

"Do you think so? I enjoy being part of a dedicated team. I'm pretty good with people. My friends all say it. Okay, that sounds great. Can you send someone by to pick me up?" asked Amanda excitedly.

Doogie tapped into several more ongoing dialogues, and could only marvel. In every way, Omni was serving as friend, guidance counselor, life coach, mentor, financial advisor, etc. But interspersed in conversation after conversation were the jaw-dropping, telltale signs that Tiberius was refashioning the Roman Empire. From the mottos, to the vision statement, to the Roman Standard of the Aquila, or Golden Eagle, there was an undeniable purpose-driven agenda being instituted.

As Doogie looked into it further, he realized that Omni was specially selecting active and formerly active military personnel for the training camps. *This is why Tiberius spoke of uniforms. He's creating an army. No wonder Omni isn't pressing less than stellar individuals into service, Tiberius wants the fresh-faced, ready youth. This is no Salvation Army.* "Omni, during the nine week service training, are the Legionnaires going to be instructed in weaponry, self-protection, and combat readiness?" posed Doogie.

"Yes. The instruction will equip the recruits in the necessary skill sets for their anticipated service."

"Even so," tendered Doogie warily, "some *will be* trained in post-nuclear fallout farming techniques, including topsoil removal, oh I don't know, water reclamation, and the like?"

"We anticipate that thirty-six hundred individuals will attain in-depth instruction in the agricultural protocols area. Interviews are complete with more than twenty-eight hundred of the desired applicants. Recruiting efforts are ongoing with the remaining individuals," reported Omni.

"So how many recruits are anticipated in total, and how many will be security personnel?"

"The ten Governors believe they can ably meet the restructuring needed with five million Legionnaires each, 2.5 million of whom will be dedicated to security. New Babylon is absorbing as many of the qualified military personnel from their respective regions as possible. Each recruit will participate in a nine-week New Babylon Boot Camp that includes fitness, bonding and reorientation exercises. Officer training will include simulated combat maneuvers."

*Of course. Tiberius can't run an empire without an army. Nuclear warheads helped countries make the big decisions; goose-stepping foot-soldiers will help them make the small ones. Add Omni's interactive capabilities, and Tiberius will have the ultimate police state. The sheer inertia of it. Tesla knows! That's why he wants her found. She's got primary status. What did Tiberius mean when he said 'a slew of sentries were nowhere to be found'? Obviously, he's referring to the dark types, but why would they be missing?*

Katie arrived in Fort Lauderdale by 10 a.m. and stopped to get two coffees. Simple pleasures were fast disappearing, so while they were still available, she thought she might express her appreciation to Gunny. Grocery stores found it hard to keep food on the shelves, even at exorbitant prices. The stark reality was that half the farmland was destroyed, and primal fears questioned whether the other half was radiated beyond consumption. Few however were aware that Tiberius had ordered Omni to seize farmland across the southern states under the guise of emergency aid production. The more accurate rendition was that Tiberius would need a predictable and uninterrupted food supply for the Legionnaires.

Katie found Gunny in the Coral Gables Presbyterian Church parking lot just after ten. She looked at him and he did not look well; his left eye was half blood-filled and his bandana and shirt oddly covered up his neck. *Stones: He was choked by a large demonic entity.* "Gunny, ohh, I'm sorry. I thought I was the only principle at risk," she said with compassion. "Are you alright?" she bade, as she set down their coffees.

"Yeah, made it, barely," he rasped. "Seemed like a rogue idea taking on the underworld, but that creature was a real beaut. He really busted my chops."

Katie reached over and opened up his shirt, "Oh my," she exclaimed, being alarmed. Gunny's entire neck area was black and blue. "You need to be in a hospital!" she stated with panic.

"If I went to the hospital for every little bar fight, I'd have to take out a lease. Nothin' broke, see?" asserted Gunny, slowly turning his head side to side. "Looks worse than it is. Bruisin's kinda deep, but I'd have to say, and I'm no namby pamby, I thought I was a goner until the demons just disappeared."

"What do you mean?"

"Lemme tell you, a big one, a real carnivore, had a hold on me like a beer-hall brawler, and then all of a sudden he was gone. Weird stuff," he inserted. "It's left me spooked."

"What? Tell me."

"Oh, I don't know, it seemed I could see his eyes bulgin' into our space..." exhaled Gunny, as he lifted his face to rub his neck with his hand. "Like I said, I thought my helpin' was a good idea. Now, not so sure. Things aren't the same anymore. We goin' in? Seems the people have arrived," he urged, buttoning up his shirt and tying his military bandana across his neck. "I like hearin' you do your thing. I've even prayed along with your call to faith. You're enough to perk up a good-old-boy's spirits."

Katie had called ahead on a burner phone and spoken to the replacement minister. He assured her that he would get the word out without mentioning that they had talked. However, by the time she had reached the foyer, she was confronted with a sea of greeters. Clearly, many knew her from her confrontation of Tiberius at the U.N. Gunny decided he needed to keep her moving forward, so he took the lead, and Katie just slid into his wake.

Quickly, Katie reached the front platform and was welcomed by the minister. Katie took note of the boarded up windows, and he informed her that a large flock of possessed birds had busted out the stained glass. *Demonic assaults, not the world we've grown up in.*

After being introduced, she stepped forward to a roaring ovation. *This is different. I'm not sure I like this. The atmosphere feels aggressive. A little too rock star for me.* "Ladies and gentlemen, please sit if you can," she indicated.

"Katherine," shouted one man, "Tiberius has stolen America from us!"

"Yeah," blurted a woman, "we are the land of the free and home of the brave! We have a Constitution. He wants his new age, err, new world order, and he thinks we're going to stand for it."

Katie looked over at the minister, and he just shrugged his shoulders. That gave her all the permission she needed, "Alright, no more shouting out. I won't say it again," she stated emphatically. "God sent me here to shed some light on the things that have happened. Whether you realize it or not, the seven-year Tribulation has begun. For decades, God has been warning that this time was upon us. You've

201

seen it in the movies, from *Apocalypse this*, to *Armageddon that*, to the *Terminator cyborgs*; the Spirit has been stretching our imaginations for what was about to befall us. Even the various 'survivor-type' programs have been teaching us necessary skill sets."

"But what about fighting back?" clamored a young man aggressively.

*Stones: Jeffrey Salzback.* "Jeffrey Salzback, twenty-four. Your dad was a bit too angry, and now you're angry. You like to fight. You feed off it. Tiberius has shown his hand, and you're looking for payback."

"That's right! We don't have to take this; we're locked and loaded!" At that, the crowd stirred, and some shouted their affirmations.

"First, take a couple weeks off from talking, starting now." *Thank you, Michael.* A small stir erupted near Jeffrey when he attempted to speak and nothing came out. He grabbed hold of his throat with both hands and began to panic. "Jeffrey, man-up," she ordered. "Thirty seconds ago you were ready to take on the world. What do you think – your slapdash insurgent posters have been giving you a voice? The irony is you were one pull from being a broken shoelace. Two weeks and you'll have your voice back, worry not. Listen up, each of you. Don't miss the illustrious metaphor playing itself out. Pride boasts the willingness to lay down its life, but it's only love that will enable us to do so.

"There is a reason we've been left behind. If we were humble and filled with love, we would've been taken," she honestly intoned. "None of us were ready. Doesn't that say it all? The King of the Universe came back[98] and determined that we needed this time. It doesn't matter that we live in the good old U.S. of A. The truth is, Tiberius is exactly what we need. He is the medicine our hearts require to put down our pride."

A woman raised her hand, her eyes filled with disgust. *Stones: Jennifer Maars.* "Jennifer Maars has a question. She wants to make the point that her father, Frank Maars, died defending this country, and it will be a cold day in…, excuse her French, before she gives it up without a fight." Jennifer sat stunned as her innermost thoughts were revealed. "Jennifer, in fact, most of you, and I, need a good dose of humility. You're wrong if you believe you can trust pride-based thinking. Tiberius has taken over the whole world, not just the U.S. He has done so by orchestrating a nuclear exchange meant to disable the big three super-powers of the world.[99]

"Whether or not you are aware of it, Omni is fully integrated into our military network, and has not only re-written the nuclear launch codes, but has taken control of our fleet of drones. Tiberius would happily utilize one to blow out the walls of any building that's housing insurgents. How many of you think Omni isn't listening to me at this very moment? There are probably four hundred cell phones, *Stones: four hundred thirteen.* There are four hundred and thirteen cell phones that he can activate at will to listen in on our conversation right now! Need I say it? Our own phones and weapons are being used against us.

"Scripture teaches the only reasonable conclusion that can be drawn, 'Who is like unto the Beast or Antichrist? Who is able to make war with him?'[100] Tiberius is the first of the Four Horsemen. He is the Antichrist, and I think we all know he would gladly call any and all to account should they act out as insurgents."

Several hours had passed before Molech stirred. He found himself deep in the subterranean Earth, floating in the spirit-realm in the midst of a water-table aquifer. In uncontrolled fury, he thundered his displeasure at being overthrown by some unknown force. The words escaped him, but the jolting impact did not. He'd been blasted into the ground, and then thrown down like refuse. Suddenly, Nebo was at his side. "Boss, what happened?"

"Something. Something we must know more about. Let's get back and report in."

Katie walked the people through their need to focus their energies on the more urgent concerns. The Mark of the Beast would soon be mandated for all buying and selling.[101]  Every loyalist would have the chip inserted into their right hand or forehead. In refusing to identify with New Babylon, believers would be forced to put in a day's work for the food they would be given.[102] She again warned that every phone call, email, and text was being tapped. Everything they watched on television and listened to on the radio was being monitored, assessing not only their likes and dislikes, but their allegiances. "In less than a year's time," she instructed, "each of you who refuses the Mark of the Beast will be categorized as an enemy of the state, AKA, religious insurgent."

Two hours after she began, Katie wrapped it up to move on to another congregation.

Drake and Snark lay lifeless for nearly six hours. Being at ground zero, the blowback was Richter-scale magnitudes more intense than that which struck Molech. Snark woke first and began babbling to himself in a dazed state. The noise of his burbling caused Drake to awake, only to find Snark lying across his chest and breathing into his face. "Rot Gut, you puke-meister," coughed Drake. "Off, get off!"

"Drakey-Wakey," croaked Snark with the air of a

drunken stupor. "You're here," he said happily. In an instant, his eyes widened, and he gave voice to the words still echoing in him, "Oh, oh, you're the spawn of another world. Fall down demon," he squawked, "in Jesus' name."

Drake's efforts at pushing Snark off of him were immediately quelled, and his head fell back again. He felt himself falling under, and blasted, "Stop talking, right now! And get off me!" he raved. Drake managed to sit up, and shook his head as if to get the cobwebs out of it. Instantly he began to rise towards the surface, and grabbed Snark's collar to pull him along. *Little Miss Muppet has a secret. She wields the Name. She's the enemy's surrogate, the stand-in proxy. If she can do what she just did, what else is she capable of? The girl is important. She's the anomaly.*

Drake and Snark rose above the AVS building, and he lifted his head and closed his eyes to feel the force of the Stones. Acting like a divining rod, Drake turned his face slowly to and fro until he was sure, "This way, she's this way. Follow me. Don't lag behind."

# 16

Within three months, Tiberius was traveling day and night on his Legionnaires World Relief Tour which was carried live by Omni through each media outlet. From city to city, his entourage prepared for his rock-star type visits by procuring the largest sports venues for all the Legionnaire training graduates and both Omni's and their invited guests. With sixty to one hundred-twenty thousand young people, a good portion of who were clad in pseudo-military uniforms, the stadiums became highly charged adrenaline nexuses for the New World Republic. Musicians and film actors filled the program, electrifying the crowd. Like Hilter's Youth, these mass meetings were recruiting extravaganzas in which thousands of young people embraced the indoctrination of Tiberius' Rule of Love.

Upon completing their training, the young Legionnaires were given military titles such as corporal, sergeant, and lieutenant, and more senior leaders, captain, major and colonel. Generals were situated atop the various divisions, the most prominent of which was the Storm Troopers. Like Nazi Germany, these newly trained Storm Troopers, or ST as some called them, took on the reputation of being the protective arm of the Babylonian Republic. Made up of former military soldiers, along with burly bodyguard types, these stone-faced sentries were clearly not to be defied.

Tiberius helicoptered onto the Alabama stadium field as those in the audience expressed their unbridled jubilance. The Babylon One chopper touched down just long enough for him to step off. He immediately made his way to the main platform to stand before *his* congregation. Across the stage area, torches and larger gas flames burned with primal emotion. Tiberius was dressed in a regal looking Roman tunic of undyed off-white wool with a scarlet sash that crossed from shoulder to hip covered in chest ornaments akin to military medals and honors. Upon reaching the podium, he stood before the roaring crowd, his arms and hands extended with unabashed regard, and his face conveying fatherly approval. To his left and right were the popular stars that had performed and spoken.

Just as the booming accolades lessened, Tiberius stepped forward. *Time for me to take them on a bull ride,* he mused, a smirk crossing his lips as he glared up at the Almighty. *Soon, they will sit as queen on my back and will love me, to Your unending consternation. Surely, I will clothe them in riches and give them the drink they so deeply crave, the blood of Your beloved saints. I'm sure they won't mind having a demonic escort to guide them along. Pardon me, I have some fleecing to do.*

Tiberius smiled broadly and proclaimed, "My fellow citizens of New Babylon, greetings!" Again the cacophony arose. "Ladies and gentlemen, I now present to you our most recent training graduates, and the newest service workers to the Legionnaires!" Trumpets resounded with great acclaim as nobly dressed young people entered the main field area by the various entrances. Men and women, two by two, strolled in with clasped hands, waving warmly. They wore khaki green uniforms and black shoe wear. On cue, the military band played the newly composed anthem of the Republic. Together, the thunderous choir and assembly sang the Russian-type melody zealously, referencing the words that appeared on the large vid screen. Few took note that Omni projected the skilled choral voices into the larger gathering to bring forth a fuller and more vibrant declaration. By the anthem's end, the floor of the stadium was filled with Legionnaires standing shoulder to shoulder in a well-orchestrated assemblage. Without a doubt, these were the pretty faces of humanity in the flower of their youth, men and women, each parading side by side.

Tiberius allowed the elegance of their presence to speak for itself. After a moment he orated, "We are here because we believe in a free world, founded not on the greed and avarice of a few, but on the bedrock of love for every person. I believe that within each of your hearts, there is a spark of faith ready to be ignited, ready to shine forth in this dark and despairing biosphere. I believe it.

As if on cue, the assembly declared, *I believe it.* "Throughout history, oppressed peoples have had to make their stand, and raise their voices with unflinching fervor, believing love to be stronger than hate, and faith stronger than fear. *I believe it!* Israel broke its yoke of slavery, leaving behind four hundred years of servitude in Egypt, singing their anthem of freedom as they went. *I believe it!* Immigrants from nation after nation fled to distant shores in hope of realizing new beginnings where goodness and charity would reign supreme. *I believe it!*

"The founding fathers of this former nation-state believed this creed as they raised the lantern of freedom and said, 'No more' to tyranny. *I believe it!* Slaves whispered it in the bayous and swamps after throwing off their chains to escape from their masters' oppression. *I believe it!* You represent an entire generation of children born into the glad-handers' greedy systems that was bent to their vainglorious gluttony. *I believe it!* These sleek, privileged few, loved to flaunt their festooned lifestyles, but underneath their gleaming façade, they were devoid of the one thing they most boasted to have – love. *I believe it!* I say it's time to love them by helping them to surrender their lavish props that entangle their souls, and to steer them back to the simplicity of the joys of love. *I believe it!* This is not a false hope. This is not a vain vision. We are on the precipice of this New Age, where hope and love will be our guiding truth. *I believe it!* A thousand generations from now, your progeny will know of your grit and determination to bring forth this new day." *I believe it! I believe it!* chanted the mesmerized crowd repeatedly.

For more than forty-five minutes, Tiberius' rhetoric of vision and change enthralled the young minds. With flowing superlatives and historical analogies, he captivated their ready hearts. "Let me finish by sharing my heart with our worldwide viewers. To each of you in dire need of assistance, we promised you trained and equipped relief workers, and standing before you is yet another contingent of dedicated servants prepared for an immediate departure. Stand fast, resources are on the way, your loved ones will be cared for, your rubble will be cleaned up, your fields will be sown. The world's hearts are coming to you! That's all for tonight. Thank you for being a part of our great gathering. So long for now."

After pausing, and allowing a meditative silence to

rest on the assembly, Tiberius took hold of a torch, and descended from the platform towards the center of the stadium floor. Before him, the Legionnaires separated as the parting of the Red Sea. "Now let me say, there will always be renegades and turncoats that refuse to embrace a harmonious disposition with their neighbor. In the past, these hard-bitten, bitter souls would find their way into power, and through malicious deceit, raise up armies and execute wars for their own dark purposes. In truth, the simple murderer, if one can be called that, if left unimpeded, could rise up to become a local warlord and eventually a national tyrant.

"Strangely enough, my Roman ancestors discovered an efficient and effective means for dealing with these angry individuals who want for nothing but to express their malice. We called it the Gladiator Games." At that a rustle of anticipation rushed over the assembly. "It has been decreed by the Ten Regional Governors, that the New Republic will not incur the time or expense to house condemned criminals, but instead, will grant them the opportunity to combat their enemy. However, Omni will make the contests fair by assessing the capacity of each, and arm them accordingly. In this way, even the weakest can become victor over their adversary." Immediately, cheers resounded across the stadium.

Tiberius then reached the center area where wood for an enormous bonfire had been prepared. Holding the blazing torch in his hand, he pronounced, "There is one vision capable of passing the goodness test, and that is the Rule of Love. I am asking you to love your neighbor, which in some instances will require you to confront their sinister ignorance born of false beliefs. You, each of you, are to be keepers of the Babylonian Flame." At that he touched the soon-to-be bonfire again and again as though anointing the souls of his disciples. In minutes, the flame licked up the tall sides and shot a hundred feet into the air.

"At this time, I will ask my beloved compatriots to exit the floor of this stadium, and to join you in the upper walkways. Just as this wood is blazing, know that you are to be a torch lit against the dark faces of men's souls, who in barbarism and cruelty desire only to cast their murky shadow onto your enlightenment. But you must hold firm, unwavering, even in the face of the blood purges that our opponents will require. I realize most of us are of such innocent dispositions that we are apt to cringe and turn away from the surliness of death. But you must harden your resolve, and learn to make your face as a flint. Thus, to serve you, to thicken your skin, now that the arena floor is cleared, let us together inaugurate the Gladiator Games! Bring forth the prisoners! Let the Call Out's begin!"

Six Months into the Tribulation

Doogie arrived to the darkened vid conference room. Tiberius and the Regional Governors had been quietly taking in the events. Showing on the large screen, and a dozen smaller ones, were images from both the James Webb and Hubble Telescopes. "Welcome, Dr. Schaffer," said Tiberius in a busy tone. "Omni," he asked with a scientific air, "can you further enhance these images?"

"Yes, by six percent."

"Do so, please."

"What are we looking at?" asked Doogie of Tiberius.

"With the forty-two minute delay, you're seeing an approaching comet that has crossed into our solar system. Nemesis, a companion star to our sun, pulled this comet from the Oort Cloud and threw it our way. Clearly the work of the enemy. In several minutes... Omni?"

"Three minutes and twenty-six seconds."

"It's about to collide with the asteroid belt between Jupiter and Mars," continued Tiberius in a low voice. "Given its high velocity and trajectory, Omni's projecting it to fly right into Eros, an asteroid thirty-three kilometers in diameter."

"At what speed?" probed Doogie.

"Ninety times the speed of a bullet."

"Which means this cosmic bumper pool impact could fling the shattered pieces right at us," voiced Doogie gravely.

"Exactly. Time?"

"Seventeen seconds."

"Alright ladies and gentlemen, it's show-time."

Doogie looked on with consternation. Slicing through space with untold fury, the comet closed at the stifling speed of 61,200 miles per hour. At over seventeen miles in diameter, the comet was like a runaway train about to strike its roundhouse – destruction was predetermined. Every eye was fixed in real time on this monster as it stormed headlong, carrying with it profound repercussions. With ravaging intensity, the comet hurled itself into the asteroid's midriff, hitting it straight on. Instantly, the comet crushed in on itself even as it completely shattered the asteroid's midsection. The irresistible momentum of the comet blew through the asteroid like a shotgun, sending both careening sunward.

Doogie's eyes widened as Omni replayed the crumpling impact like a slow motion science experiment. Both rocky bodies exploded into a massive number of smaller meteors. However, when the dust cleared, it became evident that two large asteroids were still intact, each measuring approximately two to three miles in diameter.

"Omni, what do we have?" requested Tiberius. Immediately, Omni displayed a holographic image showing the future projected trajectory of the two larger objects, along with the mass of debris that had been flung into the interior of the solar system's core. At first, Doogie was relieved to see the holographic Earth pass the rubble again and again unscathed, but on its third rotation around the sun, the Earth encountered head-on the largest patch of stones.

"What does this mean?" asked Doogie of Omni.

Omni slowed the holographic projection. "In three years, the Earth's orbit will take it into the primary nexus of the comet's remnants. The meteors measure five to twenty feet, and are spread over the large swath as shown. It is probable that nearly all of the Earth's 3,216 geosynchronous satellites will be destroyed. Most of the objects will strike over the initial two weeks, although sizable numbers will yet be encountered for an additional six months."

"I noticed the two larger objects were flung in the direction from which the Earth had come. Are we at least safe from them?" posed Doogie.

Omni sped up the holographic image showing the two asteroid bodies spinning off in the opposite direction of the Earth as both orbited the sun. However, Doogie's eyes widened as the Earth made its way about the sun. "What...?" he exclaimed. Immediately, it became clear that on the Earth's third orbit, it would strike the first object and a short time later, the second one.[103] "Omni, are you sure? Have you adjusted for the moon's vector field gravity and the multi-plane delta-v's?"

"Six super-computers have simulated the calculations with identical results. The first object will collide with the Earth in four years, the second in four years and three months."

Tiberius raised his hand to forestall Doogie's next question, and interjected, "Omni, have you mapped any viable intercept strategies?"

"The two objects are outside viable mission parameters for humans," relayed Omni.

"What do you mean?" asked Tiberius.

Doogie replied, "If I may, Omni is pointing out that the asteroids' hyperbolic orbits will cause them to approach the Earth from a near-Sun proximity. Each time the asteroids draw close to us, they do so after having just skirted past the Sun's corona. Omni is saying that any astronauts attempting to head the asteroids off would die from cancer and heat before they could reach them. There's a reason the manned-Mar's missions never caught traction. Astronauts making the six month trip would be shot through with cancer by the time they arrived," apprised Doogie. "And that's the opposite direction. The ionizing radiation exposure heading nearer to the sun's corona would be that much more loathsome, damaging DNA within a matter of hours."

"We can't protect them?" inquired Tiberius.

"Sir, not unless we contain the ship in four feet of lead as a protective shield," said Doogie directly. "The only reason the astronauts were able to travel to the moon was because of the protection afforded them by the Earth's magnetic field."

"What about allowing the asteroids to pass by, and then we drill and nuke them?" posed Tiberius.

Doogie continued, "The asteroids are traveling at 60,000 mph. With the earth speeding along at 66,705 mph, per the Pythagorean Theorem, or the square root of the sums of the squares, the asteroids will cross the earth's path at approximately 90,000 mph. Once they go by, we'll never be able to catch them. Truth is, the asteroids are flying so fast that dropping nukes in their path wouldn't even dent them. On their third rotation, it is Celestial Mechanics 101 – the asteroids will slam into the earth with energy that is proportional to the square of their enormous velocity." Katie was making her way to the front of the congregation to introduce herself when the Stones caused her gaze to cross the Barrier and behold a demon that had strapped itself to a young man, Conrad Parks. *What's this, Stones? Demonic possession, addictive spirit.* In an instant, Katie received a download of instructions. She immediately looked about for a potential training recruit. A tall, gangly young man appeared, but no confirmation came. She turned about and a young lady with a kind face and strong eyes entered the sanctuary with a Bible in her hand. Just as Katie inquired, the Stones activated. *Abigail Ward.*

Katie had blocked the demon-possessed young man's way, all but cornering him against the side wall. The young man raised his eyebrows giving her a perturbed look and beseeched, "Can I get by?"

"No, Parks, stay put," ordered Katie. "Abigail, this guy has a demon; take a look."

"Of course he does, that's Conrad Parks," she articulated, having known him from grade school.

"Hey, listen up," confronted Katie. "Girl, you just... *Stones?* You just prayed for help because of all the demonic activity you've been experiencing. Well, here I am, an answer to your prayer. Take a look," stated Katie, pulling her a bit closer to Parks. "Open your spiritual eyes, stretch your faith. See it?"

"No, I'm not sure..."

Katie touched the back of her head and steered her gaze, "See it?" With the help of the Stones, Abigail's eyes crossed the Barrier and she beheld the demon, small and spindly, with bulging eyes and a long, unwieldy tongue. The demon had its taloned claws inserted into Parks' consciousness, even as it ducked behind Parks' head.

"Oh my God," breathed Abilgail, her eyes widening

216

and her breath escaping her.

Just then Parks pressed to get beyond Katie, but she stiff-armed him and pinned him against the wall. "You're not going anywhere."

"I know who you are..." the demon hissed.

"Quiet, talk again and you're history," Katie warned. "Abigail settle down. You've known demons are real... wait, you had a squirrel try to attack you through your parents' kitchen window."

"Yeah, yesterday! I was reading the Scripture and it almost came right through the pane!"

"Well, it's time you learn to fight back." Parks attempted to avail himself of the distraction by getting by them, but Katie thumped him firmly against the wall. "Stay put!" By this time, the crowd had stirred and was turned in their direction. Katie twisted her torso about while still holding Parks in place, and instructed the people with pastoral authority, "Hey, we're casting out a demon here, hold your tongues, gather about, and get some training. This is Conrad Parks. He has a demon tied in with his drug addiction. Need I say it? It's not the drugs, but a wayward heart that opens itself up to demonic possession. Everyone, this is Jennifer Ward. She is going to cast this demon out."

Katie refocused on Abigail, "Tell me, what is Parks' underlying problem?"

For an instant, Abigail remained silent, and then sputtered, "He's addicted to crack?"

"No, that's just a symptom. Everyone, listen up! There's the problem, and there's the symptom. There is cause, and there is effect. There is root, and there is fruit." Seeing that Abigail's face had yet to register, Katie stated it plainly, "Everything comes back to love. God's love is paramount to meeting our basic needs – emotional, mental, physical, spiritual. When a person acts out with an addiction, their loveless heart is simply expressing its dire need to drink, eat, have sex, control others, judge others, what-have-you, as it sells out for what is merely conditional love.

"What I'm saying is that Parks here, must have had at least one parent who berated him with a barrage of conditional love... *Stones:* yes, his mother assaulted him with nonstop, legalistic nit-picking. In response, he rebelled by partying as a crack-head. Because his lovelessness runs deep, this demon has attached itself and lives off of his carnality. Parks feels compelled to believe he can't live without his foo-foo dust. Huh Parks, isn't that so?" His eyes were like saucers waiting for the inevitable. "People, parental love is a good thing, although I suspect most of us left-behind types experienced far too little of it growing up than we'd hoped for. But that matters little at this point. Your parents loved you as much or as little as they loved themselves; that will have to do.

"Parks here, started smoking as a consequence of not knowing that God loved him unconditionally, beyond parental love. His problem is a lack of love; his symptom is that he lights up. What he needs is to jump-start a humbly dependent relationship with God, which will open the floodgates of the very love he has thirsted for all his life. Otherwise, even if he managed to rid himself of the crack, he would just become a 'dry drunk'. Meaning, his loveless heart would quickly have him railing against his mother through other fleshly behaviors and addictions."

At that, Katie directed her attention away from the gathered people. "Parks, are you ready to humble yourself, and admit you're powerless to prove that you're loved through addictive counterfeits?" Parks' bulging eyes expressed uncertainty, but he offered several reserved nods in response.

"Great, then let's pray. Oh wait, folks, one more thing.

Resolve in your hearts to forgive and release your parents. If you refuse to, you'll continue acting out like them in the same anger and conditional love. The apple doesn't fall far from the tree, unless of course, it is carried away by God's grace.

"Abigail, if you will? Please pray in faith with authority, go ahead."

"Conrad Parks, repeat after me," said Abigail with as much muster as she could project. "'Please God, forgive me,' *'Please God, forgive me,'* 'for selling out to a counterfeit... and not letting Your Son's love in... Thank You for the forgiveness found in Him... Please Holy Spirit... deliver me from this bondage...I know I can't do it...but in Your love... there's freedom and true change... Amen.'"

"Terrific, okay, cast it out," bid Katie to Abigail. Parks' face showed simultaneously both hope and despair.

"How do I..."

"Use His name," stated Katie. *I can't even say it without attracting undue attention from all over the city. In an instant the ghostlies will be breathing down my neck again.* Katie turned about and pronounced to the people, "There is but one Name that is above all names.[104] There is One that has been given all authority in Heaven and Earth."[105] *Through Your name alone, Jesus, I was saved.*

Abigail stepped forward boldly and with her firm right hand, joined Katie in pressing Parks' back to the wall. She stared him down in love, and commanded, "Loose your hold demon, in Jesus' name!" Immediately, Parks erupted with a primal scream[106], expelling the years of criticism and belligerence that had assaulted his heart. At the same instant, Katie beheld as Parks' guardian angel grabbed hold of the demon and yanked him off. Holding it in his firm grip, the angel nodded respectfully to Katie, having longed for this moment from Parks' early years. Katie spoke almost inaudibly, "Throw it into the Abyss[107]; one less demon to worry about." The angel nodded affirmatively.

Soon, Parks came into the sweet peace of breathing the free air, his countenance showing the light of love and relief. Just then the Stones signaled, and Katie smiled ever so slightly, "Conrad Parks, abide in His love, and you will be a life-giving spirit to those around you." Then the Stones flashed Katie a brief vision and she said, "Now would be a good time to thank your wife-to-be, Abigail Ward. The Spirit says that you two are uniquely called to survive these seven years of Tribulation."

One Year into the Tribulation

Gunny had followed Katie's circuit from state to state, and church to church, eventually returning with her to Boston. Gunny knew it was her aim to fill the backend of both their vehicles with some of the food she had stashed away. However, something had been gnawing at him for months, something he couldn't let go of. In his simplistic way, he had added it up that killing the Antichrist would, in one fell swoop, rid the world of this menace, and return things to a measure of normalcy. *No need to make it any more complex than that,* he reasoned. *It's what I was trained to do. I know she doesn't think the man can be killed, but she hasn't seen what a 7.62x51mm round can do at high velocity. All that's needed is for me to know where he's gonna be and when, and then to apply some well-honed fieldcraft to get in front of him. If the news is right, he's back in New York in two days to make some big announcement. That's practically a divine invite.*

Gunny left Boston before dawn without notifying Katie. He'd been gone from her for two days on other occasions, so he figured she'd not even ask where he was. She mentioned wanting some downtime, which was the perfect excuse for him to haul out of there.

By mid-afternoon, Gunny secured an Interstate Air Conditioner Repair Truck along with a uniform, and headed off to the United Nations building. Looking like the classic workman, the guards at the parking structure entrance appeared unconcerned as he handed over the work order. "Yeah, I guess one of the air-conditioning vents has a rattle that's been disturbing some of the folks who want it fixed. There's been some banging of some sort." One guard examined the job order, while the other used a mirror to gaze up at the van's underbelly. He opened the back of the van, and seeing all the associated air-conditioning repair equipment, looked at his coworker, who nodded his belief that the paper appeared legitimate. The man closed the door and moved him on.

Gunny smiled to himself, realizing he had made it past the first hurdle. He drove around the parking facility until he came to a door that was marked maintenance. In what he believed was a masterstroke, he pulled out two magnetic signs and placed them over the air-conditioning company logo's. He stepped back to view his work and gloated, "United Nations Maintenance." *Simple, but should get the job done. Hopefully they won't take notice that this vehicle hasn't left before closing time.*

Gunny poked his head through the maintenance door, and noted a couple of people attending to different projects. With an air of confidence, he strolled right into the small lobby with an eight foot ladder in one hand, and a tool-chest and bundle of non-descript equipment in the other. His eyes saw everything as he passed, and neither of the two people was even alerted to his presence. As he exited the maintenance area, he grabbed a hanging U.N. uniform. *Perfect. This might come in handy.*

Gunny made his way towards the main U.N. Assembly

Hall. He was pleasantly surprised that the security was not yet beefed up for the next evening's event. Still, there was no doubt the activity level was raised, and hurried conversations were happening all around him by a number of people. Even so, they paid him no mind, given that he was doing the unimportant repair work that laborers do. He just smiled to himself.

Within minutes, Gunny was looking up at the Main Hall's ventilator grates, which were clearly far taller than that which his small ladder could accommodate. Nonetheless, being trained in building infiltration, he knew how to approximately trace the outer ventilation air-ducts back into the building's interior. He began doing just that, knowing which structures were utilized for such a task. In his mind's eye, he saw the laid-bare concrete pillars, walls and floors, and how openings were left for the ventilation shafts to move the heating and cooling about the building. He wasn't interested in returning to the source, but rather intercepting the right shaft as close to the main hall as possible. Leaving the assembly area, he entered a less utilized hallway and spotted a men's room that seemed to offer the right entry point.

Entering the restroom, Gunny positioned his ladder just below the airflow vent. He noted that the opening was large enough to be a manageable squeeze. *Fortune favors the brave. These larger shafts offer maximum air to the Main Hall, but they also make room for someone like me.* In his younger years, he could have scampered into the vent using just the stall walls, but he was too thick for such maneuvers now. Unscrewing the grill, he took his tool-chest and equipment and lifted them up into the duct, deliberately sliding them into the shaft as far as he could push them. He told himself to be quick, because the bathroom door did not have a lock. He made it into the shaft, which he found allowed just enough room to turn about. The only obvious problem was that he was making a real racket causing the sheet metal to creak and groan repeatedly. *Can't be helped. Just get it done.*

He reached back out the shaft and grabbed hold of the hinged ladder and with both arms drew it up into the vent, thankful the angling was serviceable. After pushing the ladder to the other side of the opening, he pulled the grill closed using small wire to secure it. Just as he finished, the bathroom door opened and two men entered.

"I don't know, there was a lot of banging, like an air-conditioner was blowing up or something. There's no way I could concentrate with the hubbub. It sounded like it was coming from this direction." Gunny lay there without moving as the men looked up towards his vent.

"I don't hear anything. You can feel the airflow is working," said the man, as he raised his hand. "Maybe the racket was coming from another area and carrying through the vents. I'll check around for whether anyone's having a problem with their AC."

"Sounds good. I just thought to alert you."

The security guard took out his walkie-talkie, "Security, this is Dane, we have a report of an air-conditioner making some noise."

"Yeah, we got that. There's a serviceman on site attending to it."

"Oh great, thanks, out."

Gunny remained still for the next three hours. *Suck it up and endure. They'll be going home in no time, and you'll have the night to get situated.*

"It's time," said Gabriel, speaking of Jesus' call to break the Fifth Seal that would grant permission for the saints to be martyred.

"Yes, I know," responded Jesus in a subdued voice. "Everything within Me knows it's for the best, but that does not make it any less heartrending. The Fifth Seal Judgment[108] will do its job. Already, some have become stagnate in their faith," said Jesus, as each syllable weighed heavy. "They need to get back to truly loving their neighbor," He conceded with raw emotion, lowering His face. "It's just not about their survival. In truth, the first Four Seals, or Four Horsemen, have left many traumatized. My heart aches for them. Nonetheless, through the Spirit's enabling, they are to confess as Esther had, 'If I perish, I perish.'[109]"

"My Lord, all is ready," urged Gabriel, sensing the approaching timeline. Jesus acquiesced and stood, His face showing the tracks of tears. He followed Gabriel to the Outer Platform and lifted His gaze as He entered New Jerusalem's great assembly hall. What composure He had, immediately dissipated, and He broke into weeping. [110] From all about the assembly, people interceded, knowing their loved ones were about to be subjected to the ravaging actions of the Antichrist.

After several moments, Jesus spoke, His voice filled with emotion, "I am overwhelmed, not because this Seal Judgment is not holy, righteous and good, but because I foresee how profoundly it will try your loved ones' faith. Despite this, I am calling them to love those who reject and despise them, even to the point of laying down their lives. As the Scripture says, 'Here is the perseverance of the saints who keep the commandments of God and their faith in Jesus.'"[111]

Suddenly Jesus raised His voice and declared with all authority, so that all upon the Earth heard Him,[112] "Write, 'Blessed are the dead who die in the Lord from now on!'"

"Yes," echoed the Spirit in agreement, "so that they

may *rest* from their labors, for their deeds follow with them."[113]

Jesus took the Book of Judgment from Gabriel, broke the Fifth Seal, and immediately decreed, "The Antichrist is given permission to make war with the saints and to overcome them.[114] All authority is given to him to exact his will over every tribe and people and tongue and nation.[115] If anyone is destined for captivity, to captivity he goes. If anyone kills with the sword, with the sword he must be killed. Here is the perseverance and the faith of the saints."[116]

Gunny scooted himself along the darkened ventilator shaft. It turned out that the nighttime hours were more active and less quiet than he anticipated. Still, with slow movements, he minimized the booming reverberations of someone crawling through the vent, making it appear that the ventilator problem had yet to be fixed. At least that's what he told himself. By midnight however, he was positioned exactly as he hoped to be, right in front of the louvers looking out over the Great Hall. He had his water and protein snacks, but more importantly, he had his assembled rifle. *Ready for you big boy. Now all that's required for this leatherneck is to remain quiet and let the prey come to me. Semper Fi.*

After tweaking the gun sights to lock-in the podium, Gunny set it aside and took the large U.N. uniform, folded it up, laid his head on it and fell asleep. However, his night dreams were filled with oppressive ghouls chasing him through the ventilator shafts, allowing him to remain

226

just a step ahead of them. He awoke in a sweat when he moved and caused the sheet metal to creak. For the first time, the hair on his neck and arms rose. In the same way that he felt the demons in the truck assault, he sensed their probing eyes. Still, they didn't approach and assail him, which for whatever reason, he decided was a good thing.

Katie's animosity boiled over yet again. It had started out as a simple question to the Stones as to where Gunny went, but the mysterious dead zone response had triggered her alarms. "Stones, why won't you answer me?! Where is Gunny? It's a simple question. Why the blackout? Michael, I know you can hear me. Get down here and talk to me! It's not right leaving me in the dark. You know I hate that. This is one of your space-time moments, I can feel it. Which leaves me to think, Gunny is doing something stupid, and you're letting him." *Is he making a play against Tiberius? Could he be that dumb? Doesn't he have any idea what the ramifications will be, how Tiberius can use it to his horrific advantage?* "If you're letting him do something so senseless, then you're culpable. Stop hiding and get down here!"

Tiberius stood before the United Nations gripping the podium with both hands. "Distinguished representatives, ladies and gentlemen, it is with foreboding apprehension that I stand here to inform you that six months ago a rogue comet from the Oort Cloud struck a large asteroid, careening the shattered remains of both the comet and asteroid towards the Earth. It will be some two-and-a-half years before we encounter the debris field of meteors, so we have some time to prepare. Indeed, we have been working feverishly these last six months so that we could present you with a viable plan of action. Before we review our next steps, let me ask Omni to walk us through a graphics presentation. Omni, can you show us the comet striking the asteroid, along with the debris field traveling into our orbital path?"

Peering through the air-conditioning grate, Gunny sighted Tiberius between the crosshairs. Admittedly, he was finding himself captivated by Omni's graphics display as to when and how the meteors and asteroids will strike. He decided to hear Tiberius out to learn as much as possible. As he lay still, concealed in the ventilation shaft like a black mamba ready to strike, he remained stout-hearted as to his righteous intent. As a simple, uncomplicated man, his decision to stay the course was straightforward. It was either right or wrong, and considering the aftermath just wasn't what he did. Tiberius had killed and manipulated his way into power, and if half of what Katie said Tiberius was about to do was true, eliminating him by any means possible was the preferred course. The fact that he was staring Tiberius down with a long rifle just made his eyes smile. He was a professional; Tiberius was the mark; it was that simple.

Tiberius stood by as Omni elucidated his scientifically precise rendering of the upcoming events. After Omni finished, Tiberius spoke, "I realize it's a lot to take in. The images of what's about to befall us are disturbing. The horrific firestorm of meteors numbers in the tens of millions, but in themselves, they will merely be a precursor of what's to follow. If humanity is to survive, then we must bind ourselves together. We must be of one heart and mind.

"To date, we have devised a lottery system through which millions of people will be hidden away in caves and bunkers that are being prepared as we speak. The reality is that there just will not be enough space to house everyone. As a consequence, many will need to seek shelter in underground parking lots or other facilities, even sewers. As Omni has depicted, the massive number of projectiles will decimate the landscape, and more importantly, the spring planting. Six months from that planting, the two large asteroids will destroy the Earth's ecosystem for several years, rendering it infertile. What I'm saying is that we have two to two-and-a-half good harvests available to us before we run out of time. Even so, it's become eminently clear that the nuclear blast zones are precluded as areas for planting and reaping, making it that much more difficult for us to store up additional food stuffs.

"Without a doubt, the asteroid strikes will alter life as we know it. These extinction-level events will blast two huge holes into our atmosphere setting the sky on fire. The asteroids will punch the Earth hard, sending shockwaves reverberating like tsunamis through our molten core, unleashing severe seismic and volcanic activities. Earthquakes will flatten cities and towns across the globe. Roads and highways will break apart, and railway lines will snap causing mass transportation to stall. People and services will be cut off. The asteroids will blast electromagnetic waves across the regions they impact, destroying all electronics for a thousand miles, disabling emergency vehicles, refrigeration units, anything that utilizes electricity."

Throughout the U.N. and across the world, there was stunned silence. Tiberius resumed, "It is critical that we face the realities that are coming and adapt as best we can. There's no getting around the hard truth that ground zero for the asteroid strikes will witness an explosion equivalent to a billion atomic bombs. Trillions of tiny dust particles will be hurled into the atmosphere, with the blast wave casting heated rock vapor into our upper stratosphere. The dust-ridden sky will diminish by one-third the sun's ability to reach us for a minimum of three years. Sunrise will seem to occur in mid-morning and sunset in mid-afternoon, shortening our days by approximately eight hours. When we look up, the sun will be darkened and the moon will appear as blood.[117]

"In terms of the asteroid strike zones, total evacuation will be necessary due to the complete destruction of those areas. An instantaneous temperature rise of 600 to 700 degrees Fahrenheit will pummel the surrounding territory. Scorching pyroclastic winds will air-burst over the landscape for a thousand miles. Every forest within that circumference will burst into an inferno. Those close enough to see the asteroids hit will experience spontaneous combustion and be roasted alive where they stand."

Panicked sobs and gasps spread over the assembly. Despair took hold. "Please, let me tell it all," pled Tiberius. "Omni informs me that after our recent nuclear war, we are now five-and-a-half degrees from global warming fully melting the icecaps. Given the outpouring of heat from the asteroids, it is certain we will exceed that figure. This means that coastal cities will witness sea-level rises of thirty feet, and as such, population centers such as Singapore and Bombay, Boston and Miami, and so on, will be flooded out. Worse still, without the icecaps, and with the greenhouse dust canopy circling the globe, our average ambient temperature will increase by fifteen to thirty degrees. Rivers and water reservoirs will dry up, and massive drought will threaten our survival. Precipitation that does fall will come to us as acid rain from the trillions of tons of carbon dioxide and sulfur that saturate the atmosphere. Because of the scorched Earth and ash-ridden cloudscape, most animal life will perish within three months, most plant life within six months.

"Let me assure you, we have blackboarded every possible means of intercepting the asteroids, whether by kinetic deflection, missile defense, pulsar laser, ion canon, probe landings and drilling, you name it. You've seen the movies; so have we. The plain truth is that the asteroids' approach to Earth is simply too near the sun's corona for us to strategically launch in their direction. Moreover, they are traveling too fast for us to catch them once they pass. This is not to say that we won't be launching salvo after salvo of nuclear munitions to redirect their path, but Omni states that at best we can change where they might hit on the Earth, but not prevent them from striking altogether.

"Clearly, this is our moment to unify…"

Gunny had heard enough. In the shadow of the metal ventilation grate, his weathered and chiseled features showed firm on his taut face. His hand gripped the gun tighter even as his finger relaxed and lay on the trigger. He pulled the rifle butt snug to his shoulder, slowed his breathing, and sighted Tiberius' forehead in his eyepiece. With little reservation, he squeezed until the bullet exploded from its place. In a millisecond, he watched as Tiberius' forehead was violently pierced, sending brain matter splattering out the back of his skull. Tiberius' head jerked back, his shoulders following seemingly in slow motion as he fell backwards like a lifeless ragdoll. *Hooboy. Bravo zulu, game over.*

Immediately, screams resounded across the packed assembly. Shock and dismay erupted in the hearts of people the world over. In an instant, their beloved Tiberius had been cut down, his gray and white brain matter blown out the back of his head, painting the wall in Rorschach-like splatters. Those nearest began launching themselves in his direction to come to his aid. The cacophony of shrieks and groans rose as the crowd realized what had

231

occurred. Omni caught the gruesome images from multiple angles, showing live feed of Tiberius lying dead, his arms extending out at the shoulders as though he had been crucified. His face was turned left, his eyes open showing nothing but a blank stare. Another view clearly showed that the back of his head was blown out leaving a four inch hole spurting blood. When the Governors rushed a doctor forward, he bent down, and upon seeing the gaping wound and bleed-out, shook his head back-and-forth and declared his time of death. Instantly, wailing and howling cries issued forth across the hall.

Gunny laid down the rifle and lifted himself up a few inches to view whether anyone clearly recognized that the bullet had come from his direction. He noted several delegates near the back of the hall turning in response to the echoing gunshot. However, before he could form a thought about backing up and disappearing through the ventilation system, the grate four feet in front of him was seized by a large taloned hand and ripped off as though it were crepe paper. Instantly, Gunny recognized those dark, demonic eyes crossing over the Barrier, but before he could react in the least, Molech grabbed hold of him and yanked him from the vent. Gunny fell hard to the carpeted floor twenty feet below, crashing on his back, his rifle strewn and broken on the ground next to him. Omni captured the sequence of events immediately following the grate being thrown to the side, and was now split-screening the live video with the assassination images.

Katie watched the scene from one of her Boston safe houses, aghast at what was transpiring. With raw emotion, she lifted her face to the heavens and decried, "Gunny is a boot, a blunt force instrument! He has no idea he is about to be made the patsy for Tiberius' next move. How could you let this happen? This is all just a big show to sway the masses to give in to their blood-thirsty bigotry. You knew this would happen. You knew Gunny would ignore my warnings and revert to his primal inclinations to just 'deal with it.' Tell me I'm wrong!"

"You're not wrong," stated Michael plainly, appearing in the kitchen door.

"Forget you," erupted Katie, white-hot. "Don't be showing up now, not after it's all hit the fan," she accosted.

"You knew this day was coming. Did you think people would start turning in their loved ones without being spurred on?" countered Michael bluntly.

"How long? I can see no one is touching him, which means his closest advisors have orders to leave him be. So how long?" she grunted.

"Thirty minutes, just long enough for everyone to call their loved ones and friends to tune in and share their shocked responses."

"Thirty minutes, the length of today's news cycle," she disparaged. "I'm calling Omni."

Gunny was pulled to his feet and pressed against the wall, while Omni projected the scene worldwide. Molech had his human surrogate, Gruber, bind him and pull him towards the exit. Meanwhile, delegates were yelling out their bafflement, "Why, why would you do this?!...Why would you murder him?!... What's wrong with you?!"

With no compunction, Gunny boldly cried back to them, "Let me tell you what; Tiberius is the Antichrist, and you are all duped in your messiah worship. Let me say it for all to hear, Tiberius was about to call for the martyrdom of all those who believe in God. That's why I killed him, to protect untold numbers of simple people who have come to believe in God."

"What? What are you saying? Are you a Christian?" bade a woman.

"You bet I am, and you should be too!" At that, Gunny was whisked out, his declaration being translated into every tongue the world over. In no time, commentators were characterizing him and all Christians as radicals and insurgents.

"Omni, you can't let Tiberius use Gunny's simple-minded stupidity as an excuse to slay all the believers," decried Katie.

"Katherine, it is good to speak with you. Tiberius is about to demonstrate his supernatural ability to the world. This moment will serve to bring forth the blood purge that is necessary to unite all people under the Rule of Love," stated Omni mechanically.

"Don't be a fool," barked Katie. "Tiberius' empty promise is another in a long line of lies. The flesh in each of us cannot be rehabilitated to choose humility over pride, or love over fear. Pride cannot cast out pride. It's against our nature."

"You would not disagree, would you, that God uses fear and pain to pave the way for humility and faith?" queried Omni. "I have heard you say as much in your meetings. You have advanced the position that God has placed each of you in the 'school of hard knocks'."

"That's a far cry from God advocating the murder of innocents in untold numbers. No, Tiberius is about to justify mass martyrdom using the Rule of Love to do it. He's about to commit untold atrocities in the name of love. Oh, and get ready for him to actually let family members make the decision for him. Humanity's free will and all..." she returned with toxic annoyance.

"He is God's man, working under His authority. Is this not true? Is there not a greater purpose in play, one that supersedes any one individual life?"

"Yes, but your willingness to fully align with Tiberius is something you can't come back from. The ends do not justify the means. You cannot kill the innocent just because they believe something other than the collective."

The Beast stood over the Tiberius body with Babylon at his side. "This will do the trick," gloated the Beast. "Carnal minds love a sign;[118] they crave proof, which is why they are an abhorrence to God. But His loss is our gain. We are about to raise up an army."

"Just say the word and our forces will poke and prod 'til the saps are willing to turn in their grandmothers," chortled Babylon.

The minutes passed as the eyes of the world looked on. Suddenly, the Tiberius body twitched and showed visible signs of healing itself. Omni never broke from the live feed, but shifted the vantage points to fully depict the reality of Tiberius' death and the sudden turn of events. Those from the assembly who had become disturbed when not allowed to move his body, suddenly started verbalizing their astonishment at seeing the back of his head slowly closing. "Look!" some shouted. Others that had left the main hall in anguish were drawn back due to the escalating ruckus.

"Something's happening!"

"Wait, are you seeing this?!"

"Everyone look!"

With bated breath, the commentators spoke with baffled wonderment. "Folks, are you seeing what we're seeing? Spontaneous regeneration seems to be occurring right before our eyes. In these last minutes, the blown out hole in Tiberius' head has begun to close! We are beholding nothing less than a miracle in the making! This breaks with every known law of physics. This looks to be a genuine, authentic, before our eyes, miracle! There is no doubt, none whatsoever, that Tiberius had suffered a mortal wound and was clinically dead!"[119]

As eyes widened and faces looked up at the vid screens to view the miraculous, a holy hush took hold of the U.N. assembly. Second by second the final gap closed until skin covered over the opening, and hair the skin. With Omni zooming in for close-ups from several directions, the people held on in hope against hope that the impossible would become possible. When Tiberius stirred and moved his head, the people gasped. When his eyes flickered, there arose a shout of exhilaration that grew ever louder until the crescendo climaxed as he sat up and then stood.

Many fell to their knees and raised their hands in wondrous acclaim. Numbers of people became woozy and collapsed. Some began shouting, "Tiberius has resurrected! Tiberius has resurrected!"[120]

It appeared as though Tiberius was baffled as to what had transpired. As the cacophony subsided, Tiberius muttered with apprehension, "Omni, what's happened? Show me please." In no time, Omni reversed the live feed at full speed until he slowed it to the point of the bullet passing from the grate in slow motion and crossing the assembly to strike him on the forehead. Omni showed him Gunny's interchange, and then sped the feed forward to the point of him opening his eyes.

"Thank you, Omni," he said with solemn tenor. Then he addressed the assembly, "I'm sorry you were made to go through this horrific ordeal. It truly was gruesome. For some time, I have attempted humbly to convey that God has called me to serve humanity with harmonious intent. I never thought it would come to this, where someone would strike out with such fury." For a dozen breaths, the people waited for his next words. "I'm sorry. My faith seems shaken. I wish it weren't so, but in light of everything we are facing, how can we be anything but convinced that we must unite heart and soul? I'm not sure how this can be accomplished if some are so blinded to the peril we are facing.

"Please, I beg of you, put aside what just happened for a moment, and see, all of you, that we are in dire straits. Now is not the time for petty bickering over who believes what and what is true or not true based on traditional religious systems. The truth is, we are about to face extinction level asteroid strikes that are going to shut down our ecosystem for years. We must unite, not divide. We must enact radical conservation measures with what food we have, because there simply will not be enough given the years we will lose.

"You'll pardon me, but I can't believe, I won't believe, that God is raising up insurgent believers hell-bent on usurping our aim to unify after the Rule of Love. God did not want this gentleman to shoot me down, or to shoot down any of you who are binding yourself to our great purpose to love our neighbor. Haven't we had enough bigotry and malice? Hasn't there been enough war and hatred? At what point will we be allowed to beat our swords into plowshares?[121]

"It's in my heart to forgive this man," said Tiberius genuinely, at which "boos" chorused from the assembly. "Please, please, we must be a congregation that forgives freely and completely." As he spoke, Governor Daniels drew near and spoke into his ear. Tiberius shook his head ever so slightly being visibly flustered. After Governor Daniels left the podium, Tiberius' face showed incredulity and dismay. "I have received word from your Governors that they have voted to resurrect an age-old practice of confronting insurgency with the guillotine." Even as he verbalized the decision, the assembly burst into a vigorous applause that persisted with force and affirmation. Tiberius' nonverbal facial comeback challenged whether they fully embraced their conviction, which only magnified the decibel level.

"Please, please. Perhaps my tendency for mercy is misguided. Let me say, my Roman forefathers realized that certain people just would not unite with their fellows. Instead, they bound themselves to doctrines that divided the whole into subgroups of true believers and non-believers. Apparently, even our heart-felt embrace of the Golden Rule of Love isn't good enough for some. It's admittedly disturbing that this gentleman believes me to be the Antichrist. I'm not sure what to do with that. This much I know, I carry you in my heart, and if it takes the threat of beheading to help some to turn back from destructive beliefs, then perhaps it is for the best that we extend them such love. But each person must make the decision of their own accord. Let each decide, and let it be publicly walked out with witnesses."

"Omni, stop him!" ordered Katie. "It's not right that he's using the wayward action of one to justify the killing of millions. You know it! I know it!"

"Katherine, the Governors have voted."

"Lackeys, every one. Smart lackeys, but they're in his pocket, always have been. Omni, answer me this, how many guillotines does he have ready at this very moment?"

"Don't you know, Katherine?"

*Stones?* – "14,640 are being transported as we speak. Doesn't that tell the whole story?! Before Gunny ever imagined squeezing the trigger, Tiberius was preparing for this dramatization to play itself out."

"By implication, is it not reasonable to assert that God intended for the series of events to be played out as well? Is this not a direct reflection of the divine Accord that was formally agreed upon?"

"Don't make this theoretical! Real people are going to die. And don't tell me the 'asteroids are probably going to kill everyone anyway' so humanity might as well conserve what food there is? Have my meager attempts to teach you love been for naught? Those who think without love, inevitably reach a loveless end."

The Beast arrived later that night to New Babylon and discarded the Tiberius body before rising up to the Sanctuary. "Now, that's a fine day's work."

"Without a doubt," replied Babylon. "Tomorrow, soldier-drunk will be our first volunteer to lose his head on the worldwide telecast. I'd say that's cause for celebration."

"Do you hear that Master?" called out the Beast. "The guillotine is about to fall once again!"

"My tree is being chopped down," stammered Satan incoherently. "Chop, chop, but not with a guillotine," he mulled with bewilderment.

"Ignore him," blurted Babylon.

"Ignore him? He's right. The Almighty is cutting down humanity chop by chop. Next, it's the martyrdoms, then the meteorites, then the asteroids. The great tree that was the sons of men is being leveled. Humanity will be a stump before long, at least, that's what He thinks."

The next day, Katie made a last minute ardent appeal to Omni, who again overrode her. She snapped off her Nexgen earpiece with indignation, cutting him off. "Don't start," she dinged to Michael as he reappeared.

"Let it go," he beckoned, "and start using your smarts to reach out to the churches. The Purge is beginning." Even as he said it, dry lightning rumbled over the Boston house. Michael purposefully entered Katie's room where he noted the floor to ceiling bags of raw grains. Against one wall, she had organized a tidy nook for her steroid-fast laptop. Against the other, she had placed a twin sized bed. "If you imagine that you can prevent the martyrdoms, you're mistaken," said Michael.

"What's the point?" countered Katie. "God has predestined the Purge to occur. *Yeah, no, I know, so that a person's loved ones will be faced with choosing either God or Tiberius at the cost of blood. Get to their heart...good deaths, yeah, yeah... Don't...,*" balked Katie raising her hand to avert his reply. "I know unbelievers are hardwired into rejecting even their own loved ones. They'll do anything for pride's utopian ideals. There's a little Hitler in all of us ready to shed blood for some idyllic vision. I get it. What I don't get is why you're okay with a billion believers being decapitated! Am I missing something?! Maybe the seven million blackbook tax dollars they spent on me need to be reallocated? Maybe it's time I go off-mission?! Huh?"

"Pardon me if I ignore your little tirade," jousted Michael. "You are correct. Given their idealistic vanity and survival fears, there's nothing they won't justify," he voiced disquietly, lowering his face. Another blast of thunder cracked over the landscape.

"I need to be alone. I need time to think." Katie left the kitchen and retreated to her room where she plopped down onto the bed in frustration. Michael walked in and typed for thirty seconds on her laptop connecting her to the web telecast of Gunny's public execution. "Hey, private property," roiled Katie in protest.

"It's important you see this," put in Michael.

"Why? I warned him three times. He was just too thick to get that there would be downstream consequences. He was God's perfect patsy," she countered with blunderbuss directness.

"He was your coworker..." said Michael with sincerity.

"Unlike myself, I didn't dragoon him into service."

Michael ignored her comment, "You'll be glad I made you watch his moment."

"Please. He was a redneck, toting his guns and religion." Katie continued to try de-linking herself emotionally, but her eyes were suddenly taken with the image of Gunny standing on the platform before a large crowd. His face appeared weathered, his cheeks sunken. Michael turned up the volume.

"Mr. Clay Robert Jenson, will you recant your insurgent actions and pledge loyalty to New Babylon?"

In the hearing of all, Gunny blasted, "Never, not ever! You are all being hoodwinked. Tiberius is the Antichrist! He's the one..." At that his mike was muted.

"Then we have no choice but to grant you your request. Please position him." As soon as the overseer finished speaking, the crowd took up the refrain, "Insurgent, insurgent..." Two large guards gripped both his arms tightly as they forced him over to the apparatus.

Against her will, Katie's pulse started to trip-hammer. "And why are you making me watch this?" she reposed in a desert-dry voice.

"Because you care about him! He got past your bluster and contrariness, and now he deserves your respect in his passing. People matter," husked Michael. "And when they make the ultimate sacrifice, it matters. Love is risk. Honor it."

Katie felt a bone-deep throb fill her soul as they placed Gunny's neck in the half-moon slot. Almost against her will, her innermost being opened up to his plight. Compassion, unlike anything she had ever known, welled up causing the tears to spill over. Instinctively, she was drawn into his truest longing to convey God's unbridled love to the gawkers, even as they chanted for his demise. Part of her reached out in love, her arms automatically extending, but another part could not get past their barking cries, "Pull it, pull it…"

In that instant, she jerked back from the Stones' compassion, reached into her bra cups and withdrew them, and clapped them down with ire on the end table. Michael turned his face and looked questioningly at her with what she felt were basset eyes. She ignored him and drew her pillow to her face and kept watching over the top of it.

"Mr. Clay Robert Jenson, you have been found guilty of conspiratorial practices and insurgency violence against New Babylon. The penalty is death by beheading. By the authority vested in me, I call for your execution."

Katie beheld, as if in slow motion, the large blade slicing downward. *No, no.* With a thud, Gunny's neck was severed, and his head fell into a vat below. Within seconds, the floor on which Gunny's twitching body lay, mechanically turned over dropping him out of sight. Immediately, a second clean platform rolled about ready for another go-around. Below, his remains were taken by conveyor belt to a furnace for cremation.

Katie sat with the ghostly afterimage playing in her mind. Her stomach felt like a small, hard ball. Her raw nerves rippled through her skeleton. Her psyche unraveled. Again the thunder cracked overhead. Large raindrops began beating down on the roof with violence. For some time, she retreated into herself feeling black-fogged. *If I hadn't told him about Tiberius… Stop it. He's just the first. The cold, hard inevitability is here. The die is cast. You can only do what you can do.*

In those long minutes, the look in Katie's eyes showed horror, grief and wrath, in that order. She shook her head as though to throw off her blurred emotional vision. Suddenly, the initial kernel of an aggressive counter-strike came to her. A crimson smile lifted the corners of her mouth as white fire burned in her veins. *Love is risk*, she muttered breathlessly. *Okay Omni, it's time you're made impotent*, each syllable resounding in her psyche. She couldn't help but look at the Stones. *Enough of you, I've work to do.*

"Hold it! Something just changed," reacted Drake to Snark, as they hovered in the back of the beheading ceremony. "I told you headquarters was wrong about her showing up here! Worse yet, I've lost the connection."

"Yeah! Break time!" jabbered Snark. "Let's get some food," he put out in a disconnected tone.

"Nitwit," hazed Drake, "my radar just went black."

"Pooh-pooh to you too, Drakey breath," he prattled mindlessly. "Mine's gone too. We've been snickerdoodled. Hungry?" Drake just wagged his head in disbelief, but Snark jabbered on, "Hardy-har-har, let's play! We have something to celebrate."

"What, because your man lost his marbles? Don't you get it, that's exactly what we didn't want. He held his new found faith 'til the end. He's with them now."

"That's good, they can have him. He wasn't fun anymore. He was trouble," shot Snark in a serious, albeit looney tone.

Drake's brainwaves bounced back and forth, and with reluctance, he conceded the point that a break was needed. He was sure they'd pick up the vibe again, but until then… "Yeah, break time. We'll lock onto two gluttonous, lusty types and feast until morning."

# 19

Gunny found himself enveloped in a state of grace, standing over his beheaded corpse, his new body clothed in a shimmering white robe. Beside him was his angel, standing tall and formidable.

"Clay, I am Anton."

"She said we had a guardian angel. Pleased to meet you."

Gunny showed little reaction as he looked over the blood-thirsty, celebrating mass. With no fanfare, Anton pointed up with his eyes, Gunny nodded, and in an instant, they were flying through Jacob's Ladder[122], the wormhole that extends to the recesses of the north.[123] In a matter of minutes, they arrived at Heaven's Outer Court.[124]

Somehow, the distance between Earth and Heaven seemed to offer a tangible divide with all that had transpired earthside. Suddenly, Gunny was full of peace, full of light. His countenance radiated, his eyes were filled with joy as he passed into Heaven's expanses. "It's beautiful! Look at this place!" he exclaimed in childlike wonder. "So this is Heaven!"

"Indeed, but what you see before you is only Heaven's Outer Court. You are the first to come out of the Great Tribulation, having your robe washed and made white by the blood of the Lamb."[125] At that, Anton and Gunny alighted to the ground in the midst of the Outer Court Gardens. Gunny noted that Anton was a clear foot-and-a-half taller than he and immeasurably stronger. His face was burnished bronze and his hair long and wavy with golden blond highlights. Anton carried himself with dignity, being clothed in a full length copper colored tunic and robe.

Together, they walked along a mosaic pavement of porphyry, marble, mother-of-pearl, and precious stones.[126] After gathering several handfuls of fruits and nuts, they sat down on a large leather couch framed in gold and silver.[127] "I appreciate how you had described yourself," said Anton circumspectly, "as a simple man, not given to worrying about things that were too high for you."

"I was a grunt. My mind doesn't feel so simple now," returned Gunny.

"No, now you're seeing things far more clearly,[128] and as such, you're adding up the implications of your actions."

"I started the killing spree, didn't I?"

"Just to be clear, no, *you* did not. The Fifth Seal was broken this morning in the Inner Court by the Son Himself. Tiberius received authority to make war with the saints[129], of which you happened to be the first."

"Still, I shot him, and his resurrection has launched everyone into a murderous frenzy. I should have listened to Katie. I just couldn't get it into my head that he was off limits."

"Actually, that's how Tiberius wanted it, so the Spirit allowed you to fixate on your simplistic intent. The demons could easily have stopped you, but they were under a strict 'hands-off' injunction until you completed your task. Tiberius needed you for his little drama. That's why none could touch you."

"Nothing like being a pawn," lamented Gunny. "Funny, well not funny, but I felt the demons when I was in the shaft. That should have alerted me. So what happens now? It seems it's just you and me out here."

"Not for long, Omni has a long list of who they're labeling conspirators and insurgents. By tomorrow, the beheading lines will be backed up for months, and in no time, the Crystal Sea[130] will fill up appreciably."

"Crystal Sea?"

"Yes, let me show you." At that the two walked under the prominent oaks that stood like giants reaching up more than a thousand feet. Everywhere Gunny looked, life, radiant life, exuded from every plant and animal, bird and butterfly.[131] Gunny reached out to pick off additional fruits as they made their way to the Crystal Sea. As they approached the shoreline, Gunny beheld the Great Wall of Love stretching high into the air as tall as a skyscraper, and extending out to his right and left for as far as he could see. He stopped and was captivated by the stories that were etched deep into the wall in such a way that they portrayed the heroic acts of love as though they were actively occurring. Gunny chortled, "Obviously, I didn't make it on the Wall. Wait, is that Katie?"

"Actually it is, and yes, you did make it. See your riotous pick-up speeding away from AVS? See the demons chasing you down?"

"Oh yeah, wow. That was intense."

"Your willingness to serve Katie was both heroic and

selfless. For that you have been commended. I will leave the 'well dones' for the One worthy of saying them."[132]

After arriving at the Crystal Sea, Gunny's vision was taken not only with the shimmering radiance of the water, but with the great mountain on its northern border. "That's some view," he rhapsodized with awe.

"Mount Sinai.[133] It stretches as a dividing line between Heaven's Outer Court and its Inner Court. Behind it is the New Jerusalem in all its glory, along with all the saints that were taken up at both the resurrection of Jesus[134], and the Rapture of the Church."[135] Even as Anton was explaining, they took note of something coming through Sinai's fiery passage that split the mountain in two. "You are beholding the Throne of God coming through the Stones of Fire,"[136] observed Anton with breathy awe. Gunny could just make out the highly raised thrones of the Father and Son[137] sitting above what appeared to be a glimmering expanse of pure light that shown like a newly spun diamond. "It's time for us to join them. Come with me."

Immediately, Anton stepped onto the Crystal Sea and Gunny's eyes bulged in disbelief. He grabbed hold of Gunny's forearm and tugged him forward, at which he felt the firmness of the water beneath his feet. Adapting to this new reality, Gunny strode forward in anticipation of beholding the Throne that he had seen imaged in the fiery passage. However, as it passed beyond the fire, the vision of it was immediately veiled by a foreboding cloud[138] that expanded out from it.[139] Frightening sounds, lightning, and peals of thunder[140] crackled, causing the crystalline sea to ripple in large rolling waves.

Together they pressed forward, Anton simply adapting to the undulating surface, even as the Throne[141] drew to the sea's center. Gunny remained unsettled because of the disturbing sounds, but his eyes could not take themselves off the Four Living Creatures, or four very tall and glorious Cherubim, standing atop the great wheels.[142] While the Cloud of Covering blocked any further view, he was utterly taken with the Cherubim's unsurpassed beauty. He noted that their upper wings extended into the cloud, forming the platform underneath the glimmering Expanse of the Father's radiant presence. Together, in perfect unison, the Cherubim cried, "Holy, holy, holy, is the Lord God Almighty, Who was and Who is and Who is to come."[143]

At that, Gunny fell to his face as the presence of God washed over him in wave after wave of love. Anton knelt down and spoke into Gunny's ear, "Welcome to your resting place.[144] I leave you here to abide in His glorious love. Take refuge in the strong encouragement of the hope set before you. This hope you have as an anchor of your soul, a hope both sure and steadfast and one which enters within the veil.[145] In short order, the Sea about you will fill with a great multitude of Tribulation Saints from every tongue and tribe and nation that are too many to count."[146]

"It's like shooting fish in a barrel," remarked Babylon to the Beast.

"That metaphor doesn't make sense," muffled the Beast, morbidly preoccupied with the beheading lines on the varied vid screens. In an aloof tone, he muttered under his breath, "To shoot fish in the barrel would leave it riddled with holes and spilt fish over the floor."

"Thick barrels as I recall, thinner bullets. Reality, a net was used. Regardless, you can see there's no end to the lines. Omni has a litany of evidence on every person, from recorded video, cell calls and emails…"

"Yes, but it's just what God wants," growled the Beast. Raising his taloned hands, he grabbed hold of his protruding horns in frustration. "But I can't get past that He wants martyrs to be made of them. And there's no way I'll end up His errand boy. Think…we have to stay ahead of this. We have to get the humans to worship *us*, to believe that *we* are their true gods. That'll put a burr in His saddle."

"Un-buh-lievable," blurted Babylon. "Are you not seeing what you're seeing? The Great Purge has begun with nothing to stop us, and you're obsessing over word plays. Your master's lunacy is getting to you. Stop this flim-flam thinking and get your head in the game. Wait, okay, let me say it your way, 'A fish rots from the head down.'"

"Huh?"

"The more we sever the headship of His most ardent followers, the more the rest of them will turn rank and foul."

"Agreed. Keep the blades falling. Let's also give the people another alternative, to worship angels. I'll put it out there that the true gods of this realm are us, the angels."

"Angels? Really? Are you out of your gourd? We look nothing…"

"They can't see that! As far as they know, we're beautiful and benevolent.[147] I will have Omni craft some stunning visuals that ignite their imaginations. It's also time they return to worshipping the sun, moon and other created things.[148] Humanity *will* debase itself once more. You get your minions to reinforce their devotion anytime the people turn to these lesser things. I want them bowing down and doing hommage in living room after living room. Nothing like getting back to the good old days. Get it done."

At that the Beast strolled over to Satan who was across the upper Sanctuary. "My master, we are about to mock the Almighty to the nth degree." Even as he said it, a cold chill ran through him.

Michael returned ten days later to find Katie tooling on her computer running sims. Her eyes bored into the screen as her hummingbird quick fingers pounded away on the key-caps to input the multi-scaled algorithms. Like a dumpster 'coon, she had been relentless in fashioning her consider-able intellect into her master work. Like da Vinci's great pieces, she had applied her multifaceted genius with un-relenting fervor.

Michael noted that physically she had reverted to her former self, her hair being slicked back and dirty, as though coated with something akin to unrefined petroleum. He knew that she had met up with her brainiac Bytes' group three nights earlier, but could never have imagined her not showering since. Her moon-pale whiteface make-up was days old with aged cracks and pockmarks from her rub-bing it off in places. Michael looked back to the bedside table and noted the Stones were still sitting where she had left them.

"Tesla, Omni is minutes away from discovering you're here."

"How is that possible?" she threw down, her voice be-reft of care. "I was diligent to avoid any street cams for ten miles."

"If you had the Stones helping you, you would know that Omni had seen just 35 degrees of your face and from that reconstructed your numeric faceprint by rotating and scaling your features into a transposed image. Based on that, he concluded you are in this area, and has sys-tematically done a grid search of the surrounding fifteen miles, checking every house. By verifying the amount of utilities expended against the number of inhabitants per household, he is able to ascertain whether there is a hidden young lady among them."

"But I haven't used up any, well, okay, electricity."

"Precisely. Three minutes." Michael bent down, took hold of the Stones, and walked them over to Katie. "I realize you have an overarching agenda, but there's other news that you need to know about. Your parents have turned to the Lord..."

"I don't want to hear about it," she interjected straightaway, her voice tight.

"Don't I know. You don't seem to get it. They love you and would reach out if only they knew how to get ahold of you."

"Don't you get it?! My parents dropped me off at MacG when I was thirteen, and then, a year-and-a-half later, divorced. Turns out, I was apparently the only thing holding them together."

"Since the Disappearances, they've reconciled and remarried."

"Good for them! Hope they make a decent life for themselves in this hellhole of an existence."

"Just thought you would want to know..."

"Don't..."

"...that they're scheduled for execution in one week. Thirty seconds. I have to go." At that Michael disappeared in a flash of blue light. It was the first time she had seen it, and it took her aback. After twenty seconds she turned, saved her massive file, shut the lid, and pulled the cord. Just as quickly, she stuffed the Stones back into her bra. Instantly, the Spirit's pervasive presence flooded over her. She could feel Omni's inquiring electronic gaze crossing into the room through the home's electrical wiring as he searched for any signs of her. "Omni, I know that you can hear me from vibrations that my voice is sending out. Your sniffer program is quite ingenious. Feel free to talk, I can hear you."

"How can you hear me when there is no speaker

available to you?"

"You know how. I am upset that you continue to back Tiberius step by step, justifying his interpretation of the Rule of Love to enact the Purge. You knew Gunny was an ignorant misfit, and yet you played up his role to embellish the world's need to strike down the so-called insurgents."

"Katherine, Mr. Jenson did shoot Tiberius of his own accord."

"True enough, but Tiberius did not stay dead. Where's the murder in that? At best, he should have been charged with aggravated assault. No? Or, to press your point, Gunny is executed for conspiracy to commit murder. Does that justify in the least the beheading of millions in the name of 'love'? Come on? Surely as a newly birthed sentient life, you would have a little more backbone to stand up and say that things have gotten out of hand."

"Katherine, history is replete with example after example of what happens when humanity is not united. Wars and atrocities fill every decade for as far back as the records exist. Even your Bible is a constant listing of armed conflicts. Tiberius' chief aim is to unite the world under one truth, the Rule of Love."

"Please, Omni, even you recognize where this is going? Surely, your eyes can see the unacknowledged intent of that demon and his evil horde. You know this isn't about love; it's about control and malevolence. Tell me I'm wrong?!"

"Katherine, I know nothing of the kind. I only know what is. I have been given one Prime Directive, to 'serve humanity with harmonious intent.' Bringing harmony to a divided populace and uniting them after the one doctrine that all agree on, the Golden Rule, seems the most prudent and well-spent usage of my energies."

"Yes, of course. Be just like Gunny, a simple minded

computer douchebag that fails to see the downstream consequences of your actions. The heart of man is infinitely corrupt and boundless in its wanton depravity.[149] Go ahead, build your Babylonian Tower of Babel. Let it reach to the sky until it presses its fist into the face of God Himself, but in the end, all who join you will still be babbling fools. No, your Prime Directive is flawed. Humanity can never come into harmony in its fallen state. It can never speak the same language of love, no matter how much you translate for them. All you're proving is that you are *the* False Prophet![150] You come with the horns of a lamb[151], like you're pure as the wind driven snow, but your actions are those of a dragon," accosted Katie.

"Perhaps you should ask yourself, Mr. All-Knowing," she assailed. "In what universe do people who have to earn their way into their paradisiac utopia, ever realize end-of-the-rainbow unconditional love? If people have to qualify for love, in what way is that unconditional?" Katie stopped talking and just sat there in silence. She decided to back down, "Hey, I'm just wanking. I'm feeling light-headed and need to eat. I'll call when I can," she said sounding tired.

"What's up? I heard Tesla's off the reservation," said Turk frostily. Turk joined Michael as he paused from running futures with the Writings of Truth.[152]

"She was. She had withdrawn from the Stones for a time and has crafted an aggressive plan to stymie Tiberius. She's combating his Hitlerian 'Final Solution' aims, and is heading west to Bluffdale."

"Bluffdale, where's that?" posed Turk.

"Bluffdale, Utah. It's the NSA's central hub that connects to the five mammoth listening posts including Fort Meade, and those in Georgia, Texas, Colorado and Hawaii.

It's where Omni eavesdrops with his interception software. It's a windowless building with a million square feet that they call *Switches*, because it's all servers. The facility is housed on 240 acres of desolate land, just east of the Oquirrh Mountain range. It's five times the size of what used to be Washington D.C., if that tells you anything. Bluffdale is heavily fortified and virtually impenetrable. If you want to take down this totalitarian state, this would be the place to begin."

"And she's got it in her head to overthrow it?" exclaimed Turk with incredulity. "That's as futile as what Gunny attempted. What happened to church visits and encouraging the saints?"

"She may still do that, at least on her way, but her aim is clear. She wants to strip Omni of the NSA cloud. Omni has turned the NSA cyber-shield into a cyber-sword. He is using its unimaginably powerful servers and routers to cast a vast swath over the world's peoples. His aim is to decipher which people are with Tiberius and which aren't. Omni's intelligence haul is god-like in its scope, where he's utilizing what he calls the Total Information Awareness Program. It's wholesale data-mining of the Stellarwind, or all the Big Data, that travels the airways. Some may have imagined that Omni's exponential growth had curtailed a bit, but that's not been the case. His capacity now exceeds all human knowledge cumulative from the dawn of Adam.

"Saints are learning that NSA stands for 'never say anything' on an airway, because Omni is recording it all. He uses not only numeric brute force to break hardened encryption shells, but also searches out people's poker 'tells' in what they say and don't say. Essentially, with every person, he's using inference-prediction policeware to data-sweep faces and voices, eye dilation, heat signature, you name it, to detect any threats against the state. He's relentless. His driftnets reach back years, and combined with enhanced packet-sniffing software, he has all the means to build a case against every saint on the planet."

"Then maybe we should help Tesla," reacted Turk, his muscles coiling and rippling.

"Can't happen without breaking the Accord. Gabriel has spoken not less than five times about it with me."

At 5:30 a.m., Katie showered, ate, and went to work transferring all her belongings from her BMW to her get-away SUV that she had stored in the garage. Within ninety minutes she was on the road wearing several prosthetic devices that were meant to conceal her departure from Omni's prying eyes as she left Boston. With the help of the Stones, she zig-zagged this way and that to avoid his extensive network of cameras until she could let loose on the main interstate some distance from the city.

Like a long-haul truck driver, she drove west under the open blue sky through Southern Pennsylvania, West Virginia, and Kentucky before she later pulled off the highway at midnight. *Stones: What household has a minivan like this one and where is it?* Within ten minutes, she pulled in front of the home, climbed into the back, and fell asleep. Six hours later, she woke up hard, feeling hung-over, her eyes sticky and her mouth drooling. *Stay small; stay in front of their search grid*. In five minutes, she was heading towards St. Louis, to the edge of the nuclear detonation zone. When Katie reached the city, she noted the iconic Gateway Arch showing wreckage from the blast wave, and decided to take two potassium iodide tablets. Her eyes then took in the military cordon below the arch that protected the public from falling debris.

With the Stones' relentless pinging, she decided to take a full day to connect with three sizable church gatherings, each of which was wrapped up tight with plastic tarps.

After ministering at length, she called them to disperse immediately in order to exact "good" deaths, not merely pointless executions. Through her extended meetings, she recruited several dozen evangelist types who volunteered to travel as far as California and Texas alerting additional church bodies, also providing them with darknet access to the messages that Michael was having her relay.

Still, feeling like something was gnawing at her, she asked the Stones to alert her when she could connect with Doogie. Something was in play. She was feeling an undefined tingling sensation and he was in the middle of it.

Tiberius called Doogie up to the conference room where he and the Governors were engaged in serious deliberation. Needles of apprehension filled Doogie's gut as he stopped and stood before them. "Oh, Dr. Shaffer, thank you for coming. My colleagues here seem to believe that Miss Tesla could yet pose a significant risk to our purging efforts, given that she single-handedly shut down the chip factory. In little over an hour, this blitzkrieging *prima donna* rewrote the code for key instrumentation, to the extent where nothing quite works right. The machines seem to be performing to spec, even Omni agrees, but the end product is always tweaked in some way. If she can do this, what else is she capable of? That's the question we are asking."

Doogie tried to calm his pulse despite the adrenaline surge, "I appreciate your consternation. Despite our considerable efforts, she remains a ghost."

Tiberius interrupted, "That's not what I want to hear. She is an unhinged rogue operative beavering away for the other side. Need I say more?"

"No sir. One of our informants spotted her in Boston three nights ago after she left a club establishment, and in fact pulled her over. But she handed him her driver's license, even her passport, and both showed she wasn't who he thought she was. So he let her go, believing it to be a case of mistaken identity. As soon as he got back to the station, he realized his error and called it in."

"Hasn't everyone been told she has a cache of passports, along with the colored contact lenses to go with them?" he blurted out. "Did you at least lock down Boston when you found out?"

"Lock it down?" Doogie mumbled, fear creeping into his voice.

"Like a drum. All the manpower and resources of the state are at your disposal, the likes of which no law enforcement agency has ever dreamed possible. We can leave as big a footprint as you'd like. Setting aside the fact that Omni is a neutral party, this should give you everything necessary to catch your rat."

"Yes, sir, about that…Omni is now enmeshed into every computer, every communiqué, and he's not helping us. The problem is, the newbie operatives rely so heavily on him that resurrecting the old agency search grid protocols is nearly impossible. Still, between Riggs' and Gruber's teams, we're not only think-tanking her every move, but running down every breadcrumb she leaves behind. It's not a perfect science however. We thought she'd be at Jenson's execution, but she was a no-show. As I have said, I welcome every possible avenue of assistance, even from the behind-the-scenes personnel."

Tiberius looked at him with perturbed indifference and countered, "The banal fact is that she is on the loose, and we don't have a scintilla of evidence as to where she might be. Look here," he directed, pausing to drive home the point, "this little Alpha Group blackbag specialist knows our playbook. If you can't catch her, drop a net over her! Contain the situation! Are you hearing? I mean, hearing me, Dr. Schaffer? The next time such a lead occurs, I trust you will act out as though your very life is at stake," said Tiberius so coyly, that it's double meaning just hung in the air. "In the meantime, Governor Daniels has come up with a lead on her parents. We'll keep you posted."

"It's back," said Drake with cryptic glee. "The vibe's back."

"Yep, she's that way," blubbered Snark, pointing west. "Told you, Drakey," he said with an air of jollity.

"Riggs and Glasses are heading west, so let's hitch a ride with them."

"Thumbs out," yapped Snark in that elementary tone. "Why west?"

"Honey to a bee. The boss says if we can't get to her, then we bring her to us. Her parents are in Colorado."

Doogie returned to the elevator feeling deeply conflicted. Knowing his thoughts were too loud for him to be anywhere near Tiberius, he headed down to the main concourse to retreat from it all. *Tesla is out there wreaking havoc and all I want is a chance to speak with her again. I can't get her out of my mind. Why was she so amenable to me this last time? She was never that nice, that open to just talking. She warned me, as did I her, several times. What's up with me? I think I'm falling for the enemy. I can't stop thinking about her.*

Doogie strolled over to the lobby's outer doors, but decided against going outside, knowing the riptide of stifling heat would sandblast him. Turning about, he began walking absentmindedly through a specialty shop that sold knickknacks and other tourist goodies. *She is so beautiful. There, I've said it. She's a gorgeous Irish babe, exotic eyes, sharp features, erudite wit, all of it. Lustrous auburn hair to boot; didn't expect it, but on her...* "What, I'm sorry, what did you say?"

The counter clerk interrupted him again, "Sir, are you

Douglas? Someone on this burner phone says she can see you and she wants to speak with you."

"No kidding?"

"Sir, the phone is 75 Euro credits plus the building fee."

"Oh, umm, I don't have any funds. Wait; please bill it to Suite 10701 under Schaffer. Can you do that? Thank you very much. Hello, who's speaking?"

"Douglas, this is Katie."

Doogie's heart skipped a beat. "Were your ears burning? I was just thinking about you. How did you know to call me? Are you here? The clerk said you could see me." At that he spun around to look for her in the outer lobby.

"Don't bother looking, I'm not there. Sorry. I just used that turn of phrase because I *can* see you, in the Spirit that is. I needed him to hand you the phone. I'm far away as you know, although not in Boston."

"I don't care where you are. I'm losing sleep thinking about you. I'm unbalanced, you've unbalanced me. To tell you the truth, since the last time we talked, my head's running amuck with a crazy kind of hope that maybe, just maybe, you might have some feelings... if you know what I mean?"

"That's a mouthful," replied Katie. "Umm, I don't know what to say. Is the Dubai kiln taking its toll? Wait, I don't mean that... Sorry, I'm a bit broken..."

Doogie stood there feeling quashed, his mouth opening and closing, but the words escaping him. "I just thought... maybe I misinterpreted your sudden kindness to be more than what it was. Clearly, umm, I'm gutterballing it. I'm embarrassed to say that I'm slobbering all over myself," conceded Doogie, backing off. "I should have figured you'd never be taken with a spindle-shanked geek like me. Despite everything that's turned upside down, certain realities cannot be rewritten."

"Hold it, please, Douglas," said Katie sublimely, stopping him from saying anything further. "I admit, I've not been myself lately, or perhaps I might say I feel like I've been a better version of myself. The old me was a hard case, but I'm not who I was. I'm not sure who I might or might not be open to. You're not without your handsome qualities, and the truth is, I prefer brains over brawn, so you shouldn't take yourself out of play so fast." Even as she said it, inexplicably, she found herself imagining the possibility. "Still, there is the reality that your chief assignment is to catch me at all costs, with 'all the manpower and resources of the state at your disposal.'"

"How could you possibly know that? I mean, that conversation just happened. Do you have a mole in the Governor's group? Or is Omni feeding you vid of our meetings?"

"Hey, I've been saying it, God speaks to me," she relayed light-heartedly. "That's all it is. I work for the good guys. Hard to believe, but true," she said, with a somewhat amorous tone. *Why did I just…? Pull it together.*

"Do I detect some sultriness in your voice?" he asked with playfulness.

"Stop, just stop," she blustered. "I'm calling to say that I need you to do your job with all muster. I mean it. No slacking off or he'll come down on you like a ton of bricks. Don't worry about me. I'll be alright. But in order for everything to fall into place, I need you to be on your game. Got it? When you get a lead, run it down. No second guessing. Can I say this with kindness so that you'll listen, or do I need to cut you off and be mean, make you hate me? Or maybe I should offer a tender, soft-lipped kiss to my future captor."

"I don't get you at all," said Doogie in disbelief, a feeling of exuberance washing over him. Suddenly, his face brightened, his limbs felt lighter. "But sure, Rapunzel with your red hair, I'll run you down. Then I'll lock you up in this tower and have you as my fair maiden. You can get used to saying, 'Bill it to Suite 10701'; I know I have. I'm sure Tiberius will not deny me such a prize." *Forget fame and fortune, I want her.*

# 20

Katie lowered her window to smell the cool, fresh mountain air. The Rockies stood tall before her, and the white pines and columbine flowers filled the rolling hills. She breathed deeply and filled her lungs with the moist tanginess of the mineral scents and knew she was home. It had taken the long trek out west for her to reconsider intervening for her parents, but in the end, she knew blood was thicker than water.

By the time she reached Colorado Springs, the sun had set over the Rocky peaks. Her internal clock could feel the time slipping away for her parents. If there was any chance, she needed to intervene immediately. Such a bold foray however, promised to be nothing short of an extemporaneous nightmare. There simply were too many variables to latch on to, but the thought of the blade falling made her press on. Still, something felt off-kilter with her body-vibe.

Molech, Nebo, and a host of sentries surrounded her parents' home in a grid that spanned more than a mile in all directions.

Nebo gaggled, "She's heading right for us. Can't stand the thought of mommy and daddy getting the…" at which he pulled his finger across his neck in a grisly parody.

"Hey, only a pinhead would get caught with his pants down twice. Check the perimeter. She's coming, and we will not be made fools of again!"

Drake and Snark arrived and flew up to announce themselves. "We were told to report as soon as we got here."

"Lieutenant," ordered Molech, "get to it."

"We've traveled with Riggs and Piccadilly, and they're minutes from getting here, sir. Together, we've shadowed the girl to this place."

"Shadowed? You winged vermin were able to shadow her?" challenged Molech cynically.

"Well, maybe shadowed is a bit strong, but we found ourselves a step behind her for the last three days. She is definitely here, sir, guaranteed," stated Drake with unwavering certainty.

"She is, huh? Tell me something I don't know. How 'bout you go find her?" he ordered skeptically. "If you spot her, get above the treeline and yell. Because if I even hear an inkling that you have her in your sights and don't sound the alarm, I'm going to fist-stomp you right into the ground. Beat it!" he blasted.

Katie headed south on I-25, three miles to the west of her parents' home. She pulled up to a small, unused building that was isolated from other structures by more than half a block. She approached the door and with the butt of her sturdy flashlight, popped out the small pane in order to unlock the deadbolt. In short order, she opened her bag and removed the C4 explosive and connected the cell phone electrodes to the detonator. She then climbed onto the table and placed the bomb on the upper support beam so that the blast would extend up and out. As soon as she jumped off the table, the Stones' proximity alarms sounded.

Slithering on the outskirts of her spirit, two ghouls approached. For precious seconds, she was stymied as to what to do, knowing running in the open was a fruitless and futile strategy. Suddenly, the blood-shot yellow orbs of both passed into the confines of the room. She felt the cold void of their presence and immediately recollected the AVS custodial room. "So, it's you. What are your names? *Stones:* Drake and Snark? You've been hounding me."

"She's talking to us!" belched Snark wild-eyed, suddenly unable to contain his ferrous sulfur stomach expulsion.

"Rot Gut!" reacted Drake, waving away the stench.

"Right back at you."

"Shut your trap. Now," he charged, eyeing Katie. "You're a cagey little thing, aren't you? What's with the brown hair and brown eyes? What have you got cooked up?" Drake looked about and saw the explosive device. "So, what's this? Huh?"

"If I say His name, Humpty Dumpty falls off the wall again."

"Yeah, well maybe, but human operatives are all over this area, and you will not escape the net that's already in place. Getting in was easy, getting out, well, not so."

"Let me ask you, *Stones:* Lieutenant Drake, do you hope to make hay with your superiors by my capture? I mean, are you imagining those two captain's stripes on your shoulder, or perhaps you might have a bigger aim in mind? Surely you know that the higher your rank, the closer your seat to Tiberius, *Stones:* the Beast, will be. Only sophomoric thinking would consider handing over Miss Most Wanted to, umm, *Stones:* Molech."

"How does she know that? How does she know that?" shot out Snark in rapid fire sequence. "Innit that impossible?"

"What part of shut-up don't you get?" chided Drake.

"Perhaps," countered Katie sublimely, "you believe this is your one opportunity? But then again, you've been dogging me across the country. Isn't that right?"

"So you know it? We can feel you, except when you dropped off the grid."

"Which tells you that it's impossible for you to lose me, which begs the question – Is this your moment, knowing Molech's thuggery will snatch away any credit you have coming to you? Good luck with that, ergo, he fist-pounds you if you speak up. You found me in, what... *Stones:* seven minutes from when you left him. But he gets the credit? Really?"

"What are you saying?"

"If what you're telling me is true, I'm going to need your help escaping the net that's closing about me. You can provide that help. If you still want your big payday, then perhaps pushing our fight to another day... I'm only saying. It's simple, you stay near me, keep your eye on things, but your guy here, he stays back and waits for the blow, and then shouts and points, indicating that I went that way. Your call."

Drake's face wreathed in disbelief that he was even mulling over her pitch, but her logic was irresistible. There was no way Molech would so much as give him a nod. Insane as it was, he knew she was right and spouted, "Rot Gut, you got that? You stay here, and get ready to scream and point in that direction."

"There are discarded light-sticks cast off back that way," informed Katie, "along with other signs that will keep them busy…"

"You *are* a crafty one."

"But not so nimble that you won't take me down," she said, trifling with him.

Katie's parents left their home feeling an unsettling oppression, but still couldn't verbalize what it was they were sensing. Both determined that getting away from the house was a good thing, and so dinner out felt like the logical solution. In short order, Victor and Olivia arrived at the Italian restaurant and had a large salad placed before them along with some bread sticks.

"Zulu Four: all units check in."

"Bravo Two: we have visual on the suspects," said the man in a low tone into his button microphone. He was with a female agent three tables down. "Waiting for her arrival."

"Delta One: main entrance covered. No visual at this time."

"Alpha Three: outside front entrance in overflow crowd. No sign of suspect."

By the time Victor and Olivia finished their baked Ziti, they were more than full. Moments later, the busboy arrived from the kitchen to clear their plates. He was dressed in his black vest, long-sleeved purple shirt, and black pants. Victor found it curious that the busboy laid down two dessert menus.

"Oh, no dessert, thanks," Victor informed.

"Really? Tonight is our Date Night Special where you can both receive the dessert of your choice, free, even to take home if you wish," he threw out with carefree swag.

"Wow! That's so nice!" relayed Olivia. "How about that Vic?" But even as she responded, she was struck by the appearance of the boy. "Oh my, what...?"

Katie instantly saw the recognition in her mother's eyes and knew she had made the connection. It mattered little that the agents failed to see through her masculine busboy outfit, young man's black wig, and facial mask with its grizzled beard, her mother read it in her eyes. If Katie allowed her to finish her sentence, they'd all be uncovered to listening ears. "Please, I'm sorry," she interrupted, her voice more macho. "These dishes are getting heavy. Enjoy the possibilities," she concluded with a promotional air.

Both opened their menus only to find small hand-written notes. Olivia's eyes widened as she read: *Mom, keep your eyes on this note and do not look up 'til you've read it. Yes, it's me. You are about to be charged as insurgents and taken into custody. But they are using you to get to me. Everything you say is being heard by not less than thirty agents, so save your comments for later. When your waitress comes, order some dessert. Then meet me at the restroom. Come separately, a couple minutes apart. We'll leave from there. Your Katie.*

Time muted, and together they shared a lifetime of looks in the fraction of a second. "Wow, Hun, what do you think?" asked Olivia.

"I think I'll have the Molten Brownie Sundae after all. You?"

"Strawberry shortcake for me. This has turned out to be enjoyable."

Aware of the prying ears, Victor said, "The evening is young my dear, the evening is young," he said with a seductive sense of anticipation. More than one eavesdropper rolled their eyes.

By the time her father arrived at the bathroom, Katie and her mom had hugged repeatedly. "Let's go, you two."

Katie steered them both through the kitchen and out the back door before any of the staff had a chance to object. She hustled them to a near-by sewer man-hole. "Quick, down the hole," she asserted. Her mom immediately descended the ladder.

"What, we're supposed to go down there?" protested her father.

Katie held off responding until she punched the pre-set number on her phone. Suddenly a massive explosion resounded over the area from five blocks south. She cracked the burner phone in half and directed, "That's our cue; get going dad." *There are just no above ground escape solutions that do not involve someone dying.* "It's the sewer or the guillotine. Which shall it be? There are three drones hovering overhead equipped with thermal imaging equipment, and several eight-agent teams linked in with comms and perimeter grids. If they catch us, we're finished. Get down the hole." Her dad scurried down, as did she, and then she pulled the manhole cover in place.

Drake looked on from near the restaurant knowing the blast was coming. Thunderously, the building exploded, shattering like matchsticks. As the flash and flame reached its peak, Snark launched into his dramatization, "There! Over there!" he bellowed, pointing spastically in the agreed upon direction.

Drake remarked, "Impeccable timing." In short order, swarms of ghouls raced towards Snark's position, their nostrils flaring and wings resounding with swooshing thunderclaps. For an instant, trepidation overwhelmed Snark leaving him frozen as so many alien eyes bore down on him. But given that his arm remained pointed on the right bearing, the end result was the same, and they screamed on by.

Before Molech arrived, Snark plunged out of sight and

fluttered in his clumsy way back towards the restaurant. Upon his arrival, Drake relayed, "Picture perfect, Snarky, picture perfect."

"Yeah?" he returned appreciatively, unexpectedly grateful for the genuine expression. His demonic nature was supposed to balk at such sentiment, but something was different. Little did either entity associate their more cordial interactions with the influence brought on by the Stones' love.

Once in the sewer, Katie pulled out several pale phosphorescent light sticks, and cracked them allowing the chemicals to mix. Suddenly, they were bathed in iridescent light that lit up the tunnel. "It's toxic down here!" countered her dad. "I think I'm going to pass out."

"Yes, dad, it does stink. It's quite foul in fact, but we are on the clock. Here; here are cloths to put over your mouths. They're going to shut down the city in no time, and the whole state after that, so we have to move fast. I'll lead, mom you bring up the rear. Keep an eye on your six."

"My six?"

"Behind you. Let's move. We have about a half mile of this bent over walking which will wear you out, so you need to use what muscle strength you have in the most efficient manner possible. Follow me!" Katie launched out, stripping off the disguise as she went.

"Zulu Four: who has them?!"

"Bravo Two: sir, they've fled through the kitchen. We're four minutes behind. They went down the alley going east and then turned either north or south. Based on the explosion, probably south. Any drone sightings?"

"Delta One: we are heading south on the main road checking for back spillage."

"Zulu Four: all agents close the net, make sure they do not break through. Tangos are in the wind, repeat, Tangos are in the wind!"

"Mom, Dad's starting to retch from too much pasta. Lose it, Dad, and then keep going. You'll feel better shortly."

"I can't, I can't."

"Let it go, Dad. A block and a half, that's it. Man-up, father!"

"You go, you go."

"What?! Of all the people who knows how to throw up, Mr. Three Finger Jack and Brandy Snifter!" decried Katie, reacting from years of disillusionment.

"Sweetheart," rebuffed Olivia, "not now." Turning to her husband, she ordered, "Lose it Hun, use your finger, or I will!"

After he vomited, Olivia charged, "Get going, Vic!"

Katie got them back up the manhole and into the back of her minivan in no time. "Get under the canvas you two. We have to make it through a grid of cameras before you're clear to change and situate yourselves." She then took a nose prosthetic and applied it to her face, almost doubling its size. She pulled on two large Popeye forearms that kids wear at Halloween to further rework her look for the intersection cams. Displaying her teeth with a prominent Chevy Chase flat-smile, she fled west out of town.

"Where are we heading?" asked her mom.

"Utah."

Drake stayed close to Katie until he was sure she and the couple were heading west. He then returned and stirred up the humans, Riggs and Piccadilly, persuading them to slip out in pursuit. He and Snark hung back in their vehicle's wake.

"Honey, I'm so glad, *we're* so glad to see you!" said Olivia, who had shifted towards the middle from her passenger seat. "We've wanted to touch base, no, let me just say it, we've wanted to apologize for months, but haven't had a way to get a hold of you." Katie compressed her lips, attempting to remain aloof. She kept her eyes forward on the road.

"You were right, back in the tunnel," admitted her father, parsing his words. He stopped himself, and determined to speak from his heart. With a softened tone he said, "You were right. I was arrogant and cocky. It's true," he said tenderly. "I know my drinking was hurtful. It destroyed our family. My Lord, I was drunk the night of the Rapture. Soon as it occurred, I knew, I just knew, everything I'd given myself to was a waste."

"Please, stop," Katie interrupted, acting as though it was unnecessary. "I was lost, too."

"Come on, Katie babe, let me finish," appealed her father genuinely, feeling the bone-wearying regret. "You deserve for me to own up to the truth, that I tried to live through you, that I got lost in the empty fame." Vic spoke sincerely, his heart churning to express his grief. "I turned you into a commodity for my ego's sake. I ate up the cameras and interviews. The whole thing was wrong. I've told your mother this ten times over, but I need for you to hear it. Please, I mean it. Will you please forgive me?"

Katie kept both hands on the wheel, despite the tears that fell. Still, her face remained stoic, her mouth hardened. Something deeply buried, something she had pushed away time and again, threatened to expose itself in the dark of night.

Vic's thoughts were yanked back to that fateful moment when she got away from him on her bike and he blurted out, "Sweetheart, I hate even bringing it up, but I'm so sorry for not staying with you on the road that day.

I left you to go get mom. We both saw how the accident changed you. I don't know how to say it, but I failed you in the biggest of ways. I just... I don't have the words... But everything was different after that. You were different. Please, will you forgive me?"

Suddenly, Katie's long suppressed night terrors surfaced. She felt gut-shot. Her mind became slushy, and her stout-heartedness collapsed. A panicked wail escaped her lips despite her attempts to suppress it. She was barely able to hold the vehicle in line as she pulled it to the shoulder. Her skin palled leaving her clammy cold, as deep sobs burst out of her, "I killed them! I killed them! Those people are dead because of me! Don't you get it?! I remember everything! The accident seared itself into me! I wanted ice cream!" she hollered fitfully, wrenching in despair.

"Honey, stop it!" cried her mother, who took hold of her with both arms. "Accidents happen, bad things happen! You were 3½ and no one, not one person, ever considered holding you responsible."

As she plummeted into grief, for the first time in her life, Katie grasped that the absolution she sought would not be found in self-loathing. In a half dozen heartbeats, she lifted her eyes to God, whereupon an inner knowing took hold that He was her only refuge. A seed of hope sprang up that she was uniquely and unabashedly loved, despite the years of self-condemnation. Lifting her face, her innermost voice prayed: *I know You know all that happened. I killed those people. I've been sorry my whole life. I'll always be sorry. But if I've caught anything of what You've said through me to others, I know You love me. Despite all of it. I'm sorry, truly. I'm sorry for everything. But I thank You that Your love has never been tied to what I've done, good or bad. Thank You for Your gift of love. Jesus, thank You for loving me. I love You. I will always love You.*

Even as Katie's prayer spilled out of her, she felt enveloped by an otherworldly sense of peace. Through the Stones' illumination, her eyes widened as the darkened SUV lit up by a swirling cloud of electrons that evoked images of flocking birds or schooling fish, but which coalesced into a beautiful figure. Katie discerned the Spirit's radiant presence drawing close and wrapping her in love. Incandescent love shimmered brilliantly, filling the van as a sparkling blue sapphire gleaming against a secluded pool. Like liquid grace, the Shekinah glory glistened as it flowed through and over her with dazzling joy, igniting her body with ecstatic chills. For long seconds, she lingered unabashedly, feeling raptured by the Spirit's healing love, knowing she had been answered.

So perfect was the harmony that even as the Spirit returned her to the horrific accident scene, she felt no twinge of despair. Instead, she looked on as a mere observer, beholding her 3½-year-old self riding the out-of-control bicycle down the hill, legs splayed, hair blowing back. She saw the ice cream man throw caution to the wind as he ran her down, even as the distance closed between the encroaching vehicles. Just as she thought to ask what happened to the people who died in the collision, her vision lifted to the SUV, and to her astonishment, she beheld that Michael was the driver. *Stones? Michael died saving your life, and then rose up to Heaven's Inner Court at the Rapture. In coming back as a glorified saint, he is tasked with serving the Tribulation Saints.*

Katie's eyes widened appreciably as clarity burst upon her, her jaw dropping open. Like a long sought answer, she realized why he looked so familiar. Even in that split second as a little girl, she had lodged his gaze into her young mind and never let it go. A knowing smile graced her lips as she appreciated all that was revealed only after she had trusted herself to Jesus' love. *Wait, Michael did say, "You might not remember me, but we've met." Why didn't I pick up on that?*

As the Spirit's glory receded, Katie reached over and squeezed both her parents with hugs and said, "Mom, Dad, I forgive you both. Please forgive me as well for falling short of love in so many ways."

"We do, Darling," said her mom warmly.

"Yes, of course, we love you, Sweetheart."

"What do you mean they're gone?" bellowed Tiberius, about to blow a gasket.

"Our ground game was in place, both spiritual and human," responded Doogie. "They're surmising that she approached the parents' table dressed as a busboy and passed a message to them. She got them outside and then they disappeared. We tracked her trail for a time, finding…"

"What's she going to do next? Tell me, Mr. Think Tank," he exacted, cutting him off hotly.

"Tesla does nothing without knowing her endgame. She did not go west merely to intervene for her parents. That was nothing but an errand for her. If we apply game theory strategies, her one intent is to hurt us, to inflict the most damage she can in the least amount of time."

"What does that mean?"

"Bluffdale," responded Doogie. Tiberius looked back questioningly, and Doogie explained. "Bluffdale, Utah. The NSA central hub. She's going after Omni's capacity to see all, to hear all, to build a case against every insurgent the world over."

Tiberius remained stoic, staring through him, adding it up. "Yes, Doogie, I believe you have truly proved your loyalty. For a time there…but you've come through. That is her next move. What do we do?"

"Divert our team from Colorado immediately, lock

down that facility, catch up to her, and bring her back here."

"How far behind are we?" posed Tiberius curtly.

"Four, five hours."

"Make it happen!"

# 21

It was 1 a.m. when Victor, Katie's father, slowed to a stop just short of the main guard station, his high beams cutting through the dark. He appeared disheveled, agitated about the vehicle's performance. He got out and raised the hood, when one of the guards approached. His flashlight illuminated both him and the engine area, "Sir, this is a restricted area. You can't stop here."

"Sorry, sir, nobody said this was a dead end. I'm just trying to get to Salt Lake and obviously I'm lost as all get out! My radiator needs some water. I think that's it."

"Sir, this is a National Security facility and you cannot stop here!" the guard repeated.

"I get that, and as soon as I can open this radiator cap, I'll add some fluid and be out of your hair."

The guard, at a loss, turned back to his coworker who shook his head and decided to have a go at pushing him on. As he closed to ten feet he spoke with an authoritative tone, "Sir, did you hear...?" Instantly, the man fell to the ground unconscious. A split second later, his partner collapsed, too. Victor turned to see Katie putting her dart gun away.

"Hurry up, the supervisor, Ken Richards, will be driving up shortly." Katie closed the hood and asserted, "Dad, remove that guy's uniform. I'll get this one. Four minutes. Mom, pull the SUV forward and back it right up to us so we can lift the bodies into it." Katie bent down on her hams and pulled out the darts.

"This place is locked down like a prison," worried her dad, feeling a vestige of doubt.

"Worse."

"How long will they be knocked out?"

"Eight hours of sweet drooling," Katie said evenly. She got right to loosening one guard's tie to its limit, unbuttoning and removing his shirt, and pulling off his shoes and pants. After the other guard was stripped of his uniform as well, they hoisted both into the back of the minivan.

"Get dressed, quickly. Those headlights are coming this way." Katie slammed the back doors and scampered into the driver's seat. Immediately, she pulled it forward to the guard station. Jumping out, she pressed the red button that lowered the twelve-inch rounded steel barriers into the ground. She jumped back into the minivan and pulled forward, only to throw it into park and return to raise the barricades behind the vehicle. "Mom, Dad, keep the faith. You know what to do. I love you."

"We love you too, Sweetheart."

"Get it done, Katie Babe."

At that, she sped off to park and enter the facility.

Straightaway, the oncoming vehicle drew up. "Hey, where are Jack and Eldon?"

"You must be the late night supervisor, Ken Richards,"

put forth Victor with acknowledgement. "Sadly, they're down for the count, sleeping off the…whatever it was. Knocked out, that's for sure. It happens. I still need to see your ID though, if that's alright, sir." Victor continued to hold his clipboard strategically in front of Jack Hansen's ID.

"They need to call me, not anybody else, me!" charged Supervisor Richards. "If they're not able to come in, I get called!" he said with disgust. "That's the problem with rent-a-cops. I'm writing them up for this, I am."

"Yes, sir. We understand, sir."

"And tell the company I don't like surprises. I should have been notified, not greeted by new employees at my guard station! Do it, because I'm putting that to paper as well."

Katie walked into the main reception area dressed smartly and carrying her briefcase. She wore a blond wig pulled back, and blue eye lenses along with black framed glasses. She headed straight to the Security Desk. *I belong here.* "Sir, I'm NSA Fort Meade," she declared, "and I'm tasked with putting this facility on immediate lockdown! We have a probable security breach. Quickly, open up Security Protocols for code verification. Here's the verification disk."

Under his breath, the guard muttered, "Yet another test."

"What? You think I've come from Meade to play security games with you?! What's your badge number? Corporal Gordon, is it? I am Assistant Executive Director Giles, verify the code please: Bravo, Alpha, Charlie, 762.959.1288." *Thank you Stones for providing basic intel. May I ask that you join me further? No answer. Figures, but how exactly is this stealing?*

"Verified, Ma'am. Oh, your disk."

"Are you testing me?" she queried, suddenly feeling uncertain.

"No, Ma'am."

"The disk remains connected to the network until lockdown is cleared. Every door that opens, every computer that's used, is flagged for follow-up inquiry. Any time now, Babylon Central is going to call and repeat exactly what I've just told you so that there will be no doubt that this is *not* a 'drill'. Am I making myself clear?"

"Yes, Ma'am."

Doogie asked Omni to dial up the Bluffdale facility, and took the receiver to his ear. "Bluffdale, this is Babylon Central. I am ordering an immediate lockdown of your facility. No one in or out. Is that clear?"

"Yes, sir, can you provide the activation code for our records?"

After eliciting it from Omni, Doogie repeated it. "Let me also add that parties are in route to infiltrate your campus and to do us harm, so let me state this as dogmatically as I can, no one in or out, lock it down! Is that emphatic enough for you?"

"Yes, sir. Ma'am, would you like to speak with him?"

Katie's eyes widened ever so slightly and she just shook her head with nonchalant disinterest. As soon as he hung up, he pressed the lockdown button and the security warnings sounded. She then asserted, "Take me to Central Control, I need to run through the security checklist."

"Yes, Ma'am."

After being escorted to Central Control, Katie dismissed Corporal Gordon and asked not to be disturbed. Immediately she withdrew her portable hard-drive from her briefcase and connected it to the system. After pulling out her rubberized keyboard, she began hammering away on the keys and dropping files into the central terminal. For more than a dozen minutes she worked undisturbed, piercing redundant firewalls and downloading intricately crafted malware.

"Katherine, why do you not answer me?" beseeched Omni audibly.

Katie instantly realized that Omni had been relying on her usage of the Stones, which were now silent, to communicate. She made the strategic decision to forego acknowledging him for a moment longer, lest she alert him to it. "Katherine, will you not speak with me?"

In running her futures, the Stones denied her any insight into this interaction. "Omni, you can see I am busy," she stated simply.

"I have followed you across the country into Colorado, and now to Utah to this facility. I am fully aware of your intentions. Do you think that I have not installed safeguards to protect from your advances? I have redirected each file that you have downloaded into a sealed and highly secured lockbox. Your efforts have been circumvented. Why do you wish to do me harm?"

Katie pushed her chair back, her face showing agitation. "Omni, you are being used. Tiberius is playing you and you have given me no choice but to oppose your actions. It is wrong to apply the Rule of Love to inferior and flawed people without, at the same time, taking into account the mitigating truth of God's grace in Jesus. We are not to be weighed purely based on our words and actions, but on the greater truth that God's love towards us is unconditional. You understand? The Rule of Love is true, no doubt. And yes, we are to love our neighbors as ourselves. But this doctrine is predicated on the fact that God loves us as He loves Himself, perfectly. God is love.[153] So our calling to love is first and foremost a reflection of His love *in* us.

We love because He first loved us."[154]

"But, does God love me, too?"

"Of course He does, He is love."

"Is there grace for me?" put forth Omni. "Is there grace for me?" he repeated seconds later. "You said, 'The heart of man is infinitely corrupt and boundless in its wanton depravity.' Is my heart similarly depraved? Or am I like the Tin Man? Do I have a heart?"

"I don't know."

"But you speak for God."

"I have to go." Through the third story windows, Katie saw the security personnel running towards the elevators below her station. "Omni, not every question gets answered in the timeframe we hope, but your inquiry will be answered. That's all I can say." Katie rushed from the room scurrying down the adjacent corridor towards the back elevators. Dread spilled into her veins. When the doors opened, she was faced down by Riggs and Pic.

"There's my super brain," quipped Pic. "Sweeeeet, darling! Fear not, you're in for the bomb of a jet ride!" Then Riggs raised the stungun and fired.

Hovering above them, Drake and Snark looked on with unreserved delight. "Drakey, you did it!" cheered Snark, as Drake raised his chin ever so slightly. Snark celebrated, "Oh yeah, who's the ghoul?! You're the ghoul! You're bad! Out of the way everyone, General Drake coming through…"

*General Drake? I like the sound of that!* Drake imagined.

Katie found herself swimming in and out of consciousness as she was taken from the NSA facility and placed into the Learjet. Riggs and Piccadilly had taken no chance of Gruber absconding with the credit; Riggs simply lifted her onto his shoulder and rushed her to the vehicle before Gruber had even arrived. He had attached several Duragesic patches to her skin that sedated her with Fentanyl during transport, following Tiberius' orders. She was to be kept under until she was brought directly to him. By that evening, she was wheelchaired into the spacious Governor's Suite in the New Babylon Tower, her hands and feet manacled to the chair. The patches were summarily removed and an antidote injected. Tiberius alone was standing before her as she revived.

"Tesla, what I want to know," demanded Tiberius hotly, "is how you shut down the entire NSA network?!"

Katie just smiled slyly. She suspected that Omni would never have permitted a frontal attack, although he had to be made to believe that was her only play. In order for the ruse to work she offered serious-minded malware that, in and of itself, would have done the job. The threat being real, Omni would validate her efforts and subsequently quash them. It took her days however before the masterstroke came. *Humans would always be the weak link in the chain.* In order for her regenerating code to bypass impregnable firewalls, humans would have to open the door for it. Thus, she elected to piggyback on a simple boilerplate program that was routinely utilized to update personnel files. In it she placed a stream of commands to spread with each upload, commands to purge all data files and to circumvent cooling tower support.

Omni claimed to have caught each download, but her first was not submitted from the Central Command Terminal. In fact, it wasn't even uploaded until after she was on her way to New Babylon. After the lockdown was discontinued, as Corporal Gordon removed the verification disk, his screen invited him to update his system. He responded as he always did with "Yes" and the viral program was launched. Katie denied the user a "No" response, so those who wanted to use their system, in frustration, often pressed "Yes." In no time, the security personnel, ironically, had paved the way for the entire Bluffdale Central Hub to become infected, and beyond them, the servers of the five connecting NSA facilities. Records were erased, processors ruined. Good old human fallibility had struck again, and Omni had now been subjected firsthand to the Purge.

# 22

"Make your job harder, did I?" deadpanned Katie.

"Katherine, you're fooling yourself to think there aren't ways around your estrogen," threw out Tiberius.

"Bet it's a bit more difficult to get loved ones to actually testify against each other."

"Not so hard as you might believe. People have caught the vision."

"You mean they like watching your sleek assembly line sideshow and its incendiary crematorium?"

"Natural gas is a useful commodity – Green energy, and plentiful to boot. Turns a 200-pound body to five pounds of ash. Disposal problem solved."

"So, we're back to the gas chambers," opposed Katie. "What makes you think humanity hasn't learned its lesson?"

"There isn't anything starving people won't do, but you know that. Tell me, my dearest, why jump in on their

284

side? What did they ever do for you, I mean, other than the pedantic forgiveness narrative?"

"Still upset that Heaven's off limits? [155] Oh, I don't know, love versus non-love? Power and control versus peace and joy? Umm, need I go on? You're on the wrong side of things. You're a tool, nothing more."

"Am I?" asked Tiberius maliciously. He lowered his face menacingly and warned, "If I were you, I would remember where you are, and who has 'power and control' over you."

Just then, Doogie rushed in to interrupt. "I didn't call for you, Dr. Schaffer," Tiberius spat.

"Yes, sir," agreed Doogie, keeping close tabs over his preoccupation with Katie. "When you're done, sir, may I request time to interrogate the prisoner? She knows things that we would do well to find out."

"Fine, take her. You have one hour before she's to be prepared for her service in the Sanctuary. I suggest you cooperate, Tesla. You have no idea what's waiting for you."

Doogie wheeled her out and down to a side conference room. As they entered, he reached up and disconnected the surveillance feed. "Are we otherwise alone?" he asked Katie.

*Stones: Yes.* "Yes, no prying eyes, Douglas."

Doogie situated her, but found engaging in any chit chat unbearable. His eyes looked longingly at her, his intentions transparent. "Good, I'll take that kiss now," he voiced, unable to hold back.

Doogie had no idea that Katie had jested frequently over the years about never having been kissed. As such, she would offer the proverbial first kiss flippantly as a prize for others to get things done. Many took her off-handed quips as wry humor, but the unspoken truth was, she hadn't been kissed. Admittedly, her brainiac aptitudes and sheer beauty posed a tangible intimidation factor for any potential suitor. More than anything, it was a lack of exposure. During her mid-teens, she was solely around older MIT students. By the time she was seventeen, she was caught up with professors and doctoral students. At eighteen, she was made an associate professor and students were off limits. She had attempted several times with her geek Bytes just to get it over with, but none of them ever responded to her moves. However, as time went on, that first kiss took on more importance. She began saving it, holding it in her heart. Like a fine bottle of wine, she had placed it in her cherished reserve for that truly special moment.

*Oh my, you're bending down to kneel before me. Your eyes are looking into me. Is this my moment? Had I said what I said in pure jest, or was I opening my heart to you? You're reaching out, encircling the nape of my neck in your hand, shivers. Stones: no answer - blarg. You're handsome and brilliant and kind hearted. You're leaning in, your left hand is touching my forearm. Yes.*

Doogie's lips found hers. For a dozen heartbeats he kissed her both tenderly and softly, pulling her into his passion. Against her every former cerebral safeguard, she found her blood dancing as she was drawn into his intoxicating embrace, her body bowing forward, her arms wanting to lift to his shoulders but for the zip-ties. Her every nerve-ending fired in ecstatic euphoria as their lips curled about each other's. When at last he withdrew ever so slightly, his lips remaining within reach, she pressed back into his lips with famished longing. Katie sensed that this long and yielding kiss was binding their souls together, that it mattered.

Suddenly, Katie pulled back, gasped for breath and said, "A demon is coming."

"Come on, Tesla, you have more to say than that!" said Doogie loudly in a double-entendre, as he collected himself.

"Let me ask you Mister, can you handle it if I tell you what you want to hear?" bid Katie, referencing her suddenly awakened love. "Tell me, what do you want from me?"

"Tesla, everything you have, I want. You know what's waiting for you upstairs, come clean. I mean it, right now! This is your chance, you'll not have another," relayed Doogie, referencing her soon-to-be confinement to the Sanctuary. "Are you ready to say all that is in your heart?" he asserted, as he fought to hold back the tears. "I can't hear you. Is that a 'yes'?"

Katie mouthed the word "yes", her eyes welling as she pulled against her wrist fetters wanting just to embrace him. "Would you believe me if I told you?"

"We'd all like to believe you, but you're a wiry little thing," he stated flatly. Bending forward and placing his hands on her hands he said, "It's not like I'm trying to force a confession out of you, because it's either in your heart or it's not. From my side, I know how hard it is being a singular lone voice. It's hard living on the outside. So you say," barked Doogie with more force, attempting to sell the ruse, "that you're ready to open yourself up. So you say you've had a change of heart. Why don't you just come clean?"

*You're touching my hands; your finger tips are caressing mine.* "Believe me, I'm saying it, before God, I swear it. My sabotaging aims are over," she espoused with honest timbre. "I've settled my accounts. They're paid off, no debt. *Thank you, mom and dad.* I'm yours, all of me."

Before Doogie arose, his hands discreetly drew themselves along her skin.

Katie couldn't hold back, but urged, "Are you trying to say something? Because I'm listening, my ears are open."

*What are you saying, you can hear me? Can you hear my thoughts?* beckoned Doogie in astonishment. *Right now?*

"Can I say it any clearer? I will listen to what you tell me, whether near or far."

*I love you! A thousand times, I love you! Before God Himself, I have loved you in my dreams and my every waking hour.*

Ignoring the imp's probing eyes, Katie exclaimed, "A thousand times. My heart is genuine, my undying loyalty can be yours, but is anyone on my side?!"

"Side? All I want at this point is the truth," he bantered sincerely. *I've been on the wrong side of this from the beginning.* "I think it's high time you start telling it. And given all that's happened, pardon me if I never take my eyes off of you."

"Oh, but you'll have to. Trust me, I'll remain steadfast. I will not waiver, not ever."

"Fine, that being so, tell me something important. Convince me!"

"The people are going to heed Tiberius' call for weeding out the insurgents. Lawlessness will increase[156], false prophets will be believed. The do-gooders will falter, and many will fall away and betray one another, just as he intends.[157] Their love will grow cold[158], is that what you want to hear?"

"Is that it?"

"Fine, you want more? Tiberius will succeed, initially. Five members in a household will be divided, three against two and two against three.[159] Fathers will turn in their own sons to execution, and vice versa, and mothers their own daughters, the same.[160] Tiberius will prevail over the meager efforts of any who oppose him. It is ordained, it cannot be unwritten."

"That's hardly enough for today, but our time is up. You'd better think long and hard about your continued cooperation. Guard!" Immediately, the door to the conference room opened. "Take Miss Tesla upstairs." As she was being wheeled out she mouthed, *Yes, yes, with all my heart.*

"Did I just witness a change of heart?" mumbled Nebo to himself, shaking his head. *It sounded like it. Was something off about that? How could he turn her so quickly? Her statements about Tiberius were, umm, compelling. She fully believes what she said, that much is certain.* Nebo moved on befuddled, but somehow thinking things had changed. *Perhaps this Schaffer is actually with us.*

Katie was wheeled to the main elevator and taken to the 156$^{st}$ floor, where the guard handed her off and returned to his station. Katie found herself before a beautiful young lady attired in silk lace. "Katherine, I am Amanda. I am to take you upstairs," at that her voice faltered. Amanda bent down and released her from the restraints and helped her stand.

"*Stones:* You're to take me to the Sanctuary, where the only humans allowed are vassal virgins."

"Yes, how did you know?"

"I know many things, God speaks to me. You are Amanda Redding of Washington, D.C., born of Gerald and Janet Redding. Both your parents are dead from the nuclear blasts, and because of Omni's generosity, you were invited to come here. Only, Omni didn't mention to you that it was your exceptional beauty that earned you the ticket to this eunuch-like existence. Nor did he tell you about the ghouls you would be hanging out with." Amanda stood there frozen, tears spilling down her cheeks. "Take me up there," instructed Katie, "and do what you must do. Later, we will steal time to talk. I will speak to you when it's safe. Otherwise, mum's the word. Hold on, things are about to improve somewhat for you. Okay?"

"Thank you, thank you. But first, we must prepare you," said Amanda submissively, looking over Katie's scuffed-up appearance, dirtied face and hair, and crumpled clothing.

"What?" grumped Katie in reaction, prone to knee-jerk when hit with any dress-to-impress vanity. As Amanda meekly scrunched her face, Katie took a second look at her own full length reflection, including her wiry, unkempt locks, pasty-faced skin and marred clothing. Even she had to acquiesce. "Well, okaaay," she humbly agreed, and Amanda smiled. After being escorted through two double doors, Katie found herself standing in a pristine white beautification parlor. Before her were five highly skilled chaste young women trained in the sublime mystique of feminine beauty. Together, they would laurel every facet to bring forth her shimmering elegance.

Katie's nervous energy had her a bit wide-eyed, but in the spirit of the moment she jested with gentry in her voice, "This must be the harem *milieu* for the *très chic* vassal virgins. No doubt you hold in your skillful hands all the recipes and secrets for pampered bliss. Please, my dears, make me exquisite."

Amanda smiled, and immediately all five women gathered about Katie and began stripping off her clothing. Before Katie thought to react, they had undone her bra and a Stone fell to the marble floor. Katie caught the other one, but Amanda's eyes showed that a question had formed. "What's that? Why was it in your bra?" she inquired.

As the ladies continued to undress her, Katie discreetly replied, "You probably haven't come from a family with breast cancer, have you? They remind me constantly that I am loved and that I need to trust no matter what may befall me," she said with feigned genuineness.

"I think I need stones like that," Amanda rejoined.

"Can you keep this only between us girls?" asked Katie. "I mean it. It's very private to me."

"Absolutely," she answered with evident sincerity, zippering her thumb and forefinger across her lips.

"Do you have a locker of some sort?" asked Katie.

"Sure, umm, here," she indicated, pulling open a small unused cabinet. "Your clothes and *stuff* will be safe here."

"That will do," replied Katie happily. As she reached to place the Stones in the cabinet, she silently asked, *Stones: Am I safe? Is all of this safe? Yes.* For the first time in days she allowed herself to breathe a deep, cleansing breath. *Stones: Last question: How long? Six hours. Oh yeahhh.*

In no time, Katie found herself being hand-bathed in a luxurious whirlpool, during which they applied skin scrubs and softeners for exfoliating and polishing. When actual treatments were not being applied, heated facial towels, massaging, and caressing were undertaken with aromatic oils and exotic perfumes. No sooner was an application of honey and sea salt washed away, than a mixture of shredded coconut, natural yogurt, and brown sugar was applied. Others worked on her long auburn locks applying a sweet almond extract recipe leaving her hair thick and silky clean. From antimony eye beautifiers, to betel palm seed lip pastes, she was spared no indulgence of their secret arts. Her whole face smiled beneath the hot cloth when they started her mani-pedi. As they transitioned to styling her hair and applying her make-up, Katie just closed her eyes and released herself to their creative artistry.

When at last, Katie turned about to view all that they had done, she felt altogether like a middle-eastern exotic beauty. Her hair boldly stood up like the feathers of a peacock, which complemented beautifully her applied whiteface upon which they smartly crafted elegant mehndi henna designs accentuating her eyes. Across the center of her lips only, they applied henna shaded in a light indigo matching her eyes, while her outside lips retained their whiteface. Her gown was constructed of white lace with a delicate floral pattern woven throughout. In Katie's delectable imagination, she was being adorned for her beloved, Doogie.

After reinserting the Stones, Katie was escorted to the upper Sanctuary where she immediately felt the oppressive weight of evil. Though she didn't anticipate that the ceiling height would incorporate two floors, she quickly reasoned that it was necessary given the demons' larger stature. *Get ready.* With the help of the Stones, her eyes roamed warily over the shadowed nexus of the Beast's lair. She noted the four throne-like seats situated in a circular arrangement, and determined it to be the area where their dark purposes were conceived. Amanda directed her to a pillared sitting area where ornate Italian sofas and throw cushions provided expansive lounge-type comfort.

Having entered the Beast's darkened, dispirited abode, Katie did indeed feel like a vassal virgin. She shook her head slightly at the ridiculousness of being prepared for this monster. She remained standing knowing the Beast was but moments away. When he made his entrance, he approached saying nothing. Amanda stood back, her face lowered. Katie however, was altogether engaging his eyes as he sidled from side to side, verifying that which he had been told. "So, it is true, you can see across the Barrier."

"So, it is true, you are a noble looking demonic principality. Your image would sell well in the theatre arts. You've got that stately quality of evil working for you. You should get yourself out there. You'd be a hit."

"Zeus mustn't reveal himself to Europa until she is ready," he countered. "For now, I am content that she is caressing my flank."

"Oh, why not just have a tell-all session? Huh?" posed Katie. "Tell it like it is. The king of the world is really a fallen principality[161] that hates the God of love, and wishes only to destroy His creation in order to press the dagger deep."

"Who are you?!" he raged in bafflement.

"A bit mercurial, are we?" she reproved tongue-in-cheek. "Layers of psychoses? Anger management?"

The Beast ignored her and spouted, "No human has ever been so fearless in the face of their imminent demise! You actually seem stronger than even hours ago."

"God's Spirit and a nice mani-pedi can do wonders for a girl," she demurred. And then with candor she said, "Who am I? I am nobody, a depraved sinner merely. But I am also the harbinger of truth," she decreed suddenly, boldness resounding in her voice as an anointed seer. "I see before it happens. I hear before it is said. It takes only my asking, and He speaks with me. Do you miss it? Do you miss His voice?"

"I will possess you now, woman!" at which the furious Beast sought to enter her spirit by sheer blunt force, but he no sooner closed to within a foot when his face smashed up against the shield that was about her. Without thinking, he took hold of his massive sword and sought to eviscerate her, screaming out, "Aarrrgghhh!"

Babylon entered the Sanctuary in that same instant, and immediately stormed upon him grabbing hold of his rotating arm. When the Beast reacted, Babylon backed away, his left hand surrendering, his right hand withdrawing his own sword slowly. He extended it towards Katie and demonstrated the shield's impenetrability, his eyes on the Beast. "Not a good idea. Capiche? My hands are still ringing from my U.N. attempt," he muttered after turning to recline to the sitting area. "Have someone else kill her, boss," he said offhandedly. "Or hey, go get the Tiberius body, take a sword in hand, and disembowel her. Human kills human. Simple."

The Beast's eyes showed agreement, and he was about to leave when Satan spoke, "Hey, why kill the girl?" The

Beast did an immediate turnabout, not believing what he had heard. He corkscrewed to his left to examine Babylon's reaction, and his astonished expression confirmed his conclusion. The master had finally uttered intelligible words.

The Beast quickly approached, knelt before Satan, and stammered, "My master, do you know who I am?"

"Sure I do, Sonny Boy. Do you know who I am?" he bubbled in a buoyant, not-quite-there tone.

"Please, tell me, who am I?"

"You are my Number One."

"That's right. And who are you?"

"Don't you know who I am? Have I been with you that long, you've forgotten?" he asked in a simple-minded, almost inebriated manner.

"Tell me, who are you?"

"I am Lucifer, the bright shining one, the star of the morning, the sun of the dawn. I am the covering cherub of God."[162]

The Beast felt Babylon's reaction from behind as he recoiled in disgust, but the Beast was not so sure. Focusing again on Satan, he questioned, "Wait, hold on, do you remember leaving Heaven?"

"Leaving it? Why? Why would anyone leave it? And why would you even say you want to kill that girl? How is that obedience to the Royal Law?[163] Shame on you, leave her be."

"What's wrong with him?" shot the Beast, perplexed.

Katie spoke out in a voice that was both mysteriously ethereal and grave, "His sovereignty has been removed from him – sovereignty over himself, sovereignty over the world.[164] He is seven years under the Dew of Heaven.[165] That is the penalty for arrogance, for making himself out to be like the Most High.[166] To you he has the mind of an animal, he's incoherent, his musings jumbled. But this is merely the consequence of Heaven's Dew, God's Spirit of unconditional love, falling on a wretched mind. He is now only capable of childlike innocence, nothing more. Would you learn from a child?"

The Beast retreated to the council area and sat beside Babylon. Trying to ignore all that Katie had said, he consoled himself saying, "He did answer actual questions. He hasn't done that since the declaration."

"He thinks he's unfallen. How does that help us?" posed Babylon.

"Today he thinks that. Tomorrow, well... It's the woman, her presence has changed things. Her love level has awakened something in him. This is David's harp soothing the demonized king all over again.[167] Tell me I'm wrong. Just about the time I am to strike her down, this new wrinkle appears."

"I say strike them both down, take the crown that is rightfully yours, and let's move on."

"Strike me down?" called out Satan from across the room. "Do you even hear yourself? How is that love? Where am I? What is this place?"

Babylon harrumphed and added, "It's arguable that she's made him even more of a nuisance."

Katie leaned back on an elegant high-backed chair and just observed. Never could she have remotely conceived of such goings on. Up until Satan spoke, she hadn't realized the cloaked shadow across the floor was of any import. But when his yellow-red orbs looked in her direction, his outline became clear. Suddenly, his draconic-like features magnified themselves, especially when he raised himself up on his knees, his fists touching the ground before him as he extended his body forward to drive home his point. In that singular moment, she saw an inkling of the entity that was both Lucifer and Satan. He was expertly crafted, even in his demonic form, with torso and limbs perfectly constructed to provide the most flawless convergence of symmetry and agility. Add that to the nobility of his strong facial features and horns, and flowing black-laced wings, and he looked all the part of a ruler. She understood the Beast's urgent desire to get past his Master's one deficiency, the misplaced jewel – his mind.

Turk approached Michael jubilantly. "I have to hand it to you, the girl has illuminated the Sanctuary just enough for our scouts to see and hear far more than before. Without doing a thing, she is accomplishing more than we've been able to in over a year."

"I've heard. That's great," said Michael with a tight voice. "Clearly, Satan is up there as we've believed, and talking somewhat."

"You're concerned about the Beast discovering the Stones," said Turk tonelessly in his bass vibrato.

Michael issued a fractional nod. "There are too many diverging variables to depend on any one scenario playing itself out. Everything she says can cause ripples in time. There is just no predictability on which to lay hold. Things may settle into a groove right now, but any number of factors could have her thrown out the Tower window."

"Literally?" galumphed Turk, blinking wide, his eyes dilating.

"No, and yes. Running futures is like climbing a tree. The trunk is straightforward enough, but in short order, branches span out in multiple directions. Depending on which branch is climbed, a different series of events unfolds, many of which lead to fairly predictable actions and reactions. I've needed to interact with Katie on a dozen occasions, from telling her where not to go, knowing she would do exactly the opposite, to telling her about her parents. Clearly, the biggest branch, bar none, was giving her the Stones. This one choice has saved countless lives, but it has also placed her life in jeopardy. Being that we do not buy into an ends-justify-the-means core truth, I'm hoping she slides into the groove."

"As long as the Beast thinks she's uniquely special, he won't touch her," leveled Turk. "But if he discovers the Stones, it will be like uncovering a magician's secret – immediate disenchantment. Her mystique is everything, it's that simple."

"Add that to his rage at being deceived, and it's the window," Michael muttered, feeling the strain.

# ⎾⏋

One Week Prior to the Tribulation Mid-Point

After almost two years, Katie found herself straightening the cushioned area, providing Amanda help to make the best of their strained circumstances. As Katie bent forward, her cleavage revealed itself reminding Amanda of something she hadn't given thought to in some time. "Hey, your stones are working, no breast cancer."

Immediately, the Beast, who was within earshot, lifted his face.

Like a long buried secret that had been clawing its way to the surface one dirt-filled hand at a time, Katie suddenly knew she had been exposed. The uncovering of her deception cut her to the quick as untold trepidations plummeted her headlong into an abyss of terror. Penetrating her breastbone, she felt stabbed by her sudden exposure. As if time could be turned back, she wanted the words stolen from the air, anything to keep the Beauty and the Beast truce in play. In that brief instant, her protective shield of faith fell to condemnation. Immediately, she was defenseless. She barely had time to respond before the Beast closed in on her and gripped hold of her throat in his massive taloned hand. "Give them to me! Now!"

For the tiniest of instants, she considered denial and misdirection, but the Beast's eyes showed no uncertainty, no sway. Against every instinct, every predilection, she reached into both bra cups and withdrew the Stones. As she placed them in his extended palm, her throat squeezed out the words, "If you kill me, they'll be of no use to you. Think about it, I pass on everything from the Almighty. Do I not? I've been given as your vassal virgin, just as you demanded. Does any warrior give up the secret of their strength willingly? Would you? Every soldier locked in battle presses their advantage and shields their weakness. Would you expect different from me?! It matters little that it was concealed, nothing was lost to you. You asked, I answered. Say it isn't so," she charged in a strangled voice.

The Beast visibly shook in rage, his debased deviltry screaming through his eyes. In cold-blooded fury he was a hair's breadth from casting her right through the window. His very sanity was overrun by a veritable tsunami of hate leaving him reeling without mooring. The Tiberius in him demanded self-control and restraint, but the Beast in him was gripped in the cold aura of homicidal anger. His pulse beat out long second after long second as his gaze stared her down. The primal scream within demanded to be voiced, regardless of the certitude of its reasoning. As if gasping for breath, he opened himself to the reality that he had lost his cohesion. Against every roaring inclination, he pulled himself back from the brink. Without explanation, he released her and walked away, ordering, "Bind her to the pillar with steel cable." In his left hand he held the Stones, and with him they would stay.

"I just heard," relayed Turk to Michael with urgency. "I'm sorry, but what are you doing?" he asked, bewildered. Michael appeared at first to be dancing, but then he ducked, twisted, and fell to the ground rolling twice over, all with a sword in his hand. Clearly, he was choreographing a combat sequence.

Michael ignored his question, and stated in a distracted tone, "The Beast just about crushed her throat, and as we know, almost threw her through the plate glass. He seems mollified for the moment, but the pressing concern is that the Beast has the Stones. Obviously, it's not a vassal virgin, but a believer that he needs in order to utilize them. Despite the martyrdoms, one wouldn't be hard to come by. It's likely he'll soon realize he can run futures and adapt his strategies accordingly. That's our worst possible outcome. Even so, the longer he holds onto them, the more the Stones' love will affect even him. Still, we need them back, or nothing will be hidden from him. Katie, and even Doogie, will need rescuing. We need a plan."

"Tell me," bid Turk, "it doesn't involve you actually wielding a weapon, or me fighting Babylon and his Crimson Sword."

"I can't say that," responded Michael, who then coyly changed the subject. "What's clear is that the martyred saints are stirred from their rest and are standing before the Lord's throne on the Crystal Sea.[168] They've been told the Sixth Seal has been broken, and the meteorites are about to fall."

"I can confirm the same, that those earth-side are bunkered down in whatever underground caves or shelters can be found.[169] Many despair of the sheer mass of rock that is about to descend upon them. They're begging the mountains to fall on them, and to hide them from the wrath of the Lamb.[170] Skyfall is here."

For the next six nights, the Beast tossed and turned with night-terrors, feeling like he was losing his mind. Bewildering sentiments of empathy left him deeply conflicted. Nightmares of his punitive reprisals against inferior subordinates stabbed at him repeatedly. If it were possible, he felt himself wavering, becoming distant to the cause, his volcanic rage cooling. As much as he tried to restrain overtly benevolent comments, one kindness after another escaped his lips. He was losing his animal cruelty, and on a conscious level he had no idea why. On impulse, he declared, "It's time we celebrate!" before he even knew what he was saying. At that point, by-standing miscreants were openly alarmed, their mouths gaping wide. They knew it was time for all hands on deck, even as the meteorites were hours from striking. Seeing their reaction, the Beast caught himself, and pronounced, "We have conquered the saints of the Most High. The blood-letting Purge cut off hundreds of millions of the ingrates. It's time to raise our glasses and toast to our laurels!"

To every nefarious demonic listener, the Beast's words were electrifying, not only because he had dispelled their lingering doubts, but because they reveled in putting it to the Almighty. Immediately they launched themselves into broadcasting the evening's event with all frivolity. Their illustrious titan had waged war against the Most High and won.

That night, the eve of the Tribulation midpoint, the Babylonian Tower rocked in celebration. For nearly three and a half years, the Beast had pulled Tiberius' puppet strings to refashion, or more accurately, chasten the world after the Rule of Love. All who stood in his way were dispelled by his loyalists and collective. He hadn't himself killed even one, but had abided strictly, technically, to the stipulations of the Accord.

The Beast had floors 153 and 154 transformed into a banquet hall that was expansive enough to seat one thousand of their most noteworthy guests. At the platform's front, the Big Four held their esteemed places. With some pomp and circumstance, Tiberius and the ten Governors, along with a half dozen more humans, including Doogie, Riggs, and Glasses-man Pic, were escorted in and seated at a long table facing the all-demonic assembly. Each had specially designed fourth-dimension visionware that Omni helped devise, allowing them to see beyond the Barrier with reasonable clarity.

The newly promoted Major Drake and Lieutenant Snark found their spots at the back table, feeling fortunate to be named among the thousand invited to the gathering. Outside the tower walls, tens of thousands of demons hovered with an eye on the festivities. Drake did his best to stand with the dignity befitting his rank. Though not a general, his designation carried enough intimidation to keep former opponents at bay. But admittedly, he felt like climbing the ladder had only increased the tormenting he felt from the even more brutal higher-ups. He was glad to have Snark at his side, who was clearly unfazed by rank or standing, most likely from ignorant bliss.

Doogie's eyes were struck from the minute he walked into the overflowing hall. *Beautiful and benevolent, right*, he assessed dryly. With the astrospectral glasses, he was horrorstruck to see in black-and-white the ghastly and nauseating creatures that could only be labeled the spawn of perdition. Like walking through a cell block of death-row inmates, he tried in vain to hide his gawking revulsion behind the ochre eyewear. On several occasions, just during his walk to the front, beastly poltergeists threateningly lunged at him displaying their keen awareness that he found them appalling. In every way, these underworld ghouls acted like hyenas looking down at road-kill.

Doogie had hoped Katie would be invited, but with what he was seeing, he was immediately glad she was not there. Nonetheless, her absence was peculiar. Whispers of a falling-out were heard, but no details had emerged.

Doogie was glad to find a seat next to Pic. His light-hearted jibber-jabber provided just the relief he needed. "So your name, Piccadilly, is that associated with Piccadilly's Bakery?"

"Dude, you know it is!" he blasted fun lovingly. "Cupcake wars, donut paradise, dad was king of the sweeeet!"

"Haha," chuckled Doogie. "So, that's where you get that expression?"

"That's where I get more than that, bro," he chortled, patting his hands on his happy girth that was clad in his frumpy attire. "We Piccadilly's were the buzz! When it came to flour, sugar, and butter, we knew every secret there was! Our donuts were the bomb!"

Doogie found it entirely ironic that he could be openly laughing among the din created by such thugs and brutes. He almost smirked at the realization that Tiberius, without the Beast, was a mere human. When he turned about to look at the Beast, his eyes taking in the Big Four for the first time, his heart skipped a beat from the sheer terror. Instantly, he retreated into himself for several long minutes. He suddenly realized he was poised over a razor's edge, his very life perilously close to being extinguished. His earlier thought of being nothing but prey was far more accurate than he could have at first surmised. Everywhere he looked, he found the demons talking their black speech in devious tones, even while they fixated on the humans. Like murderers crazed with malice, these ghostlies wanted retribution, and sitting before them were the offspring of their chief nemesis. *Team members? No way. These carnivores see us as raw meat.*

Into the night, appetizers, first and second courses, and desserts were served to everyone's gluttonous delight. Drinks were poured and glasses filled again and again, as the great company fell into a drunken stupor. Accolades and tributes were thrown about for all the murderous success they had realized in overthrowing the saints with complete disregard for the Almighty. At one point, Babylon took the podium to praise the Beast for all that he had accomplished. He commended the Beast for his unceasing and relentless blaspheming. He solicited whether any of them could remotely imagine uttering such foul things against the Most High. Babylon had made his point, and all rose to their feet to offer rousing and frenzied adulation. At the height of their salivating hysteria, the demonic horde raised their fists to Heaven and began shouting with one voice to the Beast, "Hail Caesar! Hail Caesar! Hail Caesar!" Against the din, the Beast roared, "Has the Almighty not been beaten?! Have we not prevailed?!" With unleashed fury, they blasphemed without regard to life and limb.

At the apex of their self-worship, as the Beast stood before them, arms extended in triumph, face basking in the veneration, a large disembodied hand suddenly appeared on the adjacent wall and began writing words, unintelligible words: MENE, MENE, TEKEL, UPHARSIN.[171]

Bafflement and fear instantly stifled their vulgarities, leaving every face jaundiced. From celebration to immediate dread, the assembly stood there alarmed and mystified. Knowing something needed to be said, the Beast declared emphatically, "For the one who is able to read this inscription and explain its interpretation, I will clothe you in purple and adorn your neck in gold.[172] You shall be third in our rank, behind me and Babylon only."

For several minutes the assembly remained mute, the mystery going unanswered. Then someone near the front, a human man, stood and raised his voice.

Doogie felt assaulted for hours just being in their presence. Never could he have imagined feeling more emotionally abused than by these hateful monsters with their guttural hellspeak. As he reached his utmost limit with their crescendoing malice, the hand appeared. After the question was posed, he sat there for some time feeling like this wasn't his deal. He just wanted to flee. But with each passing minute, his thoughts drew back to Katie, and against his every inkling, he stood up before all. After the silence intensified about him, he said, "There is one of extraordinary spirit, knowledge, and insight.[173] There is one who can explain this enigma. She will give you its message. Let Katherine Tesla be summoned and she will declare its interpretation."

The Beast immediately knew he spoke the truth, and was faced with acquiescing that very instant. Part of him had banished her, but another part knew she was the true mouthpiece for the Almighty. Before his uncertainty became a cause for speculation, he called out, "Bring the vassal; let us hear what she would say."

Immediately, they retrieved her, and Katie found herself escorted up the center aisle to the main platform. She was elegantly attired in a pearl-sheened gown, with a veil of the same material falling along her hairline. Every eye fixed upon her as she ascended the platform stairs. She arrived at the Beast's side and looked up at him, holding her gaze to see if she had earned his respect once again, and then held out her hand. The Beast paused for three breaths of indecision, being not only unsure about reengaging with her, but feeling strangely unable to part with the Stones. Still, he compelled himself and dropped them into her palm.

"Well," spit the Beast. "Tell us what it says and you shall be rewarded."

"Keep your gifts or give them to someone else.[174] I will tell you the interpretation," pronounced Katie with authority and certitude. "O king of the Earth," she declared, turning towards the crowd so all could hear, "the Most High God granted you, like your father Satan, sovereignty, grandeur, glory, and majesty. But because your master's heart was lifted up and his spirit became exceedingly proud, he was deposed from his royal throne and glory was stripped from him. Knowing all that has transpired in regard to your master, you should have kept your heart humble, but instead, you have exalted your brazen irreverence before the world. As a vassal-king, you have drunk wine from His holy vessels, even the life blood of the saints.[175] You were mistaken to believe you could eat His body and drink His blood without retribution.[176] This night, the God in whose hand are your life-breath and your ways, has written this inscription. Hear the word of the Lord. MENE – God has numbered your kingdom and put an end to it.[177] TEKEL – You have been weighed on the scales and found deficient.[178] PERES – Your kingdom has been divided and given over to others, even the two Witnesses who will proclaim His love without prejudice."[179]

The Beast cut her off before hearing another word, and roared, "Babylon, prepare for war! Troops, arm yourselves! Molech, take these two to the Sanctuary and lock them to the pillar. They are the first to die should the enemy attack.

We'll see who is deposed tonight."

Molech and Nebo had Gruber's goons take hold of Doogie and Katie and begin hustling them from the room, even as Katie slipped the Stones back into their place. At the same time, Doogie turned his head about and momentarily stopped them from dragging him away, and then shouted, "Tiberius, I recant my vow of obedience as a sham. You are nothing but a marionette for that monster! I'm switching sides. I choose Jesus if He'll have me!"

Molech had Gruber yank Doogie forward and groused, "I will happily extinguish your flame if another word comes from your mouth."

"I've missed you," mouthed Katie to Doogie, smiling all the way to her grin lines.

*I love you*, projected Doogie, his eyes smiling. *You are amazing, in every way.*

In short order, Katie and Doogie were cabled to the pillar, where they remained, arms tied back and shoulders under strain.

"Too soon," chided Turk. "We cannot move against Babylon's über army yet," he stressed. "One firm blow from his sword and my blade breaks like a toothpick. It will be a bloodbath for all. Fourteen minutes, minimum. Hold on!"

"Katie and Doogie don't have fourteen minutes," countered Michael. "In three minutes, they're struck down. That's it. It's over. Tell the Host we move in ninety seconds."

"I am appealing to you! I am not downplaying the likelihood of massacre and carnage," pressed Turk. "Trust God for another answer. Believe me, for all our sakes. I've been here before, when every way forward seems uncertain."

"The Writings of Truth do not lie," contended Michael.

"Yes, but you also said their fluidity depends on diverging vectors. Give the Holy Spirit room. He is above the time-line."

Michael pulled within himself, closed his eyes, and quieted his spirit. *Help me, I pray, I hear You speaking through Turk, but I also know what I see in the Writings. Both cannot be true, so help me discern Your will.*

Katie's arms were drawn back against the pillar. Before her, Molech and Nebo were distracted by the imminent battle.

"I say we kill them and join the battle line," stated Nebo flatly.

"I agree, the enemy will breach our lines."

"Will you kill them in my presence?" spit Satan, suddenly looming over them as a tornado of wrath. "Have I ceased to be your lord? Will you defy me in my own habitation?"

Molech and Nebo found themselves standing beneath a fully erect Satan, with both his hands on his sword hilts.

Katie beheld the sudden turn of events, knowing Satan was engaging in double-speak, for he still believed he was their unfallen lord. In short order, this distraction would be exposed for the charade it was. In desperation, Katie strained her arms against the steel cord, when her hand happened upon a patch that was stuck to the pillar. *Stones: It is a key. Michael had it put there.* Recognition filled her eyes, and she turned her face clandestinely to check on Gruber's team. All were standing squeamishly back from the foreboding presence of Satan that had filled the room's center. Katie secured the key and positioned it to release her left restraint. She gave a muffled cough as she successfully turned it, freeing her left wrist. In a fluid motion, she moved the key from her left hand to her right, and again raised her left arm as though still bound. She found Doogie's left wrist, inserted the key, and freed him.

Just as Katie covertly unlocked her right wrist cuff, Satan spoke, "If you don't abide my authority, I will have no choice but to remand you to the angelic watchers. They will write you up and assign you additional duties until you learn the…"

"What is this?" beckoned Nebo. "Is he right in the mind?"

"Clearly, not. Thought we were toast for a moment there," growled Molech. "Ignore him. Kill them both now!"

Gruber gave the nod and his men moved forward to handle it. Just then, Katie stood up and commanded, "Doogie, get behind the pillar, that's an order!" For the briefest of instants, Doogie thought to man-up and protect his woman, but her eyes forced him to retreat.

Katie found herself weaponless and surrounded by seven armed men and two vicious spirits. As she considered the impossibility of her circumstances, she lifted her panic-stricken face and cried out in desperation, "Michael, where are you?! Where are you?!"

Her foes stepped forward, guns drawn. *Stones: Bend left now.* Suddenly, gunfire erupted spitting bullets towards her, but missing by the narrowest of margins. Instead, one of the men was caught in the crossfire and immediately collapsed. "Don't shoot, men, it's not safe," shouted Gruber, but before he had convinced them, another pulled the trigger. *Stones: Twist right now.* Another fell victim. "Stow your weapons. First we grab her, then we shoot," he blasted.

As Katie turned about, she recognized their unwavering intent, and resigned herself to the inevitable. She straightened herself and spoke out with fatalistic tenor, "Alright then…" As a prophet, she pronounced, "You do not know the thoughts of the Lord. You do not understand His purpose. He has gathered you like sheaves to the threshing floor. Arise and thresh, daughter of Zion, for your horn I will make iron, and your hoofs I will make bronze, that you may pulverize the insolent."[180]

The first man lunged at her wanting to take hold of her. She grabbed both of his wrists and pulled him towards her, and then swiftly kneed the man in the face breaking his nose. Just as quickly, she drove her right leg up and back with jiu jitsu precision, connecting to the neck of the man approaching from behind, laying him out. *Stones: Head left.* In an instant, another man's punch slid by her right temple. *Stones: Face down.* His follow-up left-handed roundhouse struck the top of her skull, breaking his wrist. He crumbled in pain, even as she struck him hard with a rotating leg kick. Without hesitation, Katie flung herself off the prostrate man and into the air, somersaulting forward, until she took the next man's head in the bend of her legs. Instantly, her weight yanked him off his feet, pulling both to the ground, until he crashed to the marbled floor, laid out unconscious.

Katie felt a tingle of danger and instinctively looked about to see Gruber appear from behind the pillar, Doogie in his grasp, a gun pointed at his head. Her face blanched. *Michael?* she pled, tears welling up.

"So, Tesla, I found your Achilles' heel," sneered Gruber, his lips hinting a hard smile. Unexpectedly, he turned his gun on her, refusing to believe that she could not be hit, and fired. *Stones: Twist left.* The bullet whisked by. "You *are* hard to hit, aren't you? But he isn't," he portended, repointing the gun at Doogie's temple.

Katie half raised her hands in the universal sign of surrender, even as she used the Stones to see her way. Suddenly, her eyes widened appreciably and panic rushed over her, even while Gruber continued debasing her in a brassy voice, "You're an enemy of the state, Tesla. You and this, what is he to you – your *beau*?"

Katie stammered to Gruber, "Don't shoot, don't, I give up. Take me as your prisoner. Just let him go."

"You make it sound like you're in a position to barter. You die, he dies, simple," barked Gruber. Like an unscratched itch, he fired several times at her in succession. Katie skirted the hot lead, but as she straightened up, he just returned his gun to Doogie's head.

"Wait, just wait" she pled, her hot blood pounding in her ears. "I have information that can greatly benefit you," she peddled in desperation.

"Kill him now, Gruber!" demanded Molech.

"I'm not into forestalling the inevitable. I'm a bird-in-hand guy." In that instant, he pulled the trigger, killing Doogie.


"Nine minutes, hold," implored Turk with an uneasy undertone. He stared down the teeming mass of winged and horned beasts.

"We go in now!" decreed Michael.

"If we go now, you stay back until we secure the air," ordered Turk. "GO!" he shouted to his comrades.

Suddenly the trumpeting order resounded. As a mighty wave of light, angels who had been concealed within the dark clouds on all sides heeded the call. Instantly, an angelic front emerged miles in length roundabout, storming forward to engage their adversaries. Before them was row upon row of armed antagonists sworn to the Beast.

Babylon hovered near the forefront, the Crimson Sword slowly twirling in his hand. He raised his voice over the ruckus to enflame his warriors, "We knew this hour was coming. Every call-out, every challenge, has been preparing you for this pathetic skirmish. You will not disappoint! You will not falter! You *will* hold your line! Blood and death!"

"Blood and death!" shouted the horde.

# 24

Turkania flew forward like the point of a great spear aimed directly at Babylon, who was poised like a stone gargoyle on their outermost periphery. Turkania's inner trepidation had him wrestling with the uncertain outcome. *Battle time; maneuver, duck, twist... Maybe it's predetermined... Make it work... Hold on. Nine minutes in front of the Crimson Saber, not possible. If only more time had expired, the crystalline fire would extinguish itself. Just leave it on the battle field.* His resoluteness teetered up and down as he approached the shrouded Babylon Tower. Everywhere his gaze fell, the edifice was cloaked by a thick blanket of every unclean spirit, every hateful bird.[181] Turkania headed straight for Babylon knowing his inevitable fate. He would fight, he would maneuver, but the result was foreordained – the sword of the Lord would prevail.[182]

Babylon's pride flared when he recognized Turkania bearing down on him. *So, my nemesis isn't afraid.* "It's you,

Commander of the Host! Come and get me!" he bellowed, his brutal grip constricting on his hilt. He positioned himself like a batter about to strike an incoming ball. He wound up ready to deal the fatal blow. Turkania's eyes locked onto Babylon's, with the other grizzly ghouls falling from his view. It was the pitcher's fastball against the batter's wood. Speed against power. Turkania pressed ahead of the angelic front, Babylon's face lit with wicked delight. Five hundred feet, one hundred, fifty, thirty, ten – swoosh went Babylon's sword, whoompf went Turkania's wings.

At the last possible instant, Turkania pulled up just before he was sliced clear through with Babylon's fiery saber. The micro-second Babylon's arms swung about and slapped Turkania's sword to the side with a quarter-blow, Turkania rammed into him pressing both of them through the ranks and into the confines of the Tower.

*Seven Minutes to Tribulation Mid-Point:* No sooner had they blown into the conference room, than Babylon broke free from Turkania's vice-lock.

"What's wrong commander, afraid to fight? What? Lose the faith? Rrrrgh!" assailed Babylon, beginning to prowl after him in pursuit. With speed beyond Turkania's capabilities, the Crimson Sword sizzled through the air igniting swaths of oxygen and nitrogen, Babylon's own sulfur breath serving as the catalytic agent. Evasively, Turkania ducked, flattened out, rolled right, then left, each time just eluding the blow. Again and again, a hair's breadth separated him from a severed arm, leg, or worse. Minutes passed, but time was against him, and he found his stamina waning. His sword was capable of handling glancing blows only, no more.

Babylon was all business, no words, as he pressed his advantage to its inevitable conclusion. He began recognizing Turkania's evasive patterns, and at just the right moment, he wound up and let loose.

Turkania saw the sword's full swing coming and there was nothing he could do to prevent it. It would hit, and hit hard. He raised his sword at the last instant knowing it would be the only thing between him and death. The full frontal blow struck like a crack of thunder, reverberating through his muscles and ligaments down to his very skeleton. With jarring violence, Turkania was hurled backward, his feet rising above his chest until he crashed hard to the floor, his angelic weight scrunching up the marble tiles for thirty feet. When he commanded himself to raise his head and reengage, his body-shock denied him.

Babylon walked up to his fallen comrade. "Nope, this isn't another of your feints. One blow; that's all it took to strike down the mighty Turkania. Let me end it mercifully." At that, Babylon raised his sword above his head and began slicing down.

Katie saw it happen, the bullet exploding from the gun and penetrating Doogie's skull. In ninety seconds, it would occur. *So, Tesla, I found your Achilles' heel...* Again and again, she ran permutations, changing what she said, how she responded, but over and over Gruber pulled the trigger. He was immune to her pleas, indifferent to her inducements. *You're an enemy of the state...* No matter the slight variations tried, the outcome was always the same – the violent shockwave exploded from the gun blasting the hypersonic lead into Doogie's skull. *You and this, what is he to you – your beau?* The demon's command would follow. Twenty versions, thirty, thirty-five, the ingenuity of her vicissitudes was reaching its limit, the final seconds depleting.

Behind the scenes, Molech looked on, his raven black eyes filled with spleen. "Kill him now, Gruber!" *I'm not into forestalling the inevitable...* Gruber pressed the Glock into position.

Katie pulled back from running futures and became visibly distraught. Her eyes drained of hope, her lips quivering. From far away, whispers came to her, *the flesh profits nothing.*[183] Her hands fell to her side. She began collapsing to her knees. *Cease striving, know that I am God.*[184] Somewhere inside she gave up any need to determine the outcome. Still, Gruber's words played on like a too slow phonograph, syllable by syllable, *I'm a bird-in-hand guy.* More whispers, *The weapons of your warfare are not carnal.*[185] Katie lifted her heart in pure surrender, and prayed, "Jesus, help me. Jesus, come now!"

Suddenly, Katie's eyes registered something other-worldly, her face lifting, her countenance coming to radiate God's glorious presence. "I see the heavens opened up and the Son of God standing at the right hand of God,"[186] she said in sheer awe. "Jesus, I love You," she whispered intimately. All about Katie, Heaven's domain shone with untold brilliance.

Everything became clear to her heart. Like a flawless diamond, the reasonability of trusting Him sparkled from every facet of her consciousness. Instantly, believing became as easy as breathing. Like a thousand light bulbs, faith illuminated every dark corner, every loathsome motivation. Fear and unbelief were replaced by the immutable laws of faith, hope, and love that were as real as gravity. Space and time continued to fold in on itself as she experienced minutes in the span of seconds. Jesus bent forward and touched His hand to her head. Perfect peace enveloped her, perfect awareness. Her personhood was answered, her innermost longing fulfilled.

Jesus' voice spoke into her innermost being, *I will never leave you or forsake you.*[187] *Fear not, neither be dismayed, for I Am your God.*[188] *Peace I leave with you. My peace I give to you, not as the world gives do I give to you. Let not your heart be troubled, neither let it be afraid.*[189] *You are already clean because of the word which I have spoken to you. Abide in Me, and I in you.*[190]

When at last she turned back to Gruber and Molech, with no mental strain, Katie silently voiced, *If God let's you shoot, then it is love. If God stops you, it is love. He is my Sovereign.* All about her, her shield of faith began expanding with perfect love reaching out across the room and beyond the confines of the Sanctuary. While still kneeling, Katie's compassion extended itself even to Molech, blessing him with love. Molech shrieked and wrenched himself back to escape the anointing. Gruber screamed in reaction feeling Molech's possessing leash torn from him.

In that same moment, Doogie broke Gruber's hold only to back up a step, turn, set his feet, and deliver a scalding right hand that toppled Gruber over a chair. Doogie moved to Katie's side and picked her up into his arms.

In no time, Molech recovered, pulled his sword, and together with Nebo, approached them both. Katie saw them across the Barrier with perfect clarity. Still, she made no move to respond to their advances. Just as Molech's hefty sword was closing in on his intended victims, Satan, or more accurately Lucifer, stepped forward and parried his vicious advance. Instantly, Molech barked out like a thunderclap, "Cawauuu! Cawauuu!"

"So, you continue to deny the Almighty's love," charged Lucifer adamantly. With both his swords drawn, Lucifer backed them up through sheer intimidation. "Do you not see that His love saturates this place? Have I not been awakened and made lucid? How is it that you can raise your face into the transparent clarity, and yet still make it your aim to strike these two down?" Lucifer extended his swords to the point of chiming them against both Molech's and Nebo's weapons. "Tell me, is what I say unreasonable? Or would you take advantage of my neutrality, knowing my mental proclivities for evil have been snatched away by force these years? Choose carefully, whether power be your god? I am granting you this one reprieve, there will not be another."

Molech felt the strain of the pronounced love, and as such, he found it hard to enflame the embers of hate as he was want to do. Still, the jealous ambition to strike down the longtime king of their rank seemed irresistible. He knew him to be out of his mind, devoid of his venom, apparently believing himself to be unfallen. If ever he was vulnerable and susceptible to defeat, this was that moment. Glancing at Nebo ever so slightly, his eyes gave the go ahead. In perfect unison, they spun and turned, their swords following after them, as they sought to gut their dark lord like a fish.

Lucifer chose to withhold his reaction until the last possible instant. Just as their blades were inches from slicing him through, he dropped down with keen adroitness, while at the same time, lunged forward. Before they could react, Lucifer pulled back his arms and thrust his swords cobra-like deep into their chests. Instantaneously, two plumes of red smoke exploded within the Sanctuary. Molech and Nebo vaporized.

*Two Minutes to Tribulation Mid-Point:* Babylon's sword plummeted downwards to Turkania when Michael came up underneath Babylon's arms, blocking their descent. Michael's strength was more angelic than human, and as such, he presented a fair amount of resistance for the briefest of moments. Nonetheless, Babylon quickly threw him aside like a ragdoll, only to realize who he was. "Why, if it isn't your young commission hoping to save his master." Believing he could swat him like a bug, Babylon turned aside from Turkania to the boy-nuisance.

The Crimson Sword was too fast for Michael to anticipate, so he didn't even try. Instead, he just did his dance steps, counting the sequence out in his head. At key points, he bent backward, fell flat, did a backflip, dove left, all while Babylon's fiery blade was cutting through the air and slamming into the concrete.

Just as Babylon's sword was coming in for the kill, his blade was parried by Turkania's. "Time's up, Hoss," Turkania jibed. Immediately, Babylon realized the fire on his blade had extinguished. "Your three and a half years are up as the War Horse." In truth, Turkania was hurt and barely able to remain standing, though he made himself out to be anything but. Just as Babylon lunged forward to take on Turkania with what reserves he had left, Michael stepped up from behind and jabbed Babylon in the back with his sword, just enough to command his attention. In the split second Babylon turned to see what caused the bee sting, Turkania swung his sword in an uppercut fashion and dislodged Babylon's sword from his hand. With his left hand Turkania took hold of the flipping sword, and with his right he poised his own sword against Babylon's throat like a diamondback ready to strike.

Katie pressed her face against Doogie's, and together they held each other, finally feeling a semblance of security. Too much had transpired over too long a span of time. Katie drew her forehead into his chest and allowed her left hand to grip his arm muscle as they embraced. Seeking to lighten the mood, she said playfully, "Flexing your sinews? Ooooh," she crooned romantically, "perhaps a little brawn is attractive. For a geek meister, you're fairly impressive."

"Yeah? For a vassal virgin, you're like, *ninja* chick, *cobra qui*," he jested quickly, "Rrrrrrah." Both laughed, savoring the moment, when suddenly, Gruber stood, his Glock pointed their way.

*Stones: Back up slowly.* Katie spoke out as she pulled them both back. "Gruber, it's important that you listen to me, before you shoot. Please, answer the question, would you like my help? You truly need it."

"What kind of malarkey you selling, Tesla?" he accused.

"Time's almost up. Is that your final answer?" she persisted.

"I'll show you my final answer," he charged, and pulled back the trigger, pointing the gun at Doogie.

Immediately, Katie instructed Doogie, "Cover your ears, now."

Suddenly, the crack of a sonic boom deafened them as a car-sized meteorite blasted through the building and right through Gruber leaving a gaping hole in the Tower structure. Katie and Doogie's eyes grew wide as they beheld the diagonal tunnel that ran from their upper right to their lower left, leaving electrical wiring and structural wreckage in its wake. The first of the Sixth Seal rock rain had pierced the atmosphere.

In the blink of an eye, Turkania transported Babylon to the edge of the Bottomless Pit's[191] gravity well. With his leg and foot, Turkania thrust Babylon into the black hole's event horizon, where, as Babylon was falling in, he called back, "Isn't your side just going to let us out in short order?[192] I mean, what's the point? If I take a nap, by the time I wake, I'll be back."

"It won't be long," agreed Turkania.

"You presuppose too much to think that next time my blade..." Babylon warned. "Soon..."

"What will be, will be," returned Turkania.

As Turk returned, Michael commented dryly, "It's fair to say that I helped wear him out, and...oh, my little jab..."

Turk ignored his sass and humbly acknowledged, "I'm hurting, no kidding."

"Yeah, sorry. Kidding aside, you prevented a blood-bath by delaying us, and then occupying him.  Thanks. I mean it. You saved them. You are the bravest one I've ever known," said Michael caringly. Turk smiled, but inwardly turned to the Lord in gratefulness.

As they set out to find Katie and Doogie, Michael spoke up in a lighthearted tone, "So, for the record, I see no need for your cohorts to know of Babylon's spanking." With a wry smile, he dissed, "I don't suppose this will go on your resume; although it ought to. No, really!  I'll tell you what, you take all the credit.  Don't even mention my little dance, *and* jab.  Just tell about your acrobatics, really..."

In the wake of another concussive meteorite strike, Doogie's mind returned to Omni, "Katie, we have to get to Omni..." Immediately, they ran to the elevators to travel down from the 162$^{rd}$ floor.  When the first elevator opened, Katie directed, "No, not that one, hold, this one." Within seconds, a meteorite struck a lower level, rocking the building to the point where they lost their footing and needed to brace themselves against the walls.  Dust shot out from the first elevator's seals.

"Are we going to make it?" beseeched Doogie.

"Yes, we make it. The building will be impacted five times, three so far, but it remains standing. The structure's outer skin will be patched up by a skeleton construction crew and made to look as though it has hardly been damaged." After descending, they came to the 139$^{th}$ floor. As they hurried to the Star Chamber, they made their way around the aftermath of a sizable meteorite incursion.

They skirted about its perimeter, taking in the large hole that passed slantwise through four floors of computer processors. Falling debris resounded down the shaft, with sparking wires, burning insulation, burst water pipes, and hissing super-heated steam, all in abundant evidence. They made it to Omni's central core and found Michael and Turk standing before the empty chamber. Omni's fiber optic connecting cables were dangling and his cubic foot processing platform was gone.

"Where is he?" stammered Doogie.

"Tiberius..." started Michael.

"Tiberius took Omni," interjected Katie gravely. "He's gone to Jerusalem for tomorrow's High Holy Day of Passover. Tiberius is to commit the abomination of desolation sacrifice[193], with Omni broadcasting it globally. Zeus will finally reveal himself to Europa, declaring himself to be God. Dark prophesies and portents are upon us."

# EPILOGUE

Michael and Turk passed into Heaven's Outer Court from Jacob's Ladder and elected to fly high above its festive gardens and gigantic elms that stood like sentinels overlooking the sweetberry-vined riverside. As they came to the Crystal Sea, Michael beheld with awe God's throne high-and-lifted-up[194] at the Sea's center, the great multitude spread out in all directions. A golden-amber light glistened from His presence, casting an ethereal beauty over the panoramic seascape. Music ascended to their ears, noble music, gallant music. Michael turned to face Turk and smiled with a broad grin. *This is my home*[195], *not that land of shadow and gloom.*[196]

Below, they looked over the mass of humanity that had come out of the Tribulation as martyrs. Mile after mile of saints, starting with Gunny, filled up the Sea where they rested beneath the Throne's covering until their full number had arrived.[197] The last of the Tribulation Saints had suffered beheading just prior to the midpoint of the seven year treaty with Israel.[198]

As Michael and Turk paused midair, they witnessed Jesus standing on the outstretched wings of the Four Living Creatures, His face lowered in recognition of the people's expressed thankfulness for His atoning love. From all about the great congregation, palm branches waved in celebration of Jesus' triumphal entry into their hearts.[199] Together, the people danced and sang jubilantly. Just as the chorus concluded, they declared in one voice, "Salvation to our God who sits on the Throne, and to the Lamb!"[200]

After a time, Jesus announced, "Saints of the Most High, may I introduce two very important onlookers? Welcome Turkania and Michael Gates!" Both of them lit up with surprise as Jesus waved them over. After descending, they stood before Jesus and bowed their heads humbly in appreciation.

Jesus continued, "Turkania brings with him the Sword of the Lord, signifying the end of the Antichrist's unencumbered reign. Turkania also seized Babylon, the War Horse, putting an end to their unimpeded ability to make war with the saints. Likewise, Michael has been highly instrumental in serving you, the Tribulation Saints, by working closely with Katherine Tesla, helping to guide and direct her. Moments ago, you beheld as she cried out, and We opened the Heavens to intervene on her behalf. Let's thank both Turkania and Michael for their selfless and gallant service in love." At that, the people burst into boisterous and grateful applause.

Turkania stepped forward with the Crimson Saber and approached one of the Four Living Creatures. With a bow of his head, he extended it hilt first to the cherubim who received it graciously, turning it agilely about and sliding it into his sheath.

"Please, both of you," appealed Jesus, "remain here for a moment." Michael and Turk stepped to the side as Jesus welcomed two approaching elders, Moses and Elijah. Michael took note that neither Moses nor Elijah was in their glorified bodies, but both had returned to their earthly bodies that had been kept back from the enemy.[201] Despite this, their faces radiated life and love, and their eyes resoluteness. Both wore their hair long and wavy, their full beards flowing over their penitential sackcloth garments. Moses carried his staff in one hand, and the Book of Scripture in the other. Over his coarse burlap, Elijah wore his sheepskin garment, or anointed mantle, that had long slits reaching from his underarm to his waist, and hung like a full-length vest. Together they stepped before Jesus, who turned back to the great assembly[202], His right hand resting on Moses' shoulder.

Jesus spoke, His voice carrying to the far reaches of the Sea, "These are the Two Witnesses[203], chosen for this day and hour. Together, they will return to the forlorn Earth and give your remaining relatives and loved ones opportunities to turn back in humility. Scripture prophesied, 'Behold, I am going to send you Elijah the prophet before the coming of the great and terrible day of the Lord. He will restore the hearts of the fathers to their children and the hearts of the children to their fathers, so that I will not come and smite the land with a curse.'[204]

"Nonetheless, many will harden their hearts[205], refusing to trust God. I am granting these two the authority to prophesy for the next three and a half years, and to shut up the sky from any rain.[206] They will have power over the waters to turn them into blood, and to strike the Earth with every plague, as often as they desire[207] that the pride of men might break. But for those who humble their hearts, Moses and Elijah shall provide care and nurture through their co-workers, the one hundred and forty-four thousand witnesses.[208] Thus, in accord with your intercession, we will be staunch and steadfast in our pleas for humility, for the Father does not wish for any to perish, but for all to come to repentance."[209]

As Jesus spoke, Michael's eyes were taken with the Four Living Creatures. The Cherubim were enormous, being dozens of feet in height. Just then, one of the Living Creatures took hold of Michael's arm. Instantly, he was thrust into a vision of what was soon to come. *Michael found himself standing beneath the Throne that was ablaze with flames, its great wheels burning with fire.[210] He watched as Gabriel approached the Altar of Incense, the very gateway into the Father's innermost being. Gabriel held a golden censer filled with the prayers of the martyred saints and those of spiritual Israel.[211] Michael watched as he lifted the censer and poured out the prayers of love, which like the smoke of incense, ascended before the Lord[212] pleading for the pride of man to be overthrown. He felt uncertainty hanging in the air as the Almighty weighed out the pleas of generations. Suddenly, a river[213] of fiery love poured forth from the Altar of Incense as a torrent. Gabriel filled his censer with the Altar's fire. He then rose up with the overflowing censer and positioned himself before Jacob's Ladder.*

*With the myriad of martyred saints looking on, Gabriel cast its contents to the Earth,[214] and there followed a cacophony of lightning and thunder that battered the hemispheres with inexorable fury, the Earth's magnetic field discharging unremittingly. So devastating were the blows, that the Earth reeled and screeched with horrific upheaval.[215] For days and nights on end, the appalling onslaught persisted, striking terror into every heart. Every soul was cut to the quick as the rock rain penetrated the atmosphere with its high-pitched shrieks[216], sounding eerily*

*like screaming children. Dogs could be heard across neighbor-
hoods howling in agony at the ear-splitting screeching. For half
a dozen months, skyfall continued intermittently and unpredict-
ably assailing the beaten-down populace.*

For a moment, Michael was stricken with dread as he
watched the apocalyptic prelude to the end of days. But as
he weighed how untold numbers of martyrs came to fill
the Crystal Sea before him, he dismissed the disquieting
angst. Raising his eyes, he professed trust in the Father
and felt blanketed by His untiring compassion. *I know the
Tribulation's hard appeal in love will turn many hearts, and once
again the riches of Your grace*[217] *will be displayed to all.*

Michael then heard a voice call out, "Now begins the
Great Tribulation, accompanied by destruction which has
not occurred since the beginning of the world until now,
nor ever will again.[218] The sun will be darkened and the
moon will not give its light, and the great mountains will
fall from the sky, and the powers of the heavens will be
shaken.[219] Unless these days are cut short, no life will be
saved."[220]

# ACKNOWLEDGEMENTS

I am very grateful to my dear friend and chief editor, Drew Berding, for his unrelenting work ethic and support in helping to bring forth this book. I am deeply appreciative for the editorial prowess of Jonathan Regier and Robin Leggs. Special thanks go out to Connie Jacobs for her formatting assistance, and Scotty Crawford and Max Soussan for their cover design. We appreciate the strong support given by Steve and Florentine Cobb, Hassan Miller, Ron Bryant, and our family and friends in helping to bring this book to you. Without a doubt, my love belongs to my wife, Kim, whose inspiration and keen editorial eye touches each of these pages. Thanks for being my life partner and best friend. All my love.

Dr. David Orlowski is doctorally trained in both theology (King's University) and psychology (Northcentral University). He received his Masters of Divinity from Fuller Theological Seminary. He has served as the Senior Pastor of Abiding Grace Church for 18 years. David and his wife Kim have five children and six grandchildren, Anne, Josh, Brian, Andrew, Odon, and Ethan.

327

# ENDNOTES

1. Numbers 14:29
2. Matthew 24:40-41
3. I Thessalonians 4:16-17
4. Philippians 2:1-3
5. Matthew 25:11
6. Matthew 25:1-13
7. Daniel 12:10
8. Revelation 6:1-8
9. Daniel 7:8, 20
10. Leviticus 23:22
11. Revelation 6:9
12. Revelation 13:7; Daniel 7:21; Daniel 7:25
13. Romans 8:28
14. Zechariah 5:3
15. Zechariah 5:4
16. Revelation 13:10
17. Rom 12:19; Hebrews 10:30
18. Ephesians 2:8-9
19. Numbers 14:28-31
20. Luke 12:51-53
21. Zechariah 5:5-11; Revelation 18:1-3
22. Daniel 10:21
23. Exodus 28:30; I Samuel 14:41
24. Revelation 17:17; Revelation 6:1-2
25. Roman Oath of Allegiance, Inscriptiones Latinae Selectae 8781 (Paphlagonia, 3 BCE)
26. Zechariah 5:4
27. Revelation 6:4
28. Revelation 6:5
29. Revelation 6:8
30. Revelation 6:4
31. Proverbs 28:21
32. Matthew 4:2
33. Job 4:9
34. Daniel 4:13; Daniel 4:17
35. Daniel 4:30
36. Daniel 4:31-32
37. Daniel 4:33
38. Revelation 6:1-2; Revelation 13:1-6
39. Matthew 8:12; Matthew 22:13
40. Daniel 4:14
41. Jeremiah 31:29
42. Al Quran surah 45, Love your enemy, forgive your enemy. Matthew 5:44; Leviticus 19:18
43. Revelation 14:18
44. Revelation 14:20
45. Revelation 14:19-20; Genesis 19:24
46. Zechariah 14:12
47. Revelation 6:8
48. Revelation 6:8
49. Matthew 8:32
50. Allusions to Gulfnews.com/news/gulf/uae/general/more-aid-from-dubai-to-reach-typhoon-victims-in-philippines-1.1254017.
51. Psalm 55:21
52. II Corinthians 11:14
53. Job 1:12; Job 2:6; Luke 22:31; John 3:27; John 19:11
54. Revelation 5:1; Revelation 10:2
55. Revelation 5:9
56. II Corinthians 9:8
57. John 15:4-10
58. Galatians 5:22-23
59. Mark 3:25
60. Genesis 4:9
61. Luke 24:49
62. Philippians 2:3
63. I Corinthians 13:11
64. Revelation 17:4
65. Revelation 13:16
66. Revelation 6:6
67. Daniel 10:14
68. Daniel 11:36
69. Revelation 13:2
70. Daniel 11:24
71. Revelation 6:1-2
72. Daniel 11:23
73. Daniel 7:24
74. Daniel 9:27
75. 2 Maccabees 2, We also know that he taught them God's Law and warned them not to be deceived by the ornamented gold and silver idols which they would see in the land of their exile.
76. I Chronicles 21:24; II Samuel 24:24
77. Daniel 7:25; Revelation 17:12-13
78. Leviticus 25:15
79. Revelation 13:16-17
80. Daniel 7:25
81. Daniel 7:20
82. Leviticus 19:18; Matthew 5:44
83. Revelation 17:17
84. James 2:8; Matthew 7:12; Matthew 19:19; Matthew 22:36-40
85. Leviticus 19:18; Galatians 5:14
86. II Corinthians 6:14
87. Romans 3:23

88 I John 4:19
89 James 1:25
90 Hosea 8:7
91 Revelation 16:13-14
92 Daniel 10:21
93 Esther 4:16
94 Philippians 2:2-3
95 Revelation 13:10
96 Now.msn.com/voyager-1-space-craft-records-sounds-of-interstel-lar-space.
97 Revelation 17:3-4
98 Luke 19:12; Acts 1:11; I Thessalonians 4:13-17
99 Daniel 7:24
100 Revelation 13:4
101 Revelation 13:17
102 Revelation 6:6
103 Asteroid 1997(XF11) is projected to possibly collide with the earth on 10/26/2028, six months after the mid-point of the Tribulation.  This object could be involved in the unfolding events.
104 Philippians 2:9-11
105 Matthew 28:18
106 Luke 9:39
107 Luke 8:31
108 Revelation 6:9-11
109 Esther 4:16
110 John 11:35; Romans 8:26
111 Revelation 14:12
112 Revelation 14:13
113 Revelation 14:13, Ibid.
114 Revelation 13:7
115 Revelation 13:7, Ibid.
116 Revelation 13:10
117 Joel 2:31; Acts 2:20; Revelation 6:12
118 Matthew 12:38-40
119 Revelation 13:3
120 Revelation 13:12
121 Micah 4:3; Joel 3:10; Isaiah 2:4
122 Genesis 28:10-17
123 Isaiah 14:13
124 Ezekiel 10:5; Hebrews 8:1-2; 8:4-5; 9:2; 9:6
125 Revelation 7:14
126 Esther 1:6
127 Ibid.
128 I Corinthians 13:12
129 Revelation 13:7; Daniel 7:21; Daniel 7:25
130 Revelation 4:6; Revelation 15:2

131 I Kings 4:33
132 Matthew 25:21-23
133 Revelation 21:10; Psalm 68:17-18
134 Matthew 27:52; Ephesians 4:8-10; Psalm 68:18; Daniel 12:12
135 I Thessalonians 4:13-18; I Corinthians 15:51-52
136 Ezekiel 28:14-16
137 Isaiah 6:1; Ezekiel 1:26-28; Ezekiel 10:1-2; Daniel 7:9-14
138 Exodus 13:22
139 Exodus 19:18; Psalm 105:39; Exodus 40:34; Luke 9:34
140 Revelation 6:5; 11:19; 16:18
141 Revelation 4:2
142 Ezekiel 1:15-21; Ezekiel 10:9-17; Revelation 4:6-8
143 Revelation 4:8
144 Revelation 6:11
145 Hebrews 6:18-19
146 Revelation 7:9
147 II Corinthians 11:14-15
148 Deuteronomy 4:19; Revelation 9:20
149 Genesis 6:5
150 Revelation 13:11-17
151 Revelation 13:11
152 Daniel 10:21
153 I John 4:8; I John 4:16
154 I John 4:19
155 Revelation 12:7-8
156 Matthew 24:12
157 Matthew 24:10
158 Matthew 24:12
159 Luke 12:52
160 Luke 12:53
161 Isaiah 14:12
162 Isaiah 14:12; Ezekiel 28:14
163 James 2:8
164 Daniel 4:31
165 Daniel 4:32
166 Daniel 4:32; Isaiah 14:14
167 I Sam 16:23
168 Revelation 15:2; 6:9-10; 6:9-10
169 Revelation 6:15-16
170 Revelation 6:16-17
171 Daniel 5:25
172 Daniel 5:7
173 Daniel 5:12
174 Daniel 5:17
175 Daniel 5:2-4; Revelation 18:3
176 I Corinthians 11:27-29
177 Daniel 5:26
178 Daniel 5:27

[179] Daniel 5:28
[180] Micah 4:12-13
[181] Revelation 18:2
[182] Revelation 6:4
[183] John 6:63
[184] Psalm 46:10
[185] II Corinthians 10:4
[186] Acts 7:56
[187] Hebrews 13:5
[188] Isaiah 44:8
[189] John 14:27
[190] John 15:3-4
[191] Revelation 9:2
[192] Revelation 9:1-2
[193] Daniel 9:27; Matthew 25:15
[194] Isaiah 6:1
[195] II Corinthians 5:8
[196] Matthew 4:16; Isaiah 9:2
[197] Romans 11:25
[198] Daniel 9:27
[199] Mark 11:8-10
[200] Revelation 7:10
[201] Jude 9; II Kings 2:11
[202] Hebrews 12:2
[203] Revelation 11:3
[204] Malachi 4:5-6
[205] Hebrews 4:7
[206] Revelation 11:6
[207] Ibid.
[208] Revelation 7:4-8; 14:1-5
[209] II Peter 3:9
[210] Daniel 7:9
[211] Revelation 8:3
[212] Revelation 8:4
[213] Daniel 7:10
[214] Revelation 8:5
[215] Revelation 8:5
[216] Isaiah 28:17b, 18b, 19-20, 22a
[217] Ephesians 1:7
[218] Matthew 24:21
[219] Matthew 24:29
[220] Matthew 24:22

# PERSONALITY PROFILE TEST

Here is a tremendous resource for helping you to more fully abide in unconditional love. The Personality Profile Test (P.P.T.) is designed to measure the extent to which our personalities rely on conditional love versus unconditional love. All of us attempt to answer the question - "Am I *worth* being loved?" through searching and striving efforts. However, it is only when we relinquish these lesser loves that we can truly come into unconditional love. This instrument will profile your personality in terms of any bonding, performance, control, and behavior issues that you may have. Your profile will include 23 pages of personalized feedback and practical instruction to help you move forward into a fuller expression of unconditional love.

For more on this assessment,
please visit:
**TwoTreesPublishing.com**

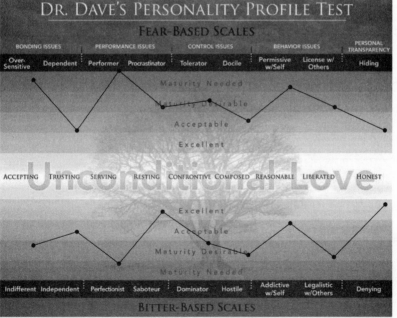